Advance Praise for

A Death at the Dionysus Club

"Scott and Griswold have triumphed again in this hot, lush Victorian fantasy whodunnit. From impeccable magic system to steamy encounters, *A Death at the Dionysus Club* will have lovers of Victoriana and detective fiction alike in stitches."
—TIFFANY TRENT, author of *The Tinker King* and *The Unnaturalists*

"Delicious historical detail, awkward sexy romance, sinister magic and a murder to solve—I can't think of a better combination for a cozy weekend read. Best served with a glass of port and a slice of Stilton in an antique leather reading chair."
—TANSY RAYNER ROBERTS, award-winning author of *Ink Black Magic*

"Difficult to believe, but this second adventure of metaphysician Ned Mathey and private detective Julian Lynes is even more enthralling than the Lambda Literary Award-winning *Death by Silver*. When amoral amateurs meddle in proscribed ancient magics, members of Victorian London's homosexual underground turn up murdered, their hearts uncannily removed from otherwise untroubled bodies. The strict grammar of modern metaphysics proves worse than useless against anarchic older powers, and a second threat appears when it seems Mathey and Lynes's secret lives must be exposed. With this series, Scott and Griswold are creating future classics of speculative and detective fiction."
—ALEX JEFFERS, author of *That Door Is a Mischief* and *You Will Meet a Stranger Far from Home*

D1178662

A Death at the Dionysus Club

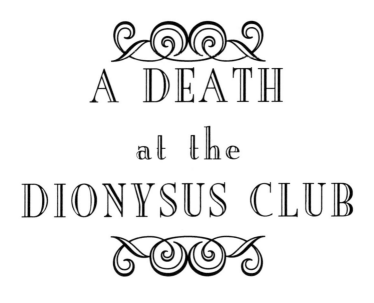

A DEATH

at the

DIONYSUS CLUB

Melissa Scott & Amy Griswold

Lethe Press
Maple Shade, New Jersey

Published in 2014 by Lethe Press, Inc.
118 Heritage Avenue ✦ Maple Shade, NJ 08052-3018, USA
www.lethepressbooks.com ✦ lethepress@aol.com
ISBN: 978-1-59021-530-2 / 1-59021-530-3
e-ISBN: 978-1-59021-086-4 / 1-59021-086-7

This book is a work of fiction. Names, characters, places, and incidents are
products of the authors' imaginations or are used fictitiously.

Set in Jenson, NewOrleans, and Warnock.
Cover and interior design: Alex Jeffers.
Cover artwork: Ben Baldwin.

LIBRARY OF CONGRESS CATALOGING-IN-PUBLICATION DATA
Scott, Melissa.
A Death at the Dionysus Club / Melissa Scott & Amy Griswold.
    pages cm
 ISBN 978-1-59021-530-2 (pbk. : alk. paper) -- ISBN 978-1-59021-086-4
(e-book)
 1. Private investigators--England--London--Fiction. 2. Great Britain--
History--Victoria, 1837-1901--Fiction. 3. Metaphysics--Fiction. 4. Fantasy
fiction. 5. Mystery fiction. I. Griswold, Amy. II. Title.
 PS3569.C672D37 2014
 813'.54--dc23
                    2014036070

CHAPTER ONE
An Incident at the Mercury Club

JULIAN LYNES LEANED BACK TO ALLOW the waiter to clear away the remains of what he had to admit had been a better-than-expected dinner. Not that it had been anything elaborate, and the fish had been mediocre, but the soup and the chop had both been excellent, and all in all it had been a satisfactory evening. The Mercury wasn't his club, and even if he'd been the sort of man who joined this sort of club, the Mercury would not have been his choice. He glanced around the still-busy dining room, its walls covered with framed prints of horses and boxers and cricketers and one stalwart oarsman, his muscles bulging under tight trunks, all of whom he presumed the membership could identify, and made himself look back at his dinner companion, Edward Mathey, whose club it was. Ned gave him an encouraging smile, one Julian returned. It was only fair that he should let Ned take him to dinner here, particularly if he had any plans to introduce Ned to private rooms more advanced than Jacobs' card room, and so far, at least, no one had commented on his own ignorance of sport, or suggested he didn't belong. In fact, no one seemed to have noticed them at all, a state of affairs that Julian found more refreshing than not.

Ned seemed to take his relaxation as encouragement. "Brandy?"

"Yes."

"We'll take it in the library," Ned said, to the waiter, who bowed and hurried away. Julian pushed himself to his feet, and followed his friend down the dark-paneled hall. As he anticipated, the library was empty, though the clatter and voices from the billiards room next door suggested that was fully occupied. Ned waved vaguely toward a pair of armchairs by the enormous fireplace. Julian settled himself opposite, stretching his feet out to the fire crackling nicely on the hearth, and another waiter appeared with a tray and two enormous brandies. He scurried away again as soon as they had taken their drinks.

Julian lifted his glass in a not-entirely-ironic toast. "I'm impressed by the service."

"It's a good part of what we pay for. For most of us – most of the membership, I mean – the idea is to have a place where you can get a decent meal and not have to put on airs."

Ned winced just a little, as though he wished he could take the words back, and Julian looked down at his drink. They had been lovers for a few months now, ever since the end of the Nevett murder case, but they had been friends since their unhappy schooldays at Sts Thomas's. They had gone up to Oxford together fully expecting the friendship to continue, and instead had grown apart over just that question of airs and tastes and friendships. Ned had gravitated to the sportsmen while Julian had found men who shared his tastes among the literary and theatrical sets; the two groups had never mixed, and the two friends had singularly failed to find a way to remain close in the face of general disapproval. Julian was far from sorry that Ned had made the effort to rekindle the friendship, and their affair, and if it meant a night or two at the hearties' club, he was prepared to make the sacrifice. To be fair, it had hardly been difficult.

"The food's quite good," he said.

"The salmon's been better," Ned said, judiciously. "But the chops were good, I thought."

"And you keep a good cellar."

"Our steward's very good. We're hardly the most wealthy club about, but the claret's always excellent."

Julian let his gaze range over the shelves that ran from floor to ceiling: a proper library, certainly, the sort of place every club had, with its tables for writing the occasional letters, but most of the books seemed to be bound volumes of magazines, and there were more than a few shilling shockers drooping at the ends of rows, or tucked in among the more solid bindings. That didn't surprise him – it was what he would have expected of the club's membership – but the frank acknowledgement of their tastes was rather charming. "You seem well-supplied."

Ned paused as though he wasn't sure what to make of the comment, and Julian looked at his brandy again, scowling. He certainly hadn't meant it badly. Ned knew how many copies of the Police Gazette decorated his rooms, but if he chose to take it that way –

There was a sudden rise of voices from the billiards room, a sharp note of alarm, and they both looked up as a figure darted past the library's open door, then stopped and turned back.

"Mathey! Thank God! Come quick, we need you –"

Ned set his drink hastily aside, the brandy slopping unheeded, and hurried after the stranger. Julian followed. There was a note in the babble that spoke of real trouble, and he stopped in the door of the billiards room, taking in the situation.

A young man hung over the end of the center table, one hand clutching at the table's edge while the other tore at his mouth. Another man had gotten shirt and collar loose, but the young man's face was scarlet, and there was something bright green between his jaws.

"Wright?" Ned said, and looked around as though searching for someone responsible. "What the devil?"

"He's never had any problem before," someone said, and Wright beat hard on the table, flailing for air.

Ned reached into the inner pocket of his jacket and drew out his wand, a ten-inch length of oak stained black in the severe Oxford style, with only the sharp silver caps at the ends for decoration. "Easy," he said, as though he were talking to a horse. "Steady, old chap."

Wright's eyes rolled up in his head, and one of the others caught him under the shoulders, easing him to the carpet as he collapsed. Ned went to his knees beside him, eyes closing for an instant as he composed his enchantment, and then his wand moved, sketching out the sigil. Julian couldn't quite see the symbols – *release*, he thought, and possibly *to make smaller* – but he caught the sulphur-match smell of a hastily-formed enchantment, momentarily stronger than the gas. Wright heaved once, and then one of the others tugged the green object from his mouth. It was a billiard ball, Julian realized, not quite sure he believed it. Wright drew a whooping breath, and another, then doubled over, coughing. Ned patted his shoulder, and pushed himself to his feet.

"Thank God, Mathey," one of the others said, and a nice-looking blond nodded.

"Yes, nice work."

"I don't think he ought to try that again," Ned said, mildly, and looked over his shoulder at Julian, inviting him to share the relief. "Wright's single great parlor trick, I'm afraid. He can fit an entire billiard ball in his mouth. Only it seems to have gone wrong somehow."

The blond heaved him to his feet and into a chair, and Wright flopped back against the cushions, working his jaw. Wright's color was coming back, though his breath still wheezed alarmingly.

Julian looked at Wright, considering the shape of his jaw, the set of his teeth and chin. "I expect it was the teeth-straightening that caused the problem,"

Ned looked at him, eyebrows rising not in question but in consideration, and Wright looked up, frowning.

"I never."

"Of course you did," Julian said absently, looking at the billiard ball. It was just a fraction smaller than the others.

Ned winced. "I imagine I'll be charged for spoiling the set."

Julian grinned. "Surely it shouldn't fall on you."

"It was my enchantment."

"I did not have my teeth straightened," Wright said, more loudly, and Julian lifted an eyebrow.

"Yes –"

Ned said, "Whatever you say, old man. Get him a drink, Forbes."

"It wouldn't have taken much change," Julian said. "I imagine there wasn't very much tolerance anyway."

Ned put his hand on Julian's shoulder, and Julian grimaced, recognizing the warning.

"Anyway," Wright muttered, "it didn't work. So that wasn't it." He subsided again, and someone handed him a glass of whisky.

"Drink up, old man, you need it."

"We'll just be going," Ned said, and Julian let himself be steered to the door.

"Why would someone put a billiard ball in his mouth?"

"Because he can?" Ned answered. There was a note in his voice that suggested he was prepared to explain why this was reasonable.

Julian sighed. "Let's finish our brandies and go home."

❦

NED HURRIED THROUGH THE GARDENS OF the Commons the next morning, angling his umbrella to fend off the chill October rain. The omnibuses were crowded in this weather, and when one had finally stopped, the inside seats had been filled with ladies, and he'd been relegated to the unprotected top deck, where the cold rain hissed and spat as the water-shedding glamours on adjacent umbrellas met and battled.

In the gardens, the bed of *Urtica mordax* was quiescent from the weather, its tendrils curled around themselves as if hugging themselves in the cold. Ned couldn't blame it. The wing of the Commons devoted to theoretical metaphysics had suspiciously few lamps burning, suggesting that many of the learned metaphysicists had chosen to sleep in. That was one of the privileges of theory; the metaphysicians who dealt in actual practice generally had no such luxury.

As he expected, there were more signs of life as he emerged from the gardens on the side of the Commons occupied by the applied practitioners. Most metaphysicians couldn't afford to take the morning off for bad weather, depending for their living as they did on their clients. Ned hoped that he wouldn't spend the morning waiting for nonexistent new clients and brooding about the previous evening.

It hadn't been a disaster, precisely. Ned had thought at first that his attempt to introduce Julian into the company of his other friends was going well; dinner had been good, and Julian had even shown signs of beginning to relax once it became clear that no one was going to mock him as a bookish little swot who wouldn't know a cricket bat from an oar. And then Wright had to go playing silly beggars and spoil the evening.

He shook his head to dismiss unprofitable thoughts and went in to his chambers, which by virtue of his junior status in the Commons were cramped and ill-lit, with a single window and no fire. Inside, his clerk Cordelia Frost was already at her desk, her clothes holding their crisp lines despite the weather and the week's issue of *The Metaphysician* at her elbow.

To Ned's surprise, the visitor's chair was occupied by Inspector Hatton of Scotland Yard. His ginger hair stood up in damp spikes, and the tweed hat in his lap was sodden. He was leaning one elbow on Miss Frost's desk in conversation, and he looked up at Ned as he entered with what Ned fancied to be a guilty expression.

"Here's Mr Mathey now," Miss Frost said. Ned raised an eyebrow at her, wondering if Hatton could possibly have been importuning her. It seemed out of character for the man, and Miss Frost only shrugged, unruffled.

"Hullo, Hatton," Ned said. "Hadn't you ought to get a properly-charmed hat?"

"I had one," Hatton said. "It only made my hair wetter." He waited as Ned hung up his own hat and coat and maneuvered himself between the desks.

"Congratulations on your promotion, by the way," Ned said, folding himself into his chair.

"Not exactly a promotion," Hatton said. "More in the way of more responsibilities for the same title and pay."

"Even so. Head of the city's new Metaphysical Crimes Squad sounds impressive."

"Somebody's got to do it. There are enough men who get it into their heads to use metaphysics to commit crimes, never mind unlicensed practitioners and two-penny enchantments that shockingly enough don't do what was advertised. After the Nevett case, and that business with the necklace, the Yard seems to think I'm an expert."

Despite his tone, Ned thought Hatton was pleased by the assignment. It was a way to distinguish himself from the crowd at the Yard, and that was always worthwhile. "Are you here on police business, then?"

"In more than one way," Hatton said. "First, and probably most important from your point of view, we've been given the budget to put a metaphysician on retainer. All I have now on the Metaphysical Squad are a couple of unlicensed men who've been persuaded to come over to the right side of the law. That's fine for the run-of-the-mill work – it's not illegal for them to use their skills, only to claim training they haven't got – but for anything out of the ordinary I need a professional…a man with an education. I had you in mind for the job."

"What about old Carruthers?"

"He's well enough in his way," Hatton said in a tone that suggested the opposite. "But I wouldn't deprive the Yard of his services in the evidence room. It needs a young man for this, someone who's not afraid of tramping through muck to look at dead bodies and figure out how they got that way." He cast an apologetic sidelong glance at Miss Frost.

"I positively thrive on reports of gruesome murder," she said.

Hatton cleared his throat. "So, how about it? We'll pay your usual rates. It won't be pleasant work, and probably not steady work, but it won't run dry, either. There's always something."

Ned hesitated. Miss Frost looked meaningfully at the accounts book. They were narrowly enough in the black as it was, and with the Commons fees coming due in the new year…

"I'll take the job," he said.

"Glad to hear it. Half the point of the Squad is to look good in the papers – oh, I know it, all right, and I'm not about to argue. Every time there's any hint of metaphysics involved in a crime, there's a hue and cry about 'Hindu death curses' and demonic creatures roaming the streets and who knows what all else. It makes people feel safer to think that the Yard has it all in hand. 'Bright young metaphysician Edward Mathey, helped to solve the Nevett murder case,

Oxford man, all the latest methods, and etc.' It's just the right sort of thing to feed the papers."

Ned flinched at the thought. Too close an examination of his life would yield the sort of publicity that Hatton would never wish to be associated with. On the other hand, the right sort of publicity would mean new clients. "I'll try to give satisfaction."

"That's the spirit. Now, I've got an extremely peculiar corpse I'd like you to come back to the Yard and look at, if you're free."

"I thrive on peculiar corpses," Ned said, although he couldn't quite match Miss Frost's pleasant tone. "What's the matter with it? Some sort of time-delayed poison again?"

"Nothing as common as that," Hatton said. "I've got an unidentified bloke found dead in the street. Not a mark on him. We opened him up and had a look. Then we figured it had something to do with the fact that his heart is missing. Simply gone, as if it had vanished clean out of his chest." He shrugged at Ned's expression. "I told you it wouldn't be pleasant. It seldom is. But I've never seen anything like this. That's why I thought of you."

"I'm flattered. I think."

"If you can explain this one, I'll stand you lunch."

Ned wasn't at all certain he was going to want any, but he refrained from saying so, and braced himself to go back out into the rain.

❦

NED FOLLOWED HATTON THROUGH THE MAZE that was Scotland Yard, not to Hatton's former office but through a courtyard to one end of a long brick stable. Inside, desks and filing cabinets had been wedged into what had once been stalls, and the floor swept down to brick. Despite whitewash and the evidence of stubborn scrubbing, the place still smelled of horses.

"They're cramming us in everywhere they can," Hatton said, nodding toward his own desk in the corner of what must once have been a loose box. "I can't say it's worse than my old office. At least you can get a breeze through this place, although I expect it'll be murder in the winter. Here, mind your step, the evidence room's up here."

Ned ascended the rickety hayloft stairs, and found the hayloft above fitted out with shelves and cabinets, as well as several long tables, one with an indistinct form on it draped in a sheet. Gas lamps, surely newly installed, threw the room into yellow light. At the end of the room, the hayloft doors were closed against the rain.

"We'll get more equipment in here when we have the budget for it," Hatton said.

"I don't need much," Ned said. "Not all that rubbish in Carruthers's den, at any rate." The Yard's old metaphysician distrusted newfangled ways, and his laboratory could have served as a museum of last century's practices, full of hand-labeled herbs and disturbing pickled things in jars.

"Here's our mystery customer, then." Hatton pulled back the sheet, and Ned got his first look at the corpse beneath it, lying in a long wooden box packed with ice. Ned made himself look squarely at what was revealed, and then swallowed hard and busied himself longer than strictly necessary with his metaphysician's bag.

"There wasn't a scratch on him," Hatton said. "Nor a stitch of clothing. I'd think it was some anatomy student's practical joke, but if having his heart taken out didn't kill him, our surgeon hasn't got a clue what did."

Ned drew out his wand from his bag and frowned at the body, professional interest starting to displace revulsion. Warning bells were sounding at the back of his mind. "You can kill someone by metaphysics. The easiest way is by magnifying some small ailment; a cold turns into pneumonia and carries you off, or an old man with heart problems has a sudden heart attack and dies."

"There are signs, though, if a metaphysician examines the corpse."

"Certainly there are, if the grieving relatives are suspicious enough to put it to the test."

"If there are any grieving relatives…"

"It's possible someone thought that removing the heart would conceal the evidence of a curse that targeted it. He might even manage to close up the wound afterwards by metaphysics, with some considerable effort." He shook his head. "But it doesn't make sense. Anyone who knew enough to do that would also know that taking out the heart wouldn't prevent a metaphysician from detecting a curse."

"Then you can?"

He held off answering, too troubled by other possibilities. "Far easier to use metaphysics to propel a physical object – although not half as easily as you can hit someone with it using brute strength."

"Like the cursed candlestick that fell on Nevett's head. Ah, but there's no sign of that here. It seems to me his heart's just disappeared into thin air."

"And that's exactly what can't be true. Making things vanish into thin air is a conjurer's trick. You can't do that with metaphysics. Not in our modern system. None that I've seen. The grammar won't allow it." Ned glanced up at Hatton's face. "The theoretical men could explain it better."

Hatton leaned back against the table. "Probably not so that I'd understand. You said 'not in our modern system,' though."

Ned let out a breath. "There are other kinds of enchantment. Non-conforming metaphysics."

"Which is illegal."

"For good reason. But you still see it sometimes with enchanted objects that are very old, where the work was done in a system that didn't have a fully-worked-out grammar. The effects produced can be startling, and when it's mixed with modern practice, they can be disastrous."

"So you think it could be a very old curse."

"Or one that doesn't conform to any regular system at all. Now and again you see that, someone fabricating a kind of makeshift system of metaphysics entirely out of his head, like a private language. Most of the time it doesn't work at all, but every once in a while the results are dangerous."

"I'd say this one was dangerous, all right."

"You have no idea," Ned said. "If he was playing around with non-conforming enchantment, we're all lucky it didn't end worse. Every college of metaphysics warns against making that kind of experiment, but there's always someone who thinks he knows best."

"You think he might have done it to himself, then." Hatton sounded a bit relieved at the idea.

"It's possible. Non-conforming metaphysics is unpredictable. It's more likely to blow up in your own face than to work as a weapon. But I can't swear to it. I can't even swear that's what killed him, short of putting it to a test."

"Let's have the test, then."

"It's not what I'd call safe."

"Neither is mucking about with criminals who've found every crooked use there is for hocus. But the men who gave me this job expect results, and that means not listing the cause of death as 'we expect it's metaphysics, but we're frankly buggered if we know for sure' except as a last resort."

"I see your point," Ned said. He wracked his brain trying to recall everything he knew about dealing with non-conforming enchantment that wasn't entirely a cautionary tale, but that wasn't much. He thought of consulting the dog-eared copy of the *De Occulta Philosophia* in his case, but was fairly certain it contained nothing relevant except a warning against objects enchanted by "men of little learning."

He took up his wand instead, resolving to try the first of the standard tests for cursework, and hoping it wouldn't go too badly awry. It was merely the metaphysical word "light," one of the simplest, sketched on the square of the Sun. He kept a small hand mirror in his bag, and he angled it to catch the light from the nearest lamp and throw it across the corpse.

"Stand well back," he told Hatton. "Just in case." He took a moment to visualize the square of the Sun superimposed over the body, its thirty-six familiar numbers standing for the thirty-six letters of the metaphysical alphabet, and crisply traced a short line between two of the letters with his wand.

The moment he completed the gesture, Ned knew something was wrong. The word should have fit into an existing enchantment, or at worst tangled with its grammar; instead it seemed to connect without closing, its energy flailing like a fish fighting on the end of a line. The mirror cracked in his hand with a noise like a shot, the pieces rattling down into the ice. The ice brightened, casting up jagged reflections, as if the corpse were lying in a box of broken mirrors with something bright glowing underneath.

"Hatton, get down," Ned said, ducking down himself behind the shelter of an adjacent table. Hatton followed suit admirably fast, scowling as he crouched like a ginger-haired gargoyle.

"Suppose you tell me –"

Hatton's complaint was drowned out by a noise like someone smashing a mirror with a piano. It was followed as a considerable anticlimax by the sound of shards of ice dripping down from the rafters and the walls. When no further alarming noises followed, Ned stood up cautiously, brushing crushed ice and splinters of mirror from his coat.

The sheet had been thrown free, and the body was lying in a box entirely empty of ice, except for the pulverized fragments now dripping down from the ceiling. Some of the shards of mirror were embedded quite deeply in the rafters.

There was the sound of hurried footsteps on the stairs, and a scruffy man in an ill-fitting tweed coat stuck his head up cautiously. "All right up there, guv?"

"In one piece, anyway," Hatton said, unfolding himself from behind the table. "Mr Mathey was just examining the corpse."

"I'd say that confirms the cause of death," Ned said.

"You don't say." Hatton shook his head and gave a nod to the newcomer. "Mr Mathey, Special Constable Garmin. Garmin, this is Mathey, who'll be consulting."

"Pleased, I'm sure," Garmin said, and gave Ned a look that seemed to size him up professionally. Ned half expected to be offered a telesm guaranteed to restore masculine virility and whiten his teeth at the same time.

Hatton drew the sheet back up over the corpse, arranging it neatly as if through long practice. "It looks like our lad was messing round with non-conforming metaphysics."

"Silly bugger," Garmin said.

"You're probably right," Ned stared down at the pale face. "But who was he?"

"I wish we knew. No one's turned up to claim him. I had thought you might be able to give us a clue about where he lived, but I don't imagine you want to try any more enchantments on him."

"I wouldn't dare," Ned said. "You shouldn't even let him come into contact with anything metaphysically active. Make sure there's no glamour on the casket when he's buried, nothing meant to preserve the body."

"If no one claims him, it'll be a plain pine box."

"I'm out of my depth with this. I'll have to do some research and see if I can find any reports of anything like it, maybe bring in a metaphysicist. There are a few of them who study non-conforming systems."

"You do that. You think it could have been an accident, though."

"There are any number of easier ways to kill a man, and most of them would be considerably more likely to pass for a natural death."

"That's what I like to hear," Hatton said. "Poor bloke, though. I hope none of his friends were in it with him. Or that this has scared them well off it, at least." He clapped Ned on the shoulder. "Well, come along, and I'll stand you that lunch."

"You needn't put yourself out."

"We'll start with a pint, and see if that gets your appetite back. You soon get used to the corpses."

"I look forward to it," Ned said as gamely as he could, as Hatton took his elbow to steer him back toward the stairs.

CHAPTER TWO
Practical Poetics

J ULIAN LYNES PUSHED ASIDE THE CURTAIN to stare down into Coptic Street, wishing the rain would let up a bit. He felt oddly on edge – nothing to do with the less than ideal ending to the previous night's entertainment, he told himself, though perhaps if he had persuaded Ned to come home with him he would at least feel satisfied. Mrs Digby's breakfast had been no worse than usual, if no better, though his patented Napieric coffee maker had been particularly balky that morning. He'd barely avoided an explosion on the first try, and the second had produced a beverage as insipid as dishwater – the fault of the barometric pressure, he suspected, glancing at the pencil marks on the wallpaper beside the barometer, but it still made for a discouraging morning.

Below him, the bell jangled with the morning's next post, and he watched idly as the postman bustled down the steps and on toward the next house. A moment later, there was the sound of footsteps on the stairs, and then a knock at the door.

"Come in."

"Post's here, Mr Lynes."

"Thank you." Julian took the handful of envelopes, fishing in his pocket for a penny. He handed it to young Digby, who acted as house page as well as errand boy, and rifled through the mail. Three of the five were bills, the fourth was a pamphlet he vaguely remembered ordering, and the fifth was addressed to him in a flamboyant yet legible hand. It looked familiar, and was anyway more promising than any of the others. He set them aside on an already tottering pile and broke the seal on the letter.

He recognized the name instantly: Auberon Kennett – who had been plain Oliver when Julian knew him at Oxford – was a rising young poet and also a habitué of many of the same clubs that Julian frequented, which did not bode well for the message. Kennett was rumored to be on the verge of releasing a new volume of verse; he would not need scandal attached to his name.

My dear Lynes, I find that I may be in need of your professional services in regard to a possible question of some awkwardness. It seems to be more professional on my side as well rather than personal but nonetheless I would appreciate a friendly eye and ear.

"What the devil does that mean?" Julian demanded, but he suspected, in spite of the obfuscation, that Kennett was being blackmailed, and that rarely ended well. He refolded the letter and locked it into his desk, then stood for a moment tapping his fingers while he debated his next move. Presumably Kennett expected him to write back, and then there would be the inevitable dance of telegrams as they settled on the time and place for an appointment, and abruptly Julian couldn't bear to wait. He reached for the bell-rope and tugged it sharply, then shrugged himself into his overcoat while he waited for his landlady to appear.

"Yes, Mr Lynes?" Mrs Digby's voice was sharper than her words, her scowl forbidding, and Julian tried to think what Ned might do to appease her. Nothing occurred to him, and he reached for his bowler, brushing yesterday's dust from the brim.

"I have to go out. If anyone calls, tell them I'll be in this afternoon. Please."

She sniffed. "I'll tell them. If there should be anyone."

Her assessment was unfortunately accurate – his practice was still relatively new – but Julian managed to bite back his first answer. "Good," he said instead, and clapped his hat on his head. He collected his umbrella from the stand by the door and clattered down the stairs before she might say anything more.

Both his hat and his umbrella were glamoured against rain, but the damp and chill seeped up through his shoes as he walked across Bloomsbury to the address in the superscription, Kennett's lodgings off Great Ormond Street. It was an odd, narrow house in a street barely wide enough to take a carriage, and Julian had to press himself close to the damp stones as a delivery wagon rumbled past. Still, the maid who came to take his card was neat and quick, and brought him up the stairs to Kennett's first floor parlor with a smile and a quick curtsy.

"Lynes, dear boy," Kennett said. He was only a year older than Julian and a head shorter, sturdily built, with round cheeks beneath red-brown curls. He was also dressed to go out, in a neat sack suit with a single yellow flower in a silver boutonniere pinned to his lapel. "I didn't expect to see you this quickly."

"I had business this way," Julian said. "And besides, I couldn't make head nor tail of your letter. Why don't you tell me what the problem really is?"

"I'd like to. You have no idea how much I'd like to. But I've a meeting with my publisher in half an hour, and it doesn't do to be late."

"Five minutes would be enough to get started," Julian suggested, but Kennett shook his head.

"I wish it were that simple."

"You could at least tell me if it's blackmail."

Kennett flinched at the word, which Julian supposed was answer enough. "Yes. Yes, I suppose it is, though it's a bit more – complicated." He pulled his watch out of his pocket, shook his head again. "I'm sorry, Lynes, there's just not time. Why don't we meet tonight – at the Dionysus? I'll be there after ten, I expect."

Julian blinked in spite of himself. "Is that wise?" The Dionysus was the least reputable of the private rooms to which he subscribed. Oh, the ground floor card rooms were more or less decent even if the stakes weren't, but the first floor parlors were often the scenes of startlingly public display, and the second floor… He shook away the thought of taking Ned to one of those little rooms, and made himself focus on Kennett. "If it's blackmail –"

"But not about that," Kennett said. He reached for his watch again, looking regrettably like the White Rabbit in *Alice*. "I really can't talk now. Tonight?"

"Yes, of course," Julian said. "Wait, hold still." He brushed at Kennett's sleeve and succeeded in grasping a single shed hair. "There, that's done it."

"Thank you," Kennett said. He let them out, and they walked together up the narrow road, parting at the corner of Great Ormond Street.

Julian didn't look back, but ducked into the first sheltered doorway he saw, folding his umbrella and bracing it between his feet. He found the strand of hair he'd taken from Kennett's coat and wrapped it carefully around the shaft of the umbrella just above the handle, sealing it to itself with a whispered charm. When he was sure it was secure, he pulled his wand from his pocket and used the finger-long slip of ivory to sketch a pair of sigils that would cause the hair to seek its original owner. It was a somewhat questionable enchantment – and Kennett should be more careful in his grooming – but it was definitely effective. He tucked his wand back into his pocket and opened his umbrella again, feeling the hair's pressure on the shaft. Back the way he'd come, then, and he stepped back into the rain.

Kennett led him a merry dance, the enchantment drawing Julian around corner after corner as though Kennett had wanted to be sure no one was following. And that was certainly interesting, Julian thought, and wondered if Kennett was trying to ward off the blackmailer or him. Both, more likely: he'd learned that most of his clients lied to him at least at the beginning of a case. Which was not to say that many of them didn't have cause, he added, with an inward grin, but it had led him to take his own precautions.

The pressure against the umbrella led him down a narrow arcade occupied by a cobbler and a pair of glovers and a dispirited-looking hatter, and then pulled him to the right. This time, Kennett seemed to be making no real attempt to conceal his destination, and Julian guessed that his quarry had convinced himself he wasn't being followed. He doubled back past the Foundling Hospital and turned onto Tavistock Place. The pressure on the umbrella increased, then tugged sharply right into Dane Court. From the feel of it, this was where Kennett had been heading, and Julian made his way slowly up the street, stepping carefully around the puddles. He wasn't surprised when the umbrella dipped sideways, trying to draw him up the steps that led to a brass-bound door with a plate that read "Delahunt Bros Publishers." Kennett was within, and Julian paused long enough to dismiss the enchantment and let the hair drift away to be lost in the muck of the street.

Literature was not particularly Julian's strong suit, but he did know the names of the more prestigious houses. Kennett was published by Lawrence and Chadburne, nearly top tier; the Delahunt Brothers weren't in the same class at all. He thought he'd heard of them, though, but couldn't make the connection – but if he didn't know, he knew someone who would.

He turned back toward the British Museum, tilting his umbrella against the increasing rain, and made his way through the maze of back alleys to one of the dozens of booksellers who kept their shops in the side streets. The bell clanged as he opened the door, and he stood for a moment in the gaslight, folding his umbrella and letting his eyes adjust to the relative darkness.

"Mr Lynes. Haven't seen you in a while."

"Mr Horrocks." Julian moved toward the desk where the proprietor did most of his work, careful to keep his umbrella from dripping on any of the pamphlets piled on the floor. "Business, I'm afraid. I hope you're well?"

"As well as anyone can be, in this weather." Horrocks hunched his shoulders in his heavy frock coat, which looked as though it had been made for a much larger man. "Out with it, then. What are you after?"

"Delahunt Brothers. What do they publish?"

Horrocks made an odd, wheezing sound, and after a moment Julian realized he was laughing. Still wheezing, Horrocks slid off his stool and disappeared into the maze of shelves, to return after a moment with a set of short volumes bound in bright blue cloth. The gilt lettering read, amid flourishes, "Miss Amabel's Deception, or, A Cautionary Tale, by Mrs Barnard Tremaine." The Delahunt Brothers' monogram, a *D* and a *B* with a hunting horn, was almost as large as the authoress's name.

Julian felt his eyebrows rise. That was where he'd heard the name: Ned had an unfortunate fondness for multi-volume novels, and Julian had seen that mark on several of them.

Horrocks nodded. "Shilling shockers, you'd call them if they were for boys, but since they're for the ladies, we'll just call them romance. Not that I'd let a daughter of mine read these, nor my wife, either."

Horrocks had neither. Julian opened Volume Four to reveal a frontispiece of a young woman in a flimsy-looking nightdress whose bound hands stretched overhead to a hook attached to the ceiling of the hovel. An old woman grinned up at her from beside the fire, and someone – the hero? the villain? – peeped in the unshuttered window. "Miss Amabel, I presume," he said, and closed the cover. He was afraid he might be blushing, and gave his most forbidding frown.

"God only knows," Horrocks said. "But that's what Delahunt publishes, Mr Lynes. They publish a lot of it, too, and make a tidy profit."

"Quite." Julian slid the book back across the counter. "Thank you for your help, Mr Horrocks."

"Always at your service, Mr Lynes."

Julian let himself back out into the rain, still frowning, this time in genuine perplexity. He couldn't imagine what Kennett's business with Delahunt might be – but the main thing, he reminded himself, was to find out what Kennett wanted him to do. That meant a visit to the Dionysus Club, which was always an adventure. Perhaps it was time to invite Ned along. They could surely find amusement while they were waiting for Kennett to appear. The thought was definitely warming, and he lengthened his stride, suddenly in a hurry to get back to Coptic Street to send a discreet invitation.

☾❀

THE FRONT PARLOR AT JACOBS' was thinly occupied early in the evening, only one table occupied by a game of chemin de fer, and by the looks of it the game was being played for money rather than the stakes of dubious forfeits that were customary later in the evening. Jacobs' could have been confused for any of the many clubs in the city, Ned thought, if it weren't for the way one of the onlookers at the table had his arms twined around the neck of one of the players.

It was Julian's usual haunt, and Julian had suggested they drop in for a drink before moving on to the Dionysus in search of his poet. On his few previous visits, Ned had avoided the tables, not sure he was willing to risk either kind of stake. Besides, he found it hair-raising to watch Julian cheat at cards.

As they came in and made their way toward the bar, Peter Lennox disengaged himself from the fringes of the card game and came over to meet them. He was a big man, taller even than Ned, and must have cut a handsome figure in youth, Ned thought; even with a receding hairline and a tendency to run to flesh in middle age, his face had a mobile humor that caught the eye.

"Lynes, dear boy…and you've brought back your paragon once again."

"Lennox," Julian said discouragingly, but Ned thought the teasing note in Lennox's voice was affectionate, with no sting in the words.

"I do strive to excel," he said.

Julian choked, and Lennox smiled in amusement that bordered on delight. "You know, I'm certain that you do," he said. He took Julian by the elbow. "Come and have a drink, my dear, before you swallow your tongue."

Ned let Lennox lead Julian a little away to the bar. They'd been to bed together, Ned knew, but he had come to believe Julian's assurance that he wasn't serious about Lennox except as a friend. And he was glad for Julian to have friends. It was only that when they were at Oxford, Julian's friends had been such an unpleasant lot, certain of their own artistic genius and quick to snub mere sportsmen.

By the time Ned had obtained a whisky and soda of his own, Lennox had one elbow on the bar telling Julian some story that was making him smile. Pleased to see that rather than Julian's habitual expression of being a dubious explorer in a strange land, Ned decided not to interrupt just yet. He looked about for a conversation to join that wasn't about plays he hadn't seen or people he didn't know.

In one corner, a freckled young man was toying with his own drink in apparent boredom, and Ned wandered over to join him out of a vague spirit of fellow-feeling.

"Mathey, isn't it?"

"It is, but I'm afraid you have the better of me."

"It's Smith. I mean, it really is, but that's why no one remembers. I hope they're not trying to make you talk about opera."

"Well, some people like opera," Ned said.

"Oh, yes, well, of course…I mean, one does. I hear that Patti is brilliant in her latest."

"I wouldn't know," Ned said, seeing little point in talking about an opera he hadn't seen with someone who didn't seem to have seen it either. "I'm afraid Bates is more my idea of brilliant."

The young man's eyes widened. "You follow cricket?" Ned tensed, expecting the next remark to be cutting, and instead found himself tugged into a chair by the sleeve. "Oh, God, come over here and sit by me," Smith said, his voice lower but fervent. "Did you see him against Kings' on Thursday? A regular demon at the bat."

He was actually enjoying himself by the time Julian came over carrying another drink for Ned as well as his own.

"And that *arse*, when he bends over to bat," Smith was saying, hands spread by way of illustration. "Just like two…" He trailed off at Julian's raised eyebrow, and Ned grinned and relieved Julian of the glass.

"Perhaps one of the poets in the room could contribute a metaphor to the cause," Ned said.

"Ode on a Cricketer's Arse," Smith declaimed somberly. "Do you think the Athenaeum would publish that?"

Julian snorted. "They might. But speaking of poets who are not in this room, we'd better go and look for Kennett."

❦

"The Dionysus Club. The name's not very subtle, is it?" Ned said once they had reached their omnibus stop and dismounted in a row of nondescript houses.

"They're not a very subtle lot," Julian said, with high color in his cheeks that Ned didn't think entirely due to the weather. "Just very lively. And besides, it's classical."

Lively was one way of describing the din inside. It had been quiet on the front steps, suggesting an enchantment to prevent noise from carrying. Inside, even with the doors into the parlors closed, the noise of loud conversation and laughter carried.

"We'll need to see the steward," Julian said once they'd surrendered their coats into a footman's care. "It's members only." The footman went to fetch him, and a harried-looking man with thinning hair emerged after a moment from a door at the back of the hall.

"Julian, darling, I'm glad I caught you. It is subscription time again, you know."

"Not until January," Julian said, but with a sideways glance at Ned he extracted his cheque book from his coat. "You can have it now if you must. I have my friend's entrance fee to pay as well."

"That's good of you. I hate to be mercenary, but if no one did, the drink would run short, and then you'd hear them scream."

Ned signed "John Smythe" in the club register, and the steward glanced at it without surprise. "What can I call you? It's Malcolm, by the way, if you need anything. Within reason."

"You needn't give your real name if you don't want," Julian said, a bit awkwardly.

"Ned." It was common enough, and he shook off the faint unease of inviting a stranger to be so familiar.

"Pleased to –" There was the crash of breaking glass from the back parlor. "Oh, Christ," Malcolm said, plucked the cheque from Julian's hand without looking at it, and threw up his hands in wordless apology as he hurried away.

Julian led the way into the front parlor. There the fire was blazing too high for the weather, its flames a livid green, an herbal sweetness mixing with the smell of tobacco smoke and sweat. On the mantelpiece, cut-glass lamps threw a fragmented light across the room. Figured velvet curtains covered the windows from floor to ceiling, and a number of velvet sofas were crammed into the room, along with tables littered with empty glasses and ends of cigars.

The walls were crowded with paintings of nude young men in classical poses, and a life-sized bronze Dionysus regarded the room with a cat's smile. Someone had draped a discarded coat over Dionysus's outstretched arm. On one wall, a large glass fishbowl was supported by silver dragons, smoke pouring from their nostrils and their scales shifting color as they writhed in place. One fancy goldfish swam round in circles, regarding the party with bulging eyes that looked perpetually startled.

The room was crowded, and while most of the men were in ordinary evening clothes, some were wearing smoking jackets as if they were at home, and a few were wearing even less. One young man was entirely undressed to the waist, leaning back in the middle of a sofa talking to one friend while another ran an exploratory hand down his freckled chest.

Ned swallowed hard, and Julian followed his gaze, then looked back at Ned as if trying to gauge his reaction.

"I did tell you they weren't subtle."

"So you did," Ned said, managing through sheer force of will not to stare. He could only catch snatches of conversation as Julian elbowed their way toward the drinks table.

"– I can't say I've heard of it, although I'm sure your little book is charming –"

"– as long as you don't mind doing it standing up –"

"– crawling with happy families on holiday, we might as well have gone to Brighton –"

In one corner, an argument seemed to be breaking out, one voice rising high and sharp over the others.

"– isn't the first time, and if you think I don't know what's been going on –"

"Ignore that, it's perpetual," Julian said. "Artistic temperament." He said it in the same tone he would have used for bubonic plague, which made Ned feel a bit better. So did a whisky and soda, which he drank thirstily. The heat was stifling.

"If it isn't dear Julian, with the catch of the day," an unexpectedly familiar voice said. Ned looked up to see Linford Farrell balancing a glass of gin. He'd been one of Julian's friends at Oxford, with a razor wit that Julian had admired without seeming to notice how mean-spirited it could be.

Farrell leaned in to kiss Julian on the cheek, which Ned wouldn't have thought anyone could do without warning and avoid being kicked in the shins. Julian allowed himself to be kissed, although without much apparent pleasure. "Linford," he said. "You remember my friend Ned?"

"Of course," Farrell said. He narrowed his eyes in what struck Ned as entirely feigned confusion. "I thought it was Hercules, though, or something very martial like that. Hannibal, maybe."

"Hannibal will do if you like," Ned said mildly.

Farrell looked him in the eye as if sizing up an opposing wrestler, and then smiled with abrupt amiability. "Of course I remember you. And any friend of Julian's…" He extended his hand, and Ned had no alternative but to shake it, and then beckoned to his companion. "You remember Ryder, don't you?"

Ned did remember Ryder Leach, primarily as having been inclined to ask people their opinions about literary greats and then explain to them why they were wrong, but he only nodded. Leach was handsome in an untidy way, his hair still too long for fashion, curling about his wrinkled collar, though Farrell had trimmed his own and had a professional polish about him.

"You haven't seen Auberon, have you?" Julian said.

"Not tonight. He might be in the back," Farrell said, sounding unconcerned.

"We'll look." Julian took Ned firmly by the elbow to steer him away from Farrell.

They found room to breathe in the lee of the fishbowl, and Ned drained his drink while Julian looked around.

"I don't see him," Julian said.

"Do tell me you didn't sleep with him."

"Auberon? Not for very long –"

"Farrell," Ned said.

"Well," Julian said. He cleared his throat. "Not for very long."

One of the dragons supporting the fishbowl nipped at Ned's sleeve, and as he extracted it from the silver teeth, he realized that the swirling pattern of color on the dragon's back was spreading across his coat sleeve. He drew out his wand and put it right, frowning at the fishbowl.

"These enchantments aren't very well done," he said.

"I expect not," Julian said, sounding grateful for a change of subject. "People experiment. Not so much on Miss Caroline herself, since the time she swelled up to twice her size and grew fangs." The goldfish regarded Ned and his wand with her protruding eyes, as if wondering if it was going to happen again, and then embarked on another circle of her bowl.

Another argument had broken out, or perhaps it was the same one, Ned couldn't be sure. There were exclamations as someone threw a drink, but only from people close enough to be in splashing range. Scraps of conversation were lost in the general noise.

"– tell you another thing, you conniving little –"

"– don't listen to a single word he says, he hasn't been sober in –"

"– haven't seen him around in days –"

"– if he wants to make a great contribution to literature, I said, he just has to resolve to write less."

The last was from a bespectacled man in the nearest armchair, who gave the air of holding court, with Ryder Leach at his elbow laughing obligingly and a pair of young men crowded onto the footstool in front of him, both gazing up at him with puppy-dog eyes.

"Pinky, darling, you're terrible," one of them said.

"No, the *book* was terrible."

Behind the same armchair, a flirtation was growing rather heated. Abruptly, the young man with his back to the armchair began unfastening his trousers. Ned couldn't help staring, wondering how far they meant to take it.

The question was answered when the man's companion went down on his knees in front of him and began ministering to him with great enthusiasm. On the other side of the chair, they were still talking about literature. Ned couldn't have thought of the title of a single book, not watching the man's jaw working and the curl of dark hair against his partner's shirt tails.

"I said it was a lively crowd," Julian said in his ear.

Ned glanced at Julian, who was watching too, obviously not unaffected. He leaned his shoulder against Julian's, and Julian pressed his knee against Ned's, as if they were merely crowded together. His pulse was pounding, and he could feel Julian breathing hard as well.

It would be so easy to press Julian back against the wall, so easy to press his mouth to Julian's throat where his collar was wilting in the heat, and no one would care. The young man groaned theatrically, throwing his head back, and there was scattered laughter and catcalls from his friends.

But Ned wasn't certain he was up for that kind of show, no matter how fast his pulse was beating. "Your poet," he managed. "We should find him."

"Yes, of course," Julian said, after a momentary pause that suggested it took an effort to collect his own thoughts. "He's probably in the back room."

"I'll meet you there," Ned said. "I could use some air."

Julian looked uncertain for a moment. Ned squeezed his shoulder in reassurance and then made for the door back out into the hall.

It was less stifling out in the hall, and shutting the door behind him brought the noise down to a dull roar. He walked the length of the hall, finding the cooler air restorative and at least somewhat effective at reducing his arousal from a fever pitch. He wasn't sure whether he'd narrowly escaped doing something he would have regretted, or if he should be kicking himself for a coward.

He was about to brave the back parlor when he heard voices carrying from an open door across the hall. He recognized Farrell's voice, rising in harsh and not entirely sober complaint.

"Some sodding club this is, Straun. Half the decanters bone dry, and here you are fluttering around like a wounded bird, moaning about money again."

"Only because everyone owes it," Malcolm said. "And I'll thank you not to bandy names. Now, if anyone can explain how broken glass got into the curtains six feet up –"

"Be a thrifty little housewife and figure it out. Now come on, *darling*, get off your arse and find someone to fill up the gin."

From the sound of it, Farrell hadn't changed much since Oxford. Ned shook his head, and went to find Julian.

JULIAN MADE HIS WAY OUT INTO the back hall, and immediately had to press himself against the wall to avoid a couple making for the stairs, so tangled in a heated embrace that they didn't seem to see him. One of them did bump against him, and mumbled something that might have been an apology, but to Julian's relief they headed up the stairs without further conversation. Damn Kennett anyway, he thought. Of all the clubs to pick… But at least Ned had looked as much intrigued as shocked. Julian licked his lips, unable not to imagine Ned on his knees, big hands quick and clever on trouser buttons – and that was a thought better not pursued just at the moment. He took a breath, thinking of Farrell and the rest watching avidly, and willed his arousal to subside.

The back parlor was just as crowded and just as hot, flames dancing peacock blue on the hearth, but the gaslights had been turned down, leaving the room lit primarily by the lamps that stood precariously on a handful of tables. It was just as noisy, too, and Julian winced as someone in the shadows gave a shriek that suggested a not entirely welcome advance. It subsided to giggles, and Julian looked away. There was a party playing cards and drinking – more drinking than cards, Julian thought – but Kennett wasn't among them, nor was he with the group that had taken over several of the sofas and was busy melting inks for what looked as though it was going to be an ill-advised enchantment.

Beyond those groups, on the more shadowed couches, couples and a few larger groups were engaging in behavior that was almost guaranteed to frighten horses. Julian let his eyes rove over them, trying not to stare, and was almost certain Kennett wasn't among them. Or if he was, he added silently, he wouldn't take kindly to being interrupted. Julian turned away, and saw with relief that Ned was hovering by the door, frowning as though he found it hard to see in the dim light. Julian joined him, and was pleased to see the frown relax.

"Any luck?" Ned asked.

Julian shook his head. "He's not here. But there are a few more rooms upstairs that we should check." He took Ned's arm, abruptly aware of the solid muscle beneath the fine wool, and draw him out into the hall. Ned turned obediently toward the main stair, but Julian held him back. "This way."

"The servants' stair?" Ned balked at the door.

"There aren't any on duty overnight," Julian said. "Well, bar the footmen and the waiter, and they have strict instructions not to come upstairs."

"I imagine that's wise." Ned followed him through into the stairwell. The gas was turned low, more of Malcolm's thrift, and Julian tugged him up the first flight of stairs to the landing.

"Here," he said, breathless, and to his surprise Ned moved first, pressing him back against the wall, his mouth finding the sensitive hollow beneath his jaw. After the first shock it was entirely satisfactory, and Julian braced himself against the wall, working his hands beneath Ned's clothes until he found skin. "Now —"

He pushed Ned away, and Ned sank willingly to his knees. They fumbled with Julian's buttons, and then Ned had freed him, and Julian gave himself over to the blinding pleasure.

Afterward, he leaned hard against the wall, and Ned dragged himself to his feet, laughing softly as he fastened his own clothes. "So is this the usual entertainment at the Dionysus?"

Above them, a door opened, and Julian flattened himself against the wall, eyes narrowing in the dim light as he tried to see who was there. The door closed again, and he relaxed, gave Ned a sideways smile. "It's not out of the ordinary."

"It's — enlightening," Ned said, and there was a note in his voice that made Julian give him a sharp glance. "But I suppose we should find your poet."

"Damn all poets," Julian said, and surprised a grin from Ned. "I suppose we'd better."

They made their way up the stairs. The upstairs hall was empty, though light and voices spilled from several of the rooms; there was no sign of whoever had looked into the servants' stair. Most of the membership tended to forget it was there at all, which was what made it such a useful space. Julian shook the thought away, surveying the hall. Three of the doors were closed: if Kennett was in any of those rooms, he wasn't intending to be interrupted. Two more were open, laughter spilling from one, and the third was set ajar, though no light spilled onto the worn carpet.

The first room with an open door held another circle writing enchantments around a particularly elaborate ink set and the second, where the laughter was still hysterically loud, was full of a group playing something like charades. A florid blond stripped to his drawers and draped in a sheet was miming either musical performance or a particularly lewd act. Kennett was nowhere to be seen, and Julian scowled. What the devil was he about, making arrangements to meet and then declining to appear? Except that Kennett was not the most reliable of men at the best of times.

He started for the final room, and Ned hesitated. "I – we don't want to interrupt anything."

"If the door's open, it's an invitation," Julian said. "Club rules." He pushed the door open far enough to see in. The fire was built high here, too, and the gaslights were turned low. An ottoman had been pushed closer to the hearth, armchairs and a small sofa set in a semicircle around it, and there was a schoolmaster's cane and a well-worn leather slipper on the nearest table. Ned's breath caught for just an instant, and one of the group lifted a hand in greeting.

"Julian. You're welcome to join us. And your friend."

Julian shook his head. "I'm looking for Auberon."

"Not here, old man, sorry. But you can have your pick of this lot."

"Another time," Julian answered, with what he hoped was passable aplomb, and backed out, Ned giving way behind him. He didn't really want to know what Ned was thinking, and fished in his vest pocket for his watch. "Bloody man. Still, he might show. Let's have another drink before we leave."

"All right," Ned said, tone and expression unreadable, and Julian led him decorously back by way of the main stairs.

The crowd had thinned a bit in the front parlor, and Malcolm had managed to get the decanters refilled. Julian mixed them each a whisky and soda, and found an unoccupied chair and ottoman in a corner away from the fire. He waved Ned to the chair, on the theory that Ned didn't need any more food for thought, and settled himself on the ottoman.

"You're worried," Ned said, his voice too quiet to carry far even if anyone had been paying attention.

Julian hesitated, then nodded. "Not that Kennett isn't the sort to forget an appointment, but – he's in trouble, I'm afraid. I expected him to be here."

"Something must have come up."

"That's what I'm afraid of," Julian answered.

Ned leaned forward to rest a hand on his knee. "We'll find him."

Several sharp answers rose to Julian's lips, but he realized with mild surprise that he actually wanted to be reassured. "We'd better," he said, and covered Ned's hand with his own.

By the time they'd finished their drinks, Julian was sure Kennett was not going to keep the appointment. He said as much to Ned, who nodded.

"Still, it was worth a try."

"I'll have to find him tomorrow," Julian went on. "But there's no point in staying longer."

He accepted Ned's hand to pull himself to his feet, and there was a soft chuckle behind him. From Ned's expression, polite and utterly bland, he wasn't surprised to hear Farrell's voice.

"Leaving so soon, Julian? Well, I can see why." Farrell gave a Ned a toothy smile. "I trust you found the club acceptable."

"Enlightening, certainly," Ned said again.

Julian succumbed to the temptation to tuck his hand into Ned's arm. "Evening, Linford," he said, and at last they achieved the safety of the hall.

Except it wasn't safety at all, he realized. The front door stood partway open, and a young man stood swaying just inside the threshold, while the footman stared at him in bewilderment. "Oh, for God's sake," he began, and Ned took a step forward.

"Go tell the cabbie to wait," he said, to the footman, and as the man jumped to obey, pulled the door closed behind him. "Now, then –"

"Oh, it's you!" The young man seized Julian's hands. Julian blinked, unable to remember if they'd been introduced – though he would have remembered such a willowy blond if they'd actually gone to bed together – and the young man gave him a tremulous smile. "It's Dolly. I know you don't *know* me, not really, but I do know who you are, and I'm in such trouble –"

"Quite," Julian said. Dolly's breath smelled strongly of whisky, and there was a smear of ink on his right forefinger that suggested he'd been indulging in enchantments as well.

There were tears in Dolly's eyes and now they spilled over, tracking down his cheeks. "I don't know what to do, and he's being entirely unreasonable, but – I have to talk to someone, don't you see?"

A lovers' quarrel, Julian thought. "Yes," he said, with what he hoped was soothing vagueness, "but perhaps another time? You must want your bed."

"I couldn't possibly," Dolly answered. "Oh, God, I don't know what to do. He's just so – he's not being *sensible*, and it's all going to fall apart, and then – then, oh, my God, it's going to be an utter disaster. You're a metaphysician, surely you can help me."

"I'm not exactly a metaphysician," Julian said, and heard Ned sigh.

"But I am," he said, and laid a careful hand on Dolly's shoulder. "If you're sure that's what you need, you can talk to me. During regular office hours."

"God, are you really?" Dolly turned eagerly to face him, wobbling, and Julian steadied him. "It really is a metaphysical problem, you know. I mean, there's everything else, and he's a bit of a rotter, really, but – at the heart, it's metaphysics. Though most things are, aren't they?"

"In a manner of speaking," Ned said. "Look, old man, your cab's waiting. Why don't you come by my office tomorrow and tell me all about it? Things will look different in daylight."

He reached reluctantly into his pocket and came up with a card, but Julian intercepted it. He took out his own wand and quickly sketched an enchantment that would erase the printing if anyone other than Dolly touched it, and handed it across. Dolly accepted it, solemn as an owl, and Julian took his elbow.

"Come on, now, your cab's waiting."

With Ned's help, he got him down the stairs, and the footman turned with relief to open the cab door. Dolly squinted up at the driver, swaying slightly as he focused.

"West Street, by St. Patrick's Church."

The cabbie made a face – it wasn't much of a fare – but touched his hat. Dolly made it into the box with only a momentary wobble, but leaned out again. "It really is a terrible muddle, and –"

"Tomorrow," Ned said, firmly, and the footman began gently to close the door. Dolly subsided, and Julian reached into his pocket for a shilling, which he handed to the cabman.

"See that he gets in all right, cabbie."

"Right, guv'nor."

He'd try to get the fare from Dolly as well, Julian knew, but at least it should guarantee the young man's safe arrival. He stepped back, and the cab pulled away from the curb.

Ned watched it go. "Did you know him?"

"No. And I don't have any idea what it was about, either." Julian shook his head.

"Well, with luck, it'll make more sense in the morning." Ned nodded to the hovering footman, who disappeared back into the club.

"Or he'll have come to his senses," Julian said, darkly. "Let's go home."

☾❀

CHAPTER THREE
A Case for the Metaphysical Squad

J ULIAN SORTED THROUGH THE ACCUMULATED MAIL with an increasing feeling of unease. He had been sure he would receive another letter
from Kennett by the morning post, but here it was almost four in the
afternoon and he'd received nothing. He set the envelopes aside, tapping his
fingers unhappily on the edge of his desk. Probably he should write himself,
except that if Kennett didn't find it safe to write to him, any other letter ran
the risk of causing more trouble than it would prevent. Discretion and cau-
tion: annoying as it seemed, he would have to practice both.

He lifted his head at the sound of footsteps on the stairs, and a moment
later young Digby knocked at the door. "I've brought the papers, Mr Lynes."

"Bring them in," Julian answered, fumbling in his pocket for a penny, and accepted the ink-scented sheets. He settled himself to read, skimming through
the political headlines in search of more interesting material. The bank rob-
bers in Islington were determined to have opened the safe with dynamite, not
metaphysics: Bolster might know a thing or two about that business, and
Julian hoped he wouldn't have cause to ask him. An unlicensed séance had
gotten out of hand in Maida Vale; the medium had vanished and the neighbors were reporting mysterious lights and sounds. A matter for Ned's friend
Hatton, Julian thought, with a quick grin, and he wished him the joy of it. A
young man found dead in his rooms from no obvious cause... Julian sat up,
his smile disappearing. The reporter had given the address as well as the name,
and while Julian didn't recollect a Charles Hall, he certainly remembered West
Street from the night before. Surely it couldn't be, he thought, but he couldn't
shake the sense of unease. Ned would have talked to Dolly, or at least got a
chastened note begging off his appointment...

He set the paper aside and reached for his Gazetteer, flipping through the pages. Yes, there was West Street, and the address in the paper was in fact near St. Patrick's Church. He tossed the book onto the sofa and reached for his hat, unwilling to wait on a telegram and reply. He'd visit the Commons straightaway, and see what Ned had found out.

There were no cabs to be seen until he'd walked most of the way to the Commons, and by then there was no point. He hurried through the side entrance and across to Ned's stairway, managing with an effort not to take them two at a time. The outer door was open, denoting a current lack of client, and Julian tapped on the inner door, but pushed it open without waiting for an answer.

Ned looked up from his desk, a frown fading. "What – ?"

"Did that young man come to see you yet today?" Julian stopped, and made himself smile and nod to Ned's clerk, who sat at her desk with a ledger open in front of her, a look of mild surprise on her face. "Afternoon, Miss Frost."

"Good afternoon, Mr Lynes."

"No, he didn't," Ned said. His frown had returned. "I assumed he'd thought better of it."

"Maybe not." Julian pulled the paper from his pocket and handed it across the desk. "'Gentleman found dead.'"

Ned swore, and then gave Miss Frost an apologetic look. She smiled serenely and turned her attention to the ledger again. "The address –"

"Is very close," Julian answered.

"Charles Hall?"

"It's always possible it isn't him. I don't actually know his name. But –"

Ned nodded. "We need to be sure." He checked the newspaper again. "They don't say what station is handling it."

"Molyneux Street, for a guess." Julian reached for his watch. "And we'll catch the end of the day shift if we hurry."

Ned levered himself out of his chair, made his way gingerly out from behind the desk. "I won't be back tonight, Miss Frost. And there's no need for you to stay, either."

"I'll just finish the books," she answered, placidly.

"Thank you." Ned shrugged himself into his overcoat. "Molyneux Street, you said?"

"If not there, then Marylebone-lane," Julian answered. "But I'm betting Molyneux Street's closer."

They caught a cab from the Commons entrance, and Julian drummed his fingers on the woodwork as the cab fought its way west through the evening traffic. "You can get us in, I assume."

"I expect so," Ned answered. "I'll tell them a young man of similar address made an appointment with me and failed to keep it. He was in some distress and when I saw the papers, I wanted to be sure it wasn't my man."

Coming from Ned, that would work, Julian thought. It had the virtue of being entirely true, if not the whole truth, and no one ever delved too deeply into Ned's statements. Even the masters at Sts Thomas's had taken his words at face value. It was not a gift Julian had ever had, and he allowed himself a sigh of envy. If he tried to spin a story like that, the local inspector would raise an eyebrow and promptly demand to know when and where the young man had made his appointment, and what they'd been doing at the time.

The station's entrance was blocked by a dray and two downtrodden horses, the latter held by an unhappy-looking constable. Another uniformed man was taking notes as two carters glared at each other, and the cabbie pulled to a stop well shy of the potential fray. Julian handed him the fare, and followed Ned up the granite stairs and into the building.

The outer lobby smelled strongly of sweat and carbolic, and there were still half a dozen people sitting on the benches beneath the row of police notices. Julian's eyes flickered over them, picking out a demure-looking pickpocket in a crumpled bonnet, her hands folded neatly in her lap. Beside her was a decently-dressed man in frock coat and top hat, a shopkeeper, by the look of him, and Julian could almost feel the twitch of her fingers as she tried not to look at the chain that hung heavy across his vest.

"My name's Mathey," Ned said, to the sergeant on duty at the desk, presenting his card, and Julian hurried to join him. "I understand you have a body here –"

"Mathey?" A graying man in civilian clothes turned sharply away from the door that led to the inner offices. "Here, you're not Hatton's metaphysician, are you?"

Ned blinked, and the sergeant turned to hand on the card. "Yes, I'm working with him now –"

"I'm damned if I know how you got here, but you're the man we need." The man held out his hand. "Inspector Thomas Brennan. I'm in charge here."

"Pleased to meet you," Ned murmured. "This is my colleague, Mr Julian Lynes."

"Delighted, I'm sure," Brennan said, with a perfunctory handshake. "You asked about a body, Mr Mathey. We certainly have one, and I expect it's more your business than mine."

"We'd certainly like to see it," Ned said, cautiously.

Brennan flung out his hand in an expansive gesture. "Be my guest, gentlemen. But I warn you, it's not a pretty sight."

Brennan led them down the passageway that led to the cells, and Julian wrinkled his nose at the smell of stale sweat and urine. And blood. There was definitely a scent of blood in the air, getting stronger as they reached the end of the row. One of the barred doors stood open, and a man in shirtsleeves and a bloody apron stood by it, greedily inhaling a cigar. He stubbed it out against the wall at Brennan's approach and stood up straighter.

"You got the 'Phys already?"

"Dr Webb," Brennan said. "Mr Mathey, Mr Lynes. Mr Mathey is Inspector Hatton's metaphysician."

"Damn good thing, too," Webb said. He didn't offer to shake hands, which Julian felt was just as well under the circumstances. "I'd say this was definitely your business, Mr Mathey. Or Hatton's, anyway. I saw that as soon as I opened him up, and I haven't touched him since."

Julian looked past him into the cell, lit by half a dozen oil lamps set on a ledge above an oilcloth-covered table. In their light, he could clearly recognize Dolly's face, skin slack beneath the tumbled hair, but what drew the eye inexorably was the surgeon's cut that had opened the body from neck to navel. Julian had seen autopsies before, had made himself learn the rudiments of anatomy, but it didn't take an expert to see that the man's heart was simply gone. "Hell and damnation."

Ned's eyes flickered closed for just an instant. "You found the heart gone when you opened him."

"Didn't I just say so? And not a mark on him otherwise." Webb shook his head. "I was guessing poison from the look of him. A nasty business, Mr Mathey."

"And Hatton's," Brennan said quickly. "Not ours."

❦

HATTON ARRIVED WITHIN THE HOUR, AND directed the body's removal to Scotland Yard.

"Nasty indeed," he said. "Suppose someone had put a preservative enchantment on the corpse without calling us in first?"

"They'd be lucky if all they did was wreck the station," Ned said.

"It is non-conforming magic, then?"

"I'm afraid so." Hatton's glance shifted to Julian, and Ned added, "You remember my colleague Mr Lynes."

"I do," Hatton said, not entirely enthusiastically. "What's his involvement in this? Was Mr Hall his client, or yours?"

"Mine," Ned said, before Julian could speak. He'd always been better at concealing the inconvenient truth without getting tangled up in outright lies. "Mr Lynes happened to be consulting with me about another matter when I read the unfortunate news."

"Any idea what Hall wanted?"

"No idea," Ned said. "Only that he had some metaphysical problem he wanted to see me about."

"I'd call that a metaphysical problem, all right."

"His heart was still in his chest when he made the appointment," Julian pointed out.

"We think," Hatton said. "For all I know, it was removed a week ago Tuesday, and he's been walking around without it ever since."

"I think that's medically unlikely," Ned said. "And metaphysically unlikely as well."

The street door opened, and Inspector Brennan reappeared, "You'll be taking charge of the case, then, Hatton."

"For sixpence I'd tell you to keep it," Hatton said. "But, no, this is one of ours."

"What now?" Ned said.

"Now we go and do some police work," Hatton said. "I'm going to look over his flat myself. I'd appreciate it if you'd come along, in case we run into any more enchantments that might bring the roof down."

"Of course." Ned looked apologetically at Julian. "Dinner at Blandings, old man? Since I never did hear you out about that other matter."

Julian looked a little shaken, at least to Ned's eyes. Ned felt shaken himself. It was a gruesome business, but it had been worse than gruesome to see a man he'd met, who'd drunkenly clung to his shoulder, opened up on the police surgeon's table. And it might not have happened if they'd only bothered to hear him out.

Self-recrimination would have to wait. He clapped Julian on the shoulder in what he hoped was a comforting manner and followed Hatton out.

"What are we looking for?" he asked in the carriage.

"Metaphysically speaking, you tell me," Hatton said. "From my end of it, any sign of robbery, although this would be an awfully baroque way of pulling one off, and a list of his nearest and dearest, because if he was murdered, one of them probably did it."

"That's cheery."

Hatton shrugged. "Most men are killed by their wives. And most reasons for killing come down to love, hate, or money. Marriage combines all three. He loved his wife, so he killed her sweetheart; he hated his wife, so he killed her; he loved her and hated her by turns, so they fought until one day he hit her upside the head with the iron; he took out a life insurance policy on his wife, and then killed her to cash it in. Some days I think we should bring in the man who invented life insurance and charge him with creating an attractive nuisance."

"He looks rather young to have been married." And there was the matter of his predilections, although Ned was aware they didn't rule out matrimony.

"If it's not the wife, it's usually family or friends. Unless he did for himself. Two men having the same accident with metaphysics can't be coincidence, though."

"I would think not. If they knew each other, they might have both been dabbling with the same sort of enchantment. Or have done it together. Our modern system of metaphysics is set up for a sole practitioner, and it's tricky to work with someone else. Some earlier systems were meant for a group."

"That's just what I need, a whole lot of these lads playing with something that makes vital organs disappear."

"We can hope not."

Hall's lodgings proved to be two rooms in a boarding house.

"Married?" the landlady said. "No, he never was. What was it that killed him? He never seemed ill." Her name was Mrs Parsons, a middle-aged widow with a pinched expression, her graying hair pulled back in a severe knot and her apron crisply pressed. She was clearly none too pleased to have the police in the house, and watched them as if she expected Hatton to pocket the cutlery.

"Did he come down to dinner last night?"

"He did not," she said firmly. "He was out at his club, I expect. My girl found him when she took up his breakfast in the morning. It was an awful shock. We've never had a lodger turn up dead before." She said it as though she felt Hall had been inconsiderate in the matter.

Hatton extracted the key to Hall's rooms from her without providing an answer to the question of how the young man had died, and went up with

Ned, leaving Mrs Parsons to bustle angrily around the kitchen, instructing a nervous scullery maid in how best to boil potatoes.

The parlor was smaller than Ned's own, with a sofa worn shiny from use and a lumpy armchair. There were clothes thrown about, an evening coat draped over the chair back, a tie discarded on the small breakfast table with a top hat lying nearby on the floor, and an overcoat crumpled on the sofa.

"Late night," Hatton remarked. He poked at the hat with one foot, but it did nothing suspicious, and he turned to run his hand over the spines of the books lined up on the windowsill. There were more stacked in corners and resting on the mantelpiece. "See if any of these tell you anything of use."

Ned hoped that all the books would reveal about Hall's interests was whether he had been dabbling in metaphysics. In fact, they were hardly revealing on either point. Most were dog-eared classics, the sort of thing Hall might have had from university, with a few cheap novels in the mix. "There's nothing about metaphysics here," he said after examining them all. "Not even a schoolboy text."

"Would you expect one?"

Ned shrugged. "If he went to a school that taught metaphysics. Most don't, though – I was at Sts Thomas's, and they do teach the basics, but that's the exception."

"Lucky for you," Hatton said.

Ned made a non-committal noise in reply. He'd learned a great deal at school, mostly at the hands of bullies given free rein to beat their juniors in the name of discipline, but Hatton wasn't to know that, and he had gotten a sound education in other ways. "He might have sold some of his schoolbooks on, if they were in good enough shape for that. These all look like they've been through the wars. Or they might be at his father's house."

"We'll have to see if anyone knows who his people are."

A search of the bedroom turned up nothing more revealing than clothes more fashionably cut than Ned's own and an assortment of toiletries, including a patent hair oil whose label guaranteed improvements to body and shine.

"Says nothing about removing your heart from your body," Hatton said.

"Do you want me to test it for a non-conforming glamour?"

"We'll take it back to the Yard, and you can test it there," Hatton said. "I don't fancy explaining to that old battle-axe how we got splinters in her ceiling."

Ned tilted the bottle in his hand. "Do you really think it's the hair oil?"

"I haven't a clue," Hatton said. "It looks like the standard kind of hocus that might curl your hair, or might stick it together like paste and make you look like a chump, depending on your luck. If it's killing customers instead, we'd better find out." He wrapped the bottle up in brown paper and tucked it away in his pocket.

They returned to the kitchen, where Mrs Parsons squinted at them. "It wasn't anything catching, was it?"

"I don't think so," Ned said after a moment.

"Tell me what you know about young Mr Hall," Hatton said. "Where was he employed? Did he have friends come to visit, or a young lady?"

"I hope you're not suggesting I run a disorderly house," Mrs Parsons said.

"In the parlor, Mrs Parsons. Men do sit with their young ladies in the parlor?"

"Well, from time to time they do," she granted grudgingly. "Though in my day, young ladies didn't go running about the city with their chaperones, or without them. When Mr Parsons, rest his soul, came courting, it was in my own parlor, with Mama there keeping an eagle eye on him, and I wouldn't have set foot out of the house with him until I had a ring on my finger."

"I'm sure that's very commendable," Hatton said, with a visible effort of patience. "Did Mr Hall have a young lady?"

"Not that I ever saw. He went out most evenings to his club. The lodgers have latchkeys, although they know I don't hold with coming in very late."

"And what club would that be?" Hatton asked. Ned tried not to react.

"I can't be bothered to keep track of the gentlemen's amusements," Mrs Parsons said, and Ned let out the breath he'd been holding. "I don't think as he ever said."

"All right. What about his employer?"

"He gave me to understand he had a private income," Mrs Parsons said. "Some little legacy from a relation."

"Paid his rent on time?"

"Not what you'd call on time. But what can you do? It's hard enough to keep the house full. I don't know how I'll get anyone for his room, if it gets around that someone's died there."

"Someone's died just about everywhere," Hatton said, but it didn't seem to take the sour taste out of Mrs Parsons's mouth. The rest of her answers were equally unedifying. No, she didn't know who his people were, except that presumably they were called Hall. Yes, she thought he'd been up at university before he came to the city, but she couldn't say which one.

"It's amazing how little these women know about their lodgers," Hatton muttered as they went back up the stairs. "They might be the worst sort of criminal, so long as they're dressed up in good clothes and have the first week's rent."

35

The neighbors were somewhat more informative. "Not a bad chap, Hall, but in with a rather fast set," Mr Stevenson across the hall from him said. He was a medical student, weedy and very serious. "He hardly ever spent an evening in. And he came in some mornings just before breakfast."

"What time did he come in last night?"

"I couldn't say. I turn in early, you see, and I'm an early riser – it's not natural virtue, only that I have rounds in the morning."

"Anyone who disliked him, do you know?"

"Not that I ever heard of. He could be a bit of a nuisance as a neighbor – he used to come up short on his rent, and go begging round for a few shillings to make it up. He always said it was the last time, and of course it never was. But he was always good for it in the end."

The lodgers in the two front rooms on the first floor were out, but investigation of the second floor produced a Mr Dane preparing to set out on his way to the offices of the *Daily News*, with his tie still unknotted.

"I don't know if you know what it is to work for a morning paper," he said. "I'm lucky to come home at midnight, and it's more often one or two."

"Would you know what time Mr Hall got in?"

"A little before two," Dane said. "I was just coming home myself – I generally walk from the Strand, it's too late for the omnibus. Hall was getting out of a cab as I came up." He frowned. "I feel awful about the whole thing. I thought he was three sheets to the wind – unsteady on his feet, and positively reeking of gin. It wasn't the first time. I helped him up the stairs so he wouldn't fall down them, and made him go to bed. I had no idea he was really sick."

"He was alone when you left him?"

"Yes, of course."

"Would you come down with us and see if anything seems to be missing from his rooms that was there when you left him?"

"Of course." Dane frowned. "I didn't think there was any question of – you don't think someone killed him?"

"We'll ask the questions for now," Hatton said. "And I'd appreciate this not featuring in your paper tomorrow."

"No chance of that," Dane said. "We do fashion and society. Hats, not robbery and murder in a rooming house."

"If it was robbery," Hatton said. "You tell us."

Dane poked around Hall's rooms, frowning. "He didn't have so much that anyone would want to steal," he said. "He had a watch he kept pawning and then getting back again. He used to pawn all sorts of things when he was short, cuff links and the like. He used to have a silver cigar-case he carried about with him, but it got sold off when he didn't redeem it fast enough once. I remember how cross he was about it."

"The watch was in his pocket when he was found," Hatton said. "He seems to have slept in his trousers."

"I put him to bed in his shirt and trousers. It seemed more trouble than it was worth to try to get them off him." Dane walked the length of the parlor, considering. "There was a box," he said finally. "An ornamented sort of writing desk, the kind you can set on your lap, with colored inlay in the lid. I noticed it because it looked expensive, and it wasn't the sort of thing he usually spent money on. If it had been a new hat, I wouldn't have blinked."

"You'd never seen it before?"

"Not before last night. I was in here, it must have been three days ago, to see if I could borrow some tea – Mrs Parsons doesn't supply tea, except with breakfast, and never mind that I'm never up at breakfast time. She's a hard-hearted woman. I didn't see the box then, although I suppose it might have been in his bedroom. But last night it was sitting there, on the sofa. And now it's gone."

"Did Mr Hall lock his door when you left?"

"Well, no. He was more or less passed out in his bed. I didn't like to go fishing in his pockets for the key, so I just pulled the door shut – it's usually safe enough, with the street door locked."

"Was the street door locked?"

"It must have been," Dane said, looking even more worried. "That is, I was getting Hall in, and I can't remember for certain – but I'm sure I would have locked it behind me, I can't have been as distracted as that."

"Thank you, Mr Dane. Can you tell me the name of Hall's pawnbroker?"

"Hartwicks, just down the street. Do you think someone came in last night and –"

"It's too soon to speculate," Hatton said. "We'll be in touch, Mr Dane."

He led Ned back downstairs to the kitchen, where Mrs Parsons gave him a long-suffering look.

"Yes, inspector?"

"Was the street door locked this morning?"

"Of course," she said firmly. "I wouldn't have it otherwise."

"Had any of the gentlemen gone out before you found Hall?"

"Yes, several. Mr Hall took his breakfast late."

"I'll have to have their names," Hatton said.

He shook his head as he and Ned went out. "Good luck finding anyone who can tell us for sure whether that door was locked first thing in the morning," he said. "I'd wager it stood unlocked from two in the morning until six or seven when the first of the lodgers went out. But it's the kind of thing lodgers don't notice, not when they're young men who don't worry about being murdered in their beds. And once the neighbors get it into their heads that Hall was killed, they'll swear the door was unlocked because the alternative worries them too much."

"You think it was murder, then," Ned said.

"It does look like it," Hatton said. "We'll have to turn the house upside down looking for that box, and try the pawn shop as well, at the same time as we try to find out if anyone can tell us for certain if that door was open. All that's my business, not yours. If I find anything out of the ordinary, I'll bring it down to the Yard for you to look at."

"I'm sure that will be a treat," Ned said. "And I'll see if anyone at the Commons knows anything about non-conforming curses that might have this effect." He shook his head. "I'd still like to believe this is an accident."

"So would I, believe me. But it doesn't follow. He went to bed at two, dead drunk, and got up bright and early in the morning to try a dangerous enchantment, made his own heart vanish from his chest, then managed to lay himself out again on his bed before dying? He had a friend come by first thing in the morning for a spot of experimental enchantment, was killed in the process, and then his friend crept back out without Parsons knowing he was ever there?"

"It doesn't seem likely," Ned admitted.

"No, it doesn't," Hatton said glumly. "In which case he was killed with a particularly nasty curse no one's ever heard of before. And we'd better find out who did it, before he gets it into his head to do it again."

❦

JULIAN CAUGHT AN OMNIBUS BACK TOWARD Bloomsbury, willing to endure the familiar annoyances of the crowd if they would only take his mind off Dolly's corpse. It was hard to forget, the bloody space where the heart should have been, and he couldn't help feeling that he'd failed. He should have seen that there was something more wrong than the usual drunken quarrel with an unreliable lover – should at least have listened a little longer and been sure rather than jumping to the obvious conclusion. It really is a metaphysical problem, Dolly had said, and for once it had been the literal truth. If only he had listened.

He shook himself then. There was nothing he could do for Dolly at the moment – though there would be later, and he would take advantage of it. It was in Ned's hands, and if he couldn't handle it himself, Ned was the man he'd choose. And, that being the case, he himself should concentrate on something he could help: Kennett, in particular.

He left the omnibus at the next stop, stepping awkwardly over feet and furled umbrellas, and made his way through the evening crowd. The street lamps were lit, islands of warm light, and more lights showed at the cracks of curtained windows: most people would be at dinner now, and that should surely give him a better chance of finding Kennett at home. Yes, Kennett was hardly the most reliable of men, but he'd been upset enough to write in the first place. That he'd chosen not to follow through was worrisome.

Kennett's street seemed darker than ever, too short for streetlights and shadowed by the overhanging houses. Julian shifted his grip on his umbrella without thinking, then frowned at his own unease. There was no reason for it, surely, no inexplicable shadows, no oddly familiar faces in the crowd passing on Great Ormond Street, and he continued on down the narrow way.

The same maid answered the door, frowning in open reproof of his bad manners, to be calling at such a time, and Julian forced a smile. "I'm here to see Mr Kennett."

"I'm sorry, sir. He's not at home."

Not at home to visitors, or actually not at home? "It's rather urgent." Julian considered a reaching into his pocket for a tip, but her attitude suggested that would only put her back up further.

"I'm sorry, sir. Perhaps if you'd care to leave your card?" Her tone expressed some doubt as to whether he would have one.

There was no way to get an answer from her. Julian reached into his pocket and brought out a card and a stub of pencil. He scribbled "tomorrow" across the back and handed it to the maid. "If I might –"

The girl dropped a curtsy. "I'll give it to him, sir." She closed the door firmly in his face.

Julian made his way back down the steps, and stopped beside the steps that led down to the kitchen area. Lights bloomed from those windows, sure sign of dinner preparations underway, and for a moment he considered trying to question the staff, but he'd get nowhere at this time of day, not dressed as he was. For a moment, he wished he'd kept the hair he'd stolen from Kennett's jacket: there were half a dozen cantrips that would have told him whether or not the man was home. Without its correspondence to draw on, however, metaphysics was useless; he'd need something simpler.

There was a narrow alley between Kennett's buildings and its left-hand neighbor, presumably for the convenience of the dustman. Julian glanced at it, and then up at the building. Kennett's flat had been on this side, in the front. The street was for the moment empty, and he slipped into the alley, counting the windows on the first floor. Kennett's flat had looked like the ordinary sort, a front parlor and a bedroom behind it, and so the windows directly above him should be the ones. The curtains were drawn, but it looked as though the bedroom was dark, and – yes, there was a light in the parlor. Someone was there, Kennett most likely, but whether he was alone or with someone… There was nothing he could do. Julian swore under his breath, and retraced his steps, heading back toward Blandings.

The worst of the dinner rush was past, and Julian was able to convince the headwaiter to give him a table in a reasonably private corner. He had just approved the wine when Ned appeared in the doorway, and Julian saw the headwaiter wave him toward the corner. He lifted his own hand in greeting, and Ned dropped heavily into the chair opposite him.

"Progress?"

Ned nodded to the waiter, who filled his glass with a flourish. "Of a sort. And you?"

"Less than I'd like," Julian admitted. "No luck finding my man." By unspoken agreement, they declined both the roast and the chops, settled instead on one of Blandings' enormous meat pies. Over the soup, Ned explained what he and Hatton had found in Dolly's rooms, and Julian nodded thoughtfully.

"It doesn't sound like he had any particular friend who was supporting him, which does make things somewhat less awkward."

"Oh?" Ned frowned.

"I wouldn't expect him to be cadging spare shillings from his neighbors if someone was taking care of him."

"Unless his particular friend was just as poor as he," Ned said. "But I take your point. Still, it's a delicate situation."

"It certainly is," Julian said, with some fervor. "If the police come sniffing around the Dionysus –"

"It's not to be thought of." Ned leaned back as the waiter returned to clear the soup and present the enormous pie. Julian waited while the top was ceremoniously broken open and their plates were filled, rich sherry gravy spilling over shards of crust and vegetables and well-cooked chunks of lamb. The remainder of the pie was set between them while a second waiter presented sauces for them to choose from, and for the first time Julian realized how hungry he was. Ned's appetite seemed to have returned as well, and they ate in silence for a few moments.

"We have to keep the clubs out of this," Julian began, and Ned looked up sharply.

"If we can."

Julian raised his eyebrows. "We'd better. If it were to get out –"

"Do you think I don't know that?" Ned kept his voice low enough that no one at the neighboring tables could have heard, but his vehemence was unmistakable. "My reputation certainly wouldn't stand it – I'd never get another client, and there's a good chance the Commons would rescind my membership, and that would be every penny I ever hope to have, wasted on a practice that I couldn't keep –" He stopped abruptly, looking embarrassed.

Julian looked at his own plate. "I know. I do know. It's not as though I'd come through any better." He made himself meet Ned's eyes. "There's no reason to think it has anything to do with the Dionysus. Or any other club, for that matter."

"And if it does?" Ned put his fork down and pushed his plate away. "We'll have to do something."

"He must have had other friends," Julian said.

"Lynes."

"We'll cross that bridge when we have to," Julian said firmly. He wasn't sure he believed his own argument, but anything was better than seeing Ned this worried. "There's always a way around. Most people don't want to know, anyway."

"I've already had to be a bit circumspect with Hatton. And I don't want to lose this position."

"Everything you've told him was true," Julian said. "That we thought he was talking about a lover isn't relevant."

Ned picked up his fork again and addressed the remains of the pie. "That we know of."

"It almost certainly isn't," Julian said. It was past time to change the subject. "What I don't understand is why no one knows where this enchantment came from."

"It's non-conforming magic. Rather spectacularly so."

"Yes, but –" Julian waved his fork in a gesture that was meant to take in the dining room and its thinning crowd. Even this late, most of the patrons were members of the Commons, conspicuous in frock coats, tall hats and a scattering of expensive walking sticks decorating their tables. "I'd expect that someone here would have made a proper study of the stuff. Surely there's someone you can ask to look at it."

"One or two, maybe," Ned said. "But no one studies non-conforming systems. Not in any practical sense."

"Perhaps they ought."

"It's too dangerous."

"The Commons sets itself on fire once a month at least," Julian said.

"That's the metaphysicists' wing," Ned said, automatically.

"Well, isn't it their business?"

"It's simply too dangerous," Ned said again. "It's against all the rules and by-laws, and if you want to take on a project that looks as though it's going to brush up against a non-conforming system, you have to get permission from the Board of Governors. And they don't often give it."

Julian shook his head. "I've seen, and experimented with, a few enchantments and the occasional device that could only be described as conforming by a great stretch of the imagination, and none of them have been that dangerous." Most of this had been work for Bolster, a more-or-less retired burglar who had once been a client and with whom Julian had struck up a cautious professional friendship. "Mostly they just don't work."

"You've been lucky."

"Or good," Julian pointed out. "I do know what I'm doing."

"Not with non-conforming magic," Ned said. "No one does."

There was a note in his voice that silenced Julian's automatic protest. "Then why hasn't something happened to me?" he asked instead. "Or to any one of the – I'd guess thousands – of cracksmen in London, never mind the surrounding cities?"

"Lots of crafts have traditional enchantments that were passed down from master to apprentice, father to son. Technically, they're non-conforming because they don't fully fit the modern system, but they're based on the same underlying grammar, just an incomplete or variant version."

Julian nodded. "All right, yes, that's pretty much what I've seen."

"Real non-conforming magic is something else." Ned pushed his plate away again. "Some of it is so old that it was written using a grammar that doesn't match up with modern magic at all, and sometimes it explodes, quite literally, when the two are inadvertently mixed. And some of it is nonsense – non-sense in the original meaning, something someone made up in his own private language with no regard to how it might interact with all the normal magic around it, and usually those interactions are nothing but disastrous."

"You're not seriously saying that everyone who dabbles in non-conforming magic is mad," Julian said.

"I could argue it." Ned lowered his voice. "Look, there's a place, the Half-House, it's by way of being an object lesson for metaphysicists who might get above themselves. Let me take you there tomorrow, it's a better explanation of what I mean than anything I can tell you."

Julian looked up sharply. He had heard that name from Bolster: a house in Clerkenwell that was so heavily warded that every thief in London wondered what was inside, and so carefully watched that none of them had dared make the attempt. The few – the very few – who'd even attempted to spy out the land came back shaken and silent and refused to discuss the matter further. "All right. I'd like to see this Half-House."

CHAPTER FOUR
The Half-House

NED BRAVED THE METAPHYSICISTS' WING THE next morning in search of Nicholas Oppenshaw, the closest thing the Commons had to an expert on nonconforming magic. Oppenshaw was white-haired and gaunt, and frowned at Ned discouragingly through his half-moon spectacles.

"The Half-House is not a tourist attraction, Mr Mathey," he said.

"Yes, I know."

"I have the dubious honor to be its caretaker, no one else in the Commons having volunteered for the position since Mr Varley left us. It is my job to keep troublemaking young metaphysicians out."

"My colleague isn't a metaphysician."

"Then he has no business there under any circumstances."

Ned took a deep breath and let it out. "I'm working with Inspector Hatton at Scotland Yard on the new squad for dealing with metaphysical crimes." Oppenshaw raised an eyebrow, not particularly encouragingly. "We've hit on one that I believe involves non-conforming metaphysics, and I'd like to show one of my colleagues what we're dealing with. To ensure he'll take the danger seriously."

Oppenshaw made a noise that sounded very like "hrumph." He squinted Ned through his spectacles. "What sort of non-conforming metaphysics?"

That had him, Ned thought, like a trout that was hooked but still needed to be carefully played in. "I thought we might go see the Half-House first," Ned said. "And then I'd be grateful if you'd let me tell you about the case and give me your advice."

Oppenshaw closed the book in front of him with a snap. "Very well. Where is the other young person?"

"Mr Lynes will meet us at the house," Ned said.

Julian was indeed there and waiting when they pulled up in a cab, looking up at the house curiously from outside the wrought-iron fence.

"I wouldn't advise touching the fence, young man," Oppenshaw said crisply.

"I know that much," Julian said.

"Mr Oppenshaw, this is my colleague, Julian Lynes," Ned said. "We were at Oxford together. Mr Oppenshaw is one of our senior metaphysicists."

"Mr Lynes," Oppenshaw said, looking him up and down before opening an elderly black leather case. He withdrew both his wand, carved in an odd spiral pattern, and a heavy ring of keys. He began unlocking the several locks set in the iron gate, sketching enchantments over some of them before inserting the keys.

Ned took the opportunity to draw Julian aside. "I may have given Oppenshaw the impression that you also work for Scotland Yard," he said.

Julian's eyebrows went up. "That would surprise a number of my clients."

"I'll try not to let it get around, for the sake of your reputation."

When Oppenshaw finished the last lock, he pushed the gate open to let them in, and then locked it behind the three of them. Unraked leaves littered the walkway leading to the imposing stone house. Beside the steps up to the front door stood a large iron lockbox, looking out of place in its modern plainness, which Oppenshaw now unlocked.

"If you have anything enchanted on your person, leave it here," Oppenshaw said, placing his leather bag inside. "Please be thorough in your inventory, if you value your possessions and your limbs."

Ned surrendered his own metaphysician's bag, along with his watch, hat, and patent cab-whistle. Julian frowned, but added his watch, with its fob in the shape of an eye that had an alarming tendency to track one's every move, and his own hat.

"Your wand as well, old man," Ned said.

Julian hesitated, and then withdrew his wand from his coat and slipped it inside the lockbox as well. Oppenshaw made a disapproving noise – metaphysicists of the old school tended to feel that only members of the Commons had any business owning wands at all – but said nothing, securing the lockbox door.

"It wouldn't do you any good inside, anyway," Ned said.

"This was a private home until 1593," Oppenshaw said. "Of course, in those days Clerkenwell wasn't built up as it is now. It may have seemed a safe place to experiment." He opened the front door and put the ring of keys away in his pocket. "Follow me, gentlemen."

Ned had seen it before, but he still felt an eerie shiver as he stepped into the dim house. Oppenshaw lit a pair of oil lamps standing on a side table, illuminating the hallway and the rooms beyond. The furniture had been left just as it had been, heavy Tudor pieces thick with dust. Oppenshaw took off his own hat, apparently not enchanted, and set it on the table.

"Upstairs, gentlemen," Oppenshaw said, picking up one of the lamps and carrying it upstairs. "Watch your step."

Ned was cautious, but still found himself stumbling on the stairs; they felt crooked underfoot, although when he looked down, the wooden stairs were straight.

"What in the…" Julian muttered from behind him.

"That's just the beginning, gentlemen," Oppenshaw said. "Up here, if you please, and step briskly to the left." Ned obeyed, Julian falling in beside him. There were heavy closed doors on both sides of the hall. In the dim lamplight, Ned could see the banisters at the end of the hall where another set of stairs led down. To the right, the hall was boarded up, planks nailed up to the ceiling.

"And now all the way down the hall to the left," Oppenshaw said. Ned knew what was coming, but he kept quiet, following Oppenshaw the length of the hall to the stairs. "And down the stairs."

There was a light at the bottom of the stairs, and Ned shook his head when he came down far enough to see the oil lamp still lit, with Oppenshaw's hat standing beside it. They were back in the front hall, facing the front door. He stepped to one side to let Julian see, and had to admit he enjoyed his expression.

Julian poked at the hat with one finger. "The stairway twists?" he said dubiously. He looked around. "But now I can't see the stairs we went up. A shifting staircase?"

"There's only one staircase, I'm afraid," Oppenshaw said. "There were two sets of servants' stairs, at either end of the hall, but they can't be used now."

Julian frowned and started back up the stairs. Ned followed. At the top of the stairs, the hall was boarded up to the right, and a hallway led to the left, with heavy closed doors on both sides of the hall. At the end of the hall, the stairs led down.

"One of the young gentlemen from Oxford brought an enchanted watch up here once, six years ago," Oppenshaw said. "We have it at the Commons. It still runs, even the shape it is now, but I wouldn't recommend putting your fingers inside to set the time."

"If you put the lamp down here…" Julian began.

Oppenshaw obliged. The other end of the hall remained dark. Julian forged forward toward the staircase, Oppenshaw at his heels, and Ned followed, putting one hand out to feel the wall as he went. Julian didn't hesitate at the top of the stairs – he'd been surefooted in the dark at school – and Oppenshaw followed him with the confidence of long practice. Ned took careful hold of the banister until the lamplight below began to illuminate the steps under his feet.

Oppenshaw's hat rested next to the lamp. Julian scowled at it. He turned and went straight back up the stairs, emerging at the top to the familiar sight of the hallway leading to the left, the lamp still sitting on the hallway floor.

"Suppose you put the lamp on the stairs," he said.

"You are a clever young man." Oppenshaw took a step back down and set the lamp on the stairs. Now lamplight illuminated the other end of the hall as well, and Ned could see a gaunt man bending over the lamp, throwing his shadow against the opposite wall. Oppenshaw straightened, and took one step up the stairs to Julian's side, and he and his shadow disappeared from the other end of the hall.

"I don't see how the lamp can be in two places at once," Julian said.

"There's only one staircase, as I said," Oppenshaw said. "And the lamp is sitting on it, so it's only in one place. It's the hall that's bent to meet it at both ends." He held up his key ring. "Like a ring, if you could bend a ring so that you can only go around it one way."

Julian looked as if he were trying to parse that. "And what's in the center of the ring?"

Oppenshaw didn't answer, but he seemed satisfied at the question. He withdrew the keys from his pocket, selected one, and unlocked the nearest door. "Step well back, gentlemen," he said. "I don't want anyone to fall."

He pulled the door open, and held up the lamp. It shone into darkness. There was no floor beyond the threshold, and no ceiling, and no visible walls or any other end to vast, empty space.

Oppenshaw fished out a penny from his pocket. "Don't try dropping anything in but pennies, please," he said. "Those don't seem to do any harm." He held the penny out through the doorway and let go. The penny fell, not down, but straight forward into the darkness, glinting as it tumbled out of sight.

Julian watched it fall. "Where does it go?"

"Fancy going in and having a look to see?" Oppenshaw said. Ned put out an arm out in case Julian chose the wrong answer. "They lowered down sounding ropes years ago," Oppenshaw added. "As far as anyone can tell, there's no bottom to it, although there was a limit to how much rope it was practical to use."

"This is where they were working," Ned said soberly.

"It might have been anywhere on this side of the house. Half the house is gone – that's what it takes its name from. The hall in the other direction simply stops; we keep it boarded up so that no one can walk into it by mistake. There's been talk of putting up a railing, but I think frankly everyone feels a bit better with a door that can be shut."

Julian shook his head. "What happened here?"

"Non-conforming enchantment," Oppenshaw said. "There's no way to be certain now what they were trying to do when it happened. We do know that at first the effect was confined to one room. The servants opened the door when the gentlemen wouldn't answer, and found…" He gestured toward emptiness. "Then the rest of the house began to go, bit by bit."

He straightened his glasses, looking thoughtfully into the darkness. "It took some months for the metaphysicists at the Commons to find a way to stabilize its boundaries. Or it might be that some natural limit kept the rest of the house intact. I am the closest thing we have to an expert on the subject these days, and I couldn't tell you myself whether anything those very learned men did actually made any difference. But we do still have a city of London, in any event. There was apparently some question, for a while."

"You were right," Julian said after a moment. "That's worse than our problem."

Oppenshaw raised an inquisitive eyebrow.

"Two men have been found dead," Ned said. There was no longer any reason to hold that information back. "Their hearts were missing from their chests, with no mark on them. As if the hearts had disappeared into thin air." He drew a penny from his own pocket and dropped it into the darkness, frowning after it as it fell. "I told Hatton they were lucky not to have done worse if they were playing with non-conforming metaphysics. I'm not sure he believed me."

"I believe you," Julian said. He poked the tips of his fingers cautiously through the doorway, looking both fascinated and appalled, and then stepped back as Oppenshaw closed the door.

Oppenshaw led them out, and they reclaimed their possessions and exited the gate with – at least in Ned's case – considerable relief.

"You must tell me about your gentlemen with the missing hearts." Oppenshaw turned up his collar against the wind.

"I'm not sure there's much more to tell," Ned said. "All I know is that their hearts were missing, that seems to be what both men died of, and the first standard test for enchantment reacted – dramatically." He explained in brief.

"You ought to be more careful with broken mirrors," Oppenshaw said.

"Yes, I ought," Ned said, knowing he should have.

"Missing hearts…" Oppenshaw stroked his chin.thoughtfully. "The question is the mechanism. It's not typically possible to remove something magically from inside a container. Especially a living container. It's very interesting." He shook his head. "It's a shame we've lost Varley. He went further toward practical investigation than anyone in a century – but, well, we know what came of that."

"I'd appreciate it if you'd look into it," Ned said.

"I will. It's a pretty problem." Oppenshaw straightened his glasses as a cab drew up. "Coming back to the Commons?"

"You go ahead. I want to have a word with Lynes."

"As you like." Oppenshaw opened the cab door, and then leaned back out. "Do be careful, Mr Mathey. We shouldn't want to lose you."

"I will," Ned said.

Julian looked sideways at him as the cab pulled away. "How did Mr Varley die?"

"We're not entirely certain that he did," Ned said slowly. "It was a few years before my time, but the story is that he was researching non-conforming enchantment, and stayed late at the Commons one evening, and the next morning, there was a duck in his chambers – a drake, I should say – and no sign of the man anywhere." Ned shrugged. "I suppose he might have drowned in the Thames or run off to Australia, but people drew certain conclusions. One of his friends took the duck home and kept it in the garden. It died a few years later. Not unnaturally old for a duck, but then Mr Varley was quite elderly, by all accounts."

Julian looked as if he was struggling to control his expression. "It's not funny, but –"

"It is funny," Ned said. "And at the same time rather horrible in its implications. Varley was the foremost expert on non-conforming magic. If there was anyone who was qualified to handle it safely, he was. And whatever exactly happened to him, I think it's safe to say that something he tried went badly wrong."

"We'll find out who's doing this and put a stop to it," Julian said. "Or else the Yard will."

Ned shook his head. "Someone had better."

❦

It was early still, but Julian stopped at a pie shop and then in a pub behind the Foundling Hospital. The public bar was nearly empty; he took his half pint and seated himself in a corner to unwrap the pie. The Half-House had been unexpectedly disconcerting, and he was glad of beer and sausage to steady his nerves. If non-conforming magic could do that, never mind apparently turning Varley into a drake – perhaps missing hearts weren't the worst that could happen. He would certainly treat the next oddment that Bolster brought him for analysis with a good deal more respect.

He took another swallow of his beer, remembering the penny tumbling straight ahead into nothing. There had to be a way to investigate where they went in some sort of safety – metaphysical means were obviously out, but perhaps some purely mechanical object. An old-fashioned mercury barometer, perhaps, lowered on a long rope; it would at least give some indication of what lay beyond. Or the mercury might react badly to the twisted magic – Oppenshaw had said not to drop anything but pennies into the void. Presumably the Commons had tried something like that already anyway.

He finished the last of the pie, brushing crumbs from his waistcoat. Right now, it was more important to resolve the business with Kennett. He made his way back to Coptic Street, passing the postman on the way, but somewhat to his surprise there was a telegram tucked under the door of his room. It was from Kennett, suggesting they meet at three o'clock at the Dubourg's Museum in Haymarket, where he would "tell all." Julian swore half-heartedly, scribbled out an answer, and then on second thought scribbled out another telegram to Ned suggesting dinner, and dispatched young Digby to the telegraph office with both of them. His Gazetteer described the museum as "a collection of startling automata, including a Lion and Horses, an Avalanche, a Corsair Attack, a number of enlightening Biblical scenes, &c." open from eleven o'clock in the morning to eleven o'clock at night, Gallery 6p., Saloon 1s., Special Exhibits 6p. additional. He swore again, more fervently – after his work for Albert Wynchcombe over the summer, he had a fair idea what "special exhibits" might entail, and had long ago decided he preferred actual *poses plastiques* to mechanical ones – but had to admit no one would expect to find either of them there.

He took the omnibus to Haymarket under gathering clouds, hunching his shoulders against the wind. Dubourg's Museum was a broad-fronted building that had seen better days, the brick façade grimed with soot and the columns to either side of the first-floor windows in need of a fresh coat of paint. Julian climbed the imperfectly-scrubbed stairs to the narrow hall, where a uniformed attendant took his shilling in exchange for a cardboard ticket to loop around a button of his coat, and offered him a guide to the exhibits for a penny more. Julian parted with the penny reluctantly, and the attendant leaned forward confidentially.

"The Special Exhibit room has some very nice items in it at the moment. Not intended for ladies and children, if you know what I mean." His breath smelled of beer. "Only sixpence additional."

"Not today," Julian answered, and made his way into the gallery. It was clearly intended as a teaser to the main attractions, with an array of smaller pieces that seemed for some reason to feature a number of lions. There was a stallion being attacked by a slightly moth-eaten lion the size of a house cat, a fight between a lion and a bear that was clearly meant to represent Roman games, a lion-tamer inside a cage of lions, Daniel in the lion's den, and, by the door to the Saloon, what seemed to be Androcles and the lion. The lion and the bear had attracted a small group of well-dressed boys, who nudged one another with whispers and giggled under the jaundiced eye of an older man who looked like a schoolmaster. A nursemaid shielded a younger boy's eyes from a scantily-clad Susanna and the watching Elders while his older brother worked the handle to send the slack-rope walker through her paces. There was no sign of Kennett. Julian sighed, and nodded to the second attendant, who swung open the door to the Saloon.

It was a much bigger room, with larger cases filled with more complicated scenes. At the center of the hall were two enormous displays, one of a naval battle that Julian decided had to be the Corsair Attack mentioned in the Gazetteer, and the other of a great number of figures crowding around a platform on which was displayed a very nearly naked woman. Two women in fashionable hats were studying it, while in front of the nearest case an elderly gentleman and a gangly boy who looked enough like him to be a grandson were debating the mechanics of Theseus and the Minotaur. The air smelled of machine oil and beeswax. It would be like Kennett to make him spend the extra sixpence for the Special Room, Julian thought, but no, there he was, just beyond the Corsair Attack, staring pensively at what looked like a snow-covered mountain. Julian made his way down the hall, not hurrying. Judith beheaded Holofernes in an unattended case, and held up the head with a flourish. A few drops of crimson liquid dripped from the severed neck, and Julian looked away.

"Kennett."

"Ah, Lynes. I'm glad you could come." Kennett looked particularly dapper in a grey tweed flecked with violet, some tightly furled blue flower tucked into the silver boutonnière at his lapel. "I'm sorry about the other night."

"You had said it was urgent," Julian pointed out.

"Yes, well." Kennett had the grace to look abashed. "As things turned out, I just couldn't. But I am grateful that you've pursued the matter."

"I'm willing to drop it if you'd rather."

"No! No, no, not at all." Kennett rested his hands lightly on the edge of the case. It was labeled *The Swiss Valley Imperiled*, and showed a bucolic winter scene beneath a looming brow of snow. "I just don't quite know where to begin.

"You said you were being blackmailed." He kept his voice low, but Kennett flinched anyway.

"In a manner of speaking. Only not – not over what you'd think."

"Not your private life."

The brow of snow collapsed with a clatter of gears, flattening the houses beneath an impressive weight of artificial snow. After a moment, tiny doors opened, and the snow began to sift away, aided by the gentle vibration of the table. A small sign on the case read, "An exact depiction of the disaster that overtook the village of Nederhorn in the Canton of Graubünden in the year 1692."

"I almost wish that were it," Kennett muttered. He shook his head. "No, not really, but – this is nearly as bad, Lynes. I'll be ruined."

"Why don't you tell me what they want?" Two very young clerks were making their way down the hall, and he touched Kennett's elbow, moving him on.

"Yes. I suppose I'd better." Kennett stalled there for a moment, then took a deep breath. "You may have heard that I have a new volume of verse coming out next month? It's received very favorable comments already. Some flattering praise, and the promise that it will be well-reviewed in influential journals. I dare say it should make my name."

Julian waited.

"The trouble is, poetry doesn't pay," Kennett said. "A man has to eat, keep the roof over his head."

"Kennett –"

"So I wrote a novel or two to make ends meet."

"I'm not sure I follow," Julian said, after a moment.

Kennett looked intently at the nearest case, where the Earl of Leicester and his unwanted wife stood together at the top of a flight of antique stairs. Julian pressed the button, and watched as Leicester sent her tumbling.

"What's wrong with writing novels –" He stopped, the pieces coming to-gether, Delahunt Brothers and Horrocks's wheezing laughter. "Oh. You wrote ladies' romances."

Kennett's eyes went wide with horror. "How did you know? It would ruin me. No one would ever take me seriously as a poet again."

"And that's what your blackmailer is threatening you with?"

"Exactly. Unless I pay him thirty pounds, he'll inform the journals that I am the person who wrote *Death in the Dooryard* and *Lady Jane's Dilemma*."

"Can he prove it?" Julian scowled as a curtain whisked across the glass, cut-ting off his sight of the scene resetting itself.

"It's true."

"Yes, but does he actually have proof, something he can show the journals? If not, you could brazen it out."

"Delahunt pays me," Kennett said. "I've impressed on them that I want to preserve my anonymity, but – their bookkeepers and my banker have to know. And of course I've signed a contract. That had to be in my own name." He winced. "In fact, I owe them another five-volume shocker before I'm done."

"Your banker won't say anything," Julian said.

"But a clerk might, if he's paid enough. At Delahunt's or at the bank. Besides, the suggestion alone – you don't know how competitive the literary world is, Lynes. The slightest suspicion that I'm – less than perfectly pure in my commitment to literature – worse, that I've written women's fiction – and the journals will drop my book in favor of the next clever young man's. This is my one chance, and it's about to be ruined."

Julian touched Kennett's arm again, and they moved off down the line of cabinets, Kennett staring blindly at their faces, though Julian thought it un-likely he saw even his reflection in the glass. Damnably, he was right: London's literary lions were both fickle and vicious, and this was exactly the sort of story to produce not sympathy but malicious laughter. And the only defense against blackmail was to refuse to pay and stand the consequences. Or, of course, to remove the blackmailer, but that was always a dicey business. "The police?" he suggested, without much hope, and Kennett shook his head.

"I might as well shout it from the rooftops."

"They are capable of discretion," Julian said. "I know one or two men who might be able to help."

"But they'll expect me to prosecute," Kennett said. "And – well, there we are again."

"What do you want me to do, then?"

"Can't you – ?" Kennett waved his hands. "I don't know, frighten him off?"

Julian sighed. "It depends on who he is. It's a difficult business, Kennett. Blackmailers don't get anywhere by being easily frightened. How did he contact you?"

"By letter." Kennett reached into his coat pocket and brought out a trio of envelopes. "I brought them in case you'd find them helpful."

"Yes." Julian gave them a quick look – cheap paper, but not the cheapest, addressed in the sort of block printing that showed little evidence of identity, postmarked W.C. – and tucked them into his own pocket. There were more tests he could make, physical and metaphysical, but they'd have to wait until he got back to his rooms. "The first thing to do it find out who he is. Then we can see how to deal with him. Has he given you a deadline?"

Kennett shook his head. "He said he'd be back in touch. He'd tell me then where to send the money."

Julian hid his dismay behind a frown. That tended to confirm what he had begun to fear, that the blackmailer was enjoying the game as much as the money, that he wanted to savor Kennett's panic. Which argued that it was someone Kennett knew, or at least someone with whom he was in regular contact, but at least that was a place to start. He frowned into the nearest case, where a chariot race in miniature was churning its way around the Coliseum, the tracks intricate enough to permit the chariots to cross each others' paths. "He wants to see you suffer," he said, "and that should buy us time. I'll be in touch as soon as I know anything."

"Thank you." Kennett shook his head. "Everything I've worked for – it's a nightmare."

"I'll find him," Julian said, and hoped that would be enough.

❦

THEY ATE DINNER IN JULIAN'S ROOMS that night, by mutual agreement that the day's events were better discussed somewhere private.

"There might be a connection," Julian said, poking dubiously at Mrs Digby's mutton. Ned felt its one virtue was that it was cooked thoroughly enough to avoid gruesome associations; it hardly seemed animal in origin at all.

"You mean, besides the obvious?"

"The obvious is what I'm thinking of. If Hall was the blackmailer –"

"Kennett's a friend of yours."

"Believe me, it's not a pleasant thought. But I can't say I know the man well enough to be certain that he wouldn't take matters into his own hands. If he were pressed hard enough, anyway."

"Murder, to prevent it coming out that he writes ladies' romances? Don't you think that's a bit extreme?"

"He'd be a laughing-stock," Julian said. "He'd never weather it, not with the very serious literary set." He cocked his head to one side curiously. "I can't help but wonder who died in the dooryard."

"I think I've read that one," Ned said. "The girl has two suitors, and one of them is arrested for murder after the other one disappears, only it turns out that he's faked his death all along to get the other fellow hung."

"Doesn't proving a murder charge usually require a body?"

"Kennett did gloss over that bit," Ned admitted. "But there's a great deal of the beautiful youthful hero falling to his knees in agonies of despair, and rending his clothes to lie half-naked and shivering on the floor of his cell, all drenched with rain."

"Inside the cell?"

"I believe there's a window. It's all rather lovingly described."

"Which I suppose does suggest the author."

"It's mostly for the benefit of lady readers," Ned pointed out.

"Are they all like that?"

"To a certain extent. Occasionally someone gets chained up. The good ones are a bit like those boys' adventure novels we used to sneak into school, only with more young women, of course, but also more burning kisses and more rending of all sorts of garments."

Julian's eyebrows went up even further. "All sorts?"

"Exactly which garments is usually left to the imagination."

"I had no idea." Julian shook his head, the glint of humor in his eyes fading. "I don't want to think Kennett did away with Hall."

"Hall didn't strike me as a hardened blackmailer, surely. More likely a blackmail victim."

"If he'd tried it, and lost his nerve…" Julian shook his head. "Then he'd have simply stopped sending letters. And if Kennett killed Hall, I don't know why he involved me in the first place. Unless there's evidence he thinks I can get back for him. That writing desk still bothers me."

"Believe me, it bothers me, too. It makes it look like deliberate murder for gain – or to get back something that was in that desk, yes. But I don't think we have reason yet to point fingers at Kennett."

Julian withdrew a stack of envelopes from his pocket and set them on the table. "Even so, I'd feel better if you'd take a look at these," he said. "I haven't been able to get anywhere with them metaphysically – whoever wrote them knew enough to cover his tracks. Which itself is interesting."

"Presumably it's a useful skill for a blackmailer. But, yes, I do take your point – it means someone else who may have moved in the same circles knows at least some metaphysics. How common is that?"

Julian considered the question. "More common than in the general populace, I think. Partly because it's useful to have ways of getting rid of incriminating evidence, like that bit of hocus I did with your card that night. And partly it's just that everyone who goes to those clubs is willing to take risks, or they wouldn't be there, so what's one risk more? But it's mostly ordinary sorts of enchantment, for amusement or convenience."

"Not experiments with non-conforming magic."

"Not that I know of. There are always rumors about certain unconventional techniques – but I think they're mostly excuses for people to, well, to brag about their adventures in the bedroom. And in other locations."

There was a certain speculative note to Julian's voice, and Ned was grateful for the distraction.

"I might prefer the bedroom," he said. "So as not to worry about the *Urtica mordax* nipping anything delicate."

"It isn't interested in anything as big as that," Julian said, and Ned laughed.

It began well, both of them hungry to forget their troubles in bruising kisses and ungentle tugging at clothing. Ned was wound tight, though, and trying overly hard not to think of other things, and he found himself uncharacteristically frustrated with letting Julian take the lead. He pushed away Julian's hands when they reached for his trouser buttons, and Julian stopped at once.

"If you don't want…"

"I do, just…let me, this time." He began unfastening Julian's shirt buttons, one by one, which Julian permitted, and actually seemed to enjoy. Julian shrugged off the shirt when it was entirely undone, and then stripped off his undershirt without being asked. With his curling dark hair, he would have made a good Dionysus himself, not the Apollonian ideal of perfect proportion, but angular and lithe, all the more attractive for his imperfections.

He seemed gratifyingly eager, his dark eyes hot with intent, and at the same time, Ned hesitated, unsure what exactly to do with the upper hand if for once he had it. It was abruptly tempting to bend Julian over the bed and tug his trousers down, the idea both exciting and disturbing – he would look so very vulnerable that way, his back bent as if for punishment. He'd always been the one to fuck Ned, not the other way around, and Ned couldn't quite bring himself to suggest it.

Instead he put his hand on Julian's shoulder to urge him downward to his knees, which seemed like a lesser liberty to take. Julian twisted away at once, and then turned back more slowly, as if steeling himself to comply.

"Never mind that, then," Ned said. "Tell me what you'd like."

"Come here." Julian caught Ned's wrist to draw him over to the bed, and pressed him down under his weight once they were there, taking him in hand. It had the desired effect, but even after Ned had returned the favor and they were sprawled together, breathing hard, he thought neither of them was entirely satisfied.

"I don't usually mind being told what to do," Ned began tentatively.

"You don't have to always do what I want."

"I don't want to make you do things you dislike."

Julian shrugged awkwardly against him. "You don't."

Yes, because you always tell me what to do, Ned thought, but it didn't seem profitable to say it. He felt at a loss for words it would be profitable to say. They both knew now about more vices than they'd ever dreamed of in their schoolboy days, and Ned felt there must be some way to discuss which particular ones Julian might not mind practicing. But Julian tended to move from innuendo to blunt requests that could be taken or left, but that weren't exactly conversational openings, and he wasn't sure how he would begin himself. Which was in a way precisely the problem.

He closed his eyes against Julian's shoulder, but his sleep was restless. In the morning, the fog outside the windows seemed oppressive as they dressed by gaslight.

"I'll see what I can make out from those letters," he said.

"And I'll ask around about Hall. Someone must know more about him than the police found out," Julian said.

"That would be helpful. Even if we can't exactly present whatever you find out to Hatton –"

"Still, it would be a start."

"It would," Ned said, and knotted his necktie, dismissing all thoughts not suitable for office hours at the Commons firmly from his mind.

☾❋

CHAPTER FIVE
A New Client

"Mr Mathey, I'm afraid I have a favor to ask you," Miss Frost said, setting down the slim stack of the morning's post. "I hate to be troublesome."

"Think nothing of it," Ned said, tipping his chair to put his back closer to the warmer wall. As a junior man at the Commons, he didn't rate an office with a fireplace, and was dependent on what heat radiated from the better chambers on the other side of the wall. He hadn't quite worked up the nerve to smuggle in some alternate source of heat, enchanted stoves being officially forbidden as fire hazards, but he was beginning to suspect that the winter months might change his mind.

"I have a letter from an old school friend, Miss Madeleine Barton. She has a problem that she'd like a metaphysician's advice about, but for a number of reasons, she can't afford to be seen at the Commons. She teaches school in Primrose Hill, and she can't see you there either – it's like being in the convent to be a schoolteacher – but she asks if she might meet you at a tea shop if you're free to meet her this morning – I know it's an imposition, but I do think she needs help."

"I'm free. If we can get clear of here before Hatton asks me to come look at any more corpses."

Miss Frost looked at him sideways as she began shrugging on her coat. "Was it very gruesome?"

"Yes, rather," Ned surprised himself by saying. "But I suppose that's the nature of the work."

"I'm not sure I should like it either," Miss Frost said. "But a professional woman doesn't have the luxury of having delicate sensibilities."

"You'd be forgiven for it more easily than a gentleman, surely," Ned said.

"Do you think so? If you had fainted, or been sick, they might have laughed at you, I suppose."

"They might have." Ned didn't think Hatton would have – he had been gruffly sympathetic to his obvious squeamishness – but he suspected that the chaffing that went on between the other men on the squad was less forgiving.

"But they wouldn't have had you taken home, and said it obviously went to show that gentlemen were too sensitive by nature for the work, and should stay home knitting."

"I take your point," Ned said. "And I can't knit."

"I can," Miss Frost said. "They encourage that sort of thing at the schools I went to, in order to demonstrate that being educated doesn't take away a woman's femininity. Besides, I quite enjoy knitting. And it saves spending on slippers."

Claremont's Tea Shop was clear of the morning rush by the time they arrived, only a few lady shoppers settled at the scattered tables. The tea lady frowned at Ned when he entered, and he was strongly aware that he was the only man in the room.

"Don't worry, it's not an unsuitable atmosphere for gentlemen," Miss Frost said, looking momentarily amused.

Ned collected a cup of tea and a plate of ginger biscuits and made his way to the table in the corner where Miss Frost's friend was waiting. She was a freckled redhead, her curling hair escaping out of its knot in wild exploratory tendrils that reminded Ned of Julian's *Urtica mordax*. She wore a black coat and skirt that he supposed were her school teacher's uniform, making her pretty face look pale.

"I can't thank you enough for seeing me," she said. "I promise you, it's not modesty that prevents me from coming to the Commons – I'm not as particular as that! – but I can't afford to be seen there right now, and I hope you'll understand why." She took a deep breath. "The thing is, I teach Practical Metaphysics at Carlyle's School for Girls. It's not meant to be a technical course, you understand, only practical things they can use in domestic life – well, that's the modern way, isn't it?"

"Mmm," Ned said noncommittally, not sure he felt that householders should really be encouraged to experiment.

"And of course it saves them money on calling in a metaphysician for every little thing – I'm sorry, that's not very tactful, is it? Or very discreet, because young ladies aren't supposed to have to worry about saving money, only of course the sort of girls who come to us instead of somewhere really prestigious actually do."

"You needn't be tactful," Ned said.

"I'm afraid it's never been a virtue of mine. And I am grateful for the position, even if it isn't a very exclusive sort of school – it's entirely respectable, just a bit shabby around the edges. Although if it did only pay a bit better, I might never have been tempted…"

Miss Frost put her fingers to her forehead. "Do explain, Maddy. You're making it sound as if you've fallen into some unspeakable sin."

"You might say so," Miss Barton said. "I wrote a book. Several books, actually, because the first one did so well, and they asked for another. The best of them was *The Governess and the Tiger* –"

"I've read that book," Ned said with genuine enthusiasm. Miss Frost looked at him askance. "The hero's been wounded in India, and there's a curse – the tiger that stalks him through all the portraits in the house –"

"Until our heroine drives it off, and it's all very metaphorical for the healing power of love, yes," Miss Barton said. "And it sold like anything. But of course it's under a pen name – all of them are – and last week I got this letter."

She produced it from her handbag. It bore no return address, but the envelope and the careful block printing looked all too familiar.

"Someone's blackmailing you," Ned said.

"He wants thirty pounds, and I can't spare it." Miss Barton raised a stubborn chin. "And if I did, he'd just come back again wanting more, wouldn't he?"

"Very likely," Ned admitted.

"So I thought I'd better find some way of stopping him."

"Refusing to pay would be simplest."

She shook her head regretfully. "I should like to send him back a letter laughing in his silly face, believe me, but I can't live on the money from the books alone. My people haven't got much, they can't give me a penny unless I want to go home and live with them in the country where I can't get work, and in fact I try to send them something when I can."

"You're certain you'd lose your position?"

"Deadly certain, Mr Mathey. They couldn't keep a teacher who'd written scandalous romances. And it's not just the romance – that might come just a bit close to the mark, but it's certainly not *indecent* – but how the heroine takes up her occupation."

It took Ned a moment to remember, the brooding hero having attracted most of his attention. When he did, he winced. The heroine, thrown upon the world with no marketable skills whatsoever, had passed herself off as a meta-physically-trained governess with sterling references through a combination of lies, half-truths, and metaphysical experimentation that Ned had to admit was somewhat hair-raising.

"It's a cautionary tale, of course," Miss Barton said. He thought he detected a gleam of dauntless humor in her eyes. "But some people might think it was intended as an instruction manual."

"Pardon me for the question, but you didn't…"

"No, she didn't," Miss Frost said. "I was at school with her, Mr Mathey, so I can testify to that. But it made you wonder, didn't you?"

"They'd all question my credentials, and certainly my judgment," Miss Barton said. "And most of all whether I'm a good moral influence on the girls. And if I'm dismissed for cause, that's the end. I'll never have a teaching job again." She set her jaw. "I want to know who sent the letter, Mr Mathey, and I want him stopped."

"Do you have any idea who it might be?"

"I can't even guess. I was trying to be so careful. I keep my writing things locked up at school, and well-warded as well, and I don't think anyone's gotten into them. I never posted manuscripts from the school, or took correspondence about it there – I have a box at the post office. I can only think that someone must have seen me do it. That's why I didn't want to come to the Commons, or go to a shop where…" She hesitated.

"Of course you didn't want to go to an unlicensed metaphysician if you think you might have been followed," Miss Frost said. "And if the blackmailer is another woman, she might perfectly well know what the 'lace shop' really specialized in. And might assume that your reasons for needing to consult the proprietress were far more personal."

"I've heard of a similar case recently," Ned said, putting the letter away in his coat. "I'm looking into it now, actually. I'll try to find out if there's a connection."

"I can't thank you enough," Miss Barton said. "This simply can't go on."

Ned nodded. "I promise you, I'll do whatever I can."

JULIAN SIPPED CAUTIOUSLY AT HIS WHISKY and soda – his third of the evening, and he couldn't afford to be too fuddled – then turned to survey the card room. Jacobs' was inconveniently thin of company tonight. There was no sign of Lennox, for one – though Patti was singing, Anstruther had reminded him, which might well explain it. Nor was Cope in any of the rooms, which meant that the two best sources of gossip were absent. Geordie MacNab couldn't remember anything more about Hall than that he had been an annoyingly fidgety model, and Hal Cochrane had admitted to a brief affair, but they'd parted amicably enough almost a year ago. He hadn't much liked Hall's circle, either, and that was the main cause of the split.

"Not that they were as bad as they claimed, I don't believe," he had said, scrupulously fair as always.

"What did they claim, then?" Julian had asked, and Cochrane had blushed faintly.

"They *said* they performed the Great Rite."

"Oh. Sex magic. To what end?"

Cochrane had blushed even more deeply. "Good Lord, I wouldn't want to know. Not that Dolly would have told me if I had asked, he was an honorable sort that way. But, you know, Lynes, I don't believe they really did it."

One or two others, when pressed, admitted to having heard the same rumors, and Summergate said he thought there was a group that had tried it on a regular basis, and that there had been some sort of incident at the Dionysus, but he couldn't say more than that. That seemed promising, but Summergate wasn't a Dionysus member, and his friend Oliver, from whom he'd gotten the tale, notoriously had a bee in his bonnet about what he called the more disreputable sort of club. Julian rested his elbows on the bar, wondering who else he should talk to before he braved the Dionysus.

"Looking for your paragon?"

Julian winced, recognizing the voice as belonging to Trefethen, one of Lennox's card-playing cronies. "He's not here."

"Abandoned so soon?" Trefethen motioned to the bartender, who obligingly filled another glass.

"I came alone," Julian said.

"Ah, but does he know that?" Trefethen smiled. "Care for a game?"

"Not tonight," Julian answered. "I don't suppose you knew Dolly Hall?" It had been a forlorn hope at best, and he wasn't surprised when Trefethen shook his head.

"The poor beggar they found dead in his rooms? Apoplexy, I heard." His tone made it a question.

"That seems most likely," Julian said.

"I can't say I'm surprised. He was in with a bad crowd, if he's the man I'm thinking of – a bit more classical than most, and not just in their vices. Live fast, die young, and leave a beautiful corpse, that's their motto."

"Hall didn't get his wish there," Julian said, in spite of himself.

Trefethen grimaced. "Poor little beast. I suppose Alfie Punton will be cut up about it. They were close at school."

"I don't know Punton," Julian said. It wasn't entirely true, in that he thought he could put a face to the name, but it wasn't enough of a lie to trip him up later.

"He's part of that crowd at the Dionysus," Trefethen said. "You've probably heard the talk, the ones who are always claiming there's some magical potency in their antics, though to my mind it's just an excuse to do each other in public and shock the shockable. If people just ignored them, it wouldn't happen so much."

"I imagine it would be fairly hard to ignore," Julian said, thinking of the men they'd watched the last time he was at the Dionysus.

"True enough. I've never been favored with the display, alas."

"But you know Punton."

Trefethen nodded. "Know him to speak to, anyway. Plays a decent game of whist, if you can get him to keep his mind on the cards. Nice-looking sort, very personable – losing his hair, but that happens to the best of us."

Trefethen's crowning glory was particularly exuberant, to match his side whiskers, and Julian found himself resenting the knowledge that he was supposed to notice. He finished his drink more quickly than he'd meant, and took himself off to the Dionysus.

It was still early enough in the night as well as the week for the crowd to be less riotous, though when he made his way into the main parlor Miss Caroline was listing at an odd angle. As he watched, she released a single rainbow-hued bubble the size of one of her eyes and straightened again, only to begin tilting to the other side a few moments later. Julian disapproved of experimenting on Miss Caroline on the grounds that it was not only cruel but largely pointless – how could you tell if your enchantment was having an effect? – and this didn't seem to be doing anything clever. He frowned, trying to think of a likely construction for an enchantment that made a fish burp rainbows, and one of the group by the fireplace drew his own wand.

"Really, Pugh, if you're going to meddle with the poor fish, at least make her do something interesting." He sketched a sigil as he spoke, and Miss Caroline righted herself abruptly, spun twice, and settled to another sedate circuit of her bowl.

"Oh, yes, don't abuse the goldfish." That was Linford Farrell, his voice unmistakable even though Julian couldn't see him through the crowd. "Otherwise,

Malcolm will have to spank you – monetarily, at least. I don't believe he's up for the other."

"Lay off, Linford," someone said lazily. "It was a club vote. Miss Caroline has enough to put up with."

Julian moved to the nearest drinks table, putting a motley group of artistes and artists' models between him and Farrell. He had liked Farrell at University – they had struck up a friendship over the classics, as so many of their sort had done, and Farrell had introduced him to the larger circle of like-minded men that dominated the literary set. For all that he could be devastating to outsiders, he'd never mocked Julian for his lack of artistic interests, and Julian had quickly learned that stating his own tastes without a visible blush earned him the right to do as he pleased. Ned had never liked him – that was one of the things that had driven them apart – but then, Ned had never really known how to handle him. Still, Farrell had changed since he'd come up to London – Julian gathered that some theatrical venture had failed, and Farrell was now a respectable junior in a merchant bank, but the failure had soured him. And keeping company with Ryder Leach had not improved matters.

Julian poured himself another whisky and added a generous amount of soda, and in turning away nearly collided with a doe-eyed young man in a slightly elderly evening suit.

"Oh, I'm so sorry," the young man said.

"Hello, Bunny," Julian said.

Bunny Manders looked up through his lashes as though he were pleased at being remembered. But then, he was usually with Raffles, the amateur cricketer, and probably didn't get noticed much in that company. And that was something else Julian needed to mention to Ned before there was an unexpected encounter. He put that thought out of his mind and smiled at Manders.

"Raffles not about?"

Manders blushed, a becoming color in his milk-and-roses complexion. "I'm meeting him here, actually. But I'm a bit early."

"My loss," Julian said, and added, more out of duty than hope, "I don't suppose you knew Dolly Hall."

Manders shook his head. "Not my crowd, that. But I believe Stephen did." Before Julian could say anything, Manders lifted his hand and waved to a homely young man on the edge of Farrell's group. "Stephen! Julian here was asking about poor Dolly."

Stephen looked over eagerly at Manders's invitation, unfolding himself from the footstool where he'd been crouching. He was very tall, and moved with the awkwardness of someone not yet used to his height, and Julian couldn't help wondering who had brought this puppy to the Dionysus. Leach, for a guess, or one of his friends: they'd find his embarrassment amusing. And Stephen was obviously only young. It seemed more than usually unkind.

"I didn't know him very well," Stephen was saying. There was a sharp spot of color in his cheeks that suggested he'd slept with him regardless. "But of course I was dreadfully shocked. I had no idea he was ill."

"I don't think anyone did," Julian said. "Although I gather he was close to Alfie Punton?"

"Who speaks the ill-omened name of Punton?" That was the literary critic from their last visit, a glass of gin in one hand and one of the artists' models in the other. "Stephen, darling, come away before you're corrupted."

"There's nothing wrong with Punton," someone said.

"Well, except that he's missing." That was an older man in spectacles, frowning slightly.

"That's melodramatic, surely," the critic said.

"Oh, I don't know." Farrell rose from his armchair to lean against the mantel, surveying the room with sardonic enjoyment. "Since our Julian is asking questions, one more might think there's more to it than a week's sulk."

Julian was aware that everyone was looking at him, and silently damned Farrell for it. "I was mostly curious about Dolly Hall," he said, carefully. "I heard from someone that Punton was a particular friend."

The critic snorted. "Punton didn't have enough money for that."

"I say, Pinky," someone protested.

Farrell shrugged. "He could be a mercenary creature, our Dolly, but he wasn't unknown to have a generous impulse now and then. But if you're looking for Punton, Julian, I'm afraid you're out of luck. I don't think he's been around for, oh, a week, at least."

"How long, exactly?" Julian forced a smile that he hoped looked easy. "It's of interest."

"You can't think Punton did for poor Dolly," the spectacled man said, and Pinky looked up sharply.

"I thought he had some kind of an attack."

"There are a few items that need clearing up at his lodgings," Julian said. "Discreetly, I mean. I don't suppose anyone knows where Punton lodges?"

"At his work," the spectacled man said. "And don't ask me where or what it is because I don't know. It just came up when we were talking once about the rooms here."

Julian nodded. He hadn't really expected anything more: most of the Dionysus's members were careful not to give away too many details of their lives outside its charmed circle. Still, he managed to determine that it had been five days since anyone had seen Punton. Five days ago, he thought, Ned was called to see a naked body that was missing its heart. Surely it was too much of a coincidence – except that Punton and Hall were close, and rumored to be involved in dubious practice...

"I do believe I may have been the last one to see him," Farrell drawled. "Unless someone else wants to claim the honor. No? Then I'm your man, Julian." He held out his hands as though he was waiting to be handcuffed, and Julian suppressed the desire to oblige him.

"Oh, for God's sake, Linford," Pinky snapped. "All this melodrama over what will prove to be a simple tantrum."

"It is odd not to have seen him," the spectacled man said. "He's here most nights –"

"He's sulking," Pinky said again. "I knew the name of Punton was ill-omened! Come, Stephen – unless you wish to remain among the philistines."

Stephen paused, the color rising in his cheeks. "I haven't – I still have my drink –"

"Well, bring it. And come along." Pinky bustled off, model in tow.

Stephen hesitated just a moment too long, then looked awkwardly for a place to set his glass. "I should be –"

"Don't go," the spectacled man said. "Pinky's an ass when he's in a mood. Stay and have another. I'm Harry, by the way."

He held out his hand. Stephen took it, gingerly, and Harry contrived to tuck it into his elbow, turning him neatly away from the crowd. Julian frowned, unsure if this was an improvement, and Manders shook his head.

"It's all right," he said softly. "'Harry' is a very nice viscount, and he'll give young Stephen a night that'll make him forget all about poets."

"Yes, I wouldn't bother interfering," Farrell said. "Though – I don't see your Hercules, Lynes. Or have you already brought him to grief?"

"That was Hephaestos," Manders said, absently, and his attention fixed on the door. "Ah. Excuse me –"

Raffles, Julian thought, and sure enough the cricketer's handsome form was briefly visible in the door before both he and Manders disappeared. "I'm here by myself," he said, and Farrell rested a hand on his sleeve.

"You don't have to be."

Julian lifted an eyebrow, and Farrell withdrew his hand.

"Look, I am sorry about your Ned, I shouldn't tease, but he's just so bloody earnest —"

"I'm tired," Julian said. "And not in the mood for company." He set his glass down and turned away, not entirely sure why he was so annoyed. It wasn't as though he wanted to sleep with Farrell again; it had gone well enough at University, but in London it had become pellucidly clear that they didn't suit. He couldn't help remember, though, one night when Alanson and Symmonds had held one of their symposia. They had all been reading Shakespeare, and Symmonds had challenged someone to recite verses in exchange for kisses. One thing had led to another, and Farrell had finally scooped the pot by reciting the entire St. Crispin's Day speech, one foot on the ottoman and his head thrown back in regal challenge. He'd done it straight, too, as though he believed in it, and the applause when he'd finished had been honestly given. Julian had been proud to go home with him that night. Where that man had gone, he couldn't say.

❧❀

It was half past nine by the clock on the bedroom mantel by the time Julian dragged himself upright. He'd slept restlessly at best, and woke from a particularly vivid dream in which Ned was buggering him in full view of the assembled Dionysus club, explaining that it was all right because they had no hearts. It was both disturbing and intensely arousing; he dealt with the latter with ruthless haste, and tried not to think too hard about it as he washed up.

Most of his breakfast was unsalvageable even with judicious use of enchantment, but he made himself eat the sausages and the cold toast and jam before writing himself a reviving enchantment and dissolving it in his second cup of coffee. He was mostly tired, not hungover, but he had a feeling he was going to need to be at his best once he'd spoken to Ned. He could see no way to avoid a conversation with Inspector Hatton, and much as he hated to expose his fellow club-men to the Yard, the Half-House had been sobering. And he couldn't honestly say that there weren't men at the Dionysus who'd be willing to take that sort of risk.

He took the omnibus to the Commons, the cool air and unexpected sunshine almost as reviving as the enchantment, and ducked into the courtyard by the Blandings entrance. Ned's outer door was open, and he knocked, composing a discreet explanation suitable for Miss Frost's ears, and pushed through into the narrow chamber. To his surprise, however, her desk was empty, and Ned was putting down a slim journal with a self-conscious air that suggested it was not a metaphysical volume. He relaxed, seeing Julian, and folded it more normally, and Julian recognized it as *Modern Sportsman*.

"Miss Frost isn't here?"

Ned shook his head. "I asked her to do some research for me – I've had another blackmail client, very similar to yours. Another author of romances who can't afford to have it known."

"That's interesting," Julian said. That meant that the blackmailer wasn't necessarily after Kennett, but was making a more general attack on people he thought he could intimidate. And that might mean it would be easier to chase him off, or persuade him to move on to easier prey. Not that Julian wouldn't rather see that blackmailer stopped, and jailed, for preference – but that wasn't really possible in this case, and he shook the thought away. "And I've turned up an interesting possibility. They still haven't identified that first body, have they?"

"Not that I know of."

"It might, and I stress 'might,' be a man called Alfred Punton." Julian ran through his discoveries of the night before. "I don't know that it is Punton, mind you, but on the one hand he was friends with Hall and dabbled in group magic and possibly sex magic, and he's not been seen for some days. And on the other hand, you have a body that's missing its heart just like Hall's. One has to ask if there's a connection."

Ned was already reaching for his pen. "I agree. I think we need to go see Hatton." He scribbled a note for Miss Frost, then collected his hat. "And don't tell me you don't want to talk to the Yard. He's going to have questions."

"That's what I'm afraid of," Julian said, but followed him down the stairs.

Hatton had a new office, but Julian wasn't sure if the faint reek of the stables was entirely worth the extra space. There was another smell as well, faint and nasty, and Julian saw Ned swallow hard. Hatton had a bouquet of violets in a glass on his desk, but they weren't doing their job.

"I came to see if you'd gotten a name for your first dead man," Ned said, "because if you haven't, Lynes may have a lead."

"No," Hatton said, "and yes, that is him you smell. We had to get an old-fashioned embalmer in here for him, and frankly I don't think he was up to the job."

"I don't imagine there's much call for it anymore." Ned was paler than usual, but obviously determined not to show that it bothered him. "Most people prefer a nice preserving enchantment, but under the circumstances –"

"No, it wouldn't do," Hatton said. "So. You have a name for me, Mr Lynes?"

"Possibly," Julian said. "I have some acquaintance in common with Hall, and it seems that one of them has gone missing. A man named Alfred Punton. I have also heard rumors that he and Hall might have been involved with a group that practiced unconventional magic."

Hatton sighed. "Sex magic?"

Julian blinked. "Yes."

"We see a bit of that," Hatton said. "Though mostly it's an excuse for an orgy. Still, there's one or two houses that – well, I wouldn't say they specialize, but it's a known sideline."

"I don't know how much good that will do you," Julian began, and stopped abruptly, unsure how to continue.

"I'm not sure the ladies in question were professional," Ned said.

Or even women, Julian thought, and kept his face expressionless only with an effort.

Hatton shook his head, but didn't look surprised. "Pity. If they'd just stick to the professionals, it would make my life easier. And they'd probably get more of what they were after anyway." He sighed. "What was the name again?"

"Alfred Punton."

"Punton. That rings a faint bell." Hatton rummaged through the papers on his desk and came up with a battered circular. "I thought that sounded familiar. Alfred Punton, MMA, reported missing by his employer, the Earl of Denbigh. It's worth a telegram, though I'd better warn them to send someone with a strong stomach."

The earl sent his secretary, who made the identification and was promptly sick. Left in Hatton's office, where the thin door did nothing to obscure the sounds, Julian tried not to meet Ned's eye or to think about the body in the loft above them. It was probably an hour before Hatton returned, rubbing his hands together in satisfaction.

"It's Punton, all right. And Mr Joshua there is going to get the earl to lean on Punton's mother – she's his only kin, and quite an elderly lady, apparently, lives down in Kent – to let the earl have him buried here and now. But at least we can move him to a chapel now."

"Just as long as you keep him well away from any enchantments," Ned said.

"Damn." Hatton brightened. "Still, there must be some impoverished and unimproved church around here that could take him."

Julian was less sure of that: mortuary improvements had been popular and common at the beginning of the century, and nearly every city church had had good incentive to make the change. From the look of him, Ned was equally uncertain, but there seemed to be no point in discouraging Hatton.

"In the meantime, gents, get your hats," Hatton went on. "You, too, Mr Lynes, if you wouldn't mind. Mr Joshua says the earl has given his full permission to look over Punton's room. Just in case he's left anything – unfortunate – behind him."

"Dangerous, you mean," Ned said.

"I think that when you're an earl's private secretary, you're not supposed to mind such things," Hatton said. "But I'd lay odds Mr Joshua does."

"You can't really blame him," Ned said. "Not after what he just saw."

"Be that as it may," Hatton answered, "we've rooms to search."

They crowded uncomfortably into a battered cab, Hatton and his disreputable-looking special constable, Garmin, on one side and Joshua wedged uncomfortably between Ned and Julian. The earl had a house on the edges of Mayfair – less fashionable, Julian thought, but certainly a good deal larger and probably more comfortable than if the family had built further into the district. Punton had been given a suite of rooms in a section of the mews that had been converted to a sort of private museum when the new stables were built, according to the secretary, and part of his duties had been to tend the collection. He also had a door of his own that opened into the alleyway, Julian noted, which would have given him the freedom to come and go as he pleased. Joshua was quick to disclaim responsibility for the entire project.

"His lordship has given strict orders that the housekeeper was to wait for Mr Punton's instructions before doing anything in this wing," he said. "And that included Mr Punton's private rooms as well as the collection."

"Probably just as well." Hatton looked at Ned. "Do we dare look for wards?"

Ned looked at Joshua instead. "This looks like a very up-to-date house. I'd guess there is a fair amount of metaphysics in use?"

"Oh, yes, indeed." Joshua sounded as gratified as if he'd created the enchantments himself. "All the locks, doors and windows both, and the skylight. Plus the usual household objects."

"Then it should be all right out here," Ned said. "He wasn't going to do anything that would react with the household enchantments and risk giving himself away. I'd be careful with any interior locks, though – cabinets, boxes, things like that."

"Right." Hatton managed a smile. "Mr Joshua, I think we can manage from here. I know you're a busy man."

"I am, rather," the secretary answered, with relief. "But send for me if you need me."

"Absolutely," Hatton said, and waited until he'd vanished into the main house before turning to Garmin. "Do the honors, then, but be careful."

"Right, guv," Garmin said, drawing something from his pocket that was not – quite – a wand. He sketched some symbols and gave a grunt of satisfaction. "He's got it glamoured, all right. But I don't know the form."

"I think I do," Ned said. "May I?"

Garmin nodded, and Ned drew his own wand, sketched a quick sigil above the lock. Julian recognized it and his eyebrows rose.

"That's the hocus Mayhew used to keep the hearties from pinching his cigars."

"Very like, anyway," Ned answered.

"Is that what they teach young gentlemen at University these days?" Hatton asked.

"Young gentlemen who are studying metaphysics, anyway," Ned answered. He sketched a counter-charm and nodded. "That's taken care of that."

"But that's not all there is," Garmin said, lifting his stick, "and it definitely ain't anything from the University. This is old London, pure and nasty."

Hatton grimaced, and Julian took a step backward, recognizing the symbols that appeared on the stone of the stairs. A fat brown spider dropped from the rafters, landed with a plop, and disappeared. There were more plops from further up the staircase, and Garmin gave a grunt of satisfaction.

"All clear, boss."

"I'm surprised he didn't blow the place up," Hatton said, but started up the stairs. Ned followed, Garmin at his heels, and Julian brought up the rear.

"Perhaps he didn't experiment at home," Ned said, and Hatton snorted.

"We're not that lucky, Mathey."

Julian stopped just inside the door, studying the cozy parlor. It wasn't large to begin with, and the amount of furniture made it seem smaller, but the things were arranged with care and taste and a certain flair for design. The curtain was too big for the window – bought ready-made, then, not sewn for the space – but the bright blue and green print made the relatively dark room feel more cheerful. There was no gas laid on, but Hatton and Ned were busy lighting the mix of oil and patent flameless lamps, and the details came clearer.

"Someone's been here already," he said.

Hatton straightened, frowning. "Oh?"

"Look at how he's left his pipe." Julian pointed to the tables on either side of the most comfortable armchair. "He's set it to the left, as though he were left-handed, along with the ashtray, but the matches are on the other table, along with the rest of the cleaning tools. He usually puts his glass to the right, too, you can see the ring. And it's the same at his desk. The penwiper and the inkwell are on opposite sides of the blotter. Someone's moved them, and hasn't put them back quite right."

Hatton nodded. "I'll buy that. And did they find what they were looking for, I wonder?"

Julian shrugged. "They clearly had time enough, otherwise there'd be more of a mess."

"I don't think they did." Ned looked at a nondescript cabinet that stood beside the bedroom door. It was painted with Japanese-style figures, and the doors stood partly open, a key with an enormous tassel resting in the lock. There was a narrow drawer above it, with a much less obtrusive lock. "Take a look at this, would you, Lynes?"

Julian approached it cautiously, torn between the desire to impress Ned and the suspicion that showing off some of his skills in front of Hatton was not entirely wise. He was abruptly aware of the desire to avert his eyes, to look anywhere other than the slender drawer. "That's interesting."

Ned nodded. "It's glamoured, but –"

"Non-conforming," Julian said grimly. His own lock picks were enchanted, and he gave Hatton a wary look. "I don't suppose you'd have a set of picks on you?"

"Constable?" Hatton said, and the smaller man grimaced, rummaging in his pockets.

"Mine are hocused, most of them, which I gather isn't a good plan." He was fiddling with a ring of tools as he spoke, and finally freed an old-fashioned Iron Betty. "This one's clear, but she's big for that."

"I'll try it anyway." Julian accepted the hooked piece of iron – nicely made, neatly curved to the hand – and considered the exterior of the lock. It looked ordinary enough, and he extended the pick, only to jerk back with an oath as a spark leaped from the escutcheon to the pick. He dropped the pick and put his stinging fingers in his mouth.

"I'd say that's not the answer," Hatton said, and handed the dropped pick back to his constable. "Mathey? Can you open it without bringing down the ceiling?"

"Maybe." Ned went to one knee beside the cabinet. "I think this is more like old magic than something entirely unrelated, and if it is, there should be hooks to catch onto. But you might want to stand back, just in case."

Julian took a step back, and was meanly pleased to see that Hatton and Garmin retreated to the doorway. Ned frowned at the lock for a moment, then carefully traced a circle around the lock with his finger. There was a brief flash of light, and Ned murmured something under his breath. That was answered by a loud pop and a curl of smoke drifted out of the keyhole.

"Right, that's got it," Ned said and tugged at the drawer, which stayed firmly in place. "Well, it's taken off the enchantment, anyway."

Hatton clapped his constable on the shoulder. "Go to it, Garmin."

Garmin gave him a baleful look, but set to work. Julian bit his lip to keep from offering suggestions, and after a few minutes the drawer sagged open. Garmin scowled. "Looks like papers."

"Well, let's see what we have," Hatton answered, but Ned got there first, lifting out the sheaf of foolscap. Julian peered over his shoulder to see page after page of familiar symbol laid out in a neat scholar's hand.

"It's notes for some sort of ritual," Ned said, "but I don't recognize it. I can probably trace it in the Commons library, though."

Julian took the pages from him, sorting them into what seemed the most logical order. There was something familiar about it, about the shape of the rite and the energies involved, old-fashioned but not quite archaic, and grounded in an earlier, earthier tradition… And then he had it, the memory flashing clear, Bolster carefully unwrapping a tiny mummified hand with candles where the fingers should have been. The palm had been empty except for a protruding nail, and the dirty rind of a sixth and larger candle.

"I do know what this is," he said. "It's a Hand of Glory. Or at least whatever this was intended to be is based on a Hand of Glory."

"Can't be," Garmin said, looking a little queasy. "You can't get the materials anymore."

"Here's where he was working out the substitutions," Julian answered, pulling out a much-blotted sheet. Ned took it, nodding, and Hatton made a face.

"Well, that's some mercy. Grease from the gibbet, tallow rendered from a hanged man, never mind the hand itself – but tell me, Mr Lynes, have you ever seen one that worked?"

"Not that I know of," Julian said. And that was true enough. Bolster had showed him the thing more as a curio than a practical tool for the business.

"Nasty things," Garmin muttered.

Ned flipped through the sheaf of papers again. "Remind me, Lynes, what are the properties of a Hand of Glory?"

Julian ticked them off on his fingers. "One, to throw the inhabitants of a house into rouseless sleep. Two, to provide a light that only the bearer of the Hand can see. And, three, to unlock any lock no matter how complex. Also, it can only be quenched with milk."

Garmin eyed him with something between worry and respect. "That's *Little Albert*, that is."

"Yes, of course," Julian said, and Ned broke in hastily.

"But what I don't see is what he – they? – were trying to do with all of this. It's not a Hand of Glory, even if it's related, but what the devil is it?"

Julian took back the papers, paged slowly through them again, getting the shape of the enchantment. He could almost see it, could almost fit the pieces together, and then abruptly it came clear. He flipped back through the sheets, but nothing else made any sense, and he lifted his head. "It's – they were trying to make a creature that could commit robberies without being seen."

"Bloody hell," Hatton said.

Ned took a deep breath. "Damn it. I think you're right."

"I am right," Julian said. "Whether it worked or just went up in smoke – I couldn't tell you that without trying it, and I'm not exactly eager to do that. But that's what they meant to do."

"That's all we need," Hatton said. "And before you ask, Mr Lynes, we have a robbery-with-metaphysics every night of the week these days, thanks to the popular press and their helpful household hints." He heaved a sigh. "We'd best be sure there's nothing else here, but then – Mathey, you take those papers in charge – see if you can figure out anything more from them, but keep them well locked up. The last thing we need is for the broadsheets to get hold of this."

CHAPTER SIX
Inquiries

HATTON STOPPED BY NED'S CHAMBERS AT the Commons late that afternoon, looking sour. "I'll tell you, Mathey, it's amazing how many householders report robberies and say it must have been done by some hocus, their doors being always locked and their servants above reproach."

"Not particularly helpful," Ned said.

Hatton sat, but kept his hat resting on his knee. He glanced over at Miss Frost's desk. "On your own this afternoon?"

"I've got Miss Frost researching Hands of Glory," Ned said. "I know we have a copy of the *Alberti Parvi Lucii Libellus*, at least, even if the librarian likes to pretend we don't." He had some concern that her sex would make the man even more reluctant to hand over books on outdated and somewhat troubling rituals, but she had assured him that she had long experience at standing up to librarians.

"I think there may be something in the *Grimorium Verum* as well," he went on. "And then they've made their own substitutions, although it seems they weren't certain about those." There were suggestions written in and crossed out in more than one hand, some of which seemed inexplicable; the powdered bran might be intended to stand in for some component of the human body, but he hadn't a clue how the tail hairs of a mare in heat came into it. "I don't suppose you have any hanged corpses conveniently missing?"

"Not officially," Hatton said. "But I'll make inquiries at Newgate and the New Gaol. It's not entirely outside possibility that they've misplaced some poor sod and kept quiet about it on the grounds that he won't be missed."

"Any robberies that seem to genuinely involve metaphysics?"

"Too many. We're going through the files looking for common elements. Here's one where the householder reports jewelry taken from a locked and warded safe; could be metaphysics, could be an inside job, but we're inclining to the former. We've got a tailor's shop with money stolen out of the till overnight – also locked up tight, and there's no mark on the lockbox. Any number where examination shows that some hocus was done over a lock, and so on. It would help if we knew what we were looking for."

"If it's connected to the missing hearts, you might look for cases where something's been taken from inside a closed container without opening it," Ned said. "A safe or a lockbox."

"Or a cash till. Or you might say that a house is a closed container, mightn't you?"

"You might. A house doesn't have a lid, so it's not generally the same as a box, but…" He frowned, thinking back to his university lectures. "We had a whole afternoon on this, the difference between *container* and *box*." He sketched the sigils idly as he spoke, by way of illustration. "There was a proposal to create some canonical form of *envelope*, but I don't know that ever went anywhere."

"They go in for high living at Oxford, don't they," Hatton said dryly.

"It's interesting if you're in the profession. There's a word for *envelope* in the Chinese system, and apparently there have been problems with incompatible enchantments in Hong Kong – the local residents understandably want to go on using the system they're used to, and if we were a little more accommodating in our own practice, there might be fewer letters turning themselves inside out or catching fire." He shook his head. "In any event, I think you could describe a house, a safe, and the human chest all as containers."

"That's something to start from," Hatton said, although he didn't look particularly encouraged. "We've got another problem as well. Seen the evening papers?"

"No, should I have?"

Hatton withdrew a paper from his coat in answer and handed it over without comment.

Monstrous Horror Stalks London! Gruesome Severed Hand Creeps into Houses Under Cover of Night; Stopped Only by Milk.

"Oh, dear." The story went on in that vein, including the startling news that Scotland Yard's new Metaphysical Squad had confirmed that dozens of unsolved murders had been committed by a disembodied hand still trailing its winding sheet behind it.

"It should be good for the dairymen," Hatton said. "But no good for me. Of course I'll send them a stern official correction, and they'll toss it in the rubbish bin and go on printing what they want. The interesting question is, where are they getting this from?"

"You can't think I said any of this," Ned said.

"No, you've got no reason to want this kind of story, and besides, if they'd got it from you, I imagine it would make more sense. There's Lynes," Hatton said, frowning for a moment, "but, no, I don't really think it of him either. I expect it's nothing more interesting than one of the servants listening at doors, curse them. But the higher-ups at the Yard won't like it one bit."

"They're used to sensational stories in the papers."

"They are. But they've been very clear that part of my job is to avoid them. Much more of this, and they'll decide that having a Metaphysical Squad is more trouble than it's worth. And then there goes my position, and your retainer."

The door rattled open, and Miss Frost came in with her arms full of books and a triumphant expression. "He made me sign a sacred oath not to damage the books." She dropped the stack of books onto Ned's desk. "I'm not certain whether he's serious that members of the Commons used to have to sign it in blood."

"Neither am I, but he tells everyone that," Ned said.

"Don't lose them, or it's entirely possible that I'll drop dead on the spot and my revenant will walk the library as a restless spirit."

Ned picked up the *Alberti Libellus* and thumbed through it, shaking his head at some of the more dubious love charms. "I see I have my evening's reading cut out for me."

"Better you than me," Hatton said. "Tell me if you unearth anything. I've got a stack of case files waiting for me back at the Yard." He glanced at Miss Frost. "I could walk you to the omnibus stop, if you're going in that direction."

"And disappoint my dear mother?" Miss Frost said. "I promised her I'd never speak to gentlemen on the street unless they were metaphysicians. Very respectable, metaphysicians, you understand. Entirely above reproach."

Hatton donned his hat. "Probably very wise," he said, and went out.

"Hatton's not a bad sort," Ned said after Hatton's footsteps on the stairs were no longer audible.

She gave him a thoughtful look. "Is that your professional opinion?"

"I mean, I've never heard anything personally to his discredit."

She looked amused. "And ought I to play matchmaker for you, Mr Mathey? Or is there a young lady already? You never say, but I imagine your detective friend could find out for me."

That was all too near the mark, and Ned winced. "I'm not in any particular need of romantic advice."

"Probably very wise. I'll leave you with the disembodied hands. That ought to be pleasant bedtime reading."

"I'll ask my landlady for a cup of warm milk," Ned said. "That ought to prove a specific tonic against both insomnia and disembodied hands."

"I'll bet that's the line the dairymen are taking," Miss Frost said, and took herself out.

❈

"THERE MAY BE SOMETHING TO THIS business of sex magic," Ned said that evening, once he'd bearded Julian's landlady and been allowed up to Julian's cluttered parlor.

"Hatton's right," Julian said. "There usually isn't much more to it than an excuse for creative practices in bed."

"Maybe not. But I've been reading through everything we have on the Hand of Glory – and I'll be the first to admit it isn't much. The couple of books we have that touch on it are grimoires in the old style, from the eighteenth century. Well after this kind of thing was non-conforming; both of these were unlawfully published, without the Commons license."

"There's an argument to be made for scholars being able to publish what they want."

"There is. Do you really want to make it when it comes to this case?"

"Not particularly," Julian granted. "But the books exist, in any event. Not just the *Little Albert*, but any number of pamphlets and even hand-copied *maledictors* based on it. I've never heard that much of it worked, though."

"I don't know whether it can have. They're not even consistent in their terms – what some of them call a Hand of Glory doesn't seem related at all. But the same grimoires are full of fairly suggestive rituals, including one mention in the *Grimorium Verum* of the magical uses of, well, of the fluids produced." Ned reminded himself firmly that he was a trained professional, and tried not to writhe with embarrassment. "I can't help suspecting some connection."

"We could make some inquiries at the Dionysus," Julian said.

"I think we should. If nothing else, I'd like to talk to Malcolm – Straun, is it?"

Julian nodded, not asking where he'd heard the name.

"If it's anything like the more general sort of club, the steward usually knows a fair bit about what the members get up to."

The Dionysus was less of a shock to Ned this time, although the sheer level of noise was still startling. By wordless agreement they tried Straun's office before venturing into the parlors, and found him writing out a cheque with a frown by the violet light of a lamp shaded with clusters of stained-glass grapes.

"A new sofa for the back parlor," he said. "What they thought would happen when they lit a spirit lamp on it, I can't imagine."

"Does that sort of thing happen often?" Ned asked.

"Far too often." Straun put down his pen and leaned back wearily in his chair. "We do have lively evenings here, and many of the members chafe under rules, even when they're intended for everyone's good."

"I remember there's a rule against using non-conforming magic on the premises. Not always honored, though."

Straun's eyebrows ascended toward his thinning hairline. "What's someone done now?"

"Nothing tonight," Julian said. He glanced at Ned, and then at the door, and Ned obligingly shut it. "You know Punton's gone missing."

"I know he hadn't turned up lately," Straun said.

"He's dead," Julian said. "He and Dolly Hall both. And it's beginning to look as if they tried some kind of inadvisable enchantment together. There are the usual rumors about sex magic – I don't know if there's much to that –"

Straun paled. "Punton and Hall…they were in that, yes, but that was years ago."

"In what?" Ned asked.

Straun looked sidelong at him, and Julian waved a hand at Ned dismissively. "I told you, I vouch for him completely. He's incorruptible."

"It was – it must be going on three years ago," Straun said. "Before your time, I think. A number of the members had retired upstairs, which wasn't out of the ordinary, but Thomas – one of the footmen – was troubled by an odd smell from the room, and found the door was locked. Well, that is out of the ordinary. Everyone knows to respect a closed door, and members don't have the keys as a rule. I went up, in case there was a fire, and when they didn't answer to my knock, I went in. I'd rather be told to bugger off than have them set the house on fire."

Straun shook his head. "They had a hookah set up, and had been smoking something that stank to high heaven – that's not strictly against the rules, but they generally stick to enchantments and drink. There were candles lit everywhere, and they'd chalked a circle on the rug with odd writing in it, and were going at one another in it."

"Did they tell you what it was meant it to do?" Ned asked, curious despite himself.

"They told me to go to the devil," Straun said dryly. "But it clearly wasn't the kind of ordinary little enchantment we allow here, and I told them they'd better all get out, and consider themselves barred for a month. They weren't very happy about it – in fact some of them were perfectly beastly – but they eventually got their clothes on and left."

"I think you were perfectly right," Ned said. "Especially with the glamour you're using to soundproof the walls. Doing non-conforming magic in a building that's had enchantments put on it is remarkably dangerous."

"Ned is a metaphysician by profession," Julian said in answer to Straun's raised eyebrow. At least Julian wasn't using Ned's surname, although Ned was uncomfortably aware that Straun could probably find it out if he tried.

"Then you'd know more about it that I do. But, as I say, it was years ago. I can't imagine it has anything to do with poor Dolly's death. And Alfie – you're certain he's dead?"

"I'm afraid so," Ned said.

"Who else was in it with them?" Julian asked.

Straun frowned. "Now, I couldn't tell you that."

"We need to find out what they did," Ned said. "I wouldn't think a ritual done years ago would account for their deaths, but if they went on experimenting, there could be some connection."

"I think those particular gentlemen have thought better of those kinds of games," Straun said. "At least, I never heard any more about it, and they never did anything like that again on the premises. No," he said, shaking his head as Julian started to speak, "no, I simply can't give you names. Not of current members, you understand, who've behaved themselves since. I wouldn't keep my position if they didn't trust me to be discreet. Not that I don't wonder sometimes why I want it."

Ned returned his wry smile. "Why do you?"

"Filthy lucre, I'm afraid. I had some setbacks – very tedious, I'll spare you the sad tale – and when they offered me a little salary plus rooms here in exchange for looking after the place, I was only too eager to accept. Wretched old place," he said, with a considerable degree of affection.

"You won't mind if we ask around, surely," Julian said.

"No, that's all right," Straun said. "I just can't be the one to tell tales, especially when it's all water under the bridge. You understand."

"It would be easier if you did," Julian said, but Straun shook his head, unmoved.

Outside Straun's office, Ned drew Julian over into the quieter corner by the servants' stairs. "What now?"

"Linford and Pinky – you remember, the literary one with admirers – both knew Punton and Hall," Julian said. "And some of the other regulars as well. You might get farther than I will with some of them; at least, they're more likely to believe innocent curiosity, coming from you."

"Is innocent really the word?"

"Naïve?" Julian offered, but with an expression that suggested he didn't feel himself on entirely firm ground there.

"I think I can manage that," Ned said. "But not the critic. I can't even pretend to have read the kind of books he probably likes."

"I haven't either, but he won't expect it of me," Julian said. "And he prefers talking about books he doesn't like, anyway. But, yes, let me handle him." He opened the door to the front parlor, and Ned followed him in. "Fenworth might know them," Julian said in an undertone, pointing out a dark-haired man nursing a drink near the fireplace. "And there's Pinky." The critic was reclining in an armchair, gesturing animatedly with his drink as he talked.

Ned nodded and moved toward Fenworth, feeling very much as if he were acting in a stage play with no lines and very little appropriate business. *Hello, I wonder if you can tell me anything about orgies* was probably not correct, although in this company, it might be.

"Hello," Fenworth said as Ned approached, at least saving him from having to produce an opening line. "I haven't seen you about before."

"I came with Ly – with Julian," Ned said.

"Ah, our Julian," Fenworth said, in a tone Ned couldn't entirely interpret. "Well, you seem remarkably unshaken by your first visit to Bedlam. You can call me Fenny, by the way."

"It is very lively," Ned said.

"You could say that."

"I heard that it was. All sorts of stories, some wilder than others." Ned tried to affect a look of scandalized fascination. "Is it true about the indecent magical rituals in the parlor?"

"It wasn't in the parlor," Fenworth said. "And, really, you don't want to get mixed up in that kind of thing. I can think of more pleasant ways to spend an evening." That was accompanied by a certain speculative look, but it didn't seem badly meant.

"It did happen, though?"

"Years ago. Pinky and some of that set were in it, I understand. They were turfed out for a month, and you'd be surprised at how much peace and quiet we had until they all came tramping back in. I don't think they were really a bit sorry, but they smoothed Malcolm's ruffled feathers, so it all ended well enough. But that kind of thing isn't safe."

"I appreciate the warning."

"You needn't worry, it was ages ago." Fenworth glanced past him at Julian, who had insinuated himself into the circle around the critic. "Speaking of warnings – you look like a sensible sort, but I wouldn't want you to take our Julian the wrong way."

Ned raised an eyebrow. "The wrong way?"

"Don't get your hackles up, now. I like Julian myself. He's not cruel, or given to pressing his attentions where they aren't wanted – doesn't have any sense of humor about that at all, which in this crowd is refreshing. But – well, he's a bit like church, you know; you spend a lot of time on your knees, without much visible return. And he's never been given to long attachments. Do try not to get your heart broken."

Ned was still trying to decide how to reply to that when someone put a hand on his shoulder.

"Hannibal, isn't it?" Linford Farrell said. "No, how silly of me, it's Edward. Back again? With or without our Julian?"

"Hello, Linford," Ned said. "Is it true you were barred from the club for practicing dubious metaphysics?"

"Is this that 'sex magic' nonsense again? What have you been telling our Hercules here, Fenny?"

"No more than I heard at the time," Fenworth said.

"Don't be an ass. Straun made that whole business up out of whole cloth," Farrell said. "He was cross because some of us owed him money, and bitter because some of us were getting more than he was. I'm surprised to see you spreading that story. I don't mind what people think of me, but it wasn't a very nice thing to say about poor little Dolly, for one."

"Perhaps I misunderstood," Fenny murmured. "And if you'll excuse me, I think I could use another drink." He raised his empty glass by way of illustration and began forging his way through the crowd.

"You never did anything out of the *Petit Albert*," Ned said.

"What's that, a French book? Does it have engravings? I've done a lot of things out of French books, at least the ones that don't require a cunt, although I do have some standards. Not like our Julian. He's never been that particular, and most of us should know. But of course he's your particular friend, isn't he? I do hope he hasn't made you any rash promises."

"You needn't be concerned that I've lost my virtue under false pretenses," Ned said, as discouragingly as possible.

"Only a little sisterly advice." Farrell patted him on the arm. "Do tell him hello for me, if you can find him."

Ned set out to do just that, but paused by the drinks table to mix himself a stiff whisky and soda; he felt at this point he could sorely use one.

☾✦

JULIAN EDGED HIS WAY INTO THE circle surrounding Pinky, who was graciously permitting a willowy blond to refill his glass. The young man was lovely, and graceful, too, and Julian let his gaze linger appreciatively. Pinky saw, though, and lifted one finger in admonition.

"Naughty, naughty, Julian! I don't choose to share. At least…"

The young man blushed to the roots of his hair, and Julian guessed there had been some – sharing – of his favors. He himself had participated in a few such groups after he'd come to London, and the young man was just the sort who'd end up buggered over a footstool in the back parlor.

"Not unless the gentleman offers," he said, with a smile, and Pinky rolled his eyes.

"Worse and worse! And when you already have a surplus of masculine pulchritude to manage. Do I mean surplus, I wonder? I suspect I do. Tell me, does he follow Sandow's regimen, or is it metaphysics? Or does it just – come naturally, as it were."

"You'd have to ask him," Julian said. "But speaking of metaphysics –"

"Were we?"

"You were," Julian answered. "I gather it's a hobby of yours."

"Now what gave you that idea?" Pinky patted the arm of his chair. "Here, sit down if we're going to talk. When you loom over me like that, it gives me a crick in the neck."

It was little enough to pay for possible information, and Julian perched cautiously beside him, very aware of the casual pressure of Pinky's arm against his thigh. "For God's sake, don't spill that. I don't want to go home reeking of gin."

"No, that's not your vice, I know." Pinky smiled. "Don't worry, dear boy, I can hold my liquor."

Julian lifted an eyebrow at that, and heard someone snicker. A flash of anger crossed Pinky's face, and he set his hand deliberately on Julian's knee. Julian let his eyebrows rise higher, but didn't move away. "But not the odd cantrip? Some odder than others?"

"Really, Julian, you're behaving like the 'tec in a shilling shocker. I have no interest in metaphysics."

"You astound me." Julian kept his tone polite and remote and utterly neutral. Pinky was lying – stupidly; his name had come up too often for there not to be some truth in the story – and behind him in the crowd someone shifted uneasily, a small, betraying movement. A moment later Ryder Leach detached himself from the crowd, heading for the back parlor.

"Except in literature, of course," Pinky said. "Now there – my dear, you wouldn't believe the things some authors dream up. I imagine it gives the old men at the Commons nightmares – except, of course, I'm sure none of it actually works. At least, one hopes not, or all London would be wandering about in a daze of half a dozen love glamours."

"That seems highly unlikely."

"It might explain some people's otherwise incomprehensible – popularity." Pinky's voice held enough venom to make the blond look up, startled.

Julian allowed himself a slow smile. "My dear Pinky, are you jealous? I won't trouble you further." He rose from the chair, well aware of Pinky's leashed fury, and paused at the nearest drinks table to pour himself another whisky. Perhaps he shouldn't have baited the critic, but it had been irresistible – and besides, it had been such a stupid lie. Even if it hadn't been obvious, Leach's reaction would have given away the truth: he had looked very much like a man attempting to avoid awkward questions. All the more reason to ask them, Julian thought, and glanced around for Ned. He was nowhere in sight, and Julian frowned. Had he been part of the group watching the byplay with Pinky? On balance, he thought not, and didn't know if he was sorry or relieved.

The next step, though, was definitely Leach. Julian collected his drink and slipped out into the hall, hoping his departure looked more casual than it felt. The back parlor was less crowded than usual, just an older group playing whist while several of their friends leaned alternately on each other and on the card-players; a couple was embracing on one of the sofas in the shadowed corner farthest from the fire, and Leach was leaning moodily on the mantel, kicking at the nearest andiron. He looked up at Julian's approach, his scowl deepening.

"I don't want to talk to you, Julian."

That was not an entirely unknown opening statement, Julian thought, and was not surprised when no one turned to look. He was just as glad Ned wasn't with him now; he was aware that his reputation was somewhat – doubtful – and that it couldn't be entirely concealed, but he didn't want Ned to see the worst of it. "Just a word," he said aloud, but Leach was not appeased.

"No." He made no move to get away, whether because Julian was between him and the door or out of a perverse desire to continue the quarrel, and Julian pressed his advantage.

"You've been dabbling again, haven't you?"

Leach swore at him in terms that were anatomically improbable. "It's none of your damn business."

"I disagree."

Leach swore again. "Challice. That little –"

"He's a friend." Julian didn't have to feign anger at that: Challice was one of the unlucky men who genuinely wanted to lead a normal life, to be a decent husband and father, but his nature brought him back to the clubs and the occasional passionate and miserable encounter. Julian had had a brief affair with the man before he'd realized the circumstances, and couldn't do anything but pity him. "If Challice was involved in this game of yours –"

"It's none of your business," Leach said again, and pulled himself away from the mantel, fists clenching. "Piss off, now, or I'll break your prying nose."

Julian eyed him warily. They were pretty much of a height, but Leach was heavier, and had something of a reputation as a brawler. On the other hand, he wasn't entirely sober –

"Oh, I don't think you want to do that," Ned said, coming up behind them. "Why don't you run along, there's a good chap?"

For a moment, it hung in the balance, and Julian felt Ned shift his weight onto his toes, ready to block the first punch. Then Leach swore and turned away, nearly overbalancing in the process, and Julian allowed himself a sigh of relief.

"I dare say I could have managed," he said, "but – thank you."

Ned's smile was just slightly smug, but he said only, "Any luck?"

"Maybe." Julian glanced around, saw the damaged sofa pushed into a back corner. It was blessedly out of earshot, and the velvet seemed only somewhat singed at the ends, though the horsehair and stuffing showed through the hole in the center of the cushions. "Here, sit down."

Ned collected their drinks first, and Julian took his gratefully. The damaged upholstery forced them to sit closer than was decent, crammed together against one arm, but that was hardly a problem, and he leaned comfortably against Ned's hip and shoulder.

"Pinky says he wasn't involved, but he's lying. More interestingly, though, Leach mentioned a man I know. That won't be a pleasant conversation, but I think it will be worth having."

"One of your lovers?" There was something odd in Ned's tone, and Julian gave him an uncertain look.

"We had an affair, yes. It didn't last long. What about you?"

"Farrell says Malcolm has it in for him because he and his friends hadn't paid their bills. He also implied that Malcolm was jealous of his sexual prowess. I believe the former more than the latter, but I'm not sure that's all that was going on."

Julian nodded. "I think you're probably right. Well, Challice may be willing to help, and I can always talk to Lennox, too." He leaned harder against Ned's shoulder, not quite daring to take further liberties in his current mood. "In the meantime – perhaps you'd like to come home with me?"

There was a momentary pause, and Ned's smile was unreadable. "Why not?" he said, and let Julian draw him away.

CHAPTER SEVEN
Concerns in Low Places

L ENNOX WAS THE MAN TO SEE first, Julian decided. Perhaps it would
have been better to have started there, he admitted, as he scribbled a
quick note and affixed a stamp, but the matter had been urgent, and
Lennox had been elsewhere. Someone had said last night that he was back in
town, or at least available again, and it was time to take advantage of the man's
encyclopedic memory for gossip. To his relief, Lennox responded by the next
post, inviting him to a late luncheon at Lennox's pleasant townhouse. They
settled in the narrow dining room, the curtains half drawn to obscure the view
of the leafless garden. A well-made fire kept off the worst of the chill as they
washed down the salmon en croûte with the last of the summer's hock.

Lennox let them finish the main course before he dismissed the housemaid,
saying that they'd serve themselves the pudding, and then directed Julian to
pour more wine while he cut them each a slice of the berry tart. "And you can
tell me what you came here to ask. You've had time enough to think up a good
excuse."

"No excuses this time, actually," Julian said. "It's just a bit – delicate."

Lennox snorted. "And where are your cases anything but?"

"This may be a bit more so," Julian said. "Sex magic at the Dionysus –"

"Not that again."

"You know about it?" Julian tipped his head to one side in question.

"What I know is that someone played a rather brutal joke on a very unhappy
man, and the whole thing should have been allowed to die a natural death a
long time ago."

Lennox was genuinely angry, Julian realized, and he chose his words with
care. "I have some reason to think it may not be over –"

87

"Do not rake this up again, Lynes." Lennox's voice was cold. "I won't help you with that – in fact, I'll stop you if I can. And don't ask any more questions. I don't want to hear."

Julian paused. Ned wasn't going to like it, but the only way he was going to get any help from Lennox was to tell him the truth. "Let me explain why."

Lennox hesitated. "You really think there's anything that would justify bringing this up again?"

"I'm afraid that there may be," Julian answered. "I hope there isn't, and you have my word that if there's no connection I'll never mention the matter again. But two men are dead, and in a rather unpleasant fashion, and it has to be stopped."

Lennox drew a long breath. "Dolly Hall. How did he die, Julian?"

"We don't know. He was found dead in his rooms, that part is quite true, but it wasn't an apoplexy or some sort of overdose. When they opened him for the autopsy, his heart was missing – just gone." Julian shrugged. "Probably that's what killed him, but we don't actually know." He saw Lennox flinch and pressed his advantage. "Alfred Punton was his friend, and he's dead, too – of the same thing, presumably, as his heart is also missing. Punton was definitely playing with non-conforming magic, and I also heard that he and Dolly – and others – dabbled in sex magic. You can see why I might think there's a connection."

Lennox reached for his wineglass, tossed back the contents, and held out the glass for a refill. Julian obliged, and Lennox took another swallow, shaking his head. "You have to understand, I don't know exactly what happened. I wasn't in town then, you understand. My father was ill, I'd gone down to Cornwall to be with him. So I was only here for the aftermath. I'm not sure I'm the man to ask, Lynes."

"You're the man I trust," Julian said.

Lennox sighed. "Yes, Dolly and Punton were part of a circle. Though I don't think either one of them was a leader."

Julian refrained from pointing out that Punton was a metaphysician and presumably had some idea of how to run a circle.

"If it hadn't been Challice," Lennox said at last. His face was bleak and old beneath his too-fashionable haircut. "Anyone but him. I don't know what they promised him – he wouldn't say – but they persuaded him that the way to get it was to let them all do him, more or less publicly, and for all they promised it would be a secret, word got around scandalously fast. It very nearly broke him, Julian. I was worried for a bit that he might – well. But it was a near-run thing."

Julian swallowed his own anger. He was fond of Challice even while he thought the man had made a series of dreadful choices, and the idea of taking advantage of that just to get him into bed… "Do you know who else was in the circle? It's relevant."

"I wasn't there," Lennox said again. "And that's why I'm not a member at the Dionysus any more, by the by. I won't be a part of that sort of thing."

"But you heard enough to be sure of Hall and Punton," Julian said.

Lennox nodded. "To be fair, Dolly thought it went a bit far. Punton denied it ever happened, the liar, but Dolly said he was there, and Dolly had no reason to lie about it. He was too upset at the time to think about causing trouble. And Punton was terrified something might get back to his employer."

"Was there anyone else?"

"Pinky Dorrington. That bounder Leach. Really, Julian, if that's what the Universities are producing these days, I despair of the Empire."

"We all have our bad apples," Julian said.

"That's all that I'm sure of," Lennox said. "Linford Farrell ran with that set, and I wouldn't put it past him, but he's too clever to get his name talked about in that sort of connection."

Farrell's malice hadn't generally been actively harmful. Though if Leach were involved – they'd always brought out the worse in each other. "There's a story that he was banned from the Dionysus for a month for performing some such ritual," Julian said.

"I wouldn't know," Lennox said. "As I said, I'm not a member any more."

Julian poured himself another glass of wine, frowning unhappily. "Logically, I should talk to Challice next."

"Don't," Lennox said. "If he's come to any sort of peace –"

"I know," Julian answered. It would be cruel to bring up something that Challice had worked to forget – bad enough to bring back memories of snatched happiness, congenial company, but to raise this ghost was almost more than he could bring himself to do. "Maybe there's another way," he muttered, but couldn't bring himself to believe it.

€✿

Julian climbed down from the omnibus at the corner of Tottenham Court Road, too edgy to ride the rest of the way to Coptic Street. Not that the delay would do any good except to postpone the moment he had to decide exactly how he was going to to get Challice to talk to him in the first place, but perhaps the walk would jar something loose. Certainly the wind was chill enough, and he hunched his shoulders inside his overcoat, tugging his hat down closer on his head.

He turned onto Coptic Street, automatically lifting his head to see the Museum rising at the end of it, white in the late sun, and a man detached himself from the doorway of the Potter's Arms. Julian caught his breath, wishing he had brought his weighted cane, and in the same instant recognized a familiar client. It was Bolster in a decent suit and well-brushed bowler, not at all his usual style, but it was Bolster nonetheless, and Julian slowed his steps, waiting to see if he should acknowledge the man.

"Mr Lynes," Bolster said with a tip of his hat.

"Mr Bolster." Julian copied the gesture. "Is everything all right?" The last time Bolster had showed up on his doorstep, rather than making him go to the docks for a meeting, Bolster had been on the verge of arrest.

"Everything's well enough with me," Bolster said. Even his accent had shifted, smoothed and tidied to match the neat clothes. "But there's one or two things I'd like to consult with you about, professionally speaking."

"Of course." Julian hesitated at the bottom of his front steps. "Mrs Digby didn't let you wait?"

"I don't like your landlady. I told her I'd come back, and then I went and had a pint while I waited. I knew you'd have to come this way."

Julian nodded, though he wasn't sure he liked his movements being that well-known, and led the way up the stairs and into the parlor that served as his consulting room. He waved Bolster to a chair and rang for tea in spite of the other man's polite demurral, then settled himself in the chair opposite. "So what's the trouble?"

"Oy!" Bolster extricated his sleeve button from the tendrils of the *Urtica mordax* – with due care, Julian noted. "You didn't tell me you kept dog-thistle."

"Is that what you call it? I only knew it as biting thistle."

"It's that, too," Bolster said, shifting himself out of reach. "And green mastiff, for the fanciful. I once knew a man who dealt in jewels who had a whole hedge of that in his garden. Very nasty stuff once it's grown. Story was, a climbing boy fell into it by accident and they never found more than his boots."

"That seems unlikely," Julian said, frowning at the plant's central bud. It was large enough to take a good-sized lump of cheese now, but surely it wouldn't get large enough to devour a human being, even a young one. And it definitely preferred dead prey.

"Probably the poor bastard broke his neck when he fell," Bolster admitted. "So he couldn't struggle. But it's true they never found a body."

The maid appeared with the tray before Julian could respond, Mrs Digby's usual dry sandwiches supplemented with pale biscuits from a tin. She poured for them both before taking herself off, and Bolster examined one of the biscuits dubiously.

"No, I don't like your landlady much at all."

"She's cheap," Julian said, "and she doesn't make a fuss about my clients."

Bolster gave a wry smile. "That's a virtue in a landlady, but it doesn't make up for the cooking."

It didn't, Julian admitted, but finding another place was likely to be difficult. He said, "So what was it you wanted to consult about?"

"Ah." Bolster took a long drink of his tea. "That's not so bad, actually. Have you been following the papers?"

"Of course."

"What's all this about a disembodied hand creeping into houses and strangling people? Dragging its shroud behind it, no less?"

"Ah." Julian paused, not sure quite where to begin, and Bolster's eyes narrowed.

"Oh, so there's something in it, is there? I thought I heard your friend Mathey'd been hired on to the 'Phys."

"Yes, he has." Julian seized on that as the easier question. "But he understands my – particular circumstances. There'll be no trouble from that quarter."

"That's good to hear. Now, what about this hand? It sounds like someone's got hold of a Hand of Glory, only they've got it sideways or something."

"That's possible," Julian said. He tapped one finger against his lips, trying to decide exactly how to handle this. "The case – the one Mathey's consulting on – is murder, and a peculiar one."

"Here, you don't mean the hand is really strangling householders in their sleep?" Bolster looked almost offended at the idea.

"No, that part's invention. But two men are dead by metaphysics, and one of them was working on an enchantment that was derived from the one that creates a Hand of Glory. The papers put two and two together and got ten."

"More like twenty-two," Bolster said.

Julian grinned. "Touché."

"This story's got people spooked," Bolster said. "More than one of my colleagues has raised the question of what they should do if they should find this hand there ahead of them on a job. No one likes the idea of being strangled by something disembodied."

"They weren't strangled," Julian said.

"But they are dead."

"Well, yes."

"So." Bolster leaned forward, careful to avoid the *Urtica mordax*. "Some of my colleagues raised the question of whether there might be some sort of cantrip or emblem or such that they might carry that would lessen the chance of their ending up like your dead men, assuming they were so unlucky as to stumble into an unfortunate situation."

"No," Julian said, thinking of the Half-House, and shook his head. "It's not that I've got any qualms, it's just I think that might cause more trouble than it prevented. This thing, whatever it is – it's non-conforming magic, and it's likely to react badly with anything I could come up with for your – colleagues."

"That old tale," Bolster said.

"It's true enough. Oh, I know, I've had my doubts before this. But I've had reason to change my mind."

"If that's the case, what do I tell my colleagues?"

Julian paused, considering. If in fact Punton had succeeded in creating a creature that was capable of stealing without being seen, and if it was wandering loose in London – quite possibly undirected, or still responding to the last commands Punton had given it before his death – no, that was not something any self-respecting burglar wanted to confront in some stranger's parlor, even if the household was likely to be sunk in unnatural sleep. "First of all, if they're using metaphysics in any form, they need to watch for any sign that it's not working properly. Lights not going off or on or picks not working right, anything like that. If that happens, I'd advise them to call the business off, and come back another night."

"Because?"

"Because if this works the way I think it's supposed to, it's going to glamour the entire house," Julian answered. "If one of your colleagues uses the wrong cantrip around it, I won't vouch for his safety. And the first sign that they're up against something non-conforming would be that their own tools don't work correctly. That's if they're lucky."

"And if they're unlucky?" Bolster took another swallow of his tea.

"Almost anything. Fire and sparks for a start, would be my guess, but that's just a guess. It could be almost anything."

"Bloody hell." Bolster shook his head. "Here, what happens if this thing tries to get in a house with one of these new metaphysical burglar-traps? Or even just an alarm?"

"I wish I knew," Julian said. In fact, it was becoming more and more obvious that he needed to borrow Punton's notes himself and see if he could make some sense of it all. Not that Ned wasn't a brilliant metaphysician, but there were things he wouldn't know to look for. "If I were making such a thing, I'd tell it to stay away from a house with any serious enchantments on it. But I don't know if the maker was a sensible sort."

"Fair enough," Bolster said. "What about milk? I do know that you have to quench a Hand of Glory with milk, that's just common knowledge, but this?"

"I've no idea," Julian said. "I suppose if you saw the thing coming toward you, and you had a pitcher of cream about you, it wouldn't hurt to pour it over the thing. It all depends on how far the maker took it from its original forms."

"A man might carry a bottle in his pocket," Bolster said. "Tightly stoppered. Just in case."

It was a ridiculous idea, but, like Varley's apparent transformation, there was something uneasily serious about it. "I could look into whether it would work."

"I'd take that kindly," Bolster said. "One professional to another."

"I might have some questions to ask later," Julian said. "But I'd be the soul of discretion."

"You always are." Bolster set his cup aside. "Fair's fair, Mr Lynes. You've answered mine, and if it comes to it, I'll do my best to answer yours."

***

It was something of a relief the next day for Ned to turn from unprofitable speculation about Julian's past conquests to his commission to find Miss Barton's blackmailer. The letter sent to her certainly looked similar to the one sent to Auberon Kennett. Laid out side by side, both were written on the same unremarkable paper in the same square printing.

"Another letter to Madeleine?" Miss Frost asked, looking at the letters spread out on his desk as she came in.

"This one's to one of Lynes's clients, a Mr Kennett," Ned said. "By someone threatening to reveal to his serious literary friends that writing ladies' romances is his secret vice. It's an awfully similar situation to be strictly coincidence."

Miss Frost frowned. "I wonder."

"If you have any ideas, please don't hesitate to put them forward."

"I know Madeleine said she hasn't any enemies," she went on slowly. "On her part, that may even be true; she's always been quick to anger and just as quick to forgive. But I think I can put at least one name on your list."

"Do tell."

"Percival Oswald. He was at London University at the same time that we were at the London School of Metaphysics for Women. I never liked him much myself, but he was one of Madeleine's more serious suitors."

"What happened?"

"Eventually it dawned on her that he liked telling her what she ought to think better than he liked listening to what she did think. He aspired to write, you see, and had a great many opinions about philosophy and literature, which he felt were more correct than those of the unenlightened masses. It all came to a head when he got his degree – he was a year ahead of her, and he proposed that she leave school at once and marry him, as surely she knew enough metaphysics already to keep house."

"I take it she didn't take the suggestion well."

"She threw a full cup of tea in his face," Miss Frost said. "It was in a tea-shop, so there were quite a number of their mutual friends to witness the occasion. I was there myself. It was remarkable how silly he looked with tea running down his eyebrows. He may have taken it even worse when she went on to tell him that she'd never liked his writing – 'pompous twaddle,' she called it – and that no one really liked that sort of thing, they only felt they ought to because it used so many long words. Which I couldn't help agreeing was true, but all the same, it was the kind of scene that might lead a gentleman to hold a grudge."

"I can see that one might," Ned said.

"Of course that doesn't prove he's the one sending the letters. I don't know what's become of him for certain; we didn't exactly make an effort to stay in touch. But I find it hard to imagine that it's been easy for him to make a living through his writing, unless there's more of a market for pompous twaddle than I've been led to believe. If he's taken up a position as an editor, or something of that nature, maybe that's how he found out about Mr Kennett."

"That would make sense," Ned said. He and Julian had assumed that the blackmailer was a member of Kennett's social circle who couldn't afford to blackmail him about his private life without risking retaliation in kind, but if he were an editor, it was possible that all he knew about Kennett was his body of work and his mailing address. "Let's see what we can get from the letters."

The simplest test was designed to reveal the name of a writer, but he was sure Julian had tried that already on Kennett's letter. Still, it was better to begin at the beginning.

He drew out his wand and took a moment to visualize the square of Mercury superimposed over the letter. It was a complex square, eight rows of numbers that were familiar only through long practice, but it was undeniably the best for framing matters dealing with communication.

When he was certain of his marks, he began to sketch the metaphysical word for "name" over the paper with his wand, connecting each number that represented one letter of the word to form an angular sigil. He added the sigil for "hand" with a possessive marker – *name your hand* – and kept his eyes on the paper. Julian had probably tried it, but there was still a slim chance that the writer's signature would appear on the paper.

The ink crazed and began to crawl across the page, bleeding out of the shapes of its original letters to form new ones in the center of the page.

HAND, it read, in the same mocking block printing.

"Oh, very useful," he muttered.

Miss Frost looked down with interest. "He's used a glamour on the writing?"

"Something to prevent it revealing the writer, yes." Ned sketched a quick sigil to dismiss his own enchantment, and the ink crept back into its original arrangement, although the letters had faded. He tried a couple of variations, but the letters remained stubbornly unrevealing. They were also consistent in their reactions to his enchantments, and he was growing more confident that they were written by the same hand.

That was worth testing itself. "It would help to have two samples of your own handwriting, just to see the effect when it's working," he said. "Related to the same subject, but not about metaphysics. They can be as brief as you like."

She took out pen and paper, and wrote "Soft-boiled eggs" on one sheet and "Toast" on the other. "My breakfast," she said.

"That should be ideal." Ned wrote "Bacon" on a sheet of his own, and laid the three sheets out on the desk. He visualized the square again, and sketched the sigils for *gather together, same,* and *hand.*

The corners of the paper fluttered, and then he felt a tug in his vitals as the two sheets written by Miss Frost skated together, stacking themselves and then stilling. The sheet in his own hand lay unmoved.

"That seems definitive enough," she said.

"Yes, but those sheets weren't enchanted. Do you know the glamour –" He sketched *name me not,* and then realized to his chagrin that he'd copied Julian's practice of using a crabbed single sigil sketched in one motion, a habit he suspected Julian had picked up from his less law-abiding clients.

"I would use *hide my name,* but if you think that's the more likely form –" She took out her own wand and traced *name me not* crisply and completely over the pages she had written.

"This still ought to work, because it's not hung on *name*," Ned said. He sketched the enchantment again. The pages moved more reluctantly, jerking and sliding about the desk, and ended up in an untidier stack, but the effect was still clear.

"And now our blackmailer's work," Ned said. He cleared the desk of notes about breakfast, dropping them into the dustbin, and laid the blackmail letters out in their place. He sketched the glamour again, correctly and completely this time, and held his breath.

The letters lay on the desk, unmoved.

"Damn," he said.

"Yes, that," Miss Frost said. "It seemed so reasonable."

"It did. But these can't be in the same hand, unless there's an enchantment on them I've never seen, nor Lynes, and he has more experience with crooked dealing. Unless…" He frowned, his eye falling on the pantograph on the windowsill behind Miss Frost's desk. She used it mainly for making out receipts, its upright pen enchanted to trace an impeccable copy of her own writing. "*Hand* has to be a living person's hand, doesn't it?"

"I did say I thrived on gruesome ideas, but…you're not suggesting a disembodied one?"

"Nothing that far afield. But suppose our blackmailer works in a literary sort of office. Don't you think they'd have a pantograph?"

"They would," Miss Frost said. "And then, no, you wouldn't say they were written by anyone's hand. But if you can't use *name* –"

"Finding out they were written by the same pantograph would probably be enough," Ned said. "But suppose we try *maker*. That should tell us if it's the same person creating the letters, whether he's writing them out by hand or by machine."

Miss Frost slid open a drawer, and extracted two receipts. "To test your theory."

He laid them out next to the letters and sketched the sigils with care – *gather together, same, maker*. For a moment, nothing happened, and then he was rewarded by seeing the letters make their fluttering way into one pile and the receipts into another.

"Eureka," Miss Frost said.

"We're looking for a single blackmailer." Ned looked down at a fluttering sound, and saw that "Poached egg" and "Toast" were making a weak attempt to climb the wall of the dustbin. He picked up the sheets of paper and set them on the desk, and they began slowly but determinedly creeping toward the two pantographed receipts.

"You don't really have to help them reunite," Miss Frost said. "They're only paper."

"Yes, of course," Ned said, feeling it unnecessary to admit that he had found the fluttering pathetic. "But it does suggest a further avenue of investigation. If we can get a sample of the blackmailer's handwriting, something we know he wrote, we can match it to the letters."

Miss Frost looked up at him. "And then what?"

"Warn him off, I suppose," Ned said, more confidently than he felt. That was more Julian's department than his own, but at least with a single blackmailer, there was more chance that he could leave that part of the business to Julian. Unless looming over the blackmailer in wordless threat seemed likely to be effective; unfortunately he wasn't at all certain that would do the trick.

CHAPTER EIGHT
Delahunt Brothers

THE DINING ROOM OF THE MERCURY Club was never full at lunch, and only a few members were settled at its long tables. Ned usually took his lunch at Blandings or the Commons dining room, but he was in the mood for a sympathetic ear for his current problems. At least, the ones that he could admit to having.

He sat down next to Ayers, who was telling Parker a lengthy story about his poor luck at the racetrack.

"I swear, the blasted horse was trying to bolt clean off the track and off over the horizon. If his jockey hadn't pulled him up, he'd have finished up in the Channel, swimming for Calais."

"Bad luck," Ned said sympathetically.

"Some attempt to ginger him up gone wrong, more like it, but who can prove that? Maybe you should go for a racetrack metaphysicist, Mathey. You'd keep the trainers on the straight and narrow."

"Horses might be simpler." Ned shook his head. "Does anyone know anything about Delahunt Brothers?"

"Never heard of them," Parker said. "Do they have a good stable this year?"

"It's a publisher," Ned said.

"Over in the Strand?" Ayers said. "I've heard of them. They do romances and that sort of thing. I know a fellow who works as a clerk there, as it happens." He looked a little defensive on his friend's behalf. "He's a regular fellow, mind you. Not the thin-blooded artistic type."

"Must be a good way to meet the ladies," Parker offered.

"Exactly so. And it pays, which sadly matters in this world."

"Speaking of," Parker said, stuffing the last of his treacle tart into his mouth, "I must get back to work." The last came out rather indistinctly, and he brushed crumbs from the corners of his mouth as he went.

"What about you, Mathey? Not chained to the old desk this afternoon, are you?"

"Actually, I've an interesting problem involving Delahunt." Ned considered carefully how much to say. "I need to get a sample of the writing of the people who work there. Just a few words would do. And I can't explain why I need it."

Ayers raised his eyebrows. "If I didn't know you better, I'd think you were working up some hocus for their competitors."

"I'm not, and I wouldn't. I can't tell you what it is about, but it's not to their detriment – rather to the contrary, if it turns out there's something in my line going on." That was true enough, he thought; having a blackmailer on the staff couldn't help the firm.

"Oh, I trust you, Mathey. You're not the underhanded sort."

"But you're right that they may think so. An introduction would help..."

"Consider it done."

"But really I need an excuse as well." He could claim the auspices of the Metaphysical Squad again if necessary, but he was afraid that would alarm a potential blackmailer overly much, and besides, he was afraid Hatton would eventually notice how much his name was being taken in vain. "It's a shame they're not all authors, or I could pretend to be an admirer after their autographs."

"Or one of those johnnies who gets up petitions."

"That might be an idea," Ned said. "If it were something uncontroversial..."

"No one reads them, anyway," Ayers said. "I expect someday I'll be arrested for having my name on some anarchist manifesto, and when they call me up before the judge, all I'll be able to say in my defense is that I only wanted the chap to go away."

"Perhaps not an anarchist manifesto," Ned said. "You'll help me bring it off, won't you? Maybe someday I can even tell you what it was about."

"Should be a lark," Ayers said. He pushed his plate away. "Better than trying to get outside any more of this mutton. Adventure awaits!"

Delahunt Brothers occupied the second floor of what might once have been a private house. Ascending the cramped stairs brought Ned and Ayers into an equally cramped waiting room, where a young lady glared at them through her spectacles.

"If you've no appointment, I'll thank you to leave your manuscript with the others," she said, jerking her head toward a tottering stack of bundled pages, a few typed, most handwritten in varying states of legibility.

"I'm here to see Mr James Fletcher," Ayers said. "It'll just take a moment."

"Hardly any time at all," Ned said, brandishing his sheets of paper as if to assure her of their harmlessness. They currently bore the names of everyone at the Mercury Ned had been able to press for their signature, on the promise of a round of drinks to be bought later, and some suitably edited version of the story to be told.

"My name is Mr Claude Ayers. I'm a personal friend of Mr Fletcher."

"That is what they all say." She shook her head at them as if trying to decide whether it was worth rising from her seat, and finally made up her mind to do so, with a final skeptical glance back over her shoulder.

It took a moment, but a sandy-haired young man eventually emerged from the creaking door at the back of the waiting room. He did indeed look more like a sportsman than Ned's idea of a publisher of novels. "Hullo, Ayers," he said. "Not taking up the literary life, are you?"

"Not hardly," Ayers said. "No, it's Mathey here – he's one of the lads from the Mercury, and a cracking good metaphysician, I hear."

"Nothing doing in that line, I'm afraid," Fletcher said, shaking his head with a regretful smile. "We looked into publishing a book on household metaphysics a while back – helpful hints for young wives, that sort of thing – but the license would have cost the earth."

"I'm not an aspiring writer," Ned said. Fletcher looked a bit relieved. "Actually, it's about the city fire-fighting equipment. It's sorely out of date, you know, and really a hazard to the populace. Some of us are urging the city to put in modern metaphysical fire alarms, the sort enchanted to detect smoke. There's some minor expense up front, of course, but it would save lives. And of course be a considerable savings in lost property as well."

"I expect so," Fletcher said.

"I thought you'd see it that way. If you wouldn't mind too much just putting your name down here as in support of the idea? We're hoping to have the businessmen of the district well represented."

"I don't suppose it can hurt." Fletcher signed in a quick scribble.

"Think you could turn out the Delahunts to sign as well?" Ayers asked. "I mean, it's only horrible death by conflagration we're talking about."

"It really is a matter of public safety," Ned said.

"I might manage," Fletcher said, looking hunted. "Young Mr Delahunt should be free. Mr Delahunt himself is reading over some manuscripts, but we can see…"

Young Mr Delahunt was round and balding, with a harassed expression. "Sign what? Oh, some sort of petition…can't Cora deal with these things? Well, hand it here. Society for the Prevention of Death by Fire, I suppose we're for that. There's no subscription involved, is there? Right then, it was a pleasure to make your acquaintance, Mr – ahem – and now if you'll excuse me."

Fletcher beat a hasty retreat, with Ned following with alacrity. "I don't suppose you need the old man as well," he said.

"It does give it so much more weight when it's the proprietor of a respected business."

"Respected, well, I'm not sure that's the word I'd use, but I do see your point…"

"I'll owe you a round of drinks," Ayers said. "Come on, be a sport. We were in school together, and Mathey's a fellow clubman, so that's nearly as good as a blood tie."

Fletcher sighed. "When you put it that way."

The senior Mr Delahunt was a more pronounced version of young Mr Delahunt – rounder, more balding, and some years further into middle age. He looked up with sharp incisive eyes.

"What do we need a metaphysician for? Don't tell me some rejected author has put a curse on us."

"Not today," Fletcher said. "Mr Mathey would like you to sign his petition about getting the city to put in metaphysical fire alarms."

"How much more do those cost than the regular ones?"

"There's no mechanical device on the market that will sound the alarm automatically when it detects a fire," Ned said. "They rely on a human observer to throw the alarm switch."

"Which any observer with sense ought to do," Delahunt said. "But, hmm, off hours, I take your point. I suppose you'd be getting a cut of the business?"

Ned shrugged sheepishly. "I can't say it wouldn't be to my advantage. But it would be of considerable benefit to the public. And it does make a difference to have prominent local businessmen behind this sort of thing."

"As long as we're not the ones paying for it," Delahunt said. He took out his pen to sign, squinting at the paper for longer than Ned liked.

"I very much enjoyed *The Governess and the Tiger*," Ned said.

Delahunt's expression thawed. "Yes, that was a good one, wasn't it? They don't all stand up to reading more than once, but that one does. Mind you, they're all entertaining, which at the end of the day is how we earn our shilling. And there are a great many more prestigious houses that can't say that."

"I couldn't agree more," Ned said.

On the way out, he stopped at Cora's desk. "Would you mind signing yourself? I hate to be a bother, but of course the hazard of fire is a concern of ladies as well."

"I have these manuscripts to review," Cora said, but she paused long enough to scribble her name. "Now if we're not expiring in a conflagration on the spot, I have to tell Mr Delahunt what I think of the tragic story of a woman who falls in love with one man, but unwittingly promises her hand to his identical twin."

"What do you think?" Ned said.

She shrugged. "It's been done better."

Ayers grinned once they were out in the street. "There you are, Mathey, all set up in style. You were very persuasive. I've half a mind to write the newspapers and ask them to put on metaphysical fire alarms myself."

"I wouldn't mind if you did," Ned said. "I expect I would get some of the business." He folded away the sheets of paper and pocketed them. "Thanks ever so much for the help. It did smoothe the way."

"I hope you get on well with your hocus. *Are* they under a curse?"

"We'll see," Ned said.

Ayers clapped him on the shoulder. "You work too much. Have you even spoken to a young lady in recent memory?"

"Very recent," Ned said, nodding back toward the office.

"You know what I mean. You're too good a catch to live like a monk."

"I expect you're right," Ned said, his spirits unaccountably sinking. He had missed the ease of the Mercury Club in his evenings in Julian's haunts, but it was disheartening to be reminded how much that ease depended on telling half-truths, if not outright lies. "But monkish or not, this bit of work needs sorting out."

"See you at the club for dinner, at least?"

"Not tonight, I think." He hoped to have dinner with Julian, even if that meant trying to figure out what to say – if anything – about certain awkward revelations. Not that he had thought Julian was an innocent, or that he begrudged him admirers, but if even his rare admissions of affection were the same assurances he had given to a dozen others before –

Ayers shook his head at him affectionately. "Definitely a monk," he said, and headed off toward the omnibus stop

JULIAN SCRAWLED HIS NAME AT THE bottom of the letter, then folded and sealed it before he could change his mind. It was almost impossible to know what to say to Challice that would be reassuringly friendly rather than affectionate, and still persuade him to agree to a meeting; the crumpled sheets of seven previous attempts lay on the desk or on the floor beside it. He rang for young Digby and dispatched him to the nearest postbox, then collected the discarded drafts and dropped them one by one into the fire. He liked Challice, that was the problem, had liked him from the day they met at one of Lennox's parties. Challice had been at Eton, not Toms', but they had both survived a hard schooling to blossom at university, and Challice was one of the few club men who was genuinely interested in the occasional lecture; they'd gone about together quite a bit for a month or three. But Challice had married young to try to cure himself: in hindsight, it could only have ended in disaster. Still, Julian had no desire to hurt him, but he couldn't see any way to get the information without causing him pain. And they did need the information: there was no guarantee that this thing that was removing men's hearts had stopped or would stop unless they stopped it. He had to talk to Challice.

There was no answer in the next post, or the one after, and by mid-afternoon Julian was certain there would be no response. He poked at the fire as his clock struck five, reluctant to take the next move. Challice was going to pretend he hadn't received the letter, would ignore it as long as possible; Julian would need to go to him, and that would be awkward at best. He closed his eyes, remembering an afternoon in Jacobs' back parlor, a stolen holiday for both of them. Challice's wife had been visiting her mother; it was February, and neither of them had any business more pressing than an assignation.

They made love in the half-light, and then Challice turned from him in sudden despair, weeping into the pillow. Julian stroked his shoulders, guiltily aware of the hard muscle beneath his hand, the planes of his back still enough to rouse desire. Challice's sobs slowed and stopped, and he rolled away from Julian's touch, dragging the sheet up between them.

"Did I hurt you?" Julian said at last, not know what else to say. "I'm sorry. I never meant –"

Challice flung back the sheets – much washed and badly mended, club sheets as common as the club bed – groped shivering for his discarded clothes. Even in the dulled light, he was very handsome, long-boned and quick, white-blond hair curling at his temples. Nothing at all like Ned, Julian thought, helpless, nothing like Lennox, or Farrell, or Bell, not at all like anyone except himself. He sat up, hugging his knees.

"Challice…"

"This is wrong." Challice scrambled into his clothes, tangling the sleeves, his fingers clumsy on the buttons. "So very wrong. I'm a married man, Lynes. I made vows I meant to keep."

But why? Julian could no more have spoken those words aloud than he could have struck the man, and the latter would have been more kind. Challice was neither a fool nor a coward; to set himself a goal so wholly against his nature seemed Sisyphean.

Challice was fumbling at his collar with hands that shook badly enough to be seen, and Julian could bear it no longer. He pushed himself out of the bed, glad he was still wearing drawers, and picked up a dropped stud.

"Here, let me help."

Challice jerked away, his face crumpling as though he might cry again. "Don't touch me."

Julian dropped his hand as though he'd been burned. No one had said that to him since University, and it stung more than he would have thought possible.

"I mustn't," Challice said. "I know I can't, but – oh, God, it's so hard."

"You've done no harm," Julian said. Done no wrong, either, but in the face of Challice's misery those words wouldn't come.

Challice laughed. "More harm than you know. My wife –"

"What she doesn't know doesn't hurt her," Julian said. That was the wrong thing entirely, he knew it even as the words left his tongue.

"It's wrong. It's a rotten schoolboy vice, not worthy of grown men. My God, I'm so ashamed."

"We are what we are," Julian said, carefully.

"No. You may be, but I'll change. Somehow. But I will change." Challice shrugged himself into his coat. He looked no more disheveled than a man who'd spent a busy day in town and been jostled in a crowded omnibus. "I can't bear it. Just – stay away from me, Lynes."

Julian froze, cold filling him the way it had at school when the senior men mocked him. "I expect that won't be difficult."

Challice slammed the door, leaving Julian standing shivering in the empty room.

They'd made it up, of course – Challice had apologized handsomely, and Julian had still found him congenial company, though he'd resolved never to sleep with him again. He'd more or less kept his resolution, except for once or twice when Challice had been too pleasant, too seductive to resist. But it was always a mistake, always left him baffled and annoyed, pity and regret and unfamiliar guilt knotting uncomfortably in his gut. He'd managed to avoid him for almost six months before he'd taken up with Ned, and was grateful Ned didn't know the full story.

But it made it hard to ask for favors, particularly when Lennox had made it clear what he would be asking. And Challice clearly had no intention of making things easy. The only real choice was to try to catch him as he was leaving work, awkward as that would be. Julian seized his hat and coat and left before he could change his mind.

Challice worked for a tea importer that still kept its offices in Mincing Lane, and Julian managed to catch an omnibus with relative ease, at the price of shivering in the open top deck. The owners were some sort of cousin of Challice's, he remembered, and Challice's wife was a niece of the senior partner – one more thing that had sent Challice into paroxysms of guilt, particularly since he'd been promoted over men who were his senior. It had done no good to point out that Challice was as knowledgeable as the best of them, and more so than many. As far as Julian could tell, though, he'd proved himself worthy: he'd been promoted again in the past year, and Lennox said he was likely to be made partner as soon as the owners could justify it. Which, of course, was yet another reason that he wouldn't want his frailties to come to light.

Julian left the omnibus at Leadenhall Street and made his way down Lime Street toward the river. As he turned off Fenchurch into Mincing Lane, the wind stiffened, carrying a sudden smell of smoke and spices through the gaslit dusk. Most of the other pedestrians were clerks in badly-cut frock coats and inexpensive hats; their superiors' coats were indefinably better, their shoes shined and well-heeled, their hats that fraction taller. They moved like great steamers through the crowd, lifting a silver-bound cane to hail a passing cab, pausing to strike an enchanted match and savor the smoke of a new cigar, while their juniors traveled in shoals, queuing for the omnibuses or vanishing into the nearest noisy eating house. Julian's bowler and second-best suit marked him as a stranger, but not noticeably out of place – a tea man, possibly, or a marine agent, nothing worth a second glance.

He knew where Challice lived, and Goodridge and Neale's offices were prominently marked; it was easy enough to position himself in the lee of a busy chophouse where he could see any possible route Challice might take. And, sure enough, there he was, coming out of the door with an older man while a page in livery held the door and touched his hat. Julian grimaced – he couldn't approach Challice in company – but the two parted at the curb, and Challice turned toward the omnibus stops at London Bridge.

Julian drifted after him, timing his steps to overtake the other at Tower Street. He was still very handsome, his coat cut to emphasize a willowy height, and Julian couldn't help admiring him even now. They both stopped at the curb, and Julian gave his least threatening smile. "Challice."

"Lynes." Challice turned to face him, the first flash of pleased recognition turning to recoil. "What the devil are you doing here?"

At least he'd had the sense to keep his voice down. Julian said, "You didn't get my letter?"

Challice hesitated, not able even now to voice an outright lie. "We can't talk here."

"Let me buy you a drink," Julian said. "Sangster's, or Foy's." They were both respectable places, intended to reassure, but Challice shook his head.

"No, thank you. I don't have anything to say to you."

Passersby were beginning to give them irritated looks, and Julian stepped back, out of the main thoroughfare. For a moment, he thought Challice would seize the chance to walk away, but the other man followed, and they drifted to a stop against the railing of someone's areaway.

"I need your help," Julian said.

"No."

"It's a matter of life and death."

Challice shook his head again. "Can you give me your word it doesn't have anything to do with – more personal matters?"

Julian hesitated, tempted to lie just to keep him talking, but that would only make things worse in the long run. "Two men are dead of non-conforming magic. Alfred Punton and Dolly Hall."

Challice looked up sharply at that. "How did they die?"

"Something removed their hearts from their chests," Julian answered.

"Singularly appropriate." An odd smile flickered across Challice's face. "And you thought I might know something? Thank you very much, Lynes, I didn't think you'd throw that at me."

"I'm not –"

"I can't help you," Challice said, and turned away.

Julian didn't follow, all too aware that he had not handled the matter as well as he might. Another letter, perhaps, an apology for the insult he hadn't meant and another plea – no, he couldn't make himself believe that it would work any better. He swore under his breath, and started back toward Coptic Street. Perhaps Ned would be home, and willing to share dinner, though Julian didn't want to go too deeply into explanations for his own black mood. But at least it would be company.

❧

By the time he'd reached Bloomsbury, it was late enough that the Commons's gate was locked. Julian didn't bother asking the porter if Ned were still there, turned instead into Blandings and stood for a moment, blinking at the noise. At least it was the end of the dinner rush, the tables clearing, but he couldn't see Ned anywhere. Usually he wasn't hard to spot, either, his height and fair hair both conspicuous. He shook his head at a waiter, and heard his name over the roar of voices.

"Lynes! Over here!"

Julian turned, the knot in his chest easing unexpectedly, to see Ned waving from the doorway of one of the side rooms. He waved back, and threaded his way through the tables until he could answer without shouting. "I'm glad I caught you."

"We were just talking about you," Ned said, and Julian realized Hatton was with him. He controlled his frown, and nodded a greeting.

"Hatton."

"Speak of the devil," Hatton said. "But you're the man we want, and no mistake."

"Sit." Ned waved for a waiter. "Join us, why don't you? We've only just ordered. Chops and potatoes and rather a decent claret."

Hatton lifted his glass in agreement, and Julian settled into the seat next to Ned. Ned finished with the waiter and joined them, while another waiter brought a third glass. Ned poured, and Julian accepted it gratefully, taking a long swallow of what was quite a decent wine.

"What was it you wanted?" he asked, looking from one to the other, and to his surprise it was Hatton who answered.

"Have you seen tonight's paper?"

"The afternoon editions only," Julian answered.

Ned made a face. "Not precisely encouraging."

"They're still going on about a creeping hand," Hatton said. "Questions should be asked, et cetera. I've had my men compile a list of odd and possibly metaphysical burglaries, but even narrowing it down to things that might be described as removing objects from closed containers, I've got thirty-five possibilities on my list. It occurred to me that you know some potentially interested parties. They won't talk to me, of course, but you might be able to get them to cross some of these off my list."

"No names," Julian said. "Nothing that would identify any particular person."

Hatton raised both hands. "You have my word."

"I'll ask," Julian said. "I can't promise, but – I'll do my best."

"Thanks," Hatton said.

"I told you Lynes was the man to ask," Ned said, and topped up their glasses as the waiter arrived with the soup.

"You think the key is *container*?" Julian sketched the sigil with his finger.

"That's the best I could come up with," Ned answered. "I'm not sure what else would connect robbery and missing hearts."

And the thing Punton was trying to make surely had been meant to commit burglary, Julian thought. But if you took that away, surely the key word was *heartless*. That was something he couldn't say in front of Hatton, not without more explanation than was wise, and he nodded. "I see what you mean. Is there a chance I could get another look at Punton's notes?"

"I promised not to let them out of my office," Ned answered, "but you know you're always welcome there."

The words were unexpectedly warming, especially under Hatton's nose, and Julian grinned in spite of himself. "I'll make an appointment, then. And I'll do what I can with your list, Hatton."

"I appreciate it." Hatton reached into his pocket to produce a much-folded sheet of foolscap. He handed it across the table, and Julian tucked it into his own coat as the waiter arrived with their chops. The conversation became more general then – Hatton had a tart tongue and shared Ned's fondness for the variety stage – and Julian allowed himself to relax.

Hatton excused himself after the pudding, but Ned seemed inclined to linger over the cheese, and Julian had no desire to hurry him. It was pleasant to sit and talk of ordinary things, warm and snug in Blandings, and he sighed when the waiter came with the bill.

"Come and have a nightcap with me," Ned suggested, and Julian nodded. "I'd like that."

They made their way back to Ned's lodgings through the gaslit streets. Ned let them in with his latch key, and they climbed the stairs to his rooms, keeping quiet out of long habit. Inside, Ned turned up the gas, warm light spilling over the comfortable furniture. Julian poured them each a brandy while Ned built up the fire, and settled himself at one end of the sofa, arranging himself in a way intended to invite company. Ned seated himself at the opposite end, however, frowning slightly.

"Did you have any luck with – what was his name, Challice?"

Julian winced. "No."

He'd meant his tone to be forbidding, and Ned's frown deepened. "Another of your lovers."

"I broke it off a long time ago." Julian regretted every time he'd let himself be charmed back into Challice's orbit, which was not what he wanted to be thinking about at the moment.

There was a little silence, the coal ticking in the grate, and Ned shifted against the cushions. "You seem to have been friendly with quite a few of the members at the Dionysus."

There was an obscene quibble there that Julian hoped was unintentional. "They're my friends."

"I mean, been to bed with them." Ned met his eyes with a look that Julian remembered only too well from their schooldays, the one that meant he was for once determined to get an answer.

"Some, yes."

"Was it sport, or were there genuine feelings involved at the time –"

"Damn all feelings." Julian drained the last of his brandy and shoved himself up off the sofa. He crossed to the sideboard and concentrated on refilling his glass without spilling anything.

"Not that I have room to judge," Ned said, "if it was only sport."

That was gracious, if unlikely, and Julian managed to smile, lifting the decanter in question. Ned nodded, and Julian refilled his glass before returning the decanter to the sideboard. Ned was still sitting at the far end of the sofa, and Julian settled himself beside him. He felt Ned stiffen, and said quickly, "I would like to look over Punton's notes."

"Hatton was serious about keeping them in my chambers," Ned answered. "Under lock and key."

Under other circumstances, Julian would have protested on principle, but this was not the moment. He nodded. "I can understand that. It's not a cantrip one wants to see getting loose."

Ned relaxed slightly. "At your convenience, then. If I'm out – God knows, that's not terribly likely, but if I am, I'll tell Miss Frost to let you have them."

"Thanks." Julian took another sip of his brandy. "What I don't see is why Punton would meddle with such a thing. Presumably he wanted money, but I'd have thought he was decently settled in Denbigh's household."

"I wouldn't think being a private secretary paid all that well," Ned objected.

"Well, no, but he had room and board, and his clubs for amusement." That was skating a little too close to thin ice again, and Julian hid a grimace. "Though I suppose you're right, most men always want more. It just seems like an unreasonable risk."

"I haven't had much more chance to look at the notes than you have," Ned said, "but it seems to me whatever it was he was doing was meant for group work."

Julian risked leaning back against Ned's outstretched arm, and after a moment's hesitation, Ned shifted to accommodate him. "A lot of older magic was, wasn't it? If that's what he was drawing on."

"Yes. And of course we've moved away from that in the modern system, to the point where group work is almost non-conforming by definition."

"And so is sex magic – almost by definition, again, though I suppose self-abuse would be somewhat effective."

"But easier to raise – well, energy and other things – in a group." Ned was blushing faintly, and Julian couldn't help remembering him watching the young man at the Dionysus receiving service. He'd seemed more fascinated than shocked, the blood rising in his cheeks and his breath coming short.

"Certainly that." Julian pushed the memory aside. "But that's a bit different from creating something to steal for you."

"I suppose it depends on what they were trying to do."

Seduce Challice, Julian thought, though exactly what they'd promised him was unknown. And that was the last thing he wanted to be thinking about. "I suppose." He set his glass aside. He turned into Ned's arm, reaching out to run a finger down his cheek, the almost-invisible stubble rough under his touch. "And I'll look into it. But for now, I'd like…"

He let his voice trail off, and Ned let his head fall back in surrender. They moved from sofa to bed, and in the aftermath Julian lay sprawled on top, fingers digging into Ned's shoulder. He closed his eyes, holding him as close as he could, as though he could drive back memory in the press of bodies, and felt Ned wince beneath him.

"Sorry," he said, releasing him, but as he dressed and made his way back to his own rooms, he couldn't suppress the unhappy feeling that things were going wrong again.

☾✺

CHAPTER NINE
Scotching the Snake

"CLEARLY YOU MISSED YOUR CALLING," MISS FROST said, looking down at the list of signatures as Ned spread it out on the table. "You should have been a petition taker."

"If I only had to collect signatures for entirely unobjectionable causes." Ned laid out the blackmail letters next to the list, and prepared to repeat the test he had tried earlier. He sketched the metaphysical words for *gather together, same,* and *maker,* hoping to see the letters slide smoothly atop the list of signatures. Then it would only be a matter of distinguishing between them, possibly with the aid of a pair of scissors.

Instead the pages remained stubbornly motionless. "So much for that."

"At least you've ruled out the publisher's staff."

"That's something." He looked up as the door opened. Julian came in, shaking the rain from his hat, and cocked his head curiously at the papers on the desk.

"Any progress?"

"It's no one at Delahunt Brothers," Ned said. "Not unless they're using some means of producing the letters that I can't divine. It might still be Oswald, but as we haven't got a sample of his handwriting –"

"As a matter of fact," Miss Frost said, extracting an envelope from her desk and presenting it, if not quite with a conjurer's flourish, at least with a distinct look of satisfaction.

Ned turned it over. "How in the world?"

"I wrote Madeleine for it, of course. It seemed the logical next step."

"Of course it was," Julian said, sounding approving.

"Well, yes." Ned opened the envelope, and withdrew the title page of a book. *ON HEROIC VIRTUE*, it read, *BY PERCIVAL OSWALD*. It was inscribed as well, in a flourishing hand: *For the fairest of all ladies, from the hand of your own parfait gentil knight – oh, grant me the merest token of your love in return!*

"Madeleine said he asked for her glove," Miss Frost said. "If he'd asked for one of her stories instead, she might have married him."

"Useful that she kept the book," Ned said.

"She says it's useful to remind herself that if that sort of rubbish can be published, anything can." She shook her head. "I don't want to give you the impression she's heartless, though."

"That word again," Julian said under his breath. Ned raised an eyebrow at him, and he shook his head, clearly dismissing the matter until later.

"The contrary, if anything. I think she cared very much. As far as I could tell, she really believed that he would be content for her to carry on with a career once they were married, right up until he dispelled that illusion." Her tone was very dry. "Madeleine is a romantic, you see."

"Better for our purposes than if she had carefully burnt all his letters." Ned repeated the test over the page, to the same disappointing result; it made no move toward the blackmail letters, lying impotently limp on the desktop. "Which leaves your theory, Lynes."

Julian's eyes flicked toward Miss Frost for a moment. "One of Kennett's personal circle," he said.

"Yes. I think we ought to pay a call at his club."

"Don't forget the notes on the ritual," Julian said. "I want to go over them again. I know you're the expert on metaphysics –"

"You're the expert on crime," Ned said. "And when it comes to that, the expert on the kind of dodgy metaphysics this seems to be based on. Although I should talk to Oppenshaw again and see if he has any ideas."

"Assuming he hasn't turned into a duck," Julian said.

"I expect I would have heard."

"Most likely," Julian said, although he sounded a bit dubious. They took an omnibus to the Dionysus, as Julian agreed that Straun would be more amenable to conversation if they could catch him before the membership started arriving for the evening. The footman who answered the door informed them that the club was not yet open, but reluctantly agreed to go and ask Straun if he'd see them.

Ned was struck by the quiet inside; in the light of day, the club could have been just another townhouse, albeit one decorated with a magpie's sensibility. The door to the front parlor stood open, the windows open to air the room despite the rain. After a moment, Straun came down the stairs wearing a smoking jacket and a harried expression.

"We're not strictly speaking open this time of day," he said. "I can make arrangements, but I do appreciate a little advance warning."

"I am sincerely sorry," Ned said. "There's a delicate matter we need to speak to you about.

The blood went out of Straun's face. "Who's dead now?"

"Not that matter," Julian said. "We have another problem. Someone's been blackmailing a member, and we have some reason to believe he's a member himself. Or one of the staff – I take it they know a great many things that go on here."

"They'd have to be blind and deaf not to," Straun said. "But they're all men with similar habits. Not for the members' entertainment – some do make arrangements of that sort, but I make it clear it's not part of the servants' duties, and I discourage money changing hands on the premises. But it's an assurance of their discretion to know that they'd be equally at risk of exposure."

It wasn't precisely an equal risk, Ned thought; he suspected that if one of the members and a servant with a spotty history behind him tried to blacken each other's characters, he knew who'd be believed. But he did take Straun's point.

"Someone's run the risk," he said. "One of the members or one of the servants. I can find out who metaphysically, if you'll let me match the blackmail letters to the club book."

"Oh, come now, I can't possibly do that," Straun said. "We assure the members that their identities will be protected. If they choose to use a pseudonym, that's sacrosanct."

"You have a blackmailer in your midst," Ned said. "How long do you expect anything to be sacrosanct?"

Straun frowned. "Do you really think there's a risk he'd go through with his threats?"

"I do," Ned said. He suspected Straun believed the blackmail was over sexual adventures, not dubious literature, and didn't care to disabuse him of the notion. "With disastrous consequences to at least two careers."

Straun's smile twisted. "You needn't tell me that. Believe me, I'm well aware of the consequences of exposure."

"Then –" Julian began, but Ned nudged him to keep quiet.

"Were you blackmailed?" he asked softly.

"Oh, nothing so baroque. I was caught. I had a position as a private secretary to a prominent gentleman. There was a career in it, or so I thought. Then I made the mistake of inviting a friend of mine back to my room – I lived in, you understand. Well, he had been drinking – we both had, but I generally keep my head – and I couldn't make him be quiet. Before breakfast my employer knew all about it. He sacked me, of course. He wouldn't give me a character, and he said if anyone inquired, he'd tell the truth about what sort of practices I'd been up to under his roof."

There were two spots of feverish color in Straun's cheeks, although his voice was steady. "So much for my ambitions. One of my friends let me know that the Dionysus was trolling for someone silly enough to agree to be steward, and I said I'd do it for room and board and a little stipend to keep body and soul together. A stopgap, I thought, at first, but – well, I'm used to the place. It has its compensations."

"I am sorry," Ned said.

Straun shrugged with a determined sort of nonchalance. "Ancient history. But not history I'd care to see repeated. This place is a madhouse, but at least I've always been able to say that it's a discreet one." He let out an unhappy breath. "I'll fetch the book," he said.

He brought back both the club book and a well-worn ledger. "The servants sign for their wages, at least with an *X*," he said. "I don't know if that's enough for you to go on."

"It should be enough," Ned said. Straun pushed the ledger toward him. He was perversely tempted to open the club book first, but it was to the servants' advantage to clear them if they were innocent, and to no one's advantage to let them go on indulging in blackmail if they weren't.

He withdrew one of the blackmail letters and laid it face down next to the book. He sketched the now familiar sigils – *gather together, same, maker* – and held his breath.

The letter began to flutter, as if filled with skittering energy. It twitched its way across the table toward the ledger, and then past it, draping itself over the closed club book and clinging there as if it had abruptly grown tired.

"Hell and damnation," Straun said.

"I'm sorry," Julian said, opening the book to the latest pages and evading the letter's flapping attempts to crawl between his fingers. "But we do have to know."

"I know it."

The letter plastered itself to the right-hand page. "That's clear enough, but not precise enough," Ned said. "Have you got a penknife?"

Straun produced one, and Ned peeled off the letter, handing it to Julian to hold, and began slicing the names apart, taking care to discard scraps of paper where two men's writing overlapped. He was halfway down the page when one strip of paper tore itself free before he had finished cutting, soared for a moment like a bird, and rustled to a halt nestled against the letter in Julian's hand.

Pinky, it read, in a neat copperplate hand.

"Pinky Dorrington," Straun said. "I believe his Christian name is Alfred."

"I thought you weren't supposed to know real names," Ned said.

"He hardly makes his a secret. He's a critic – he writes reviews for the *Athenaeum*. All the boys with literary aspirations make a dead set for him in hopes of sweetening his pen, and that's just the way he likes it. You must have noticed his string of admirers."

"A critic," Ned said, his eyes meeting Julian's. A perfect reason to be in and out of publisher's offices, and perhaps to ask, in all apparent innocence, who could possibly have written such a book…

Julian nodded. "He's the one."

❦

"I HATE BLACKMAILERS," JULIAN SAID. THEY were sitting in one of the small parlors, a decanter of rather better whisky than the usual on the table between them, but neither of them had managed more than a few sips of their drink. Straun had provided a scratch supper, cold beef and salad, but neither of them had eaten much. "And it's low, even for Pinky."

Ned gave him a sharp glance, but seemed to think better of what he'd been going to say. "How do you propose to stop him?"

"That's the question, isn't it?" Julian pushed himself out of his chair and began to pace the length of the faded carpet. "We need to frighten him enough to put him in check."

"Well, there's the obvious," Ned said, looking meaningfully around the room. There were rather more classical statues than one might expect, Julian thought, and all of them lissome youths. "But that seems like playing with fire."

Julian nodded. "It's too dangerous – too easy for him to turn the tables."

"What, then? You've done this before, I gather."

"Blackmailers are an inevitable part of my business," Julian admitted, "and there's never a good answer. Oh, I can try to frighten him, but there's no guarantee that he'll stay frightened, any more than there's a guarantee he'll stay bought. And clients lose their nerve."

"No fear of that with Miss Barton," Ned said. "She's game as anything. What about Kennett?"

Julian shrugged. "He wants to be a famous poet, so he knows what he has to lose. I wish there was time to get in touch with Bolster, he's been a great help in some of these cases – but I'm afraid if we wait, Pinky will hear something. This club lives on gossip." He caught sight of Ned's appalled expression and shrugged again. "Except where it matters, of course, they're discreet enough there."

"Of course. You've used Bolster's thugs to threaten people?"

"They can be very effective." Julian grinned. "This time, you'll have to do."

Ned gave him a rather doubtful look. "It might be a good idea to have something more than my physical prowess to threaten him with."

"Well, yes, I'm working on that." Julian took another sip of his whisky. The trouble was, it wasn't the swots and the milksops who could be intimidated by physical threats. If they were gentlemen, they'd almost certainly survived worse at school, and resented it deeply. It was the former hearties who caved to threats. And Pinky was perfectly capable of exposing both Kennett and Miss Barton for pure revenge. No, stopping him required the right lever.

The noise in the halls was growing louder as the club opened for the evening. Julian glanced over his shoulder, wondering who he should talk to, who could help, and the door swung open abruptly. That was against all the club rules, and Julian lifted an eyebrow, unsurprised to see Dorrington in the doorway.

"My dear Pinky," he said, and put his hand on Ned's shoulder, willing him to stay seated. "Think what you could have interrupted."

"Nothing of surpassing interest, I'm sure," Dorrington snapped. "What the devil do you mean, casting enchantments over my name?"

"What?" Ned said, in spite of himself, and Dorrington gave him a venomous glance.

"Oh, don't play coy, I know exactly what you were doing. I have my sources, after all."

"Servants will talk," Julian said. His blood was up, every nerve taut, his whole attention fixed on Dorrington. "But, alas, they're not always accurate. No one's been casting enchantments on you, Pinky. It's more that we've been uncovering what you've been doing."

Dorrington paled. "I have no idea what you're talking about."

"Unoriginal," Julian said. "Do close the door, unless you want the entire club to hear what we have to say."

It hung in the balance for a moment, and then, reluctantly, Dorrington shut the door behind him.

"That's better." Julian didn't dare give the other man time to recover himself. "Sit down, and let's discuss this in a civilized fashion."

"I don't want to sit." Dorrington glared at him, hands on hips, but Julian thought he read fear beneath the pose.

"Suit yourself," he said, and lifted his hand from Ned's shoulder. Ned took the cue, rising to his full and not inconsiderable height, and Dorrington bit his lip.

"I tell you, I have no idea what you're on about."

"I think you do," Julian said. "You've sent some very ill-advised letters, Pinky."

Something flickered across Dorrington's face, a look almost of shock, but then he recovered himself. "I send any number of letters every day, and some of them could be construed as ill-advised. I don't know what business it is of yours."

"When you threaten people with exposure of secrets, it becomes my business," Julian said. "I've been asked to put a stop to it, and I intend to do so."

Dorrington achieved a sneer. "How very noble of you, Julian. I wonder which of your many paramours – oh, Auberon, of course. Dear Oliver, to give him his more fitting name."

"And Miss Barton," Ned said.

"The conquering hero," Dorrington snapped. "And does the lady have any idea of your tastes, I wonder?"

"You're not in any position to throw stones," Julian said.

Dorrington took a breath. "Perhaps not. But, then, neither are you. I believe we are at a stalemate."

"Not at all." Julian gave what he had been told was a thoroughly unpleasant smile. "The literary world is, as you've made very clear, a fickle place. A man may be respected one day and derided the next."

"The *Athenaeum* knows my worth."

"For now. But suppose the editors were to find out that their favorite critic was just as silly and superstitious as the lady authors he derides? A man who consults tea leaves, and plans his reviews according to the phase of the moon."

"That's not true!" Dorrington looked genuinely offended.

"No, it's not," Julian agreed. "But I can bring three mediums who'll swear that you're their best customer – gypsy ladies of impeccable pedigree, with fine flashing eyes and sun-browned bosoms that they'll be happy to display when they tell their tales to your editors. You'll be the laughingstock of Bloomsbury."

Dorrington collapsed into the nearest chair. "That's not fair. Kennett and the Barton female at least wrote those dreadful books."

"I'm not really concerned with 'fair,'" Julian said. "I've been engaged to put a stop to your threats and letters, and I intend to do so. So. Let me be plain. Unless your threats cease immediately and never resume, I will see that your editors receive information that you are addicted to the cheaper superstitions, with full and most embarrassing particulars."

"You'd never be able to prove it," Dorrington said.

"I don't have to."

Dorrington's shoulders sagged. "They're dreadful books."

"I don't really care."

"Oh, very well. It was mostly the annoyance, you know. It's not as though I need the money." Dorrington pushed himself out of the chair again.

"How fortunate," Ned muttered.

Dorrington turned to look at him. "I will do your pretty Miss Barton an entirely undeserved favor – perhaps you could speak well of me to the re-doubtable Mr Lynes."

Ned lifted his eyebrows, unspeaking, and Dorrington hurried on.

"The lady has an enemy – the suitor she rejected, whom she has driven to seek consolation elsewhere."

"Oh, really, Pinky," Julian said. "You've got him on your string, too?"

Dorrington smiled, and moved toward the door. "Well, he does have a novel coming out soon. It shows promise. And now you'll leap to defend his virtue, I'm sure."

"Not I," Julian said, and Ned shook his head.

"How forbearing of you." Dorrington opened the door, looked back over his shoulder. "He's a much better writer than either of those two."

Julian swallowed a profane retort as the door closed behind him.

"Well," Ned said, after a moment.

"A thoroughly nasty piece of work." Julian refilled his own glass and downed half of it, then poured another for Ned and topped up his own.

"Will he keep his word?" Ned took his glass.

"I think so." Julian nodded. "He knows I'll do it. And that I can."

"Gypsy fortune-tellers provided by Bolster, I suppose?"

Julian managed a smile. "Yes, if necessary. They're very convincing."

"I dare say." The humor faded from Ned's face. "An unpleasant business all around."

"Blackmail usually is," Julian said, and drained his glass.

€❀

THE NEXT MORNING, JULIAN WAS STILL unsure if he'd done more than delay the inevitable. Pinky was silenced for the moment, but he doubted it would hold him forever. And he'd certainly made an enemy there. Pinky wasn't one to let an opportunity for malice pass him by. He stirred more sugar into his coffee, wondering if he wouldn't be better off asking Bolster to recommend someone who could resolve the problem permanently. Of course, that was murder – hanging if he was caught, not to mention the risk of bringing Ned down with him, and anyway Ned would never forgive him even if he got away with it. He wasn't fool enough to think Ned wouldn't find out, either.

He did need to talk to Bolster, though, both to make sure Dorrington was scotched and to inquire about Hatton's list of burglaries. He set his cup aside and moved to his desk, where he scribbled out a note addressed to Bolster at the Poll and Anchor. It was a new meeting spot, a bit more pleasant than Bolster's previous choice, and Julian guessed he was rising in Bolster's estimation. The thought was amusing, but not one that he cared to share with Ned. He sealed the letter and dispatched young Digby to post it, then stood for a moment, contemplating his next move. Punton's notes, he decided, and seized hat and coat before he could change his mind.

It was an unexpectedly sunny day, scraps of blue sky visible between the scudding clouds, and he decided to walk to the Commons in spite of the brisk air. To his disappointment, however, Ned wasn't in his chambers – he'd been called out to a client, Miss Frost said calmly, but professed herself happy to fetch him the notes once he'd explained the situation. He settled himself at Ned's desk to read, trying to ignore the way the chair smelled ever so faintly of Ned's hair oil, and spread Punton's papers in front of him.

By modern standards, the ritual was a mess, unbalanced, ill-formed, the grammar crabbed and awkward, signifiers left dangling. By the older standards, however, it made a bit more sense, and Julian looked up from his own notes. "Do you still have that copy of the *Little Albert*?"

"Yes." Miss Frost rose gracefully from her typewriter and collected the volume from Ned's locked cabinet. She set it on the desk in front of him, and Julian's eyebrows rose.

"That's the original edition. Or an original edition."

"The second printing, I believe," Miss Frost said placidly.

Julian touched the calfskin binding with respect. "I've never actually worked with it, only the modern versions."

"The illegal ones," Miss Frost said.

Julian gave her a sharp glance. "Yes."

She smiled back at him. "Having looked into it, I can quite see why the Commons won't license a modern edition."

"I'm not sure how you'd bring this into conformity." Julian glanced at the table of contents, and turned to the section that dealt with the Hand of Glory. "If you even could. But Punton doesn't seem to have cared about that."

"What was he aiming for?" she asked. "I admit, I've looked at it, and I can't really make sense of it. There's the Hand of Glory, yes, with all its unsavory ingredients – and I don't understand the pattern of substitution at all – but I don't recognize the other things he was trying to weave into it."

"There were some attempts to come up with substitutions for blood and bone at the beginning of the century," Julian said, "conforming ones, I mean, and there are unlicensed men in the city who have their own personal lists. Not that some of them don't use the genuine articles when they can get them – there's a modest trade in things like owl's blood and bones, poachers bringing them in from the country, and of course no pure black cat is ever entirely safe."

Miss Frost made a face. "Poor things."

"I wouldn't like to be one, no," Julian agreed. He looked back at the pages that held the notes on substitution, frowning again. It looked as though Punton had started with Mainwaring's work in the 1830s, but added others that seemed to come from at least one of the unlicensed practitioners that Bolster and his colleagues favored. And that might be something useful to know. He jotted down the substitutions that didn't come from Mainwaring. He didn't recognize the source, but he suspected Bolster would.

"But what's it for?" Miss Frost asked again. "I understand the purpose of a Hand of Glory, and people do know about it. But this is – it seems different to me."

"It is," Julian said. "And I'm not entirely sure what was intended. I've been trying to translate it into more normal metaphysics, and I'm not really getting very far. I think it was meant to steal, not just to allow someone else to steal, but that's all I have."

"The thing that they made was supposed to steal – what?" Miss Frost cocked her head to one side, looking a bit like a curious robin.

"It couldn't have been too big. And yet it had to be worth stealing, so – banknotes, perhaps, or jewelry? There's a place to set a signifier, even if the grammar is peculiar." He reached into his pocket to check the time, and grimaced as he saw how late it was. Bolster's reply should be waiting, if he was able to meet today. "Damn it. I'll have to come back. Tell Mathey I've been here, would you?"

"Of course." Miss Frost jotted a note on her blotter. "You and Mr Mathey were at school together, I gather?"

Julian hesitated. "Yes, we were."

"It's nice when childhood friendships mature," she said, and Julian let himself out, not wanting to think about what she might have meant.

He caught the omnibus back to Coptic Street and found, as he had expected, a reply from Bolster wedged into the door. It set a meeting – the Poll and Anchor, as expected – and required no reply unless Julian wasn't able to make it. He checked his watch again, and saw that he had time to change before he ventured into Shadwell.

The Poll and Anchor was a bright new public house on Narrow Street by the river, with a gaudy parrot perched on an anchor for the sign, and an even brighter bird chained to a perch at the end of the bar. Julian gave it a wide berth as he collected his pint, then went to join Bolster at a quiet table in the back of the public bar.

"Mr Bolster."

Behind him, the parrot screeched and flapped, and Bolster gave it a baleful glance. "Mr Lynes. If I'd known they were going to get a real bird, I'd never have picked the bloody place."

"It's very nautical?" Julian took a cautious sip of his beer, discovered it was good, and took a longer drink.

"That's as may be," Bolster said, "but it's bloody loud."

As if to prove the point, the parrot shrieked again – *avast ye, avast ye, avast ye* – until the barman gave its chain a few quick jerks and settled it down. Bolster shook his head.

"Either the bird goes, or I do. What's your business, Mr Lynes?"

"Three things," Julian said. "First, I may need a few of your lady-friends to back up a tale." He explained about Dorrington's blackmail, and what he'd threatened, and Bolster nodded.

"Done. I don't hold with that trade."

"Next, I'm looking for a supplier of metaphysical goods who'd make these substitutions." He slid the slip of paper across the table, and Bolster took it.

"Frank Timmins on the Litchfield Road, he's one who deals in this. Leroy O'Malley, maybe."

"By the Battersea Bridge?"

"That's the one." Bolster slid the paper back to him. "But he's getting almost respectable in his old age. And maybe Ikey Bevans on Paradise Road, but that's Rotherhithe, and he generally likes men who know their business, not the trade, if you know what I mean. Frank Timmins, for my money. What's the second?"

"I've been asked to do a favor for the Yard," Julian said. "Specifically, for the 'Phys."

"Go on."

"It's about these peculiar deaths." Julian reached into his coat and drew out the list Hatton had given him. "Looked at from a metaphysical angle, the thing they have in common is that something has been removed from a closed – locked or sealed – container. This is a list of burglaries where the same thing has happened."

Bolster snorted. "I don't see as how that moves you any forwarder. There must be thirty or forty addresses on this list."

"Exactly. But if there were some way to eliminate some of the thefts – prove that they weren't done by this same person or persons who's taking men's hearts – it would be possible to focus on the ones that are linked to our man, and ignore the rest."

"And by 'ignore' you mean?"

"I mean Hatton says the 'Phys won't bother with them." Julian paused. "Well, unless there's some other reason to drew his fire. But he gave me his word that's what he wants the information for, and that he's not the least bit interested in any identifying features."

Bolster considered for a moment, drawing his finger along the grain of the wood. "Hatton's word's good, I'll give him that."

"I've found it so," Julian agreed.

"Right, then." Bolster unfolded the sheet of foolscap, turning it so that Julian could also read the neat secretarial copperplate, then hunted in his pockets until he found the stub of a pencil. "Let's see what we can do."

He worked his way methodically down the list, ticking off one address after another. At one, he shook his head and looked up at Julian. "That one didn't lose four hundred quid worth of silver. Someone's trying to put one over on their insurance."

"You really don't want Hatton paying extra attention, do you?"

"No, I suppose not," Bolster answered. "But it goes against the grain."

Julian grinned, but said nothing as the other man made his way to the bottom of the list.

"Well?"

Bolster shook his head. "There's still more than a dozen I can't say one way or another. If you'll let me take this for a few days, I expect I can get a few friends to say yea or nay."

"That would be helpful," Julian said. "Thank you."

"I'll tell you this for free," Bolster said, and turned the list again. "This one here, Taber Road, by the Artillery Ground. The pawnbroker died, right?"

Julian nodded. "I remember that one, it was in all the papers. Died of shock, they said he had a weak heart."

"I'm not sure the old bugger had a heart," Bolster said. "McGill was a nasty old man who liked his work, and God help you if you got on his bad side. But yes, something killed him that didn't leave a mark, and as far as I know no one's ever claimed the job. Or fenced the goods, though mostly it was bank notes that were taken. I'd tell Hatton to take a second look."

"I'll do that," Julian said. "Thank you."

He pushed back his chair, but Bolster held up his hand. "There's one more thing might be of interest."

"Oh?"

"There's a story I heard from a colleague of mine," Bolster began. He was weighing each word with even more than usual care, and Julian frowned. "It seems he's acquainted with a young man of no fixed profession and expensive habits, who occasionally allows certain older gentlemen to take liberties."

Julian kept his face expressionless, though it took an effort. This was not a part of the city's life that he'd expected to cross Bolster's path, though he supposed Bolster had connections to almost everything. Bolster was watching him uneasily, and Julian made himself nod. "A Mary-Ann, you mean."

"Occasionally."

Julian nodded again. "I understand."

Bolster relaxed fractionally, though his eyes were still wary. "It seems my colleague and he were swapping tales, and this young man had an odd one of his own. It seems he went to visit a gentlemen of his acquaintance, only the man was in a panic and paid him double his usual rate to dispose of something for him. And then the gentleman turned up mysteriously dead. It's your man Punton, I make no doubt."

"Hell and damnation," Julian said. "That is interesting. Would the young man have a name?"

"You're not surprised," Bolster said.

Julian froze, then made himself shrug. "I'd had some reason to suspect his tastes. It's no concern of mine, but I want to talk to the boy."

"And I don't want to talk him into trouble. There's no harm in him, bar some silliness. And he can't help his looks."

"I give you my word there won't be any repercussions," Julian said. Not least because I'm just as guilty, though at least I had the sense to stay away from the Mary-Anns. "If he knows anything useful – we need to find that out."

Bolster nodded again, apparently satisfied. "His name's Godding. Jonathan Godding. I don't know where he lodges, but I can find out."

"Will I find him in Piccadilly Circus?" Julian asked, and Bolster looked away.

"You might well."

"I'll find him, then," Julian said. "Thank you. I'm in your debt."

"I'll remember that," Bolster said, and drained his pint.

CHAPTER TEN
Seeking Answers

ICCADILLY CIRCUS WAS CROWDED WHEN NED and Julian climbed
down from the omnibus. Young men in evening dress moved in groups,
making their way into the Criterion or the Pavilion, clambering in and
out of cabs, and loitering to smoke or eye the women passing by. The best-
dressed ladies were on the arms of older gentlemen, who squired their pretty
companions with an exaggerated version of the gallantry they would have
shown their wives.

Then there were dollymoppish young women in bright best dresses, their hair
teased and their cheeks flushed in a way that spoke of rouge or enchantment;
they giggled when young men approached them, and carried on teasing conversation as if excited by their own daring. Shopgirls and maidservants, Ned
thought, and whether coin would be changing hands or whether something
more like courtship took place over a pint and a meal was still in question.

Other women were more frankly offering a service for sale, their skirts hiked
up nearly to the knee and their bosoms on frank display, their lips scarlet and
their cheeks apple-red. They paid no mind to the gentlemen entering the mu-
sic halls, setting their sights on those leaving, and thus more amenable to being
invited to end the evening with a visit to a cheap rented room or a conveniently
under-lit alley.

Their male counterparts were harder to distinguish from the general crowd
at first, but Ned had learned the trick of it; there was a certain way of standing
that was an advertisement to those in the know, an outthrust hip and cocked
head. It went along with a certain speculative look thrown at gentlemen passing by, especially older gentlemen without female company in evidence.

Ned returned one such look deliberately, and drifted closer, Julian trailing behind him. Julian cleared his throat as if feeling Ned was being indiscreet, or possibly suspecting he was mistaken, but Ned chose to ignore him. The boy was younger than Ned had preferred even in his University days, perhaps generously sixteen, but he had sharp observant eyes.

"A fine evening," Ned said.

The boy shrugged. "Not such bad weather as we've been havin.'"

"We're looking for a young man," Julian said.

The boy's eyes lit with momentary humor. "Then I'd say you're in luck, guv'nor."

Ned returned the smile, while Julian tried again. "A particular young man by the name of Jonathan Godding. I understand he can usually be found about these parts."

"I'm not a soddin' city directory," the boy said. Ned produced a coin, and his expression softened. "Try over by the Criterion. He hangs about the gas-lamp on the southwest corner, sometimes."

There was indeed a young man reclining lazily against the gas-lamp, exchanging measuring glances with passersby. He was older, perhaps Ned's own age, with curling hair that tumbled artfully over his forehead and a coat and trousers that looked secondhand but had been made over well.

"I'm told you might be Jonathan Godding," Ned said.

"Not if he owes you money."

"Nothing of the sort," Ned said easily. "More the contrary, I should say."

Godding smiled lazily. "That's a different matter, isn't it?"

"Care for a drink and a chat, if you're free? With me and my friend here."

Godding's eyes flicked over Julian and returned to Ned, with a certain resignation. "Three's not so much of a crowd. Where do you want to go?"

Ned shrugged with put-on indifference. "Have you a usual place?"

"I've a room where we could settle down and have a talk," Godding said. He slipped his arm through Ned's, in what might have passed for a gesture of drunken camaraderie, and Ned let him take the lead.

He brought them to a rented room a few streets over, slipping coins to the boy who opened the street door in a way that suggested that the room wasn't his usual sleeping place, but one rented by the hour. The bedclothes were already tumbled, and the room needed airing badly.

"Who's first?" Godding said once he'd shut the door. He shrugged off his coat and unbuttoned his shirt halfway to the waist. "And what's your pleasure?"

"We only want to talk," Julian said.

Godding's expression grew closed. "You don't look like police. Don't tell me the do-goods have started going after honest working boys? I hear the girls are plagued by gents who want to save their souls, but I never heard of your kind taking notice of Mary-Anns."

"I won't meddle with your soul," Ned said. "Believe me, I'm not any sort of saint. Another time…" He let his gaze travel deliberately up and down the length of Godding's body. "But right now there's information we're willing to pay for."

"What sort of information?"

"About a gentleman named Punton, and something you were asked to dispose of for him."

Godding frowned. "Was it yours? Because I haven't got it anymore."

Ned made a small stack of coins on the nightstand, and tapped them to make them clink. "My friend here knew Punton. We want to find out how he died. That's all."

"And go running to the police?"

"If there's anything we feel the need to tell the police, it won't include any mention of you," Julian said.

Godding bit his lip. "Was the thing cursed, then? I was afraid it was."

"Sit down and tell me all about it," Ned said. There was nowhere to sit but the bed, which creaked alarmingly when Godding perched on its edge.

"Punton was a regular," Godding said. "Thursday nights, most weeks – the gent he worked for went to the theater Thursdays. He had a room in this posh house, out in Mayfair, and he liked for me to come to him, like the dairyman. Well, he made it worth my while, even with the omnibus fare, and he didn't want anything out of the ordinary. He wasn't much for conversation, either, which was all right by me. I'd rather not pretend we're sweethearts when we both know what's being bought and sold."

Ned shrugged. "Sensible of you."

"He had just let me in, and we were about to get down to it, when he stopped stock still, like he'd seen a ghost. I thought at first there was someone at the window, and was getting ready to clear out, but he told me to stay where I was, sharp-like, and picked up the poker. Well, I didn't know what to think, then. I wasn't sure whether to be more afraid of him – that he meant to come after me with it – or that he'd seen a snake."

"That's hardly likely in London," Julian said.

"You see it in the picture papers, girls menaced by cobras some gent brought home from India – maybe that doesn't really happen, I don't know. Anyhow, he took the poker and prodded at this box that was sitting there on the sofa in front of the fire."

"A box?"

"One of those sort of writing desks you can put on your lap. He was pale as anything. Finally he threw the poker down and picked the box up. He turned round and sort of shoved it at me, so that I couldn't help but take it in my hands. And then he pulled out a note from his pocket and shoved that at me too – far more than we'd bargained for, I can tell you that – and told me to take the cursed thing away and drop it in the river. And that I wasn't to open it no matter what I did."

Godding shrugged one slim shoulder. "Well, at first I meant just to get out of sight and then to see what was inside, like anyone would. But then I started wondering if it might really be cursed, and what might happen to me if I did. The pawnshops were closed, and I didn't like the idea of having it my room for the night – I share the room with two others, and I would have had to use it as a pillow to keep it from being nicked. They're not bad to lodge with, but not what you'd call honest. Well, somehow I didn't fancy that. So I hid it out back of the rooming house, figuring I'd pawn it in the morning."

"And did you?"

"Never got the chance. It was gone when I went back and looked for it. Some rag-picker got it, I expect, and the curse with it, if there was a curse. Only then Punton turned up dead all the same. But I haven't so far."

"I think you're safe enough," Ned said, although he had to admit he only hoped that was true. "Punton didn't say any more about why he was frightened of the box?"

"He kept mum about that," Godding said. "I don't even know that he was frightened of it – maybe it was some kind of warning. That's part of why I mentioned it to a friend of mine – he's got some dangerous sorts of friends himself. But he said he'd never heard of threatening a man by leaving him a sodding writing desk."

"Nor have I," Julian said.

"You've been very helpful," Ned said. "And I promise we won't involve you further."

"I think I'm done with going back to other gents' rooms, all the same," Godding said. "Better to get it done quick somewhere where there won't be any surprises. Speaking of which, are you sure there's not something more you'd like? We've got the room another quarter-hour, and I can't fetch another punter back here in time to take advantage."

"I should hate to rush," Ned said.

"I can get the room for longer, if you're willing to pay according," Godding said, and ran his hand speculatively down the knee of Ned's trousers.

Ned shook his head. "Not tonight."

"As you like," Godding said, with a resigned shrug. He stood and did back up his shirt buttons, straightening his collar and smoothing his hair by touch. "It's too bad about old Punton. It's hard to get a regular."

"Were you fond of him?" Ned couldn't help asking.

Godding snorted. "I wouldn't say that. You don't expect a hired cart horse to be fond of its drivers, do you? But they do keep the cart horse in oats." His tone was arch, but then he added more naturally, "I've my own friends. But that's a different business."

"And none of mine," Ned agreed. "Thank you again for your time."

"I hope the box wasn't cursed," Godding said, as if it were an afterthought, but he sounded unhappy at the thought.

"I hope that myself," Ned said, and knew it the best reassurance he could offer.

❦

It was too late to get dinner from either of their landladies, so they stopped at a cheap eating house just off Oxford Street. It was not one of Julian's regular haunts, for which he was grateful, as he found himself unaccountably tongue-tied. Admittedly, this was not the place to talk about menacing writing desks, not in the middle of a crowded room where one practically had to shout to be heard above the hubbub. Nor was it the place to ask the other questions that crowded his mind, all of which boiled down to *precisely how did you get so familiar with picking up boys in Piccadilly Circus?* It seemed entirely unlike Ned, and yet there was no mistaking the evidence of his own eyes. He wolfed down his pie, barely tasting the mutton and savory gravy, and was pleased so see that Ned seemed just as eager to finish.

Julian's room was closer, and they made their way back to it without further conversation. Julian locked the door behind them, and Ned stooped to build up the fire. It had been allowed to die down to the barest embers, and the room was cold enough that Julian considered suggesting heading straight to bed. Instead, he turned up the lights and mixed them each a whisky and soda. Ned took his with a nod of thanks, and settled himself on the sofa.

"I think that was useful," he said.

Julian seated himself at the opposite end of the sofa. It was hard not to wonder what it would have been like to take Godding up on his offer – hard, too, not to imagine Ned dictating the terms of the encounter. The thought sent a jolt of heat through him, and he shifted uncomfortably, forcing his mind back to the problem at hand. "Still, a menacing writing desk?"

"Why a duck?" Ned shrugged. "That's what the metaphysicists always say when you ask them about something that seems utterly absurd and unlikely. It must make some kind of sense, just – not the normal kind. And that fellow, Hall's neighbor, he said there was a fancy writing desk in Hall's rooms."

"Dane," Julian said absently. He had a good memory for that sort of thing, and didn't mind showing it off. "And he mentioned fancy inlay, too, didn't he?"

"He did," Ned answered. "But that doesn't answer the question of why a writing desk."

"I wonder." Julian closed his eyes, conjuring up Punton's scrawl, the pattern of his ritual. "I almost think – I think Punton's enchantment was meant to be cast on something of the sort. That's the piece I was missing, that there was supposed to be a box or container at the center."

"The desk?"

Julian sat up sharply, almost spilling his drink. "Why not? It's not exactly conspicuous, and it's already got a compartment into which the spell abstracts the goods."

"If Punton made it, why did it frighten him so badly? And it didn't sound all that inconspicuous, either."

"It sounds to me as though he lost control of it," Julian said. "And of course you'd notice it if it popped up in the middle of your sofa."

"Godding said it was worth pawning."

"That doesn't mean it's actually worth that much money. It just has to be nice enough that it wouldn't look out of place in a respectable household."

"Surely someone would notice," Ned said again. "And before you say anything, more people's rooms aren't as cluttered as yours."

Julian grinned. "You haven't been in some of the drawing rooms I've visited. I've sometimes wondered how they could tell that anything was missing – there have been one or two clients where I'd swear they wouldn't notice if you added a stray dog or an extra child."

"But they did know they'd been burgled," Ned pointed out, and Julian nodded.

"True enough. Wait. Where would you not be surprised to see a moderately expensive object appear on a shelf even if you'd never seen it before?"

Ned shook his head.

"A pawnshop," Julian answered. "What was Godding's first thought? Pawn the thing, don't destroy it. And if that was the logical response, how many people would carry it to their nearest uncle and take the money, never intending to redeem it?"

"It's possible, I suppose," Ned said. "It would be a way of moving it without needing to handle it yourself or involve an accomplice."

"And there was one job that Bolster couldn't place, didn't know anyone who claimed to be involved, and that was robbery at a pawnshop. The pawnbroker died."

"And you can almost count on a pawnshop to have small and valuable items lying about," Ned said. "And if you choose right, they might even be stolen goods that the victim wouldn't dare report. I'll need to pass this to Hatton."

"There were other pawnshops on the list," Julian said, "but I left my copy with Bolster."

"Hatton will check. It does make sense."

Julian turned the idea over in his mind. It did fit, assuming that Punton had in fact meant to create a creature that would steal for him. Pawnshops were a reasonable target, and being able to abstract objects of value from a locked container, be it a display case, strongbox, or safe… "It does rather beg the question of why it killed Hall and Punton. And I imagine it would be wise to exhume the pawnbroker."

"A lovely thought," Ned said, with a grimace, "but yes."

Julian took another sip of his whisky. He was close, he thought, not quite there but close, and there was nothing more he could do until he'd heard what Hatton and Bolster had to say about the pawnshops. He glanced sideways at Ned, caught again by the gleam of the gaslight on his fair hair, the strong lines of shoulder and thigh. "How did you know how to handle the Godding boy?"

Ned looked for once faintly embarrassed. "When I first came up to London, I spent a certain amount of time in Piccadilly Circus."

"Hunting up Mary-Anns?"

Ned's mouth quirked into a wry smile. "Girls wouldn't have done me much good."

"Do you have any idea how dangerous that is? Never mind the clap, the number of men who are blackmailed for lesser sexual peccadillos –"

"I didn't use my real name," Ned said. "Besides, I did think it would have been obvious that I didn't have enough money to be worth blackmailing."

"Even so."

Ned shrugged. "I don't mind a bit of risk. You should know that."

That was true enough, something Julian remembered all too well from their school days, but he shook his head. "Still. It would have been safer to come to one of the clubs."

"I didn't know anyone who could introduce me," Ned pointed out. "And the ones I did know made it clear they didn't like me. You're the exception there."

"So it's better to pay young men for their services?"

"No, I –" Ned stopped, frowning slightly. "Lynes, are you jealous?" His voice was neither teasing nor angry, more honestly curious.

Julian hesitated a moment. "It's not my place to be."

Ned's frown deepened. "Then let's leave my previous vices out of the discussion."

"Fair enough." Julian leaned back in his corner of the sofa, aware that he was coming perilously close to sulking. Perhaps he was – not jealous, but envious, at least of Ned's ability to manage a situation that he himself had always avoided. "One thing. How did you know what to do, the first time?"

Ned blinked, and his frown dissolved into a rueful smile. "Muddled through somehow. I probably paid the boy more than his usual, and he certainly wasn't the best I ever had, but – God, I was desperate for it by then."

Julian's breath caught, imagining Ned with some young stranger. He wished again that they had taken Godding up on his offer, but realized that he didn't exactly want to share. What he wanted, in fact, was to see Ned in charge, to let him do what he wanted. "You don't have to be desperate any more."

Ned blinked again. "I'll take that as an offer."

"Do." Julian set his drink aside and stood, holding out his hand to draw Ned to his feet. Ned responded willingly enough, let himself be led to the bedroom, though he hesitated for an instant at the door. Julian shed his jacket, pulling off collar and tie and began unbuttoning his shirt. He wanted to say *tell me what you want me to do*, but at the last minute he couldn't manage the words, afraid he might not be able to carry through. "Why don't you fuck me?" he said instead, and Ned paused, unbuttoning his own shirt.

"Are you sure?"

"Of course." Julian dropped onto the edge of the bed, kicking off shoes and stockings, and a moment later Ned joined him, pressing him down under his weight.

❦

JULIAN LINGERED OVER HIS BREAKFAST, FEELING vaguely dissatisfied. Ned had left before midnight, which was part of it, of course, and partly he had to admit he was still perturbed by the notion of Ned in Piccadilly Circus. Not that he disapproved, even if he'd had any right to, but it woke all sorts of uncomfortable feelings that he really didn't want to think about today. Particularly since the previous night's indulgence had been less satisfactory than he'd expected, though he couldn't have quite said why. And if he couldn't say why, he couldn't fix the problem, and the whole thing would spiral down to nothing the way every other affair had done.

And that was another thought he didn't want to entertain. He poked unhappily at the bloater that had been provided for his delectation, unable to muster further appetite, then rang for the maid to take the plates away.

The first post was dismal, a letter from his banker and a note from a former client to distract him. The former was nothing more than a reminder that the dividend on his small inheritance was coming due, and that it would be deposited to his account unless he wished to handle it otherwise; the client was a bookmaker with an unhealthy fear of metaphysics who claimed to have a new problem with a man he'd sacked for taking money off the top. Julian was tempted to toss the letter on the fire and deny ever receiving it, but the man did pay well and promptly, and he made himself write back suggesting a meeting the following week. He took it to the corner postbox himself, but neither the prompt action nor the brisk wind gave him a sense of virtue. He dawdled instead, stopping at a pie shop behind the Museum to make up for his uneaten breakfast, then checking the news vendors for any special editions, before he returned to his rooms.

The next post had arrived in his absence, the letters slipped under his door, and he collected the envelopes eagerly, hoping that one of them might be from Ned. None was, of course; one was from Lennox, though, and he slit that one open first, unfolding the creamy paper.

My dear Lynes, if you're still determined to pursue that matter we spoke of, you'll be interested to know that Rudolph Ludgrove is back in town, quite possibly to stay. He was well acquainted with Challice at about that time, and might be able to answer some of your questions – but be kind. He's still quite fond of the old boy.

Julian refolded the note, started to put it in a pigeonhole of his desk, then reconsidered and dropped it into the fire, watching to be sure it burned without his having to resort to the poker. Not that there was anything compromising in it, but it was safer in the long run to keep no records, no mementos. His next move, then, should be to look up Ludgrove, preferably in some setting congenial enough to be sure he was able to talk freely. Ludgrove had always been an avid card-player, perhaps Jacobs' would be the place to look – or perhaps it would be better to get Lennox to make the connection, in which case Jacobs' was still the place to start. Surely Ned would be willing to join him, and surely that would take away some of the awkwardness of the previous evening. He scribbled a note before he could think better of it, and dispatched young Digby to post it.

He didn't expect a quick response – Ned had said that he was going to talk to Hatton, and that was likely to occupy a good part of his day – so the knock at the door came as a surprise.

"Yes?"

"If you will excuse my saying so, Mr Lynes, I am not the post office." His landlady brandished a grubby envelope at him. "And while I realize that you must take all sorts of client, I'd thank them to do their business in an ordinary way."

Julian grabbed the envelope, noting the lack of stamp and the penciled address. "And how the devil am I supposed to make them do that?" He made himself stop, remembering Ned's suggestions for staying on Mrs Digby's good side. "But, yes, I'll speak to whoever sent this."

"I would appreciate it if you would," Mrs Digby retorted, "being as no one here has time to search the hall for letters dropped at random through the mail slot. And, mark my words, if it's ever anything more than letters, you will be the first to hear about it, Mr Lynes."

She closed the door hard behind her in punctuation, and Julian swore. He rather doubted the woman had a good side, no matter what Ned said. The letter was from Bolster, of course. Julian tossed the envelope on the fire, and unfolded the plain inner sheet. It contained a list, in neat secretarial copperplate, of four addresses where burglaries involving sealed containers had taken place, and underneath it a different pen had added, *unclaimed burglaries from your list.* Julian scanned the names, and cursed again. Two were pawnbrokers'; the others were variously a private house and a business, and the rest of the pawnbrokers that had been on the list had obviously been eliminated. That didn't bode well for his theory about pawnshops. Of course, half of the burglaries were pawnshops, but – probably the best use of his time was to take another look at Punton's notes.

He rode the omnibus back up the Tottenham Court Road, shivering a little in the chill wind, then ducked through Blandings rather than go round the block to the Commons's main entrance. The outer door of Ned's chamber was open, and he knocked politely on the inner door. To his surprise, Ned opened it himself, his eyebrows going up in matching startlement.

"I was just about to send you a note."

Miss Frost's desk was empty, her hat and coat missing from their usual hook, and Julian relaxed in spite of himself.

Ned saw where he was looking, and perched on the edge of his own desk. "I sent Miss Frost back to the library to look out some other volumes. I think Punton must have used some other *maledictor* in his preparations, but I'm damned if I know what. I'd ask Oppenshaw, but he's out of the Commons for the day."

"It would be a grimoire, not a *maledictor*," Julian said absently, and shook his head. "But I think you may be right. I got an answer from Bolster."

"Ah. Were they pawnshops?"

"Two were and two weren't," Julian answered. "Which doesn't prove it, and doesn't rule it out either, though there were enough other pawnshops on the list that I'm inclined to think I was wrong."

"I wrote Hatton about the pawnbroker who died," Ned said, "and he says he's going to apply for an exhumation order."

Julian grimaced. "Makes me glad I'm not part of the police."

"Yes, well.

"Lennox wrote me that a friend of Challice's is back in the city," Julian said, after a moment. "He may know something about the ritual he was involved in."

"And that's why you invited me to Jacobs'?" Ned asked.

"Among other reasons." Julian shrugged. "I thought we could get dinner – at Blandings, maybe – and then see if we could find Lennox or Ludgrove. Ludgrove's a demon for cards, though."

Ned winced at that.

"I promised I wouldn't play at the Mercury," Julian said, "but the easiest way to get Ludgrove to talk is to lose a few hands of écarté."

"It's not your losing that worries me," Ned said.

"Win or lose, I'll control the cards," Julian answered. Ned seemed inclined to make something of it, and he hurried on. "In any case, are you game?"

"I've nothing better to do." Ned gave a slow smile, and in spite of himself Julian shivered with unexpected anticipation. Perhaps there would be time to make amends for the previous evening.

They made a slow dinner at Blandings, lingering over the wine and the cheese tray, but even so, they were early to Jacobs', and the main parlor was nearly empty. Lennox was there, however, settled at a favorite table by the massive bar, and he waved them over.

"Lynes and his paragon. Come and join me, my dears."

Julian leaned against the back of the nearest armchair, not wanting to encourage too much conversation. Ned was physically just the sort of man Lennox liked, but they had little else in common. "I got your letter."

"Oh, good, that saves complicated explanations." Lennox smiled up at him. "Ludgrove's here, up in the blue salon. I'd tackle him him now, if I were you, before he gets too involved in the cards. Don't worry, I'll keep your paragon company."

Julian swallowed a profane remark, knowing Lennox was right. "I should. It'll be easier for him to talk when there aren't too many strangers about."

"Go on," Ned agreed, with a smile. "Lennox and I will be fine."

There was nothing for it but to obey. Julian climbed the stairs, glancing back from the landing to see Ned fetching drinks for both of them. Not that he thought Ned would be interested – Ned was no fonder of opera than he himself was, and as a regular diet Lennox's artistic tastes were wearing – but Lennox was still quite good-looking, and, more to the point, had a graciousness about him that Julian knew he lacked. And that was not the point, he told himself firmly, and made his way to the blue salon.

It was nearly empty, too, with only the smell of tobacco and the curl of smoke rising from an armchair to betray that anyone was there. Julian made his way toward the drinks table, nodding to the man in passing, and saw with relief that Lennox had been right. Rudolph Ludgrove was a stocky, red-faced man, his evening dress just slightly out of fashion. He nodded at Julian's approach, and then his eyes narrowed in recognition.

"Lynes, isn't it?"

Julian nodded. "Hello, Ludgrove. I was hoping I might find you."

"Did I owe you money?" Ludgrove grinned, but there was a faint note of worry in his voice that belied the smile.

"Not me," Julian answered, with perfect truth, and lifted the decanter. "Can I freshen yours?"

"Don't mind if I do." Ludgrove let him refill the glass, watching with eyes that seemed lazy but were more alert than Julian remembered. "So what did you want from me? I can't think you sought me out for my *beaux yeux*."

It was a situation where the truth had a certain shock value. Julian said, "You remember that I'm a consulting detective?"

"Now I do." Ludgrove set his cigar aside. "Am I a suspect? Something dashingly desperate, I hope."

"You were friends with Challice," Julian said.

"And so were you. What of it?"

Julian seated himself on the hassock opposite the other man, close enough that anyone entering couldn't hear the conversation. "There was a very ugly story going around a few years back."

"I had nothing to do with that!"

"I never thought you did," Julian answered. "You were fond of him, too."

Ludgrove hesitated. "I was, the poor beast. In spite of all his scruples. And if you're fond of him at all, Lynes, leave that matter lie."

"I can't. I think it's connected to something that's been made my business –"

Ludgrove snorted. "Let it go. It can't be any worse."

"Two men are dead," Julian answered. "Perhaps a third."

"There are things worse than death."

There was nothing melodramatic in Ludgrove's tone, and Julian nodded slowly. "Agreed. I'd like to prevent any of them from happening."

Ludgrove sighed. "I'll tell you what I can, but I don't know much – I only heard about it after the fact, and Challice didn't want to give me details. But it was a cruel thing to do to the man, and all for what? Just to get one more chance at him."

"Was that all?" There had been a note of doubt in Ludgrove's voice, and Julian wasn't surprised when he hesitated.

"Certainly there was spite involved. That bloody Dorrington had it in for him, I'm not entirely sure why. I don't know what else they could have gotten from it. But then, I'm no metaphysician."

Julian nodded, unsurprised. "Do you know what they did? Any details of the ritual?"

Ludgrove blushed. "It's not nice telling."

"I don't doubt it."

"I don't think there was any real metaphysics in it," Ludgrove said. "Just spite and vice." He stopped, shaking his head. "I gather they cast a circle with all sorts of pomp and ceremony – incense, too, Challice mentioned that particularly, something very strong and smoky that made them all a little dizzy. And then Dorrington said some sort of cantrip over him and they took their turns buggering him. And they wouldn't let him come until they were all done, and then they mixed the result in wine or something and made him drink it." He shook his head again. "Sheer nastiness, I think, and told him so. Or was I wrong?"

"I don't know," Julian said. On the surface, no, it didn't make a great deal of sense, but it bore a certain resemblance to some of the sexual enchantments he'd heard of, and some of the correspondences from Punton's notes seemed to have had a sexual intent. "I don't think it would do what was promised, no. But I don't know what was intended instead, if anything."

"There probably wasn't." Ludgrove tossed back the last of his drink, and Julian took their glasses and refilled them. "Challice turned Dorrington down flat – said he wouldn't if he was the last man on earth, and a few less complimentary things."

"You were there?"

"Oh, yes. I can't say that I disagreed, but it wasn't precisely tactful. And Dorrington's one to hold a grudge." Ludgrove shook his head again. "That must have been a good year before the other."

"It was a group ritual," Julian said. "Dorrington was involved –"

"It was his bloody idea," Ludgrove said.

"Who else, do you know?"

Ludgrove shook his head. "Challice wouldn't tell me. I only know about Dorrington because I guessed."

"You must have some idea."

Ludgrove sighed. "Well, where there's Dorrington, there's usually Leach. And he's no nicer in his tastes. I'd lay money on him, but for the rest? I simply don't know. Farrell was part of that crowd. That poet, what's his name – Kennett? And that journalist, Sparkes or Peacock, whatever he calls himself these days."

"Peacock," Julian said.

"Tubby Barnes, and the Cochrane who wasn't in the Navy. But I don't know if any of them were involved in the ritual, Lynes. They're just people who were friends of Dorrington's."

"I understand," Julian answered. Kennett's was not a name he had expected to hear, or the non-naval Cochrane, but he hid his surprise. "What about either Dolly Hall or Alfred Punton?"

"Punton. That's vaguely familiar. Some sort of secretary or something?"

"That's right."

"He might have been part of the group? But I don't know Hall. Sorry."

"You've been very helpful," Julian said. The club had been getting busier while they spoke, more voices and footsteps in the hall, and now the door swung open to admit a trio that Julian knew only by sight. "Thank you."

"I doubt it's much help, but you're welcome," Ludgrove answered. He shook himself, set his glass aside with a determined smile. "Now – care for a hand of écarté? I've missed decent play living down in Kent."

It seemed only fair, and Julian nodded. "Why not? I've a friend to meet later, but there's plenty of time."

CHAPTER ELEVEN
A Game of Cards

JULIAN'S INVESTIGATION WAS APPARENTLY GOING WELL, Ned thought, as he accepted another round of drinks from Lennox. At least, he had been closeted in the blue salon with Ludgrove for some considerable time. Ned told himself there was no other probable explanation for the fact. All the same, he found himself draining his drink more thirstily than was probably wise.

"How did you ever meet Lynes?" Lennox asked, considering Ned over the rim of his own glass with frank curiosity. "Not that I can fault his taste in this instance, but I will admit you're something of a surprise."

Ned felt the itch of curiosity himself. Julian had assured him that he harbored no romantic interest in Lennox, but he spoke of him with more genuine warmth than some of the rest of his circle of acquaintances. If acquaintances was the word for gentlemen one had carnal relations with.

The question distracted him, and he found himself replying more honestly than he intended. "Because his taste is generally poor?"

"Well, I do like to except myself," Lennox said with good humor. "But even that wasn't the best of matches. You seem more well-suited, and at the same time not at all what I think anyone would have placed their wagers on."

"Lynes and I were at school together," Ned said. "We were in the same house at Sts Thomas's. That's where we met."

Lennox shook his head in apparent amusement at the mental image thus produced. "It's hard to imagine Lynes as a schoolboy."

"It didn't suit him. I can swear to it that he was in fact a child when I met him – we were all of twelve years old – but he never did get on with other children."

"I should think not. Rather brutal, public schools."

That cut a bit close, but there was no mockery in Lennox's eyes. And Julian trusted the man, from the way he spoke of him. Julian might not have been discriminating in his choice of bed partners, but Ned was well aware that his trust was never given lightly.

"It was a bit rough and tumble," Ned admitted. "And Lynes had never been in school before, you know – he'd had tutors when he was younger."

Lennox shook his head more soberly. "I can't imagine what his father was thinking."

"Neither of his parents was living, even then. I gather some elderly relative brought him up, as much as anyone did." It seemed a more tactful way of saying *Lynes was raised by wolves.*

"That may explain a great deal about Lynes," Lennox said.

"Lynes is a particular friend," Ned said, a little defensively.

"And you're devoted to him, I can see that, dear boy. I'm very fond of Lynes myself. But not in the same way, there's no cause to for you to bristle. Lynes and I make far better friends than lovers."

"He never has liked opera."

"One of his faults," Lennox said, but his wry smile made it clear the joke was on himself as much as on Julian. "Lynes is an utter philistine, and better off with a companion who won't want to throttle him for sleeping through the second act. Besides, I don't have much taste for being ordered about, at my time of life."

"I take it he's always like that."

"Always to my knowledge."

"It's not that I dislike it," Ned said. It was the drink, probably, that made him speak so freely, that or the singular chance to talk to someone who might possibly understand. "It's only that I wonder sometimes if he prefers always winning to actually doing what he'd like. Whatever that is."

"Well, Lynes does like to win," Lennox said. "I don't know if you've ever played cards with him –"

"Not for stakes I minded losing."

"That's probably best." Lennox's eyes sparkled for a moment. "Where did he learn to cheat at cards so well? Surely not at an upstanding public school."

"Out of a book of conjurer's tricks, if you can believe that," Ned said. "He smuggled it into school so he could learn how to escape from knots – he said it might come in handy if we were ever stranded in the Amazon, or that sort of thing."

"A practical modern education."

"I don't know if he ever managed the rope tricks, but he did learn some shocking tricks with cards. I take it he's practiced them here."

"On many occasions."

"There do seem to have been many occasions," Ned said. "He seems to have made friends quickly."

"Jealous?" There was no criticism in the question, only the tone of a physician listening to a recitation of familiar symptoms.

"Perplexed," Ned admitted. "I can't fathom his taste. Present company excluded."

"Very kind, dear boy." Lennox shook his head. "Lynes turned a great many heads when he first joined us, and I don't think he was used to the attention. I think at first he simply said yes every time he was asked."

"Which was often."

"You must admit he's handsome."

"Well, I think so."

"Take it from me, you're not the only one."

"He does seem to have...burned some bridges in the process."

"Mmm, well. I don't think Lynes is particularly gifted at making friends." Ned suspected that was also a tactful way of saying *Lynes was raised by wolves.* "And some people will persist in hearing promises that were never made."

"You don't think he..." Ned faltered on the words, feeling far too exposed, but forged doggedly onward. "Professed false affections in order to obtain..."

"I don't think he generally needed to," Lennox said. "I haven't heard any credible report of Lynes ever professing affections for anyone at all. If he's declared himself to you, you may take it as a singular honor."

"Some of his friends seem to feel otherwise."

"Some of his friends will take 'I want to fuck you, bend over' to mean 'let us now consummate our undying love,'" Lennox said. "I understand some young women suffer from the same affliction. Lynes may have been slow to recognize the telltale signs – I wouldn't put it past him to put a tendency to gaze calf-like into his eyes down to myopia – but I don't believe he did anything to lead on his admirers. Besides go to bed with them."

"As long as they did whatever he liked," Ned said.

Lennox tsked. "Not to your taste?"

"No, I...most of the time I rather like it," Ned said. He'd never considered the matter as something that could be baldly weighed over drinks. It was certainly not anything that could ever have been broached at the Mercury, even if young women had been involved. "But there are times when I admit it's wearing. And sometimes I'm not even certain it's what he truly wants."

Lennox drummed his fingers thoughtfully on the rim of his glass. "I think that there are things he dislikes," he said. "Strongly dislikes. And as long as he has the upper hand completely, he won't be asked to do them and have to refuse."

"He can't imagine I'd want him to do anything he didn't like," Ned said, a bit indignantly. "Why wouldn't he simply say..."

"Does that seem like the sort of thing Lynes would say?"

Ned let out a frustrated breath. He had to admit that Lennox had a point. Julian hated to show any weakness; he'd never liked to, even at twelve, and he'd learned in their school days that flinching was a reliable way to attract more punishment. There was usually no need to talk about the things that troubled them, as most of their nightmares about their school years were shared ones.

But perhaps not all, and then they'd drifted apart at Oxford. He had the helpless feeling that he'd missed something then, some critical period when Julian was exploring what he liked and didn't, without Ned there alongside him. And now he didn't know, and all his efforts to determine where the lines were seemed to end in the mutual decision that it was easier for Julian to simply tell him what to do rather than tell him what he might like.

"Not at all," he admitted.

"I think you ought to tie him up and make him tell you all about it if he wants you to untie him." It was hard to tell from Lennox's tone whether he was teasing or not. "He might enjoy that."

"He'd probably escape from the knots," Ned said.

Lennox shrugged and sipped at his drink. "Only if he wanted to."

JULIAN COUNTED UP THE FINAL TRICKS, added the last points, and nodded across the table. "Your game," he said, and pushed the stack of coins toward Ludgrove, who accepted them with alacrity.

"Care for another round?"

Julian shook his head. It wasn't hard to lose to Ludgrove, who was a good player; it didn't even require manipulating the cards as he dealt them, just that he make one or two bad choices – accept an exchange when he should have kept his hand intact, or play his strongest card too soon. He tried not to begrudge the money – he could certainly afford it, the stakes had been small enough, but he hated losing even when he knew it was politic. "I promised a friend I'd come and find him."

"I heard about that," Ludgrove said. "Someone told me you'd found your match at last?"

Julian could feel the blood rising under his skin, and hoped the gaslight hid his blush. "People do talk," he said, in what he hoped was a suitably repressive tone of voice, and made his escape.

Neither Ned nor Lennox were in the main parlor. Julian fetched himself another drink, dodging an invitation to join the party getting up a chemin de fer table, and turned back to the card rooms. He found them in the smaller of the ground floor salons, settled at the corner table with a decanter to make the rounds, and for a moment he simply stood and watched, caught again by the strength of Ned's profile, the sure movements of his hands as he fanned his cards and made his discard: poker, the game was. Lennox smiled knowingly from the opposite side of the table, and Julian came to lean on the back of Ned's chair. Ned glanced up at him with a quick half-smile of his own, and returned his attention to his cards. At Lennox's left, Jesperson shook his head.

"Be careful, Mathey, Lynes is a demon for cards."

"I think I'm safe for the moment," Ned answered, and slid a counter into the pot. "Call."

Julian watched the play, unsurprised to see Ned fold when the draw failed to improve his pair of sevens, equally unsurprised to see Jesperson almost carry the pot with a bare-faced bluff and a pair of threes. Lennox won the hand, amid much surprised laughter, and he immediately pushed back his chair.

"That's it, I'm done for the night. Lynes, why don't you take my chair?"

"Unfair," Squires said, with a grin. "I didn't come to play with him."

"Afraid of me?" Julian asked, and slid into Lennox's seat.

"I've played with you before," Squires retorted, but he took the deck from Ned. "Everyone else in? The game is five-card draw, gentlemen."

Julian accepted his cards, aware that Ned was watching him with something between fascination and horror. There was very little he could do if he didn't have the deal, and he concentrated instead on the pattern of play, the small betrayals he'd learned over the last several years. Squires would draw two cards when he had three of a kind; Julian folded demurely, and watched Ned lose the pot to Alec Anderson.

He refrained from manipulating the cards when it was his turn to deal, and saw Ned relax slightly as the hand played out without surprises. The deal went round again, the stakes low enough that even Squires, who had been losing steadily, couldn't say he'd lost more than a few pounds, but as the clock on the mantel struck one, Squires pushed away his last hand.

"That's it for me, gentlemen."

"One more round," Anderson protested.

Squires shook his head. "I've lost as much as I care to, thank you."

"Are you sure you're not a Scot?" Jesperson asked.

"Change the stakes," Anderson suggested. "Shilling bids."

"I've a better idea," Jesperson said, with a grin. "Let's play for forfeits."

There was a murmur of amused approval from Anderson, and Squires hesitated. "One hand, then."

"What are the bids?" Ned asked. To Julian's relief, he sounded more curious than either shocked or unhappy, and Anderson gave him a grin.

"Kisses, usually. Though if you'd like to bid higher…"

"We'll see," Ned answered, with a slow smile of his own, and Julian caught his breath, all too aware of the tightening in his groin. It was his deal, he could force the cards, give every one of them the hand he chose. And if he chose… The thought of bending Ned over the card table was astonishingly arousing, and he met Ned's eyes squarely.

"If you're in, so am I."

Squires passed him the cards, and Julian weighed the deck in his hands, glancing around the table as he began to shuffle.

"We're all agreed, then, gentlemen? A game of forfeits, and we'll each risk a kiss to start? And whatever else we dare?" As he spoke, his fingers were busy, shifting cards as he shuffled, each move smooth and easy, covered by the daring words. He received a murmur of agreement, and a nod from Ned, but paused one last time. "All certain? Last chance to change your minds."

"Get on with it, man," Anderson said.

Julian smiled. "Here you are." He dealt the cards neatly, knowing exactly what each man had and what he would have to deal next to control the outcome. Two fives for Jesperson, enough to keep him in the game at least one more round but not good enough to win; two clubs for Anderson, possibly enough to tempt him to try to draw for a flush; three aces for Ned, second best at the table, two diamonds for Squires, and the beginnings of a straight for himself.

Jesperson smiled and slid a shilling across the table. "Let's call that a kiss."

"Done," Anderson said, and matched him with a shilling of his own.

Ned did the same, an odd smile on his face, but Squires shook his head, and slid the cards away face down. "I'm done."

Julian slid a shilling of his own into the pot, smiling, and looked at Jesperson, who looked at his hand again.

"Three," he said, and laid his discards face down on the table.

"Three for me, too," Anderson said, and Ned pulled a single card from his hand.

"One."

"Two for me," Julian said, suiting his action to his words, and picked up the deck. He knew the next cards, knew no one but himself would be getting anything of any use, and he dealt the cards with careful precision. Jesperson frowned for the briefest instant, but slid two shillings toward the center of the table.

"A kiss and a feel."

Anderson shook his head, turned his cards face down. "I'm out."

Word of the stake had spread, Julian realized; Lennox was leaning on the mantelpiece, murmuring something arch in the ear of the painter MacNab, while three or four others were watching with frank curiosity.

"Agreed," Ned said, and pushed two shillings into the middle of the table.

"And for me," Julian said, and did the same. With the draw, he had dealt himself a ten-high straight, enough to win against anything at the table; now it was just a matter of managing the stakes and waiting for Jesperson to realize he couldn't win.

And, on cue, Jesperson looked at his hand again, and heaved a sigh. "I'm out."

Julian smiled across the table, knowing he'd won, and Ned studied his hand again. "Why don't we make this interesting?" he asked. "The winner can demand whatever he wants of the loser."

There was a murmur of interest from the growing audience, and Julian had to wet his lips before he could answer. "All right. Yes, I agree. Winner takes all."

Ned smiled, and laid his hand on the table. "Four aces."

Julian caught his breath. That was not the hand he'd dealt him – three aces, yes, but not four – and he just had the presence of mind to close his mouth sharply over his automatic protest. He turned over his own cards, revealing the losing straight, and there was a little patter of applause.

"Oh, well played," Lennox said, and went so far as to pat Ned on the shoulder.

Julian took a breath. However Ned had done it – and Ned had cheated, there was no other way he could have obtained that result – he had won outright and he could collect his forfeit. There was nothing to do but go through with it, and the thought stirred unexpected excitement in him. He spread his hands. "You win."

"Yes." Ned pushed back his chair, and came around the table. Julian rose to meet him, and Ned took his face in both hands, kissing him thoroughly. The room erupted with laughing approval, and Ned caught his breath. "The rest – let's find a room upstairs, shall we?"

"I'm at your disposal," Julian answered, and let Ned steer him from the room.

€✿

NED SHUT THE DOOR OF THE upstairs room behind them firmly, and then turned to enjoy the look on Julian's face.

"You *cheated*," Julian said, as if he'd been trying to hold back the words since the moment Ned turned over four aces.

"So did you."

"That's not the point."

Ned tried not to look too smug. "Didn't anyone ever tell you not to play cards with metaphysicians?"

It had been a simple variation of the same *gather together* enchantment he'd been using all week, simple enough to trace idly on the bottom of the table while Julian's attention was occupied with sleight of hand. Useless if the missing ace had been already dealt, but he knew Julian's practices at the card table through painful experience, and he'd been certain that fourth ace was still in the deck to come when he called.

Julian let out a breath in rueful amusement. "You usually let me win."

"So I do," Ned said. "But not tonight. And now you owe me a forfeit." He watched Julian's face, half-expecting him to argue that the bargain wasn't a fair one if Ned hadn't won fairly, and never mind that Julian had been dealing off the bottom of the deck.

Instead Julian drew himself up, his whole body taut with what might have been either arousal or reluctance or some volatile combination of the two. It was impossible to be sure, and his tone gave no clue. "Tell me what you want, and I'll do it," he said.

It was a heady prospect, and Ned couldn't deny the surge of arousal he felt at hearing the words. He ran his hand down the line of Julian's jaw, feeling the light rasp of stubble under his fingers, and Julian turned his head, his throat working hard.

"Anything I want." Ned could feel Julian's pulse hammering against his hand. He worked his other hand into the knot of Julian's necktie, holding him by it, their bodies pressed close enough that he could feel Julian's erection, Julian's breath coming as fast as if they were already grappling. His original plan was beginning to seem needlessly complex compared to the craving to tug Julian downward and tell him to get to work.

"Those were the stakes," Julian said, raising his chin, and took hold of Ned's lapels as if to steady himself on the way down to his knees. It was his expression that stopped him at the last, not arousal but a determination not to flinch that Ned remembered all too well from their schoolboy days. He took a deep breath, reason reasserting itself.

"Very well," Ned said, letting go with an effort that felt herculean. "What I want is for you to tell me what you like and dislike in bed. In complete and explicit detail."

Julian let go of Ned's lapels as if they had burned him. "You want what?"

"You heard me."

"But…"

"Anything I want. Those were the stakes."

"But surely that's not what you want."

"It's exactly what I want," Ned said. It was what he'd wanted for some time, and there might never be as good an opportunity again to get it.

Julian opened and closed his mouth like a fish. "Wouldn't you rather fuck me instead?"

"No, I don't think so."

"I could suck you off."

"Do you actually like doing that?"

He could see Julian hesitating, torn between the impulse to shrug off the question and the knowledge that the forfeit was fair, and he owed it. And he wanted to answer, Ned thought, at least in part, or he would have argued his way out of the bet as easily as he could have slipped free of any knot that bound him.

Julian let out a breath. "I would rather not. Not that in particular. But I don't mind being fucked. You could tell me to –"

"I want a list," Ned said firmly.

"A list."

"Of everything you can think of to do in bed, and whether you like it or not."

"And suppose I don't know?"

"You mean to say you haven't tried it all already?"

"Well, not everything."

"Then say so."

"Well, I suppose I…" Julian began, and then seemed entirely unable to go on. Ned felt a certain degree of mercy was indicated.

"You could write it down, if that would be easier. And then we could burn the list once I've read it."

Julian sank into a chair by the small writing table, where pen and ink stood ready. "Can I have a drink first?"

"Of course," Ned said, and poured him a stiff one.

Julian took up the pen, and then hesitated. "I'm not sure there's anything else I wouldn't at least try. That is – with you."

Ned rested his hand on Julian's shoulder, understanding how much of a declaration that was coming from Julian. "Make the list." After all, there might be things worth trying that he'd never thought of.

Julian's cheeks were flushed by the time he had finished, but he had produced a neatly ruled list in three columns, headed *yes*, *possibly*, and *no*. The no column was short, but blessedly informative; the other columns were intriguing.

"I don't think I should like to do that," Ned said, taking up the pen to point at an item a bit too reminiscent of brutal school punishments. "Or that."

"I didn't think you would," Julian said. "But you said to be thorough –"

"Just so." He considered the rest of the *possibly* column. I don't suppose I have actual objections to wearing ladies' clothing, but I can't say I see the point of it."

"I don't either, particularly, but if you particularly wanted to try it…"

"Not my taste, old man. And I'd look absurd."

"Admittedly, you would."

"On the other hand, the idea of having other people watch us is…" He couldn't help thinking of the Dionysus. "Interesting," he finished.

Julian's eyebrows went up, and then came back down as he frowned. "It would depend on who was watching," he said slowly. "And what exactly we were doing. I don't think I would like to be bent over a footstool for an audience."

Ned went down on his knees in front of Julian's chair, sitting back on his heels to look up at him. "And suppose I were on my knees to you for an audience?"

"You wouldn't," Julian said, but his lips twitched in the beginnings of a smile.

"Are you certain of that?"

"No," Julian said, with what sounded like interest. "No, I'm not certain at all."

"We can burn the list now if you like," Ned offered.

"Yes, please," Julian said fervently. Julian handed the piece of paper to Ned, who straightened and went to feed it to the fire. Julian leaned over the back

149

of the chair to watch, not settling back until the paper had been entirely consumed by the flames.

"I don't always mind being told what to do in bed," Ned said. "I rather like it."

Julian looked up at him soberly. "That's good to know."

"But you might *ask* if you can tell me what to do."

Julian blinked. "Yes, I suppose that's fair."

"And sometimes I should like you to do as I ask without too much argument. If it's something you're certain you like."

"That also seems fair," Julian said, with an expression that combined arousal with a degree of tension that suggested he had been pushed nearly as far as he could bear at the moment. There was no need to push him further, not when they'd established there would be other times for that. Ned came back instead and settled down on his knees again in front of Julian's chair, raising his chin to look up at him.

"Now do you want to tell me what to do?"

"God, yes," Julian said, and caught Ned by the shirt front to pull him in. His instructions after that were blunt and breathless, and Ned was well content to follow them.

☾❀

CHAPTER TWELVE
Another Death

J ULIAN SIPPED HIS COFFEE WITH SOMETHING approaching contentment, which was somewhat surprising, considering the previous night's events. Of course, it helped that he'd figured out how Ned had beaten him, and perhaps he would prefer to avoid Jacobs' for a week or so, at least until the smirks and speculative glances had died down, though most of the comments he'd heard as they'd left had been along the lines of *so Lynes has met his match*. There was something oddly gratifying about having his connection with Ned acknowledged, just as there was something alarmingly exciting about Ned's telling him what to do. The thought was enough to make him blush, and to stir the blood elsewhere, and he turned his thoughts firmly into other channels.

He needed to speak to Kennett first of all. Kennett needed to be told that Dorrington was the blackmailer, and that he was, at least for the moment, scotched; Julian also wanted to have a word with him about Ludgrove's assertion that he'd been part of the circle that had tormented Challice, but he wasn't at all sure this was the time for it. Ned would probably argue that it was unethical to accuse your client of non-conforming magic at the same time as you solved their problems, and it certainly made getting paid for one's services a bit more dicey even than usual. And yet… Julian shook his head. He'd have to see how things played out, and the first step was arranging a meeting. The man was damnably hard to lay hold of at the best of times, but he drafted a quick note and sent a copy to Kennett's most respectable club as well as to his house. If that failed, he'd try the clubs directly, always assuming they'd let him in. Perhaps a closer shave and a better suit were in order.

Kennett's answer came by the eleven o'clock post: an invitation to join him for a late lunch. Julian suppressed a groan – the Fine Arts Club had a reputation for stultifying propriety – but scribbled his acceptance and dropped it in the post.

He presented himself at the main entrance promptly at two o'clock, soberly dressed in his best frock coat and top hat. An elderly steward admitted him and brought him to the Visitors' Lounge, where thick velvet curtains shut out the watery sunlight, and a meager fire burned in the enormous hearth. The gaslights had been turned low, and the room was chilly. Julian eyed the nearly empty coal scuttle, trying to think of some metaphysical trick he could use to improve the fire but without fuel... He suspected someone would notice if he burned one of the expensive magazines that reposed temptingly on the sideboard.

The door opened to admit Kennett, very neat in a dove-gray suit and a pale green waistcoat, a spray of tiny white flowers in his buttonhole. "There you are, Lynes. I'm glad you could join me. I hope there's some good news?"

Julian nodded. "I think we've settled the matter."

Kennett's eyes fluttered closed for just an instant. "Thank God. You don't know how worried I've been." He broke off, shaking his head. "But I promised you luncheon, and they're just at the last seating. Let's eat, shall we, and you can tell me how you did it."

The dining room was on the first floor, a long, narrow room with tall windows that overlooked a severely tended garden, the now-empty beds converging on a chaste and rather chilly-looking Muse. The curtains were drawn back to give a full view of the dead leaves swirling across the brick walks, and Julian couldn't help lifting an eyebrow.

"That's atmospheric."

Kennett gave it a distracted glance. "Oh. That. There's been a disagreement on what should be done with the design, and there's not been a decisive vote. It's all we can do just to keep it maintained while the Board argues about it." He turned his attention to the waiter who appeared at his elbow, and Julian let him order, offering only monosyllabic agreement as Kennett debated the choice of soup, and considered the relative merits of hock and the new *vin primeur* before settling on the latter and a salmis of pheasant.

At least Kennett's taste in food was reliable. Julian had to admit that the soup was better than anything he'd get at any of his usual haunts, and the light *vin primeur* was a perfect complement to the delicately spiced salmis. He said as much to Kennett, and saw the waiter roll his eyes.

Kennett pulled an apologetic face. "Some of the older members feel it's too spicy. Too many foreign kickshaws to give them liverish complaints. But the chef does try to include at least one more sophisticated choice."

The waiter rolled his eyes once more before withdrawing. Julian hid his smile. "As I said, I do have good news. I believe Mathey and I have resolved the problem. Assuming you haven't heard anything more of it?"

Kennett shook his head. "I hadn't, though I hardly dared hope. You're sure?"

"As sure as I can be." Julian poured them each another glass of wine. "I pointed out that I could hurt him just as badly, and therefore it would be to his advantage to let the matter drop entirely."

"You didn't −" Kennett broke off with a gasp, and Julian shook his head, guessing the question.

"Of course not."

"No, no." Kennett forced a smile. "I'm sorry, Lynes, of course you didn't. This has all been a bit wearing."

"I'm sure." Julian glanced around the dining room, not particularly crowded, at least not so late in the day, but there were still too many occupied tables, not to mention the busy staff, to risk a frank conversation. "I'd be glad to give you all the details, but perhaps someplace more private."

"Quite." Kennett gulped his wine as though it were a tonic. "Yes. And I am grateful. Have you read Morrison's latest?"

"No." Julian hoped his flat refusal would end that topic, but instead Kennett nodded.

"Quite right, it's dreadful twaddle. Amusing, in places, but ultimately nothing more than trifles."

"If you say so."

"Oh, I assure you."

"The only Morrison I know runs a receiver's shop in Somers Town," Julian said. "A reasonable man, in his way."

Kennett stared at him in horror, then burst out laughing. "My God, Lynes!"

Julian shrugged, and applied himself to the salmis. Kennett continued his monologue through the salad course and the pudding, then suggested they end with a whisky in the library.

"I thought you wanted to talk privately," Julian answered, but followed him down the thickly-carpeted hall.

The library was much as he'd expected, a large, generously-proportioned room with floor-to-ceiling shelves and heavy furniture. Here the curtains were brocade, and closed, and the gaslights flickered in the enormous chandelier;

more lamps stood on the half-dozen individual writing tables, and the fire was warm and well-tended. One large case held dozens of morocco-bound volumes, each with the club's shield on the spine: the members' books, Julian guessed, and found Kennett's name among them. The room was empty, and Kennett led them to the sideboard where he mixed them each a whisky and soda.

"Let's sit by the fire, it's the only comfortable spot in this drafty pile."

"So why isn't it occupied?" Julian settled himself in what proved to be quite a comfortable armchair with a good view of the only door.

"My dear, none of this lot actually reads." Kennett took a quick swallow of his drink. "So, out with it. How did you fix things?"

Probably none of the members wanted to expose their taste to too many questions, Julian thought, and put his own drink aside barely tasted. "First of all, we put a name to the letters. Pinky Dorrington."

"Pinky?" For a moment, Kennett's face was blank with shock, and then he flushed deeply. "That – oh, the bastard. You're sure?"

"Absolutely." Julian watched him closely, but he could read nothing more than anger and embarrassment in Kennett's face.

"That's – it's just like him." Kennett shook his head. "And he's stubborn, once he gets his teeth in an idea – but you said you'd stopped him."

"I've put myself in a position to cause him as much trouble as he'd cause you," Julian answered. "If he reveals your secret, he'll lose his stature in the literary community as well."

"I'm glad somebody's got something on him," Kennett said. "He's a menace." He glanced sideways at Julian. "I don't suppose you'd care to share this threat?"

Julian shook his head. "It's something only I can do, I'm afraid. I must say you're taking it well. I'd heard you and Dorrington were old friends."

"I don't dare be anything but," Kennett said bitterly. "Not with his reviews in the *Athenaeum* and the *National* and a monthly column in *The Sketch*. Why do you think he has so many admirers? It's not for his dulcet tongue." He drained the rest of his whisky. "And now, my dear, I really must be going. Send me your bill at once, you've earned every penny of it."

❦

"AND THAT," JULIAN SAID, SETTLED ON Ned's sofa with the last of the claret and a wedge of shortbread from the Harrods' tin on the sideboard, "is exactly as far as I got with Kennett about his friendship with Dorrington."

"Do you think he was trying to cut you short?" Ned asked, stretching his legs toward the fire.

Julian shrugged. "He does work, I'll give him that. He keeps regular hours, just as if he were at an office. I couldn't really tell." He finished the last of the shortbread as he considered. "I don't think he likes Dorrington –"

"I'm shocked."

"Yes, well. Not a lovable man, Pinky. But, no, I think Kennett actively dislikes him."

"That doesn't preclude him having been in some sort of circle with him," Ned said. "Though I'd prefer to do that sort of thing with someone I at least trusted."

"How many men could he know who dabble in non-conforming magic?" Julian asked. "There can't be that many of them. Maybe it's all a quid pro quo, you help with my idea, and I'll work on yours."

"That's possible," Ned said. "And for a ritual that's so sexual in nature – no, I wouldn't think you'd have a large pool of men to draw on."

"The trouble is, I can't be sure of any of them." Julian grimaced. "Except Dorrington, of course, and that's not precisely helpful."

"I can't see an easy way to get answers there, no."

Julian sighed. "I'll talk to Kennett again, I suppose. Peacock, though I haven't seen him around much these days. And there's Leach, God help me." He gave Ned a sidelong glance. "I might want your company there."

Ned lifted his glass. "Any time, old boy."

"Of course, the person who'd be the most help is Challice, but –" Julian shook his head. "I'll start with Kennett. Have you had a chance to give Miss Barton the good news?"

"I asked Miss Frost to pass the word," Ned answered. "She could do it much more discreetly than I. Though I'd be sorry if she gave up writing altogether."

"If you say so."

"You might like *The Governess and the Tiger*," Ned said, mildly. "Though the metaphysics are a bit harrowing."

Julian glanced over his shoulder to be sure the door was locked. "I know what I'd like better. That is, if you were willing."

"Very likely," Ned answered, and Julian caught his lapels to pull him closer.

❦

NED WOKE TO THE SOUND OF knocking, and blinked in the pre-dawn light.

"Mr Mathey?" Mrs Clewett called from the hall outside.

Julian pushed himself up on one elbow, startled, but hardly needing Ned's warning gesture to be quiet. Ned threw on his dressing gown and went to answer the knock, taking care to shut the bedroom door behind him.

"I'm sorry to wake you, Mr Mathey, but I have this letter for you," Mrs Clewett said, handing it over. "The boy who brought it said it was urgent police business." She sounded impressed by the last.

"I hope he didn't wake you," Ned said as he opened the envelope.

"Bless your heart, Mr Mathey, it's gone six. I haven't slept as late as this since Mr Clewett passed. I'll have your breakfast up to you in no time."

The message was terse, in Hatton's scrawl: *We've got another one*, followed by an address.

"Never mind breakfast," Ned said. "I'm afraid I had better go straight away."

"Poor lamb," Mrs Clewett said, and Ned retreated back into his flat to avoid being lectured on how keeping early hours was surely ruining his health.

"It's all right," he said, and Julian emerged cautiously from the bedroom, buttoning his shirt. "Hatton's found another corpse." It occurred to him as soon as he'd spoken that "all right" was probably not the most tactful way to describe the situation, but Julian didn't seem to notice.

"Who's this one?"

"No idea. We'd better go round and take a look."

Ned felt privately certain the invitation had been extended only to him, but he wasn't about to turn down Julian's company if he was going to have to look at another corpse before breakfast. Besides, it might well be another one of Julian's fellow clubmen – which would be a reason to spare him, if Ned didn't know Julian well enough to know that he'd hate being kept in the dark worse than any gruesome sight.

"Just give me a moment to dress," he added.

Their cab deposited them outside a townhouse, once someone's fashionable town address, now cut up into flats and sinking into genteel decay. The maidservant who opened the door to them was wringing her apron into nervous knots.

"We're with Inspector Hatton," Ned said.

She nodded, eyes wide. "First floor," she said, not much above a whisper.

Ned ascended the stairs, Julian at his heels, and stopped at the open door to the first floor flat. "Hatton?"

"There you are, Mathey," Hatton said. "Lynes. We've got another customer. Maid came in to lay the fire and found him as you see him. Housekeeper tried some domestic enchantment to keep the blood from spreading, and the hearthrug caught fire."

"When was this?" Julian asked.

"Maybe five a.m. We were called in directly – apparently it's gotten through to some members of the public that it's the Metaphysical Squad for enchantment run amok."

"Those household charms can be tricky," Ned said, and then stopped short as he stepped far enough into the room to see the corpse.

It was Pinky Dorrington, sprawled on the hearthrug in pyjamas and dressing gown, his glasses askew on his face, one lens cracked. Blood had dried on his forehead, arms, and face from what looked like dozens of shallow cuts.

Julian stayed frozen for a moment himself, and then circled the corpse, looking down. "These marks don't make sense," he said.

"I know," Hatton said. "They're not defensive wounds, and not what you'd see in an explosion – these aren't shrapnel wounds. So what are they?"

Ned went down on one knee next to the body, trying not to let his mind race over possibilities – had Dorrington been a member of the circle experimenting with non-conforming magic? Or had his habit of blackmail finally caught up with him? They'd told both Kennett and Barton who their blackmailer had been –

"You're thinking it may be non-conforming magic," he said.

"The hearthrug made me think," Hatton said.

"Better safe than sorry." One of the cuts extended under Dorrington's collar, and Ned frowned and peeled the fabric away. "I think there are more wounds under his clothes."

"He might have been dressed after his death," Hatton said.

"He might have been," Ned agreed cautiously, opening the man's pyjama top.

"But he wasn't," Julian said. "Look at the way he's bled –"

"The blood isn't smeared," Hatton agreed. "It's soaked in as if someone laid a cloth directly over the wounds. Not like he pulled on pyjamas over them, much less like someone wrestled them onto him."

"Which suggests enchantment," Ned said. He hesitated, uncertain how much to say. "Not one of the usual curses. It may well be non-conforming."

"In which case we'd better get him back to the Yard and open him up," Hatton said. "I'd be interested to know if his heart is missing."

"It seems likely, doesn't it? The visible wounds can't have been fatal."

"He didn't bleed to death, no," Hatton said. "There's not enough blood here for that." He stood and considered the sitting room, which was lined with bookshelves and cluttered with still more books. "I suppose we'll have to go through this lot for any signs that he was mixed up in metaphysics. Like finding a needle in a haystack."

"I can help with that," Ned offered, wondering what else might lurk in the depths of Dorrington's book collection.

"Good of you. This one's an Alfred Dorrington, by the way. Literary critic." Hatton fingered the sleeve of Dorrington's dressing gown, a heavy China silk. "Never heard there was much money in that. It'll be worth looking into where he got his."

Ned met Julian's eyes for a moment unhappily, but he said nothing.

It was some time before they could talk in private, after Hatton had gone off with the corpse and left Garmin to assist them in rummaging through Dorrington's papers. So far they had found nothing on metaphysics besides a few authorized volumes, annotated with notes like *Will be bought by the same poor bastards who always buy this kind of thing. Christ, who'd be a metaphysician.*

Julian had unearthed several pornographic books in Dorrington's bedroom, including one which Ned found himself thumbing the pages of with a certain fascination before he remembered himself and tucked it carefully behind a book of poems (in which had been scrawled *Thinks he's Wordsworth. Isn't.*).

He heard the door to the flat open, and then the sound of Garmin in conversation with the maidservant. The conversation didn't sound entirely professional, Garmin's tone wheedling, and after a moment, the voices receded beyond the front door.

"We have to tell Hatton about the blackmail," Ned said.

Julian looked at him soberly over a stack of books. "And suppose one of our clients did it?"

"Well, yes, that's my point."

"You could argue he deserved it."

"Lynes."

"We should at least talk to them first and hear their side of it. And they may not be involved at all. If it was non-conforming enchantment, it could be the same killer again."

"Who might be Kennett."

"But probably not Barton."

"Probably not. But there's been enough in the papers that one of them might have gotten the idea that the best way to hide a murder was in a series of other murders. And that might explain why this one wasn't identical to the others."

"Possible," Julian granted. "But if his heart is missing, and one of them did him in – but not the others – it suggests that anyone who's read the papers and knows something about illicit metaphysics can work out a foolproof method of murder."

"A bit troubling, yes. Or else we're back where we were before, the victims involved in non-conforming magic and it backfired and killed them –"

"Or someone else killed them because they were involved."

"You're thinking of Challice."

"I don't want to think it of him. But – God knows he had reason."

They were interrupted by Garmin returning, whistling tunelessly between his teeth. Ned put a hand on Julian's shoulder in mute comfort, and then returned to the task at hand.

It was clear by mid-morning that the flat was going to yield nothing further of interest. If Dorrington had possessed written evidence to use against any of his blackmail victims, it was probably hidden away in a box at the post office. Ned stacked the books that bore on metaphysics neatly for Hatton, but none of them seemed likely to bear at all.

Outside, a chill wind was blowing, and Julian hunched his shoulders unhappily against the cold. "Where do you want to start?"

"Miss Barton first," Ned said. "We'd better collect Miss Frost for that – we can't very well go barging into Carlyle's School for Girls. Then Kennett, if we can find him –"

"We'll find him," Julian said grimly.

"And then you had better talk to Challice."

"If he'll see me. I've been trying."

"If you want to hear his side of it –"

"I know," Julian said, his voice even more grim.

"The Commons first," Ned said, and looked about for a cab.

❦

MISS BARTON MET THEM AT THE tea shop, her expression stormy.

"Cordelia said you had important news," she said, throwing herself into a chair incautiously enough to make the teacups rattle. "I hope it is important. You don't know how much I had to bow and scrape to get someone to watch my lunch table for me. Little beasts, if you leave them alone for a moment they're throwing halfpenny buns at each other and getting butter in their hair."

"My colleague, Julian Lynes," Ned put in, nodding toward Julian.

Miss Barton gave him a skeptical nod. "If they've gotten into the jam again…"

159

"Madeleine, Alfred Dorrington was murdered last night," Miss Frost said bluntly.

Miss Barton paled, her freckles standing out dark against her bloodless cheeks. "Over blackmail? Do the police imagine I had something to do with it?"

"The police don't know you had anything to do with Dorrington," Ned said. "Not yet. But I may have to tell them he was blackmailing you."

"But I didn't kill him," Miss Barton said. "Oswald I could have killed. I probably would have married him, you know, if he'd only taken the trouble to ask me what I wanted rather than telling me. If he'd ever even had the courage to apologize…"

"You can be a bit intimidating," Miss Frost said.

"He hasn't seen anything yet. He'd better not come near me when I have a teacup in my hand. But I'm not going to kill him. And I certainly wouldn't risk going to prison to kill some dirty little blackmailer."

"If you felt your position was threatened…" Ned suggested.

"But it isn't, is it?"

"Certainly not anymore," Julian pointed out.

"I didn't kill him."

"They may still suspect you did."

"I *couldn't* have killed him. Not last night."

Ned opened his mouth to say that the murder had been carried out through metaphysics, and that establishing her whereabouts probably wouldn't leave her conclusively out. Julian trod on his foot, and he quieted.

"Where were you last night?" Julian asked.

"At the school. The mistresses sleep in," Miss Frost said, but Miss Barton was shaking her head.

"I wasn't there. Not after lights out."

"*Madeleine.*"

"I went out after dark and climbed the garden fence. To meet a man."

Ned cleared his throat. "Who was the gentleman?"

She was flushing, now, but she carried on doggedly. "A friend. We walked for a while, and then ate a late supper. And then we…walked for a while longer."

"Madeleine," Miss Frost said through her fingers.

"How late was it when you said goodbye?"

"Near dawn."

"You spent the entire time walking about?"

"We were discussing the state of popular literature," Miss Barton said firmly.

Julian looked about to say *is that what they call it?*, but Ned trod on his foot before he could utter the words.

"I suppose your…fiancé could be produced to vouch for your whereabouts?" Miss Frost said, in a somewhat strangled tone.

"He's not my fiancé," Miss Barton said, her chin stubbornly up. "And I'm afraid it would be awkward for him, because he's married."

"Madeleine!"

"That was why he wanted to see me last night. To tell me that his wife finds it…uncomfortable that he's been spending so much time with me. And that he had better not see me again."

Ned wasn't sure whether saying he was sorry was the appropriate response or not. "If it were necessary for him to speak confidentially to the police, if you were seriously suspected of the crime…"

"I expect I could persuade him to," Miss Barton said. "I do think he was more than a bit fond of me. And besides, there's the gardener."

Miss Frost, who had taken a restorative sip of her tea, seemed to be choking on it. "The gardener?"

"He caught me as I was coming in," Miss Frost said. "Thankfully he's willing to take bribes to keep his mouth shut. But it was a bad moment, and by the time I'd gone back to my room to get something to bribe him with, it was breakfast time, and worlds of people can swear I was at breakfast."

"You might as easily have been sneaking back into the school after poisoning Dorrington," Julian said. Ned started to correct him, and then realized the slip had been deliberate in time to save his foot from being trodden on again.

"But I wasn't," Miss Barton said. "I suppose I could have if I'd wanted to – we've got chemicals and things for science demonstrations. I could have found his house and broken in and poisoned the port decanter. If he has a port decanter. I imagine him as having one."

As far as Ned knew, Dorrington hadn't possessed a port decanter, but he made a mental note to check with Hatton to be certain. "But you didn't."

"No. I never thought about Dorrington last night at all." A touch of humor lit her face. "Of course, you only have my word for it. But if I have to ask my friend to vouch for me…"

"I hope it won't come to that," Ned said. "I'm afraid I am going to have to tell the police that Dorrington was blackmailing you."

"They won't have to tell everyone about the books?"

"I should hope it won't have to come out at a trial. But it might put them on the right track. It's entirely possible that one of his other victims was responsible for his death."

"It serves him right," Miss Barton said.

"Madeleine," Miss Frost said, despairing.

"Never mind blackmail, have you seen the things he said about everyone's books?"

Julian raised an eyebrow at her. "And you weren't tempted to take your own revenge?"

"Oh, I was planning on it," Miss Barton said. "I've been making some notes for my next book. Our heroine is menaced by a blackmailer who just happens to be a literary gentleman. I thought he might be eaten by a crocodile," she said dreamily.

"In London?" Julian asked, as if he couldn't help it.

"In Egypt, or somewhere else with good local color. Are there crocodiles in South America?"

"Piranha," Ned offered.

"Piranha might do nicely." Miss Barton grew sober again. "I've got to get back to the school, Mr Mathey. I can't think what I'll do if the gardener tells the headmistress about last night. Or if she notices I've heartlessly abandoned the little beasts and run off to a tea shop with detectives."

"Has you ever considered," Miss Frost said carefully, "that you might not be entirely temperamentally suited to teaching?"

Miss Barton pushed her hair wearily back from her face. "More than once," she said. "But the alternative is men like Oswald, and I'm not sure I'm temperamentally suited to them either."

Miss Frost looked thoughtful. "You might see if Inspector Hatton needs a police matron for the Metaphysical Squad."

"I don't think that's a job for a…" Ned began, and then faltered. *Respectable lady* didn't seem to fit well in the same conversation as adultery and fictional blackmailers being eaten by crocodiles.

"Now, there's a thought," Miss Barton said. "Inspector Hatton, is it?"

"You might wait until you're not a suspect in a murder case," Ned said.

"That's sensible of you," Miss Barton said, but she sounded a bit disappointed. "Nothing to do now but go back and face all those shining little faces. Probably shining with butter." She bit her lip, looking suddenly worried. "They can't really think I killed him?"

"As long as you didn't kill him, I don't think you have anything to fear," Ned said.

Julian nodded cautious assent. "Especially not if we can find out who really did it."

CHAPTER THIRTEEN
Regrettable Choices

O UT ON THE SIDEWALK, JULIAN CONSULTED his watch, while Ned
and Miss Frost carried on a low-voiced conversation. Miss Barton had
fled, and Julian silently wished her well, though he thought Miss Frost
was probably right about her choice of profession. She did not seem suited to
the molding of young minds.

Behind him, Ned whistled for a cab, and when one pulled up to the curb,
helped Miss Frost aboard and gave directions to the cabbie. As it pulled away,
he turned back to the sidewalk, rubbing his hands together in the chill wind.
"Kennett next?"

Julian nodded. "We'll start at his house. Then his clubs."

"His servants may know his direction," Ned said.

"They're a close-mouthed bunch," Julian answered, and turned toward
Bloomsbury.

It was past two by the time they reached Kennett's house, but to Julian's
surprise, the housemaid accepted his card, and returned a moment later to say
that Kennett would see them. She led them to an upstairs sitting room, snugly
furnished, the curtains drawn against any possibility of a draft. Kennett was
standing by the well-fueled fire, wrapped in a splendid Chinese brocade dressing gown. It was enough like the one that Dorrington had been wearing that
Julian's eyebrows rose, but he reserved comment.

Ned had no such compunction. "Where did you get that?"

Kennett smoothed the black silk facings with an attempt at complacence.
"Rather fine, isn't it? A gift from an admirer."

"Not Pinky Dorrington," Julian said.

"Good God, no. I have better taste."

164

"Then your admirer has worse. Dorrington has one just like it."

"Really, Lynes, I'm surprised you'd admit to knowing that in front of your ever-so-special friend."

Julian flinched at that, and Ned said, "Dorrington was dead when we saw it. Murdered last night. Scotland Yard is asking questions."

Kennett swayed slightly, and steadied himself on the back of the armchair. "Surely not."

"As the proverbial doornail," Ned said.

"He can't be. Who'd want to –" Kennett stopped abruptly, grimacing, and Julian stared at him.

"Besides yourself?"

"I most certainly didn't want him dead!"

"Don't be conventional," Julian said. "It doesn't become you."

"Where were you last night?" Ned asked.

Kennett shook his head. "At my club – the Fine Arts, Lynes, don't look at me like that! At my club until ten or so, and then home in my bed. Virtuously alone, too, which seems to have been a poor choice."

"Not to mention unusual."

Ned set his hand on Julian's shoulder, and Julian subsided.

"Dorrington's dead," Ned said again. "Scotland Yard is involved, and they are going to find out about the blackmail."

"Not unless you tell them," Kennett snapped.

"The police aren't stupid," Ned said. "They've already noticed that Dorrington lived rather better than one might expect from what critics are paid. It would be a good deal better to tell them he was blackmailing you about your pseud-onymous books than to let them find out what else it might have been."

Kennett swayed again, then stiffened his knees. "But then they'll think I killed him."

"Did you?" Ned asked.

"Of course not!" Kennett looked faintly ill. "Don't be stupid."

Julian looked around the room, deliberately ignoring the others' voices. This was obviously Kennett's private sitting room; the books in the tall cases were eclectic and well-thumbed, and the furniture was chosen for comfort rather than fashion. The rug was worn but cheerful, the lamps unmatching but cho-sen to give good light for reading – and they had been moved recently, and set back imperfectly. He looked more closely, and realized that the furniture had been moved as well, as though to clear a space in the center of the room. There was a candle on the glass-fronted cabinet – a large one, for a room that had both lamps and gas, and one that had been recently lit. Frowning, he turned back the corner of the carpet, and found a smudged mark, like chalk.

"Mathey." He flipped the rug back a little further, and Kennett winced.

"Don't –"

"That's interesting," Ned said, and crouched to examine the marks more closely. "This looks like part of an old-fashioned protective circle."

"What have you been up to?" Julian asked, and Kennett flinched again.

"It's not what it looks like."

Ned folded back more of the rug, trying to work around the furniture, than rose to his feet, letting the carpet fall back into place. "It's not precisely a non-conforming structure, but it's certainly nothing I'd expect to see in reputable practice."

"Dorrington was killed by metaphysics," Julian said. "You'd better tell me exactly what you were doing."

"It had nothing to do with Dorrington," Kennett snapped.

"You can't expect me to believe that."

For a moment, it hung in the balance, and then Kennett's eyes fell.

"I didn't kill him. I couldn't have killed him."

"What did you do?" Julian asked.

"I…" Kennett flushed to the roots of his hair. "I wanted to pay him out, all right? He served me a nasty turn, and he deserved something unpleasant in return. I'd acquired a *maledictor* some months ago, for a poem I was working on, and – well, I thought I'd try something."

Ned muttered something under his breath that sounded like a curse. Julian said, "Let me see the book."

"I'd rather not."

"Kennett. If you want to get out of this with any of your secrets intact, you're going to have to cooperate." Julian glared at him, and the poet heaved a sigh.

"Oh, very well." He went to the small roll-top desk and produced a slim board-bound pamphlet. "This is what I used. The marker's even still in it."

Julian took it, flipped the soft pages until he reached the page marked by a thin strip of ribbon. "Plagues of Egypt: Exodus 9:8-12," he read aloud, and looked at Ned.

"Boils." Ned's mouth twitched, as though he was suppressing a smile, and Julian was hard-pressed not to laugh with him.

"It would have served him right," Kennett said, sulkily.

Julian was tempted to look to see if there were spells for frogs or lice – or deaths of firstborn sons – but made himself focus on the enchantment in question. Like many cantrips he'd seen in *maledictors*, it was old-fashioned, though not, strictly speaking, non-conforming. The ingredients were modern, no owl's blood or cat gut or dried bat wings, just colored chalk and the Powders of India that you could buy at any half-reputable chemist, and he handed the book to Ned. "What do you think?"

"I think he's lucky not to have set himself on fire," Ned answered frankly. "I think – Dorrington must have already been dead when Kennett tried this, or it would have had worse results."

"You think this is what caused the cuts," Julian said, and Ned nodded.

"I do. An intent to cause boils in all those locations, but with the man already dead, and the other non-conforming magic present, it just opened the skin."

Kennett looked paler than ever, and Julian grimaced at the thought. "So the worst you could charge him with was desecrating a body."

"Assuming that I'm right, of course," Ned said. "But, yes, I'd say so."

"I certainly didn't mean to do that," Kennett said.

"You were lucky it didn't do worse," Julian said. He looked at Ned. "If you tell Hatton this much –"

"I imagine it would be enough that we wouldn't have to mention other matters," Ned agreed.

"My reputation," Kennett said. "If it gets out that I wrote ladies' romances – God, I might as well shoot myself."

Ned looked as though he was biting his lip, presumably to keep from commenting on the quality of those romances. Julian said, "We'll do the best we can." He held up the book. "We'll keep this."

Kennett shrugged. "If you must. Lynes – I give you my word I didn't kill him."

"I believe you," Julian said, and refrained from adding *thousands wouldn't*.

❦

THEY STOPPED AT THE CORNER OF Millman and Great Ormond Streets, Julian hunching his shoulders against the wind. He hadn't worn his overcoat the night before, and he was feeling its absence. At least there would be time to go back for it before he went in search of Challice, and he dug his hands into his pockets.

Ned gave him a wary look. "I need to talk to Hatton. The sooner I can tell him something, the better."

"I know. If you can get him to keep the reason for the blackmail secret –"

"I can only try."

"The newspapers would love it," Julian muttered.

"I know," Ned said again. He rested his hand on Julian's shoulder for a moment, and Julian leaned gratefully into the touch. "Would it be any help if I came with you? I think Hatton could wait till morning."

For a moment, Julian considered it – perhaps a third person might convince Challice of his good intentions – but he knew he was deceiving himself. "No, but thank you. You talk to Hatton. I'll see if I can't persuade Challice at least to listen."

"Good luck," Ned said, and turned toward the nearest omnibus stop.

Julian made his way back to Coptic Street, where he changed into clean linen and a more appropriate suit. Mrs Digby had his tea ready by the time he was finished, and he wolfed down the sandwiches and chutney and finished the pot.

Fortified, and bundled in his overcoat, he caught the omnibus to Leadenhall Street, then wound his way through the narrow streets to Mincing Lane. It was still an hour to closing, and for a moment he considered approaching Challice at his office. But, no, if he sent his card in, Challice need only refuse to see him, and that would risk starting the scandal they both wanted to avoid. And it would warn him, give him some reason to take another way home. Instead, he found a spot in a nearly empty pub where he could nurse a pint and still keep an eye on Goodridge and Neale.

It was warmer out of the wind, even if he was sitting about as far from the fire as possible, and he rested his elbows on the wobbling table, letting the exhaustion of the early morning wash over him. It was a bad business – not that Dorrington was any loss to England, but it might have been possible to force him to tell at least some of what he knew. As it was, they were no closer to knowing what was stealing hearts.

It was hard not to think that the metaphor was somehow significant, but he couldn't place it. Certainly the group who'd performed the non-conforming rituals could be described as heartless themselves, particularly where Challice was concerned, but there was no proof that they were the same people who had attempted to make the modified Hand of Glory. Admittedly, it was likely – how many groups were there who indulged in non-conforming magic, particularly ones who shared the same circle of friends? But there was no proof that would stand up in court. A clever barrister could make nonsense of his arguments, and Hatton wouldn't be fool enough to agree to bring charges unless he had a good deal better to go on.

He looked down at the scarred wood, idly tracing sigils across the grain to set off tiny blue sparks. Talking to Challice wouldn't necessarily prove anything, that was the problem. Even if Challice was willing to name the men who'd tricked him, there was a good chance it wasn't the same group, or that the group overlapped only at Dorrington. And that would make all his efforts, and all Challice's misery, for nothing.

And yet there was no other choice, at least not one that he could see. And that meant hurting Challice, just in case there was something he'd missed. It was moments like this that he wished he'd had the sense to be a simple metaphysician – no, he couldn't believe that even at his most maudlin. He'd never have made a metaphysician, not like Ned, whose talents had been obvious even before University. There was the police, of course, but he lacked the certainty that would let him work for them even if that had been a suitable job for a gentleman. This was the price of the work he was best at, that he loved.

The businesses along Mincing Lane were beginning to close, the last customers ushered to the street, the first clerks hurrying down stairs and along sidewalks, heading for the omnibus stops on Leadenhall Street. Julian took a deep breath, bracing himself, and found a spot between a news vendor and a chophouse where he could watch Goodridge and Neale's doors. The streets were the usual scrum of clerks and newsboys, with the occasional senior man pushing through the mob, but at last he saw Challice making his way down the building's steps. He looked tired and pale in the gaslights, and Julian couldn't repress a pang of guilt. But it had to be done, and he dodged across the street, fetching up on the sidewalk at Challice's elbow.

"Challice."

The man shied like a frightened horse, and for a moment Julian was afraid that he might shout for the police. Challice controlled himself with an effort, and turned his head away. "I told you, I've nothing to say to you."

"Pinky Dorrington is dead," Julian said. "Murdered."

"Oh, God."

"I need a word with you."

"I've nothing to say."

"It doesn't have to be here," Julian said. "Have a drink with me – Foy's, for choice."

Challice hesitated, then shook his head. "Walk with me."

"As you wish."

"Dorrington's dead."

Julian nodded. "Yes."

"The same as the others?"

Julian lifted an eyebrow, and Challice glared at him.

"Oh, don't look at me like that, I'd have to be an imbecile not to guess it."

"Almost certainly."

"Not certainly?"

"The autopsy wasn't done when I left," Julian said. "But I'd be shocked if it wasn't."

"And you've come to me." Challice gave a bitter smile. "Thank you very much."

"I think that whatever they did with you is related to these deaths," Julian said. "And whatever they've done is still in effect. More people are going to die."

"And why should I care if more of that lot die?"

"Because there's no reason to think it will stop with them."

"Hah. If they've brought it on themselves –" Challice stopped, pointed his umbrella at the door of a dram-shop. "You're right, let's not talk on the street."

"Probably easier," Julian agreed, and followed him into the narrow, crowded shop. They each bought a tot of gin; Challice tossed his off and ordered another, then tilted his head toward a corner by the door.

"Over here."

Julian trailed after him, and arranged himself against a pillar between Challice and the door. They were far enough from the bar that the area wasn't crowded yet, and if they kept their voices down, they could talk without being overheard.

"If it's their twisted idea of metaphysics that's gone bad on them, why wouldn't it stop with them?" Challice demanded. "If it's some sort of side effect of their practices."

"It's possible," Julian said. "It depends on what they did, how they structured their enchantment, but – yes, it could work that way."

"Well, then." Challice downed the second tot of gin.

"But it might not," Julian said, as patiently as he could manage. "I don't know what their general practice was, except that it's non-conforming."

"I am not going to discuss the substance of their – practice." Challice's voice was thin with anger. "Not here, not ever."

"I'm not asking that," Julian said, and felt a pang of guilt again for lying. He most certainly would ask, if he thought he would get an answer. "I'm trying to prevent more deaths, Challice."

"They can all go hang as far as I'm concerned," Challice said. "I've nothing to say to the matter."

"You're the only one I can trust to tell me the truth," Julian said, and saw Challice flinch.

"What can I possibly say?"

"You can tell me who was involved in the circle," Julian said. "I've heard names, but I don't know who to believe. And if there is anything at all you can tell me about structure –"

"There was no structure," Challice said. "Just a vicious game. As for who – three of them are dead, Lynes, and I'm not the slightest bit sorry. If all the rest of them were to die the same way, I'd be a happy man."

"Dorrington, Punton, and Hall," Julian said.

"Don't pretend you're greatly grieved."

"I felt sorry for Dolly Hall," Julian said, deliberately, and there was a flash of something on Challice's face.

"Yes, all right, he was a pathetic little beast. He claimed he didn't know what they were planning –" Challice broke off, shaking his head.

"I've heard other names," Julian said. "Farrell, Leach, Kennett, Barnes –"

Challice shook his head again. "Don't you understand? I'm not going to help you save them. If someone is killing them, I say he deserves a medal."

Julian grimaced. "Should I be asking you for your alibi, Challice?"

"And now we come to it," Challice answered. "Do you really think I'm that incapable?"

"That's not what I meant."

"Yes, it is. You don't think I'm man enough to want revenge, much less to take it."

"You're not a metaphysician."

Challice waved a hand in dismissal. "You don't have to be, do you? Not with this non-conforming business. It's all different rules, and the truth is, if you find the right book, you just have to follow along."

"It's not generally that simple," Julian said.

"So, yes, you should be asking for my alibi, and no, I'm not going to tell you anything." Challice caught up his umbrella, holding it like a club. "I don't care if they all die, it's only what they deserve."

His voice had risen, and Julian saw heads turn, everyone curious to see if the clerks would fight. He took a step back, and Challice shook the umbrella at him.

"Leave me alone, Lynes. This is your last warning."

Julian lifted his hands in surrender, and Challice stalked away, shoving through the door into the street. Julian was aware of the eyes on him, and hunched his shoulders as an aproned man pushed through the crowd.

"Here, you, this is a respectable house."

"I don't want any trouble," Julian began, and the publican shook his head.

"And neither do I. Go on, get out of here."

"Right," Julian said, and headed for the door, all too aware of the censorious stares. On the sidewalk, he stopped to button his overcoat, all too aware of the glaring problem with the conversation. Oh, he'd made noise enough, but – Challice had not denied the accusation. Julian swore under his breath. Challice also wasn't a metaphysician, and surely you needed metaphysical training to commit these murders. Surely. "Why the devil couldn't you just answer a simple question?" he muttered, and started back toward Coptic Street.

❦

Ned found Hatton in the offices of the Metaphysical Squad, attempting to unearth his desk from new stacks of teetering files.

"I need to speak with you, if you're free."

"There's no such thing in this job," Hatton said. "But go ahead. Have you found out anything new about our corpses?"

"Two of my clients have been blackmailed," Ned said bluntly. "I think their blackmailer was Alfred Dorrington."

Hatton sat down in his chair and looked up at him. "Tell me how you figure that one."

"Both of them are authors," Ned said. "Both writers of ladies' romances, under assumed names, and they're both keen to keep that from the public."

"Who are they?"

Ned felt a stab of guilt, but there was nothing for it. "One of them is a Miss Madeleine Barton, a schoolteacher. The other is Auberon Kennett. He's a poet, with very serious literary ambitions."

"God help us," Hatton said. "All right, where does Dorrington come in?"

"Both of them were acquainted with Dorrington," Ned said. It seemed unfair to feel as guilty at lying as at telling the truth. "Literary circles, you know. I tested the blackmail letters against samples of the writing of a number of people who might have been involved, and they matched Dorrington's handwriting."

"You should have come straight to the police," Hatton said.

Ned frowned unhappily. "I know. But I was hoping to sort it out discreetly."

"You know, we're not in the business of tormenting blackmail victims. We couldn't bring in a conviction without your clients taking the stand, but we could at least have warned Dorrington off. But, all right. You understand, though…"

"That they're suspects," Ned said. "Yes. And I actually believe that one of them is responsible for the condition of the body, although I don't think he's the one who killed him."

Hatton rocked his chair back. "Explain."

"Kennett has a temper. He tried a curse he found out of a *maledictor*, intending to inflict the man with boils. But I think Dorrington was already dead, killed by non-conforming enchantment, and when Kennett tried his curse, the result was the odd pattern of wounds we found on the corpse."

"Or else Kennett used the curse to kill him."

"I don't think it could have done that," Ned said. He handed Hatton the *maledictor*, and Hatton thumbed through the pages. "The original enchantment isn't meant to kill, and I think it's more likely that it wouldn't work than that it would prove fatal. These old-fashioned methods weren't particularly reliable."

"It's Greek to me," Hatton said. "I take it there's nothing in here about removing hearts?"

"Was Dorrington's heart missing?"

"Just the same as the others. Can you swear to it that the curse in here would produce marks on a dead body like the ones we saw?"

"I'm afraid I can't," Ned said. "Unless you're willing for me to experiment."

"We've got no shortage of corpses."

"It'll have to be Dorrington's corpse, though – I suspect the previous non-conforming enchantment is what caused the odd results. Or one of the earlier victims, I suppose."

"They're already in the ground," Hatton said. "It didn't pay to wait, when we couldn't use enchantment to preserve the bodies. There's only so much you can do with ice. We've got Dorrington upstairs. How likely is playing about with him to set the building on fire?"

"Not likely," Ned said, but Hatton didn't look entirely persuaded. "We could do it over at the Commons," he said. "That way Oppenshaw could look on. He's our senior man when it comes to non-conforming enchantment."

"Better your place than mine."

They arrived at the Commons with both Dorrington's corpse and the corpse of some unfortunate who had died entirely explicably of being hit over the head in a drunken brawl. As Ned had expected, Oppenshaw frowned at the idea, but clearly couldn't resist the opportunity to get a closer look at the corpses.

"Bring them right through here, if you please," Oppenshaw said. Ned was used to the metaphysicians' laboratory, with its cluttered shelves full of a jumble of ingredients modern and antique, and its workbenches always littered with books and trade magazines. By comparison, the metaphysicists' experiment room was simply a bare room, its aging wooden floor sanded down but not polished and smelling of chalk dust. The walls, however, were each inlaid with large and elaborate protective circles, words and symbols in real if tarnished silver covering the wood.

Hatton reached up curiously as if to trace the curve of the nearest circle with his finger.

"Please don't," Oppenshaw said. "The walls of this room date from the sixteenth century, although the paneling has been moved from its original site. They have been observed to limit a broad spectrum of metaphysical effects to the boundaries of this room. As the method used is now technically non-conforming, we cannot legally reproduce them. So don't touch."

"Yes, sir," Hatton said, and stuck his hands in his pockets.

Two police constables laid out Dorrington and the other corpse side by side on the floor, and Hatton motioned them out. Oppenshaw lit the beeswax tapers set into sconces on the walls and then closed the door of the room behind them, which seemed to shut out a surprising degree of noise.

"Very well, Mr Mathey," he said. "What experiment do you propose to make?"

It felt very much like being back at Oxford. "According to my client, he performed a curse from this *maledictor*, intended to produce boils, specifying Alfred Dorrington as his target. I believe from the effects that Dorrington was already dead at the time, having been killed by non-conforming enchantment. I intend to test the curse on both Dorrington's body and the body of a man killed by ordinary means, to see if I can duplicate the effect."

"The Commons bylaws strongly discourage experimentation with non-conforming metaphysics," Oppenshaw said. "However, I would very much like to see what happens. Inspector, it would be prudent for you to leave the room."

"I'll stay," Hatton said. "I want to see this, too."

"Set this outside, at least," Ned said, and handed Hatton his metaphysician's bag, after removing his wand and the ingredients for the enchantment. "First the protective circle –"

"Around the entire room?" Oppenshaw said, in a lecturer's tone of careful disinterest that made Ned look for the catch in what he'd said.

"Not around the corpses," he said. "Because Kennett was working inside the circle, but Dorrington was outside." He chalked himself into a carefully drawn circle, and added the prescribed figures, barely recognizable as sigils simplified to scrawls. He folded himself to sit on the floor within it, the *maledictor* in his lap, pen and paper and the packet of black Powders of India laid out on the floor in front of him.

He wrote on one sheet of paper *Alfred Dorrington*. "What was the other man's name?" His bulldog face was slack and pale in death, a sheet wrapped round him below the chin.

"James Oakes," Hatton said.

"We're certain of that?"

"There's a Mrs Oakes who says so. But when you put it that way, there's likely more than one James Oakes about."

"Clear intention should spare them boils," Ned said. "But it's best not to get the name wrong entirely." He wrote *James Oakes* on the other sheet, and laid them out in front of him. He took a deep breath, and began reading from the *maledictor*. "Be this a true image of my enemy, O Lord, and may your judgment fall upon him."

Carefully he sketched the prescribed figures around the names, feeling the grammar building itself up around them, hooking itself to the names and forming a hook that should take a verb. *Raise up boils upon the named*, that was the way it probably ought to be done in the modern style, although he would have to look up "boils" in a volume on the metaphysical treatment of illness. Whether it would work or not was a good question.

"And the LORD said unto Moses and unto Aaron, Take to you handfuls of ashes of the furnace, and let Moses sprinkle it toward the heaven in the sight of Pharaoh."

He tipped the black powder into his hand – the black was charcoal scented with asafoetida, he suspected – and blew gently, letting it fall like rain across the two pieces of paper. A physical symbol rather than a sigil, with more weight of side associations, but he felt it hook all the same. He held his breath as the ash settled.

For a moment, darkness dappled Oakes' face, like freckles of shadow. Then the light seemed to shift and the spots of shadow faded, leaving the corpse untouched.

"Very good, Mr Mathey," Oppenshaw said. He was looking down at Dorrington's corpse, watching more slashes open bloodlessly across his face and arms. Ned looked long enough to be certain of the effect, and then looked away.

"All right, Mathey, you've proven your point," Hatton said.

"If you want to see the effect on a living man, I'm sure Mr Mathey will be willing to demonstrate," Oppenshaw said.

"I'll pass on that. You're certain this couldn't have been what removed his heart? If he'd been dabbling in non-conforming enchantment already, and then this curse were used…"

Oppenshaw shook his head. "There's no indication here of anything being removed. And your earlier victims were free of marks, were they not?"

"They were," Hatton granted. "So this doesn't tell us anything except that your Mr Kennett is lucky that he tried this lark after Dorrington was already dead. I'm not going to drag him in on a charge of attempted assault against a gent who was past worrying about it. We've got other work to do."

"It might give some clue to when he died," Ned said.

Hatton followed his gaze to Dorrington's corpse. "I see that. He bled when he was cursed the first time. Not great amounts, but enough to mark his clothes. He can't have been dead half an hour when Kennett tried this business."

"Which might give Miss Barton an alibi for the time of his actual death."

"Does she have one?"

Ned frowned. "One she's unwilling to call on except in extremity."

"Like that, is it?" Hatton shook his head. "That kind of alibi's not worth much. A gentleman friend who'll inconvenience himself to testify for a lady is likely to be wrapped round her finger enough to say anything she wants. But we'll take it into consideration."

"If you're quite done, gentlemen, I'll thank you to remove the corpses for the sake of the floor," Oppenshaw said. "It is troublesome to sand. Thank you, Mr Mathey, this was quite interesting. I would encourage you to write it up for the *British Journal of Metaphysics*, but I very much doubt you'd be allowed to publish."

"Cheer up, Mathey, you'll be paid for your time regardless," Hatton said. He threw the door open. "All right, lads, let's get these poor sods out of here."

☽❈

CHAPTER FOURTEEN

Indelicate Investigations

ULIAN DREW OFF THE LAST OF his coffee, the patent machine dispensing it with a mournful hiss, and added an extra spoonful of sugar as though that would help wake him. He had slept badly, his dreams filled with bleeding bodies and heartless men, and he still had no idea what to do about Challice. Perhaps Ned would be able to help, though that would require embarrassing explanations. Of course, the best thing of all would be to have never been involved with the man, but it was far too late for that.

Mrs Digby knocked at the door, her firm hand unmistakable, and Julian turned, frowning. The maid had collected the breakfast tray an hour ago, and it was too early for the next post; his rent was paid, along with the extra for Ned's frequent presence at meals, and he was reasonably sure she hadn't decided to acknowledge the enchantment on the bathroom geyser, at least not without further provocation.

"A lady to see you, Mr Lynes," she announced, holding out a card. Julian took it, the name in plain script leaping out at him: *Mrs Henry Challice.* He opened his mouth to deny that he was home, and saw her already in the doorway, tall and elegant in a steel-blue visiting dress. There was nothing for it, then, but he still had to swallow hard before he could speak.

"Thank you, Mrs Digby. Mrs Challice." He waved generally toward the visitors' chairs, and she came a few steps further into the room, looking over the clutter without expression. Mrs Digby let herself out, not without a backward glance, and Julian considered his visitor. He had met her before, of course, once at a public ball and once at the opera, but he had never expected to see her without her husband, much less in his consulting room. She looked steadily back at him, and he realized that he was watching her the way a bird watches a snake, which suited his feelings well enough, but was hardly flattering.

"If you would care to have a seat?" he asked, warily. "Perhaps a cup of tea?"

"No. Thank you." She did sit, however, settling straight-backed on the edge of the best chair. Both bustle and corset were moderate, and he suspected they had nothing to do with the tension in her spine or in her gloved hands. They and her hat were so dark a blue as to be almost black; all the rest, bodice, skirt, buttons and trim, from the fringe to the bow on the neat and faintly mannish hat, were the same steely blue. It was a color that flattered her, and Julian guessed she had chosen it as armor. She was a handsome woman, with honey-colored hair swept up in a severe style, but faint unhappy lines marked her face.

"What can I do for you?" he asked, and seated himself opposite her.

She paused as though she was considering the question, her gloved hands folded in her lap. It occurred to Julian that she had to be as uncomfortable with the conversation as he, but he didn't find that particularly reassuring. "I understand you are my husband's friend."

There were several ways of taking that, and not all of them were alarming, but, meeting her bleak stare, Julian couldn't bring himself to believe she meant any of those. "I have been."

"And are you his friend now?"

"I hope I will always be his friend," Julian said carefully. "But we're not as close as we once were."

She drew a breath, sharp and unhappy, but inclined her head. "Thank you for being honest."

"I don't think we're well served by anything else," he answered. Nothing that had been said so far could not be denied; if worst came to worst, he could always claim she had misunderstood. She read the thought, and the lines that bracketed her mouth tightened.

"I fear I have come to impose on that…friendship. My husband was taken ill last night, and has not left his bed today."

"I'm sorry," Julian said, tentatively, when it seemed she would not continue.

"He was feverish overnight, and your name was spoken. When I taxed him with it this morning, he said that it was nothing, that you were an acquaintance that had importuned him the previous evening. But I had inquired about you before, you and Mr Lennox, and I understand that you are some sort of detective. And my husband also spoke of murder and metaphysics. I expect you can understand my concern."

"Yes," Julian said again.

"I would like to know if there is anything to his ramblings – what trouble he is in." Her hands were still folded on her lap, the gloves hiding any hint of how tightly she wove her fingers together.

Julian hesitated, not at all sure where to begin, and she lifted her eyebrows.

"Mr Lynes, let me be frank. This conversation is deeply distasteful to me, and I would not be here if I were not gravely concerned for my husband's health. I had hoped that your feelings for him, however depraved, might persuade you to assist him."

"You mistake me," Julian said, stiffly. The blood was pounding in his temples and he knew he was scarlet with mortification. "I have been the recipient of certain confidences that I cannot break."

"I am his wife, sir."

"And if he had wished to share them with his wife, he's had ample opportunity to do so." The words were unforgivable. Julian winced, but she barely moved, only the flicker of an eyelid betraying that she had heard him at all.

"Let us begin again," she said, after a moment, and Julian nodded sharply. "I am afraid for his health, for his nerves and his general constitution. Do you believe that?"

"I do."

"Without violating his confidences, I would ask you to answer several questions."

"As far as I can," Julian said. "And if there's anything else I can do, I will."

"Thank you for that," she said again. "He spoke of metaphysics. Is he under a curse?"

Julian opened his mouth to deny it, closed it again with the words unspoken. "I don't know," he said, after a moment. "If an enchantment were involved, and I do not know for certain that one has caused this breakdown, it was one he sought. But it is possible that something went wrong." Or that malice was involved, but Mrs Challice did not need to hear that, not now.

She paused for a moment, considering that. "I believe you are a metaphysician yourself?"

"I was trained as one, yes."

She nodded. "So you would know. He also spoke of murder."

"There have been three murders so far," Julian said.

"And you suspect my husband?" Her voice scaled up in spite of herself, anger and disbelief, and Julian spread his hands.

"I don't know. He – believe me when I say he had good cause to hate the dead men, just cause. But I find it hard to believe he's a murderer." Julian paused, then made himself say what he believed. "He's a better man than that."

She blinked once, then twice, her eyes momentarily bright with what might have been tears, then stiffened her spine again. "Then why were you questioning him?"

"Because I may need to be able to prove it. The police are involved, and if I can show he's innocent –" Julian swallowed the rush of words. "My intent was to spare him as much as I can."

She stared at him for a long moment. "Why couldn't you leave well enough alone?"

Because Dolly Hall asked me for help, and I didn't give it. The unwanted truth was far too much, and he shook his head. "I have a client –"

"Surely that's a matter for the police."

"Not everyone wishes to parade his troubles at Scotland Yard," Julian answered, and thought a shadow of distaste crossed her face.

"And so you make it your profession."

"You may yet find it useful," Julian said, stung again.

To his surprise, something like a smile flickered on her lips. "Indeed. And if you are sincere when you say you want to help my husband – I want you to come home with me."

"What?"

"He's angry and afraid – possibly he's afraid of you, but I now believe he is mistaken in that – and he is making himself ill. I want you to convince him that he is wrong and that he is safe."

"The only way I can do that is if he will answer my questions," Julian said.

"He is not a murderer."

"I don't believe he is," Julian answered. "But I need proof."

She paused, considering, and then nodded. "Very well. And if there is a curse, I want you to remove it."

"That's a metaphysician's job," Julian said automatically. Oh, if he could only persuade her to let him bring Ned – except that would mean explaining exactly what had happened, and why Challice's wife was now demanding his help, and he wasn't sure he could manage that, particularly not if she were listening –

"You said you were trained. But no matter. You can diagnose one, surely?"

"Yes."

"Then that is what I want from you." She rose to her feet, and Julian rose with her. "Talk to him. Prove he's no murderer and that there is no curse. And then leave us both in peace.'"

"That would be –" Julian broke off. *That would be Challice's business*, he would have said, and he didn't need to offer provocation. "I'll talk to him," he said, and rang the bell for Mrs Digby.

The cab arrived in good time, and Julian offered his hand automatically to help her up the step. She hesitated just for an instant, then accepted it, resting her gloved fingers on his for the least possible time. Julian paused as she settled herself, drawing her skirts neatly around her.

"I don't actually know your address."

She lifted an eyebrow at that, but Julian met her eyes squarely.

"Thirty-four Hamilton Terrace. St. John's Wood."

"Thank you," Julian said, and repeated it to the cabbie, then climbed in after her. It was a nice address, perhaps a bit better than he would have thought: an expensive location for an up-and-coming businessman, not yet a partner in his firm.

"I brought a small portion to our marriage," Mrs Challice said. In the shadows of the cab it was hard to tell, but he thought there were small spots of color on her cheekbones.

"I see." And he did, that was the trouble. Challice had married late, and chosen a woman who would advance his career – and why not, when he didn't want much of anything else from her? But Challice would never have admitted that to her, and she was too intelligent not to know that something was wrong. Perhaps it would have been better to make the bargain openly, but that wasn't what Challice wanted. He wanted marriage to cure him, and there was little chance of that.

It was a long ride through the busy streets, made longer by Mrs Challice's determined silence. Julian made no attempt to break it, either, worrying instead about what he would say to Challice, if Challice would speak to him at all. Perhaps Mrs Challice was right, and there was some lingering effect from Dorrington's ritual. That was something he could diagnose easily enough, surely, and if he couldn't resolve it, Ned certainly would be able to. For a moment, he wished he had insisted on bringing Ned, but the thought of explaining the situation made him wince. Better to see what he could do alone.

The house was even nicer than he had expected, not just one of the handsome townhouses that formed the bulk of the street, but a larger, fully detached Regency house, with a low fence backed by a well-clipped hedge, and a creamy white façade disguising the brick behind it. Mrs Challice's portion had been rather more than "small" if it allowed them to buy the lease here.

Julian handed her down from the cab and paid off the cabbie, then followed her up the front steps. A neatly uniformed maid took his hat and stick, and Mrs Challice removed her own hat and gloves.

"This way, if you would."

"You don't think it would be better to give him some warning?" Julian asked, but followed her up the main stairs.

"I doubt it," she answered. She paused at the door of what was surely one of the bedrooms, stiffened her shoulders, and pushed it open. "Henry, I've brought someone to see you."

The room was in shadow, the curtains drawn against the daylight, the air chill and scented with camphor. Julian could just see Challice reclining on the old-fashioned tester bed, one arm flung across his eyes. He lifted his head at his wife's voice, and pushed himself up on his elbow, sleepy confusion turning to an angry scowl.

"How could you?" he said, to Julian, and looked at his wife. "Lucinda, my dear –"

"I brought him here," Mrs Challice said, her voice cool and remote. "I – it is my expectation that he can help you, if you will allow it."

"I don't want to talk to him." Challice folded his arms across his chest. He still looked feverish, Julian thought, and Mrs Challice seemed to think the same. She crossed to him, touched his forehead with a frown, and poured a glass from the pitcher that stood ready by the bed.

"You promised me you would drink the barley water."

"Yes, very well." Challice sipped at it, grimacing, but under her watchful eye he drained the glass. "Lynes, I don't –"

"Mr Lynes is, by all report, both a competent investigator and a trained metaphysician," Mrs Challice said. "Talk to him, Henry. And then we'll never have to speak of this again."

Challice drew breath, then, stopped, shaking his head. "If you insist."

"I do." Mrs Challice took his glass and set it on the table, then turned toward the chairs that were lined up beside the door. "I will sit here, in case you need anything."

Julian suppressed a groan. He had hoped for privacy, but clearly that was not an option. There was a straight-backed chair beside the bed as well, a novel opened face-down on its woven seat. He picked it up, set the marker in it, and moved the chair closer to the bed. "Challice."

"My wife has made a mistake," Challice said. His voice was low enough that Julian couldn't be sure it would carry to the woman by the door. "It would very much oblige me if you would tell her so and then – go away."

"Listen to me." Julian took a breath, marshaling his thoughts. "You're the one who's raised her suspicions, and that's not going to help you if this goes any further. Help me, tell me the truth, and I swear I will do everything I can to keep you out of it."

"I'm ruined already," Challice said.

"Not unless you insist on it." Julian couldn't help glancing toward Mrs Challice, still sitting silent and unmoving in her chair by the door, her hands folded decorously in her lap. "She wants to help you. As do I."

"There's nothing you can do."

Julian swallowed a curse. "Yes, there is." And if you'd just answered my questions before, it wouldn't have come to this. "I don't believe you killed Dorrington, Punton, and Hall, and before you get your back up, I believe it because you're a better man than that. But you know who else was in their circle. Tell me, and let me find the real killer."

"I'm still not sorry they're dead," Challice said.

"Dorrington's no loss," Julian agreed. "But I can't be sure it will stop with them."

"No. I suppose not." Chalice closed his eyes. "I can tell you who – was there. Who participated. But that's not all of Dorrington's friends."

Julian nodded. "It's a start. And it's more than I have now."

"Dorrington," Challice said. "Punton. Hall – he tried to tell me he was sorry, and I wouldn't have it. That he didn't know what was going to happen. He wasn't very clever."

Julian waited, not daring to speak. If Mrs Challice heard, she would hear only names, names that could mean nothing to her. She had no context, surely, from which to guess what had happened.

"Leach," Challice said. "Farrell. Always those three together, them and Dorrington. A man called Barnes, that I didn't even know…I heard he went to India not long after."

"Not Kennett?" Julian asked, after a moment. "Peacock?"

Challice shook his head. "No, neither of them. Though Kennett – he was close to Dorrington. But he wasn't there."

Farrell and Leach. The names were no real surprise at this point, and knowing for certain that they were involved, Julian could think of a few metaphysical tests he might try. And of course it made it much easier to push them, now that he knew for certain they were involved.

"Lynes." Challice reached out abruptly, caught his sleeve. "Is it possible they cursed me?"

Julian covered his hand with his own, all too aware of Mrs Challice watching from beside the door. "It's always possible. For that matter, they may not have meant to, just gotten something wrong."

Challice breathed a sound that might have been a laugh. "That would not surprise me. I was a fool to trust them."

Yes. It was no kindness to say it, and Julian tightened his hold briefly. "Will you tell me what they promised?"

Challice laughed again. "What do you think? To make me more – capable –"

He stopped abruptly, and Julian flinched. To make him more capable with his wife: that was a particularly refined cruelty, and if he ever got the chance, he would take pleasure in paying Leach back for it. "Forgive me, but did they give you anything?"

Challice closed his eyes again. "A packet…"

"Let me take it with me," Julian said. "I'll make sure it's doing you no harm, and then –"

"Then throw it on the fire," Challice said, loudly enough that Julian saw his wife stiffen in her chair. "I should never have kept it this long. Get rid of it, Lynes."

"I will," Julian answered. "I promise. Where is it?"

"In my collar-drawer." Challice nodded to the chest of drawers that stood between the windows. Julian went to it, found the right drawer on the second try. The packet was unmistakable, small and square and wrapped in stained blue paper; he sketched a quick testing sigil over it, but nothing happened. He palmed it reluctantly, and came back to the bed.

"This?"

Challice nodded again, and looked away.

Julian slipped it into his pocket, suppressing a grimace of distaste, and touched Challice's hand again. "It's done."

"Lynes –" Challice stopped, as though he wasn't certain himself what he wanted to say, and Julian shook his head.

"It's over, Challice." He turned toward the door. "Ma'am. We're done here."

"And you've succeeded at what I asked?" She rose gracefully to her feet, her hands still clasped before her.

"To the best of my ability," Julian answered, and she opened the door for him.

"Thank you, Mr Lynes. I trust we shall not need your services again."

"I doubt you will," Julian answered, and did not look back until he was in the street. There was nothing to see, just the pale elegant façade and the blank windows. He swore under his breath, and started walking toward Maida Vale and the first omnibus he could find.

❦

By THE TIME HE REACHED HIS lodgings, a chill had seeped into his bones. He added a few lumps of coal to the fire, building it up regardless of expense, but the steady flames didn't seem to warm him. He held out his hands, noting with some exasperation that they were trembling, and turned to the sideboard to brew another cup of coffee. It took a moment to get the machine assembled, and then he very nearly forgot to adjust the relief valve properly, but at last he poured off the thick hot brew, and dropped four lumps of sugar in it. After a moment's thought, he unlocked the tantalus and added a generous tot of brandy.

He returned to the fire, standing close enough that he could feel the heat through the toes of his boots, his hands wrapped around his cup, but nothing seemed to shake the inner chill. He closed his eyes, trying to focus on what he had learned. Six men had been involved in the ritual with Challice; Punton, Hall, and Dorrington were dead, and Leach, Farrell, and someone called Barnes were still alive. If Challice was right, and Barnes had gone to India – and Julian was prepared to accept that; it wasn't a name he'd heard around the clubs – then that left Leach and Farrell. Julian shook his head. He had liked Farrell at University, had enjoyed the sharp tongue and caustic wit as much as he'd enjoyed Farrell's inventiveness in bed once they'd renewed their acquaintance in London. Ned had never liked him, of course, and to be fair Farrell had never liked Ned, but this – this seemed more like Leach's sort of trick. He'd always been overbearing, and if he'd never seemed clever enough to think of such a thing before, it was perfectly possible that he'd learned new skills since University. Either way, though, what they had done to Challice was unforgivable.

He wouldn't see Challice again. That hurt more than it ought, for all that he knew it was a decision he should have made a year ago. Or that he should have held to. But he had liked Challice, and it had been nice to have someone to go about with who also shared his tastes, and it had been so easy to assume that Challice would come to the same acceptance that so many others had found.

That he hadn't, that he might never find a way to reconcile the things he most desired, and that there was nothing at all Julian could do about it – he drained the last of his coffee, barely tasting the brandy.

He returned to the sideboard to pour a glass of neat brandy, and tossed it back. It wasn't that he was in love with Challice, or ever really had been, though it probably didn't bear examining that thought too closely. It was much easier to say that he was beginning to regret Farrell, and at least he could say he'd never had Leach. At least he had Ned now, for as long as he would stay, and maybe that would be longer than he had thought, if Ned had gone to the trouble to cheat at cards himself. But it was all horribly complicated, and the bewildering ache in his chest wouldn't go away.

He considered another glass of brandy, but there were more effective remedies. He unlocked the sideboard instead and took out the morocco-leather case that held his enchantment kit, then searched his shelves for the thin notebook that held the formulae he'd collected over the years. He didn't often want this particular cantrip, hadn't used it enough to have the proportions memorized, and it was a formula where one would not wish to make mistakes.

He set the notebook on the sideboard, pinning it open with the brandy glass and the empty plate that had held his breakfast toast. The handwriting was unfamiliar, not his own, and he frowned for a moment, trying to remember whose it was. At University, they'd all had books like this, and scrawled new cantrips in each other's pages as they'd learned them, certain they were advancing metaphysics more than any mere practitioner. He'd never quite had the nerve to show it to Ned, though, and then they'd stopped seeing each other on any but the most public occasions; at this point, he couldn't think how he'd begin to share it.

He shook the thought away, and began to collect the required ink tablets. A quarter of red, a few shavings of silver, a full pellet of the best blue, and a pinch of the opalescent Selene's Dust; he had no more isinglass, but the cantrip would work well enough without it. He lit the spirit lamp and tipped the ingredients into the small brass bowl, then set it over the flame to melt, glancing again at the sigil sketched out in the notebook. He remembered how to draw it, starting at the lowest part of the sweeping curve, curling up and into the center so that he finished the fine lines of the center with the last of the ink. Or at least that was the intent. He gave the ink a stir with the set's brass rod, then laid out a square of the special paper. He took a breath, focusing his will, then dipped the pen and began to draw.

He laid out the sigil first in careful strokes, then retraced the lines with careful intent, watching them darken and thicken with each pass, until there was no more ink left in the bowl. He blew out the spirit lamp, then laid the ink-sodden slip of paper in the bottom of a glass and reached for the brandy bottle. He hesitated for an instant then, not sure if this was in fact the oblivion he wanted, then poured a generous glass. The paper dissolved in a cloud of purple and tiny sparks, the ghost of its presence hanging like smoke in the amber liquid. He swirled the glass to make that disappear as well, and downed it in a single gulp.

A knocking at the door roused him from dreams that smelled of amber and ice. He pushed himself upright on the sofa, momentarily at sea, and ran his hands through his hair. It was dusk already, nearly dark, and the lights were out and the fire burnt to embers…

"Mr Lynes!" That was Mrs Digby, pounding on the door again. "I'm sorry, Mr Mathey, I'm sure he's here."

Ned said something, his voice indistinct but soothing, and Julian dragged himself to his feet.

"I'm here, Mrs Digby. Just a moment."

He fumbled with the lock, his fingers cold and clumsy with enchantment, but managed to draw back the door without stumbling.

"Sorry, old man," Ned said, but then his face changed as he recognized the enchantment set and Julian's disheveled appearance. "Thank you, Mrs Digby, that'll be all."

Julian let him take the door and close it, and concentrated on returning to the sofa without tripping, let himself drop heavily onto the cushions.

"Lynes? What's happened?"

Julian considered the question. What hasn't? he wanted to say, but instead found himself giving the plain truth. "I spoke to Challice today."

"Ah." Ned's breath caught just for an instant, and he moved toward the sideboard, tilting his head to read the still-open notebook.

"His wife came to see me," Julian said.

Ned looked back at him. "Oh, dear."

"Quite." Julian closed his eyes, the cantrip tugging at him. "He didn't do it, Mathey."

"Did you use this?" Ned asked. "Lynes. Is this the cantrip you took?"

"Yes…"

Ned said something under his breath that Julian decided he didn't want to decipher, and tugged at Julian's arm. "Come on, up with you."

"I just want to sleep," Julian said.

"I do dare say. That cantrip would stun an elephant. But you'll sleep better in bed, old man."

That was quite possibly true. Julian let himself be pulled upright, and flung his arm across Ned's shoulders. He was warm and solid and smelled of wool and shaving soap, and Julian let his head rest on Ned's shoulder.

"Not yet," Ned said. "Just a little further, that's right."

Julian let himself be steered into the bedroom, and shifted unceremoniously onto the mattress.

"That's right," Ned said again. "Let me get your coat off – yes, like that."

Julian loosened his own collar, then sprawled against the pillows. "Don't – I'm glad you're here."

Ned hesitated for a moment, then sat on the mattress beside him, running a hand gently through his hair. "That bad?"

"Not pleasant," Julian said, and turned his face into Ned's hand.

"I'm here," Ned said, after a moment, and Julian let the cantrip wash over him again.

☾☀

JULIAN WAS SUBDUED IN THE MORNING, and Ned refrained from commenting on his activities of the night before, although he did steal a look into the cantrip-book while Julian was still dressing. Most of the enchantments contained therein were essentially harmless, if dubious in their purpose. He considered pocketing Julian's store of violet ink, and decided that was both unworthy and unlikely to be effective.

Julian came out of the bedroom knotting up his tie. "Leach and Farrell were both in it," he said flatly. "All the dead men as well. And Barnes, but he's gone to India, by all accounts."

Ned let out a breath. "You think one of them is responsible for the deaths."

"I think one of them must have been," Julian said. "Leach more likely than Farrell."

"Funny, I would have put my money on Farrell."

"He was never this malicious –"

"Never to you. And you may not remember him on the subject of sportsmen who wouldn't know a tragedy from a music-hall farce, but believe me, I do. He was very funny, in a vicious sort of way. And made it quite clear that I didn't belong in his set."

"I don't give a damn about the theater either."

"But you fit in well enough that he never went after you. I suppose in retrospect that it's not a mystery why he had it in for me particularly, since he was making a dead set for you –"

"While you were making every effort to become normal."

"I've said I'm sorry for that."

"If I fit and you didn't, it was the first time that was ever true," Julian said. "It was a revelation, finding men like us –"

It was on the tip of Ned's tongue to say he wasn't like Farrell. "They didn't think I was like them," he said instead.

"I expect they thought you were the sort who used to torment them in school. And you were going about with girls, which you have to admit made it harder to tell."

"We were all very young," Ned said. "Even Farrell. But you can't say he's improved with age."

"Hardly improved," Julian said unhappily. "And I truly don't know whether it was Leach or Farrell. Or whether the deaths were accidental or planned."

"We're going to have to tell Hatton," Ned said, although he shrank from the idea.

"We haven't got hard evidence of a connection between the two rituals."

"Lynes…"

"I know, I know." Julian withdrew a folded packet of paper from his pocket, and held it out to Ned. "This is what they gave Challice," he said. "As a charm for potency with his wife. He would have done anything to be ordinary in that regard. That's why he let them do as they liked."

Ned wanted to put an arm around Julian at the brittleness in his voice, but he wasn't sure that was a good idea at the moment. "Did it work?" he said.

"Apparently not. He's half convinced they cursed him."

Ned took the packet, turning it round to see the unbroken wax seal that held it closed. "Do you want me to take a look, old man? If it's doing him any harm, it would be best to know what."

"I promised him I'd burn it," Julian said.

"I will. As soon as I've had a look." He hesitated, not sure what else he should say. It was possible that he ought to feel jealous. Instead, what he mainly felt was sorry for Challice. He'd expected himself when he was at Oxford to develop appropriate feelings for some young lady, and had been troubled when they failed to materialize. But he'd never been willing to marry without them, not even for the sake of having children.

And he'd already known Julian. It had been impossible to think of the feelings that had sustained them through their schoolboy years as wrong, even when he'd been wrongheadedly trying to put them aside. If his first experience had been at the hands of someone like Farrell – if the choice had been to embrace wholeheartedly that cattish and backbiting set, or to marry and struggle against his nature – he might have ended as badly.

"I'll do whatever I can," he said.

"Carefully. If it's also non-conforming –"

"I know. But it's possible that understanding how this was done will help me work out why some of this same circle have died. And then…" He trailed off, and Julian didn't step in to fill the silence. None of the choices then would be good ones. But information was their most pressing need.

"You know where to find me," Julian said.

❈

Ned went back to his own lodgings to change, and then laid the small packet on the breakfast table and cracked the wax seal with a letter-opener. There was another folded packet of paper within the outer wrapper, this one bearing possibly unwholesome stains. Ned pried the inner packet open gingerly with the tip of the knife to reveal a lock of white-blond hair and one of a darker honey color, tied up with black thread and pinned to the paper.

Beneath them was a sigil in an unfamiliar style, a crabbed shorthand layered on top of itself and embellished with odd decorative flourishes. He was tempted to make a guess at some of its elements and test for them – it would be easy enough to tease out the meaning that way – but he knew it would be reckless.

Instead he took himself off to the Commons, the packet refolded and sealed in an envelope in his pocket, and spent the morning attempting to determine whether the Commons had any useful resources on sex magic.

The head librarian, an elderly gentleman Ned suspected had been chosen for his total lack of a sense of humor, fixed him with a steely gaze. "You are aware that membership in the Commons is dependent on maintaining appropriate morals and good character?"

"I'm not planning on putting anything in these books into practice," Ned said, hoping his face wasn't actually scarlet. "A client of mine may have become involved in some questionable practices. I'm trying to find out whether it's doing him any harm."

"It's degrading to the morals, Mr Mathey, and you know that kind of thing can lead to nervous debility. We weren't meant to use our fluids that way."

Ned resisted the urge to cover his face with his hands. "Please, might I just have a look at the books?"

"On your head be it," the librarian said, and went off scowling into the stacks.

Several hours later, he felt he had learned a considerable amount, both edifying and appalling, but none of it solved his problem. The sigil in his pocket didn't match anything in the few cures for impotence that he found in the Commons's volumes. Most of the writers tended to assume that masculine vigor was not in short supply, and focused on either the more dubious magical uses for its by-products, or on means of acquiring compliant young women to enjoy it with.

He closed an intriguing if probably opium-fueled volume by Sir Richard Burton and stacked it with the others to return. Miss Frost was eating her lunch at her desk when he returned, the crumbs from her sandwiches neatly restricting themselves to their outspread wax paper wrapper.

"You could have gone out," Ned said.

"And miss finding out if there's been another murder?"

"Not this morning," Ned said.

"That's almost a shame. We have letters from four clients who are desperate for protective enchantments against the Hand of Glory."

"Tell them I'll be happy to do a general touch-up of their household wards," Ned said. "But I can't promise a counter-charm I haven't got."

"One of them wants to know if saucers of milk will help. She says they're attracting cats."

"It'll keep down her mice?" He shook his head, dropping wearily into his chair. "I honestly don't know. But I doubt the public is in danger." Except that there was no certainty there, not when any married man might still have some connection to Farrell and his circle. "I've had the most harrowing morning in the library."

"Do you want me to try them? I know how to deal with that stare." She gave a good impression of the librarian's most intimidating scowl.

"I don't think it would help in this case. It's…well, it's rather a delicate matter."

"I see. Unsuitable for a lady's ears."

Ned started to say that it was, despite the look she would give him for it, and then reconsidered. When they'd been investigating the Nevett case, Miss Frost had given him an edifying introduction to the world of women who practiced metaphysics without a license under the cover of shops where respectable women could go without question. He'd gotten the distinct impression that some of the problems they offered to solve were decidedly personal ones.

"Certainly unsuitable for discussing in mixed company. But I do wonder if you might not be able to shed some light on the metaphysics involved."

"And yet to find out, you're going to have to tell me what we're talking about. I see that it's a dilemma for you."

"I don't want to mortally offend you to the point of quitting," Ned said. "Because then where would I be?"

"If the dead bodies haven't driven me away, Mr Mathey, I think our professional relations can survive admitting that we both know how the human race perpetuates itself."

With some reluctance, he withdrew the packet from his pocket and unfolded it. "This was given to a client as a cure for impotence. The ritual used to produce it was certainly unorthodox, very possibly non-conforming, and done by someone who I don't think had my client's best interests at heart. It doesn't seem to have worked, and I'm trying to ascertain whether it actually did some harm."

"I don't recall getting that particular client letter."

"It's a friend of Lynes's."

"Mmm." Her mouth tightened in what might have been repressed amusement for a moment, and then she sobered, examining the parcel carefully, and using the end of a pen to brush the hair aside to get a look at the sigil. "It's an odd style."

"Idiosyncratic. Even knowing what it's supposed to do, I can't make hide nor hair of it."

"I think you're mistaken," Miss Frost said. "And I wonder if whoever produced this has their own interest in your client's young lady."

"His wife," Ned said. "Why do you ask?"

"This isn't a charm against impotence. It's what you might call an anti-love charm. The two locks of hair bound up in black thread – usually you'd see black ribbon. And then a pin thrust between them, just here – I can't say much for the style or the handwriting, but I think this is supposed to be 'remove from the heart,' although it's written just as 'heart' and a negative –"

"Heartless," Ned said.

"A bit too poetic to be practical. And the whole enchantment is a tangle. Amateurish, and I'd frankly be surprised if it did anything at all. But the components are the sort of thing you'd get in a lace shop, or maybe out of a *maledictor*.

Whatever your client wanted, I think what he got was a charm to destroy his wife's feelings for him."

"Or his feelings for her," Ned said. And in a perverse way, he could see that Challice's friends might have thought that a mercy; if he didn't care about the woman he had married, he might also be freed from his guilt. But it was still an appalling betrayal, and he didn't think the use of "heartless" could possibly be a coincidence.

"Either one."

"I don't think it worked," Ned said. "But I think there may be some connection between this business and the murders. Thank you."

"I'm always pleased to be of help," Miss Frost said. "Inspector Hatton also stopped by to see if you had solved the case yet, but I told him that I expect when you do, he'll know."

Ned rubbed his neck, feeling a pang of guilt at everything he hadn't yet told Hatton. And that reckoning was surely coming soon. "I hope you had a pleasant chat."

Miss Frost frowned for a moment, and then looked amused. "Have you been under the impression that he's courting me?"

"You could do worse."

"I suppose he has been, but not in the sense you mean. He offered me a position on the Metaphysical Squad."

Ned felt a sudden stab of betrayal. "You never said."

"I am sorry. But I needed time to think about it."

"And have you?"

"I turned him down," she said.

"I hope not entirely on my account," Ned said. "I would very much like to keep you, but if it's a better position…"

"It's a position as a police matron," Miss Frost said.

"I'm certain you would be excellent."

"Maybe so," she said. "But what I want is to be a metaphysician."

"I do believe the Commons will come around to admitting women one of these days," Ned said. "But I have no idea how long that will take."

"Neither do I. But I'm twenty-three, Mr Mathey. If it takes them twenty years, I won't be an old woman yet. I'm willing to take the gamble. Even if it means not having any suitors, in the conventional sense."

"There are men who wouldn't mind…"

"Like Hatton? I expect there are. But if a metaphysician isn't going to be a man, she must certainly be a lady. She can't be a policeman's wife. And even being a metaphysician's wife is generally a full-time occupation."

"I'm sorry," Ned said after a moment.

She shook her head, dismissing sympathy. "I've always known what I was getting into. And I don't have Madeleine's…complete temperamental unsuitability to life without men. Perhaps I'll find a nice spinster to share a flat with, once Mother gives up her hopes of buying me a trousseau." Her eyes lit with amusement. "I'm told that way of life has its compensations."

Ned wished he could be certain whether she was teasing him, and just how much she knew. He opened his mouth, not at all sure what he intended to say, and then shut it again as the door opened.

It was Julian, his hat under his arm. "I hoped you'd be here," he said.

Ned stood, pushing his chair back. "Not another murder?"

"No, it's Kennett. I've had a cryptic note demanding that I go round to see him. Given that he's still a murder suspect …"

"I'll come and try to make sure you don't get murdered," Ned said. "And tell you what I've found out about the other business on the way."

CHAPTER FIFTEEN
Choices

NED PAID THE CAB FARE, FEELING that murder and impotence were
not best discussed on an omnibus. He explained what he had learned
as they jounced over the cobblestones.

"Heartless," Julian said, frowning. "There must be a connection. But if they
botched the ritual with Challice that badly, why did it take months for them
to begin dying from it?"

"I don't know," Ned said. "And I wouldn't think that little charm would back-
fire badly enough to kill them. Women all over the city do this sort of thing,
apparently, and we haven't seen a plague of gentlemen dropping dead with
missing hearts. But then with non-conforming enchantment, it's always hard
to be certain. And that business of substituting 'heartless' for 'remove from the
heart' – metaphor is dangerous in modern metaphysics. You shouldn't try to
be poetic."

"If it was all merely an accident, we might not have to do anything about it."

"Punton was frightened of a writing desk. Or of something in it. It wasn't an
accident that some of this set did a ritual to create a Hand of Glory."

"But it might be a coincidence. If they tried to create a Hand of Glory – or
did create one, or at least something like it – and then people started dropping
dead, Punton might have assumed the Hand of Glory was the cause, when
really it was what they did with Challice."

"There's still the delay to explain," Ned said in frustration, as the cab drew up
outside Kennett's townhouse. "Let's see what Kennett has to tell us."

The same maid let them in, and somewhat to Ned's surprise, showed them
up immediately rather than leaving them waiting in the hall. The little parlor

upstairs was overly warm, a fire blazing, but Kennett was wrapped in his silk dressing gown, and he didn't rise when they entered.

"What's the matter?" Julian asked.

Kennett frowned. "I have a metaphysical problem I want to consult you about. Actually, since you've brought Mathey...I'd rather just tell Mathey about it. No offense, Lynes."

"What sort of metaphysical problem?"

"A personal one, damn it."

Ned looked sideways at Julian, who shook his head. "Given that you're still a murder suspect, you'll understand if I'd rather not leave you alone with Mathey at the moment."

"All I did was that curse out of the *maledictor*," Kennett said stubbornly. "That couldn't have killed him."

"No, probably not," Ned allowed. "Suppose you tell me what you want my help with?"

Kennett scowled. "It's about the curse I did. I'm afraid it's...well...backfired." He shifted uncomfortably in his chair, and Ned managed, by dint of great effort, to maintain a professionally solemn expression. A sideways glance at Julian showed he wasn't being nearly as restrained.

"That's rather outside my realm of expertise," Ned said. "I could refer you to someone who specializes in medical complaints –"

"But I couldn't tell them what I did," Kennett said. "You must be able to do something about this. They're all over my –"

"All right, yes, I'll see what I can do," Ned said hastily.

"On one condition," Julian added, whip-quick. "That if there's anything you haven't told us that might bear on Dorrington's death – anything at all – you tell us now."

"That's not fair, Lynes."

"This isn't a game of forfeits. Three men are dead, and if we can't sort it out, we won't be able to keep the Yard out of the clubs forever. Do you really want your name splashed across the morning papers that way?"

Kennett looked unhappy. "It's going to sound worse than it was, really. Probably it doesn't anything to do with the deaths –"

"Tell us," Julian said.

"Do something about the damned boils, and I'll tell you."

Kennett stretched out on the sofa looking martyred, his dressing gown open to reveal the problem, and Ned set about trying to solve it. It was a tricky piece of work untangling the amateur grammar of the curse, and wondering the whole time whether some non-conforming element was going to combine disastrously with his attempts to remove it. Julian sprawled in the armchair reading a book, looking up from it every now and then with eyebrows raised.

Finally Kennett sat up, belting his dressing gown firmly and straightening the collar as if it could restore his dignity with it. "Thank you," he said grudgingly.

"I'll send you a bill," Ned said.

Julian sat up and put the book aside. "Now, what do you know?"

"There was a ritual at the Dionysus," Kennett said.

Julian's expression turned abruptly grim. "That business with Challice?"

"Challice wasn't in it," Kennett said, shaking his head. "It was Farrell and his set. Leach was there, and Dorrington, and Punton. Oh, and little Hall."

"You mean to say, all of the murder victims?" Ned said, his own voice rising a little in indignation.

"Farrell and Leach haven't come to any harm."

"Yet," Julian added.

"Nor have I."

"Yet."

Kennett went on doggedly. "It wasn't intended to hurt anybody. It was just a notion Punton had for how we could get our hands on some money."

Julian regarded him levelly. "What for?"

"What does anyone need money for? Do you think this house is easy to keep up by writing potboilers?"

"You might live in a flat," Ned couldn't help saying.

"And grow my hair out like a Bohemian painter," Kennett said with distaste. "Well, it may come to that, and then everyone can have a good laugh."

"Tell them you're suffering for your art," Julian said unsympathetically. "What about the others?"

"They all needed money. Pinky said he didn't make much as a critic, the bastard. Well, we all know now how he was making ends meet, don't we? But I suppose he wasn't satisfied with sticking to blackmail. Farrell and Leach both have debts. I think Punton wanted to see if it would work more than anything, but I'm sure he could have found some use for the money as well. And Dolly never could find anyone who'd keep him in the style he preferred."

"What did you do?" Ned asked when it seemed Kennett had wound down.

"Punton had some books with instructions for how to create a Hand of Glory."

"Which books, exactly?"

"We mixed together bits. Some of it was out of the *Little Albert*, but of course there was no question of getting the actual hand, so we used a different enchantment, one for conjuring a sort of a serpent into a box –"

"That's out of the *Grimorium Verum*," Ned said, the pieces falling abruptly into place "I've been assuming they enchanted an actual hand, or some modern substitute for it, but – what the *Grimorium Verum* calls a Hand of Glory is a sort of serpent that breeds gold."

"The *Grimorium Verum*, that sounds right. We were going to send it out to rob people who we felt deserved it. We could all think of someone – we'd all been drinking, you know, and everyone likes to get indignant in a good cause."

"Who were they?"

"I hardly remember. There was some relative of Farrell's who wouldn't give him an advance on his expectations; I think Punton named the gentleman he worked for, and Leach some old lover. I remember the top of the list was some pawnbroker who'd sold off some of Dolly's things when he didn't claim them fast enough."

Ned looked sideways at Julian. "McGill, on Tabor Road?"

"I don't know where he had his shop, but that sounds like the name. You must understand, I wasn't paying any mind at the time –"

"It didn't matter to you who you stole from," Julian offered.

"We deserved it more than they did," Kennett said, but his eyes slid away from Julian's. "We all agreed to try the pawnbroker first, because he was certain to have valuables about the place. We wrote the enchantment out on a bit of paper, and put it in the box –"

"A sort of engraved writing desk?" Ned prompted.

"That's right. It was Pinky's originally. And then we did the ritual over the box. And absolutely nothing happened. It just sat there, and after a while we opened it up, and there wasn't a serpent in the box, or anything else, either."

"Was the slip of paper still in the box?" Ned asked.

"No, it was gone. That was the only thing that happened. Apart from making the paper vanish, the ritual didn't do anything."

Ned let out a frustrated breath. That should have been a sign that the ritual had done something, something extremely worrying, but he suspected none of these men had known that much about metaphysics. "Who actually wrote the ritual? Punton?"

"He came up with the bones of it, and then I sort of polished it up a bit. You know, just to make it sound a bit more impressive when we did it, give it that poetic touch –"

"The poetic touch," Julian said, his voice low and dangerous, and Ned followed his thought at once.

"Tell me you didn't use the word 'heartless,'" he said.

"I believe I did," Kennett said. "Yes, I did, because I was trying to work out the sigil for it, and Punton said he'd worked it out already for some other bit of hocus, and he showed me how to write it. It was in the part of the ritual that summed up our complaints against…" Kennett's voice faltered, as if even he were putting it together.

"Against the people you felt deserved to have something stolen from them," Ned said, every word falling like lead.

"It didn't work. I swear to you, Mathey, nothing happened. The box just sat there, and eventually everyone got tired of waiting for it to do something interesting, and the evening broke up. And the people who've died weren't people who were ever on the list −"

"The pawnbroker is dead," Julian said.

"My God." The blood was draining from Kennett's face. "But Pinky, and Dolly, and Punton − my God, you don't suppose the enchantment backfired −" There was sweat standing out on Kennett's forehead.

"No," Ned said slowly, thinking it through. "I don't think it backfired. I think it snagged on an earlier enchantment, a curse that also used the word 'heartless,' one that was worked by Dorrington and Punton and Hall." A curse worked in an older system of enchantment, one that relied far more on intention than on precision in language − and Challice had kept the talisman they gave him, marked with the sigil *heartless* and stained with their vital fluids, keeping it near him while he brooded over their cruelty.

"But the serpent shouldn't have been able to go out and do anything at all without being fed," Kennett said. "Punton promised −"

"What did Punton promise?"

"Well, some of us were a bit nervous about it. That it might get out of hand. And Punton said the serpent couldn't go out and fetch gold unless you poured bran in the box to feed it. We had some to hand, but we never used it."

Julian glanced at Ned. "Mathey?"

"That's how it's given in the *Grimorium Verum*. You looked over Punton's notes −"

"Damn it, I think he's right," Julian said after a moment. "If that's what they were basing the ritual on − it shouldn't be able to go out without being fed. Though if it's not fed when it expects it, it may turn on its creator, and get free of him that way."

"And the devil only knows what it might do then. But then someone must have fed it, and must have kept on feeding it even after the deaths started."

"We never sent it out," Kennett insisted. "I told you, we didn't think it worked."

Julian's eyes narrowed. "What happened to the box?"

"I suppose someone took it home."

"Who?"

"I can't remember. We were all three sheets to the wind –"

"A fine state to be doing metaphysics in."

"Think," Julian said.

"All right. Dolly and Punton left first, together. Then Pinky, and I remember he left the box behind, and Leach and Farrell were bantering back and forth about which one of them ought to take it away with them if Pinky didn't want it –"

"Which one of them took it?"

"I don't know. I went down the hall for a minute, and when I came back they'd both gone, and the box was gone with them."

"One of them took it home," Ned said, certainty settling in the pit of his stomach. "And the serpent appeared, or something like it, and one of them fed it bran and sent it out after the pawnbroker. That way he wouldn't have to share. And then after that..."

"There are two ways it could have happened," Julian said, his tone hard. "One way, it was always about the money. He sent out the serpent again and again, hoping for another box full of silver and gold, and when his friends began to die, he didn't care."

Kennett shook his head, appalled. "You know Leach and Farrell, Lynes, you were at Oxford with them –"

Julian's jaw was set, his tone perfectly cold. "The other way, he panicked. The serpent killed Punton, and he saw the position he was in. He'd used non-conforming enchantment to create a creature that had already killed – how many, by then? The pawnbroker, at least. Maybe more. But he wasn't the only one who saw it."

"Dorrington was a blackmailer," Ned said. "If he realized that Farrell or Leach had been sending the creature out –"

"Not just Dorrington," Julian said. Ned could see the lines of unhappiness on his face despite the coolness of his tone. "Dolly Hall realized what was happening. I don't know if it was the pawnbroker, or if he found out about Punton, but I'm certain that's what he wanted to tell us, that night. A metaphysical problem –"

"And I wouldn't hear him out."

"Neither would I," Julian said grimly. "But remember what he said? 'He's being entirely unreasonable.' 'He's not being sensible, and it's all going to fall apart.' He had already talked to someone else about it. Maybe urged them to go to the police, or to destroy the box. Or at the very least stop using it."

"And instead he sent it out again that night," Ned said, unable to deny how well it came together. "It wouldn't have mattered if he knew much about metaphysics, because it was already linked to Hall, already considered him a proper target. He fed it, and he gave it Hall's name –"

"He sent it to kill Dolly Hall," Julian said. "And then he sent it to kill Dorrington. And if I were the only other living person who was present at that ritual, I'd be a bit worried, myself."

Kennett stared at him for a moment, and then shook his head vehemently. "I can't believe it. It must have been an accident. Someone took the box home with him, and perhaps he played around with it a bit and something terrible went wrong, but cold-blooded murder – no. Not one of our friends."

"Think what you like," Julian said.

"I think you had better go. The both of you."

"Very well," Ned said before Julian could reply. He caught Julian's arm and steered him out, not stopping until they were out on the street outside. Julian stood for a moment on the front walk as if unsure where he meant to go from there.

"It was Farrell or Leach," he said. "It can't have been anyone else."

Ned put a hand on his shoulder. "What are we going to do about it?"

Julian shook his head. "I don't know."

❦

THERE WAS NO POINT STANDING IN the street freezing and drawing unwanted attention, not in the end of the afternoon when the first wave of homing residents was about to begin. The British Library would be closing soon, and the neighborhood was a haunt of scholars. Julian shook himself and started for Guilford Street, Ned silent at his side. Farrell or Leach, Leach and Farrell – much as Kennett would like to pretend otherwise, there was no mistaking that one of them was the murderer. Farrell had proved himself capable of the cruelty, and he was clever enough, but in the past he'd always kept his hands clean. Violence was always Leach's first resort, but he'd never been particularly bright, preferring to follow someone else's lead in everything except fisticuffs. Perhaps they were in it together, Farrell's brain and Leach's ruthless determination would explain most of what had happened. They'd always been worst in each other's company, better, more bearable, on their own.

He realized that Ned was talking, had been talking for some time, and stopped abruptly. "What?"

Ned gave him a look of exasperation. "You haven't heard a word I've said."

"No. I'm sorry, I was thinking."

"What are we going to do?" Ned said again.

"That's what I was trying to figure out."

"You can't just decide that on your own and expect me to go along with it," Ned said sharply, and Julian touched his arm in apology.

"No."

Ned gave him a look, and Julian elaborated.

"No, you're right, and no, I won't."

They had reached Mecklenburgh Square and Julian led them past it, turned down the side street that brought them to the gates of the cemetery that served the Foundling Hospital. He worked the iron latch, but Ned balked at the entrance.

"What are you doing?"

"I need to think," Julian said. "We need to think. And this is more private than most places."

"It's also cold," Ned muttered, but followed, closing the gate behind them.

As Julian had hoped, both the cemetery and the long promenade that ran back toward the Foundlings' grim housing were mostly empty. A frock-coated teacher led a double line of boys into the building, while a pair of women in respectable blacks moved along one of the cemetery's further paths, escorted by a sexton. The rest of the ground was open, sparse winter-brown grass and badly graveled paths between rows of graves marked primarily by numbered plaques. There was no one to overhear, no one to see, and Julian drew a breath.

"We can't go to the police."

"We have to," Ned answered.

"You know what will happen if we do."

"I know." Ned's voice was unhappy, but Julian spelled it out anyway, keeping his voice low and cold.

"If we go to the police, they will arrest Leach and Farrell. They will charge one of them, and when they do, whichever one is charged will make sure that everyone knows exactly what sort of clubs they and their friends frequented. If they're at all clever, they'll try to discredit us that way, but, however it falls out, they'll ruin everyone they can reach."

Ned made a sound that might have been a protest, but Julian went on heedlessly.

"Leach would do it to hurt. He's a bully and a fool, and if he's wounded, he'll damage anyone within reach. Farrell will try to bargain, weasel out of it by threatening anyone of any sort of social standing, but murder is murder, and the Crown won't let him plead to anything less – at least not without compelling evidence that this was some sort of bizarre accident, and it clearly wasn't. It's murder in the course of robbery when you come down to it, and that's a hanging offense. So he has no reason not to bring us down, too."

"Surely it would only make matters worse for him," Ned said, without conviction.

"He'll hang. What's worse than that? He might as well take us with him."

Ned's face was gray in the late afternoon light. "He'd have to prove it. And the Crown will have to want to prosecute."

"He can make enough of a scandal that the Crown will have no choice." Julian stared blindly at the barren ground and the worn stone markers. "I've been careful, of course, and so have you, but – it's true. The proof is there if anyone looks." He pinched the bridge of his nose, trying not to imagine Ned in the dock, back straight as he answered the damning questions. *Have you ever had unnatural relations with* – well, fill in the name, it didn't matter who. They could lie, but a zealous prosecutor could find witnesses; their landladies would swear that they spent nearly as many nights together as apart, and Farrell or Leach could tell them where to look for more evidence of an improper relationship. He cleared his throat, forcing the thought away. "They'd have to prove actual buggery for a conviction, though, and I don't think any jury in the kingdom is going to take Farrell's word over ours. Not when it's life in prison."

He was proud that his voice stayed steady on that. The thought of prison, of confinement and regimen, stone walls and mindless labor and endless empty days, frankly terrified him. He would rather die, rather kill himself – and he had the means – but that would leave Ned to face it alone. He cleared his throat again.

"But I doubt we'd be convicted. Almost no one has been."

"It doesn't matter," Ned said. "A trial – even the suggestion would ruin me. The Commons would revoke my membership, and there's an end to my practice. I'd never hold a license again."

He didn't say what he had to be thinking, for which Julian was grateful. Even the breath of scandal would ruin Ned, but he himself might well survive. Admittedly, he'd lose his respectable clients, and some of the criminal classes could be surprisingly prudish, but he could probably continue, thought with a reduced and much more questionable practice. The thought was depressing, and he shook his head.

"We could try to brazen it out, say that Farrell and Leach just want to ruin us –"

"The Commons would still eject me." Ned's face was bleak. "You have to be certifiably of good moral character."

"Like a bloody footman," Julian snapped. It felt good to be angry, and Ned put a hand on his shoulder.

"I knew the rule when I joined."

"Damn it." Julian squinted toward the back gate, where the sexton was taking his farewells of the two women. "So we don't go to the police –"

"And Farrell or Leach keep on robbing and killing people." Ned shook his head. "We can't have that, old boy."

"We dare not." Not least because they'd be next on the list of persons, inconvenient, to be got rid of, and Julian had no desire to spend the rest of his life fending off attacks.

"We have to go to the police," Ned said again, miserably.

Julian hunched his shoulders. "Or we deal with him ourselves."

"How?"

"Kill him." Julian met Ned's eyes squarely. "We find out which of them it is, and we kill him."

Ned's mouth opened and closed. "And if we're caught, we hang."

"So we don't get caught."

"Easier said than done. The Yard aren't fools." Ned managed a grim smile. "And neither you nor I are precisely experts in the business."

"I could hire an expert. Bolster's bound to know someone."

"And have him blackmail you for the rest of your life? I don't think so, Lynes. It has to be the police."

"And ruin ourselves into the bargain." Julian's voice was equally bleak.

"There's no other choice."

"There has to be," Julian insisted.

Ned kicked unhappily at a marker. "I have to tell Hatton first – I owe him the chance to sack me before this all goes wrong."

Julian checked his watch, the numbers hard to read in the fading light. "He'll be gone home by now."

"I know. But surely it will keep until morning."

"And maybe we'll think of something else," Julian said, and didn't believe it. Outside the cemetery walls, the streetlights cast a familiar blurred light as the fog began to gather, and he swore under his breath. "I told Mrs Digby I wouldn't be home for dinner."

"We'll find something on the way," Ned said, and laid a cautious hand on Julian's shoulder.

They stopped by silent agreement at a restaurant neither of them had ever frequented, and Julian poked unenthusiastically at an indifferent pie while Ned wrestled with a stringy cut of mutton.

"We'll have to leave the country," Ned said, setting his knife aside, and took a gulp of the astringent claret.

Julian felt like downing the rest of his own glass, but made himself swallow the tasteless potato. "How does that help?"

"If we change our names," Ned said, his voice soft but steady, "change our names and go abroad where no one knows us – we could still work then. I could still practice, and so could you."

Leave London. The thought was enough to make Julian shudder. He had loved London since the first time he'd set foot within the bounds, ten years old and dragged after his great-uncle because they were between tutors and there was no one currently at the country house who could be trusted to take charge of him. He had loved the noise and the crowds and the stink, the museums and the back alleys and the endlessly fascinating people, and had spent the rest of boyhood plotting ways to get back. He had saved pennies, cheated at cards for shillings, and spent it all on tickets to Town, and taken the resulting punishments willingly enough. After University, he had taken his inheritance and found lodgings in Bloomsbury and never looked back. He knew London better than he knew most of his lovers, liked it better, too, and the thought of leaving was a knife to the heart. A part of him would almost rather hang, foolish as that was, and he shook his head. "We can't talk about that here," he said, and Ned looked away.

By the time they returned to Coptic Street, the fog had thickened, muffling sound and hanging in smoky halos around the street lamps. Julian let them in, for once grateful for Mrs Digby's stubborn refusal to mind the door after eight o'clock. He turned up the gas, sighing at the amount of clutter crowding the consulting room. Books and newspapers and a few large scrapbooks were stacked in two of the four chairs and on the floor, interleaved with markers and scraps of paper. Most of the table was covered with books and papers, too, and Mrs Digby had left the breakfast tray with its plates smeared with congealing egg and grease. He had left the coffee pot and the milk jug on the sideboard, the latter holding down a stack of unpaid bills, and he swore under his breath. Mrs Digby had won this battle in their on-going war – she was currently refusing to move anything that might threaten to disturb his working papers, but surely she could at least have taken the dirty plates. The flat was cold, too, and smelled of fog, and Julian looked irritably for the open window. It was the one by the bedroom door, and he slammed it closed, turning to the sideboard, while Ned knelt to rekindle the fire.

"Drink?"

"God, yes," Ned said, and rose to join him, dusting his hands on his trousers.

Julian poured them each a generous double measure, and they retreated to the sofa, sitting at opposite ends as though that would somehow make things better. The *Urtica mordax* pulled at Julian's hair and he shifted out of reach.

"If we left the country, we wouldn't actually have to go through a trial," Ned said. "And I have to say that appeals."

"Well, yes." Julian took a long drink of his whisky, letting it burn its way down his throat. "I don't deny that is a benefit."

"We can't brazen it out, so we might as well salvage what we can." Ned managed a wry smile. "Australia is traditional, but the ties with Britain might be a bit too close."

"And it's the other side of the world. Why not Paris?"

"I don't speak French," Ned answered. "Neither do you, unless you've learned since University."

"No." Julian swirled his drink thoughtfully in its glass. "Berlin? Or Vienna?"

"I don't speak German."

"I do. At least, I read it. A bit."

"There's America," Ned said, after a moment. "What about New York?"

"Too primitive," Julian said. "Do they even have metaphysicians?"

"Lynes, you may be able to pretend this doesn't matter, but I simply can't. There's my family to think of, too."

"Yes, of course." London or Ned: the choice was simple when it came down to it, and he took a deep breath. "Of course you're right, and of course I'll come."

The look on Ned's face was reward enough. He reached out to take Julian's hand, and Julian returned the grasp, holding on tightly until he was sure Ned believed him.

"I still think we should consider Paris. I could learn French."

"You never managed before."

"Well, neither did you."

"And it's something of a specialized vocabulary," Ned went on, as if he hadn't heard. "I think we need to go someplace where they speak English."

"New York is closer than Australia," Julian said. He refused to consider the possibility that they might never be able to return. "And it might be wise to be outside the Empire."

"New York, then," Ned said, and they touched glasses.

Julian glanced around the flat, wondering what he could take with him. He had to bring his books, they were the core of a highly specialized library, and there were volumes he would never be able to replace – and there was his inheritance to think of, too, the small sum currently safely invested. Presumably the dividends could be sent overseas? At least they would have that to live on, if nothing else. He'd never considered the question.

Ned drained his glass and leaned forward to pat Julian's knee before heaving himself to his feet. "Another?"

"Why not?" Julian handed him the glass and leaned back against the cushions. A hangover would hardly improve the impending conversation with Hatton, but nothing could make it worse. And there were cantrips to cure hangovers.

It was still cold in the flat – if anything, it seemed colder than before, in spite of the now crackling fire. He pushed himself to his feet, and Ned's voice froze him in his tracks.

"Lynes. Has that – is that your writing desk?"

"Not funny, Mathey." Julian stared at the plain brown box half hidden beneath a drift of papers. It wasn't his, he'd never owned any such thing, considered traveling desks a toy for maiden aunts and fussy travelers like his great-uncle. And surely it couldn't be the desk Godding had described, that had been inlaid, elaborate, something to pawn, not so plain that it could linger unseen in the shadows. The dark wood shimmered, revealing scrolls and curlicues, brass and mother-of-pearl breaking through the varnish like sunlight through clouds. The paper around it rustled, as though from an unfelt breeze – or as though a snake moved through the jumbled mess.

"Mathey –"

The air above the box yellowed, curdled, thickening into strands like solid smoke. They rose from the box – no, the box dissolved into them, became them, winding together to rear upright in a shape like a striking cobra. Tiny gold sparks flickered for an instant where eyes should have been, and Julian licked his lips.

"Ned…"

"The serpent in the box," Ned whispered.

CHAPTER SIXTEEN
The Serpent in the Box

THE CURLING SMOKE SWAYED LIKE A snake. Ned reached into his coat and drew out his wand. He hesitated, clutching it tightly in his hand. There were curses he could try, enchantments that might halt the thing where it stood or force it back into its other form. Any of them might also react disastrously to set the room afire or collapse it into endless void.

"We have to get out," Julian began, but the creature was between them and the door.

"You go. I'll try to hold it off." The only way to do that was to try some enchantment. Ned brandished his wand and tried to steel himself to do it, knowing that in a moment he might be engulfed in flames, or, worse, horribly changed.

"That thing eats hearts, Mathey." Julian stood up, and the serpent swayed toward him at once, uncurling itself in his direction. It was slow enough that Julian had time to back away from it, but it circled him, cutting off their path to the door.

"I know." It was drifting toward them both, now, weaving back and forth, and as they both stepped backwards away from it, Ned realized it was herding them both back against the fireplace. It swayed closer, and Ned couldn't help thinking of gruesomely opened bodies with horribly empty chests. He gritted his teeth and raised his wand.

"Mathey –"

He ignored the warning note in Julian's voice, and sketched a sigil in the air in front of him like a shield, a simple cantrip to clear away fog or smoke.

He could feel the enchantment go wrong the moment the sigil was fully formed, twisting away from the creature in front of them and escaping his control. Every stack of paper in the room rustled, as in a growing breeze, and then wind began whipping through the room. Loose books and papers went flying, dishes rattling and crashing to the ground.

The coils of yellow smoke still hung in the air, drifting undisturbed.

"Bloody hell," Ned said.

"I take it that's not what you were going for." Julian's voice was even, although his whole body was tense, as if it were taking all his self-control not to bolt.

"I'm afraid not."

The creature drifted forward, extending itself almost curiously toward Julian. Julian flicked his own wand in a less textbook enchantment – Ned thought the word was *freeze*, but it was so crabbed in the execution it was hard to tell – and the dying wind turned cold. Behind him, the fire shuddered and died, and the gas lamps guttered, throwing the room into shadow.

Julian swore. As the lamp flames steadied, Ned could see the serpent rearing back, flecks of gold once again glittering like eyes beneath a smoky hood. It looked like it was poising itself to strike. "If we run –" Julian began.

"It can only come after one of us," Ned finished. He waved a hand to attract the creature's attention, and then broke away in the direction of the window. The curls of smoke uncoiled toward him, shockingly fast. It had just been playing with them before, he realized – it could move as fast as a striking snake –

It writhed in a circle around him, wreathing him in trailing fog, and then reared up in front of him like a cobra. Ned put up his wand to fend the creature off, but before he could even begin to trace a sigil in the air, the serpent struck out at his breast.

The sensation as it touched him was horrible, like a hand reaching through skin and muscle and bone, hideously wrong. He clawed at his aching chest, trying to fend it off, touching only smoke, and the ache strengthened to a stabbing pain. He couldn't speak, could only look up in the desperate hope that Julian had made it to the door – but Julian was grabbing up something from the mantelpiece, and turning to fling it at the serpent.

Something wet spattered Ned's face, and the pain vanished at once. The smoke exploded into a drifting cloud and then swirled away toward the window, which opened for it as if nudged by an invisible hand. Ned staggered back to sit down on the sofa, clutching reflexively at his crumpled shirt front. His hand came away damp, and he blinked down at it for a moment before realizing it was wet with somewhat soured milk.

"Apparently milk will do the trick," he said, although he found his voice inexplicably unsteady on the words.

"It seemed worth a try," Julian said, going down on his knees in front of the sofa and feeling at Ned's shirt front as if he expected it to be rent in pieces. His voice was odd as well, and he tightened his hand in Ned's shirt as if unwilling to let go. "Are you all right?"

Ned put his hand over Julian's and pressed it to his chest so that he could feel his heart beating. "I seem to still have all the usual parts, so, yes."

"I couldn't think what else to do."

"I can't complain, old man. I expect you saved my life."

Julian rested his forehead against his hand for a moment, and then raised his head. "Are you sure we can't kill him?"

"It's more likely to get us arrested than telling the truth."

Julian let out a breath. "All right. Let's go and do it."

Ned looked at the complicated clock now lying overturned and somewhat battered beside the sofa, its enchanted face still glowing although some of the more complex bits of its machinery looked bent. "It's the small hours of the morning," he said. "Hatton won't be there, and if we tell it all to whoever's on duty at the Yard, we'll only have to tell it over again when Hatton gets in."

"You're probably right," Julian said, getting to his feet. He went over to shut the window, giving it a dark look as he did.

"It may not be able to come back tonight. It has to be fed each time."

"Even so – I don't think we'd better both go to sleep."

"I don't think I could sleep," Ned said. He wasn't sure which was making his heart race in his chest, fear that the serpent might return, or the prospect of having to confess the truth to Hatton in the morning. "You can if you like."

In the end they spent some time straightening the mess Ned's enchantment had made of the room, and then spent the night on the sofa, each of them dozing fitfully for a while, never quite dropping off into sleep. They left as soon as it was light, neither of them wanting to face Mrs Digby and the breakfast tray, and took a cab to the Yard.

❦

NEITHER OF THEM SPOKE FOR SOME time as the cab rattled across the paving stones, although Julian put his shoulder against Ned's.

"New York," Ned said when the silence had grown too much to bear.

"New York," Julian said, his chin set with determination, and then turned to gaze out the window at the streets rolling past as if already saying goodbye to an old friend.

Ned was afraid they would find the offices of the Metaphysical Squad still shuttered, but one of the younger constables was there, and greeted him pleasantly when he came in.

"That's nice timing, Mr Mathey," he said. "The guv'nor's out on a case, but I'm sure he'll want to see you when he gets in. We've got another one, looks like."

Ned and Julian exchanged glances. "Another what?"

"Another man dead with no mark on him. Could be he went off in the ordinary way, but it seems he was a friend of that Punton. I don't know how long the inspector's going to be; want me to send round for you when he gets back in, or do you want to wait?"

"We'll wait," Ned said, and sat down to do so.

It was mid-morning by the time Hatton came in, and Ned was beginning to wish he'd had breakfast, hunger starting to make itself felt even through deadening dread. He stood up when Hatton arrived, and Hatton nodded to him before hanging up his hat.

"Mathey. We have another one."

"Who is it?"

"A Mr Ryder Leach," Hatton said, and Ned couldn't help glancing sideways at Julian. That meant it was Farrell, and Julian knew it as well as he did. "It seems he knew Mr Punton, according to some of his fellow lodgers. We've brought him in for the surgeon to open up just to make certain that his heart's missing like the rest, but I wouldn't give odds on his having died of anything in the usual way."

"Inspector, may we speak with you in private?" Ned said. "There's something you should know, something that bears on the case, but I'd much rather – it would be better discussed in private."

Hatton turned, startled, and looked him over. "All right," he said. "There's an odd corner we've been fixing up to use as an interview room. Will that suit you?"

"Perfectly."

They followed Hatton out the door of the converted stable and around a corner, into what had clearly once been a shed but was now a clean if cramped room with chairs on either side of a table and a door that Hatton shut behind them. Ned took one of the chairs facing the door, and after a moment's hesitation Julian took the other, leaving Hatton to sit facing them like a stern headmaster considering a pair of errant schoolboys.

"Now what's this about?" Hatton rubbed his forehead tiredly. "I've been up for hours dealing with another corpse, so I'll thank you to stick to essentials."

"I know who the murderer is," Ned said. "Linford Farrell. He and the other dead men were members of a circle practicing non-conforming metaphysics. They were trying to create a Hand of Glory – at least, some kind of artifact they could use to commit robberies. But the creature they created killed its victims as well." He took a deep breath. "I believe Farrell has been sending out the Hand of Glory, and it's been killing the other men who participated in the ritual. I thought that might be partly accidental, but after last night –"

"The thing came after us," Julian said. "It tried to kill Mathey."

"I'm afraid he's killing off the witnesses to the ritual that created the creature, and anyone else who knows about it."

"And how do you know about it?" Hatton said, fixing him with a steely expression. "Tell me you weren't involved in creating this thing."

"I wasn't," Ned said, although he abruptly saw that might seem a plausible explanation. It wasn't really a better one, though, and Farrell would still tell the truth as soon as he was arrested. "I'm…acquainted with these gentlemen, and Lynes and I have been making inquiries among our mutual acquaintances. They're all members of a club to which we also belong."

"Well, why in the devil didn't you say so when we were hunting high and low for some connection between the blasted victims? I understand there's a club tie, Mathey, but when it's a case of murder –"

"There's more," Ned said, and took a deep breath. "It's a club for sodomites, Hatton. That's why it wasn't public knowledge that the dead men were members. Or that I am."

Hatton leaned his head back for a moment, regarding the ceiling. "Christ."

"I owed it to you to tell you in person," Ned said. "Of course I'll consider myself dismissed."

"Hang on just a bloody minute," Hatton said. "You're not going anywhere until we get some things straight. This thing, this Hand of Glory – it really is a hand that attacks people?"

"It's a box, an ornamented kind of writing desk – at least, that's how it looks some of the time. When it attacks, it transforms itself into a sort of a serpent made out of smoke."

"Created by –"

"Farrell, Leach, Dorrington, Punton, Hall, and Kennett," Ned said.

"Kennett," Hatton said, scowling at Julian.

Julian nodded stiffly. "He came to me because he knew me," he said.

"Through this perverse club of yours."

"Yes."

"I didn't know until last night that Kennett had been involved in the ritual," Ned said. "According to him, most of the participants didn't think it had worked. But Farrell took the Hand of Glory home with him, and it seems he's been using it ever since."

"To commit robberies, or murders?"

"Probably both. The pawnbroker who died – Kennett says they meant to rob him. But the others, the members of the circle – Punton may really have been an accident, I don't know. I think Hall was pressing Farrell to stop using the Hand of Glory, or even to confess to the police. And Dorrington tried to blackmail him about it, just as he was blackmailing Kennett and Miss Barton about their literary efforts."

"And you're pursuing him, I see that much. What about Leach?"

"Farrell's panicking," Julian said flatly. "As long as there are people who know about his role in the ritual, he's in danger. Even if they're his friends."

Hatton looked at him levelly. "Were you his friend?"

"I thought I was."

Hatton considered them both for a long moment. "Right, then. I'm bringing both Kennett and Farrell in for questioning."

"I don't think Kennett meant any harm," Julian said.

"Whatever Mr Kennett meant or didn't mean, there are at least five men dead, and a writing desk that eats people menacing the city. I know I for one will feel better when Kennett and Farrell are both under arrest."

"Am I also under arrest?" Ned forced himself to ask.

Hatton rubbed his forehead again, looking exhausted. "I ought to haul you up on charges for obstruction of justice. That would be easier to do if you hadn't just solved the crime."

"I meant –"

"I know what you meant, Mathey. That would be a fine scandal, wouldn't it? Especially when the Metaphysical Squad is already on thin ice."

"If I resign at once –"

"You can't resign until we've got Kennett, Farrell, and the damned writing desk safely in custody," Hatton said. "Let's keep our priorities straight. We round them up, and then we'll talk about what to do with you."

"If your men do find the Hand of Glory – it sounds absurd, but we were able to drive it off by throwing milk at it," Ned said. "You might have some standing by as a protective measure."

"I will," Hatton said. "But it looked as though Leach had that idea as well. We found an empty bottle of milk by the body, and the floor splashed with it. If he tried to drive it off that way, he didn't succeed."

Ned shook his head. "It's not actually a classic Hand of Glory. It may be that the milk doesn't affect it as strongly – that it found it unpleasant, but it's discovered it doesn't truly hurt it."

"Or it's getting stronger," Hatton said.

Ned nodded unwillingly. "Or it is."

€✦

It was an hour before Hatton's men returned with Kennett, during which time Julian paced, Hatton smoked moodily, and Ned tried not to think about what was going to happen to them once Farrell was in custody.

Garmin and a uniformed constable marched Kennett in, unshaven and looking suspiciously hung over.

"Take a seat, Mr Kennett," Hatton said. "You'll be assisting us with our inquiries."

"What are you playing at, Lynes?" Kennett snapped. "You're supposed to be helping me."

"I think Mr Lynes has given you more than enough help," Hatton said. "In fact, I think Mr Lynes has had more than enough to do with this investigation."

"I thought we had helped you solve the case," Julian said, a dangerous note in his voice.

"*Mathey* helped solve the case. I don't recall employing you."

"You could do worse. There have been enough times when the Yard could have used the help."

"Yes, I'm certain that employing a disreputable private detective will cure what ails us. Do you have any other advice on the running of this department, Mr Lynes?"

It was nerves, Ned thought, nothing more than that; Julian was strung tight waiting to find out what punishment they were facing, and ready for the excuse of a quarrel to distract him, and Hatton's nerves couldn't be in a good state either knowing that a writing desk that ate hearts was menacing the public. He was bracing himself to step in when Kennett motioned to him urgently.

"As a matter of fact..." Julian began, and Ned turned his back on him with an inward wince, drawing Kennett aside as far as he dared.

"What is it?"

"Farrell knows you've found out about the creature," Kennett said.

"How?"

"I told him. Last night."

"For God's sake, Kennett."

"He's – well, maybe not a friend," Kennett said. "But one of us. Surely you can understand that. And I can't believe he meant to kill anyone. It was an accident, it must have been. I thought if he understood that people were dying, and saw how serious it all was, he'd agree to go to the police. We could tell some story..." He trailed off, with a sideways glance at Hatton.

"It's too late for that," Ned said. "Farrell tried to kill me and Lynes last night."

"He can't have."

"He did, if you'll get it through your –" Ned broke off, aware that any moment Hatton would stop exchanging barbs with Julian and notice that Ned was interfering with his witness. "Is that all?"

"No. He was furious when I told him, and he said – well, a great many things. But he swore he'd bring everyone down with him if he was arrested," Kennett said. "That he'd tell all. And I said surely he didn't mean to do that, and that he'd better clear out of town, but he said he had business that had to be finished first."

"Disposing of the witnesses," Ned said.

"He wouldn't."

"I've seen nothing that persuades me you're right."

Julian was still lecturing stubbornly on. "In fact, if I were in charge of establishing a sensible modern police force –"

"But you're not, Mr Lynes," Hatton said, sounding more weary than anything else. "For which you should probably thank your lucky stars. Was there a statement you wanted to make, Mr Kennett?" he added, raising his voice.

"Not without my solicitor," Kennett said.

"Then you may be here a while." Hatton broke off as a messenger boy came in with a note, and unfolded it to read it.

"Leach was found dead this morning," Ned said, and was rewarded by seeing Kennett flinch.

"An accident," he said, but he didn't sound as if he believed it.

"You may be fortunate you're here," Ned said. "It's likely the safest place for you as long as Farrell is still at large."

"And speaking of which," Hatton said, "I don't suppose you have any idea where we might find Mr Farrell? He's not at his lodgings or his place of business."

"I don't know. I swear, I don't. He might have gone to France."

"I thought you said he wasn't planning to leave town," Ned said.

"Damn it, Mathey, where's your sense of loyalty?"

"I'm supposed to have some for the man?" Ned was aware he was succumbing to temper himself, but felt he deserved it. "He's cruel to people he dislikes and not much kinder to his supposed friends, and if you had asked me when this sorry mess began which of our acquaintances was most likely not to care if he got people killed, Farrell would have been at the top of my list."

Julian looked a bit pale at that, and Ned was a bit sorry the moment he'd said it, but Julian didn't argue. "That in itself didn't mean he was a murderer," he only pointed out.

"No, it didn't," Hatton said. "There are plenty of unpleasant men and women in this city who aren't murderers. But a word of advice, Mr Lynes, since you've given me so many of yours. It takes a hard man to kill for money. Generally that shows itself in other ways as well. It's not a bad idea to ask if there's anyone in the victim's circles who makes himself disliked."

Ned repressed the urge to say that everyone in the victims' circles had made themselves disliked. It wasn't fair, and more to the point it wasn't actually true. There were a number of people he had liked, and his heart sank at the thought of Farrell ruining them all. But he couldn't summon up a spirit of fellow-feeling for Farrell himself, and didn't feel particularly inclined to try.

"We'll check the train stations," Hatton said. "And see if he turns up at home or work."

Ned tried not to look directly at either Julian or Kennett. If Farrell couldn't be found, the next obvious step was for Hatton to ask for the address of his club. And both providing it and refusing to provide it seemed equally unthinkable.

He cleared his throat. "If we're not presently under arrest – I should like a chance to change my clothes, and to deal with some pressing business I've left undone at the Commons. I give you my word I won't go farther than that."

"I don't have much chance of safely disposing of this thing without a metaphysician," Hatton said. "If you're contemplating the idea of doing anything drastic, I'll thank you to remember that."

"I'm not going to make away with myself, if that's what you mean."

"And am I to take it that Mr Lynes give his word he won't leave town as well?" Hatton sounded as if he questioned the value of that.

"In fact I do," Julian said, although Ned wasn't certain either to what extent Julian considered his word to be a sacred obligation. "We've got to find Farrell and dispose of this creature before it kills anyone else."

Hatton considered them both. "All right," he said. "Go home, the pair of you. Wash up and have something to eat and then get yourselves back here. God knows this business doesn't look like it'll soon be finished."

"Then may I –" Kennett began.

"Not you," Hatton said firmly. "And you two go before I change my mind."

JULIAN FORGED ON THROUGH THE CROWD until he was sure they were out of sight of Scotland Yard, then stopped, so suddenly that Ned nearly ran into him, and had to clutch his shoulder to keep from knocking them both off balance. Not that it would have been hard: he felt profoundly unsettled, keyed up to face Hatton's wrath and whatever punishment he intended, and then released without further comment. It was in its own way worse than school, and he shrugged his shoulders unhappily, old fears tightening his muscles.

"Kennett told Farrell," Ned said, his voice empty.

"Damn the man." Julian closed his eyes for an instant. "So that's who we have to thank for last night?"

Ned nodded. "And he plans to name names – tell all – if he's arrested."

"Christ." Julian ran his hand over his chin, stubble rasping where he'd been less than careful in his hasty shave. He'd expect nothing less from Farrell, and while most of his acquaintance should be able to avoid the scandal, Farrell's closest circle would certainly go down with him. As would he and Ned, but he'd more or less accepted that by now. New York loomed, bleak and distant and not London, and he shoved that thought away. "I take it he's not going to be sensible and leave the country."

Ned shook his head. "We have to stop him."

"How?"

"At least warn people. We need to do that anyway – you know Kennett will give Hatton the addresses for all the clubs if he presses him."

He would, too, Julian thought. Damn the man again. "You're right." He closed his eyes again, summoning up names and places. Jacobs', the Dionysus – poor Malcolm would have an apoplexy – the Admiral's Hat, and there were certainly more where Farrell was known, too many to cover themselves. He shook his head. "We need to talk to Lennox."

The cost of a cab didn't seem to matter at the moment. Julian crossed his fingers as they made their way through the crowded streets, hoping that it was early enough still that Lennox would be at home. At Lennox's door, the starched housemaid contrived to express her disapproval of their battered appearance, but brought them into the breakfast room where Lennox sat resplendent in a Chinese brocade dressing gown.

"What in heaven's name brings you here so early, dear boy?" he began, but stopped, seeing them more clearly. "Sit down, pour some coffee, and talk to me."

The breath caught for an instant in Julian's chest – he had not known until that moment how taut his nerves were strung – and he saw the same flicker of relief cross Ned's face.

"Thank you," Ned said, and crossed to the sideboard.

"There isn't time," Julian said. "I'm sorry, Lennox. We're – there's some trouble, and we're the inadvertent cause of it."

"There is always time for coffee," Lennox said firmly. "Or at least for tea, the Empire was built on it, but what I have is coffee."

"Linford Farrell is the man behind the murders at the clubs," Julian said. "And he's threatening to name names and bring everyone else down with him if he's arrested."

Lennox gave a moue of distaste. "He would. I told you he wasn't a nice man, Lynes."

"He means it," Julian said. "There's not much we can do about it, Mathey and I, not if we're going to give evidence, but there has to be a way to save everyone else –"

Ned handed him a cup of coffee, sugar and milk already added, and he took it helplessly.

"Sit down," Lennox said again. "Both of you. Let's look at this calmly."

"But –" Julian dropped abruptly into one of the breakfast chairs, setting the cup on the table in front of him. "You've done this before."

Lennox nodded. "Do you think this is the first time someone's threatened to name names?"

"I hadn't thought," Ned said, sitting beside him with a sigh. "We were – it's been a busy night and now day."

"You look it," Lennox said. "I think you'd better have some breakfast and tell me everything."

It took the better part of half an hour to cover the essentials, at which point Lennox held up his hand to stop them, and wrote out several telegrams to useful men of his acquaintance. He dispatched them with the housemaid, who still looked disapproving, and had them start over again, filling in more details. By then it was early afternoon; they had relocated to Lennox's pleasant study, and Lennox had mailed several more letters to friends who would be able to help.

"You're quite certain he's guilty," he said, not for the first time, and Julian nodded. He felt wrung out, but at least the sense of utter helplessness had vanished. They might still be heading for New York in a few days, but at least it seemed less likely that everyone else would be ruined.

"Yes." Ned said. "There's no question."

"And it can be proved," Julian added. "The Crown won't have any trouble making its case."

"Then either Lord Grey or Archie Sinclair should be able to make it clear to him that he will only hurt himself by naming names."

"He's going to hang," Ned said, looking faintly queasy himself. "How can anything be worse?"

"Mm, well, that might be negotiated," Lennox said.

Julian lifted his head at that, bridling in spite of himself – the man deserved to hang – and Lennox fixed him with a look.

"That may well be the price of bringing this off safely, Lynes. His life for his silence."

That was the one thing that Farrell might want enough to forgo his revenge. Julian nodded slowly.

"I won't say I like it," Ned said, "particularly if we're ruined along with it – and we've already had to tell Hatton more than I ever wanted."

"Hatton mightn't keep you on," Julian said, "but it wouldn't do him any good to say why he let you go. You might come out of this all right – if Lennox's friends can make a bargain."

"We'll know that once they catch him," Lennox said firmly. "In the meantime – you said Kennett will talk?"

Julian nodded. "Sadly, yes."

"Then I think it would be best if Farrell's usual clubs didn't open tonight," Lennox said. "I'll send some telegrams – Jacobs', certainly."

"And the Dionysus," Ned said. He sounded grim, and Julian pressed his shoulder.

"Yes." Lennox looked disapproving. "I'll telegraph Straun – he's still steward, isn't he? – but I'd take it as a kindness if you'd go round yourselves and make sure he closes. He's not the most – he doesn't take a firm hand."

"It's a difficult crowd," Julian said, moved by obscure loyalty, and it was Ned's turn to touch his shoulder.

"We'll do that," he said. "And I had better send a telegram to Hatton, as well, to tell him we're detained, or he'll think we've left town. You have clothes at my place, Lynes. Let's change, and then we can take care of this. And – thank you, Lennox. We were in a bit of a bind."

Lennox waved his hand in dismissal, but didn't look displeased. "I'm glad to be of service, dear boy. Besides, I'm a member at Jacobs' myself, and I'd hate to have to find a new club."

☾✷

CHAPTER SEVENTEEN
Hide and Seek

P REDICTABLY, MRS CLEWETT PROVED WILLING TO produce an early tea, and Julian wolfed his share of the potted ham sandwiches before retreating to the sofa while Ned hunted out a change of clothes. It was warm in the flat, and quiet, and it had been difficult night; he woke with a start to Ned's hand on his shoulder.

"Sorry, old man. But we should be going."

"Yes." Julian shook himself. "Yes, of course."

He had left his second-best evening suit in Ned's flat some days ago, and with one of Ned's shirts and a borrowed vest pinned to take in the extra fabric, he looked merely rumpled. He scowled at his image in Ned's cheval glass, but there was no help for it, not unless he wanted to go back to his own lodgings, and he felt utterly incapable of dealing with Mrs Digby at the moment. He didn't have his evening pumps, either, but his ordinary shoes were at least passable. He snagged a last biscuit from the tray and straightened his shoulders.

"Shall we?"

Mrs Clewett stopped them on the way out. "A note for you from Scotland Yard," she said, handing it to Ned, who waited to open it until the front door had closed behind them.

"Hatton says there's no sign of Farrell," Ned said. "So thankfully he doesn't require us at the Yard at present. He suggests we get a few hours sleep."

"I'm all for that, once everything's squared away at the Dionysus."

"Surely Malcolm will have kept the doors closed," Ned said, and they headed out into the gathering dark.

As they made their way up the street toward the Dionysus, it became obvious that Ned had been overly optimistic. Julian swore, seeing the lights on and a footman greeting a new arrival, then swore with more feeling as he realized that the footman was trying to turn the man away, and the man was having none of it.

"You aren't closed, I can see Fenworth right there –"

"Oh, dear," Ned said, and they dodged across the street.

"I'm sorry, sirs," the footman began, wearily, and Malcolm appeared behind him, propelling a dark-haired man ahead of him.

"No, Fenny, you can't stay, not even if you don't want service. It's an emergency –"

"There's no bloody emergency, and I can see it," the dark-haired man answered. He looked past the footman to the man on the doorstep. "Oh, hello, George. I'm sorry, I'll have this sorted in a moment."

"No, you won't," Malcolm said, and Fenworth ignored him.

"I don't know what he's in an uproar about, but not to worry –"

"Police," Julian said, and was meanly pleased by the sudden silence and the blanched faces turned his way. He saw Fenworth recognize him, and overrode whatever the man might have said. "That's the emergency. I'd clear off, if I were you."

"You can't be serious," Fenworth said, but Julian saw the flicker of concern in his eyes.

"Dead serious," Ned answered. He looked at Malcolm. "How many people are here?"

"Only half a dozen. But some of them are expecting friends, and – it's a bit of a mess, that's all."

"It'll be a bigger one if you can't get the place closed," Julian said.

"I know that." Malcolm scowled. "And if you'd care to help –"

"Of course we will," Ned said.

Julian looked at Fenworth's friend, who was no longer trying to bull his way past the footman. "If you're fond of him, I'd find somewhere else to meet. There's every chance of a police raid tonight."

"You're sure?"

"I'm afraid so."

It hung in the balance for a moment, and then the man looked away. "Fenny! Come along, let's be out of here."

"Very wise," Julian said, and pushed past him into the hall.

Malcolm had been right, there were only half a dozen men in the main salon, and Julian was relieved to recognize some of them as sensible. He gave them the same story – *likely to be a police raid, better leave while you can and let Mal-*

colm close the club – and followed them like a sheepdog until the last of them was out the door. Malcolm had already told most of the staff to go home, and there were only a trio of footmen at the front door, ready to turn people away.

"Tell them there's a problem with the gas," Malcolm was saying as Julian joined them. "There isn't, but that's a perfectly respectable excuse. Oh, Julian. Is that everyone?"

"I think so." Julian looked around, and Malcolm read his thought.

"I asked Ned to make sure the back locks were secure. And, while I'm thinking of it – I have our account books glamoured against prying eyes. Could I ask you to be sure everything's up to date? I didn't like to ask your friend."

"Probably just as well," Julian admitted. "Are they in your office?"

"Yes." Malcolm fished for his keychain, and unhooked a small silver key the general size and shape of a watch key. Julian nodded his approval – it was unlikely anyone would notice one more key among such a bunch, nor was it unlikely for anyone to have an enchanted watch and key – and went back down the hall to Malcolm's office.

The room was cold and dark, and Julian muttered a curse as he turned up the gas. Saving Malcolm might be, but surely there was no reason not to have a decent fire in the grate. The account books were stacked on top of the club's safe, and he hauled them down, setting them on Malcolm's desk before he saw the curtains stir. He reached for his wand, his breath coming short, and realized that the window was open behind them. Instinctively, he sketched a cracksman's sigil in the air between him and it – *reveal trap*, one of the oldest and most basic – and flinched as he remembered what had happened in his flat when they'd tried ordinary magic. The sigil flashed for an instant, gold against the dark green curtains, and disappeared: nothing here. He drew a shaken breath, not sure whether he was more annoyed at his reaction or his fear, and stepped back into the hall.

"Malcolm?"

"Yes?"

"Did you leave your window open?"

"What?" Malcolm frowned. "No, of course not, not in this weather."

"It was open when I went in," Julian said grimly.

Ned came up behind the steward. "What was open?" The same uneasy note was in his voice.

"What's going on?" Malcolm looked from one to the other.

"The window," Julian said. "Malcolm's window was open."

"Ah." Ned took a deep breath. "Perhaps we'd better make sure, then."

Julian nodded.

"What the devil are you talking about?" Malcolm demanded.

"Linford Farrell has made a non-conforming – object – that kills," Julian said. "That's what killed Punton and Dolly Hall and three more men that we know of, and – it's possible it's in here."

Malcolm's face went even paler than before. "I thought this was just – well, sodomy."

"I'm sorry," Ned said. "It's murder, and it's possible that Farrell might have sent the thing here."

"But why?" Malcolm's voice was more indignant than frightened. "Damn it, we're – he's one of us."

"I don't think he sees it that way," Julian said.

"We should search the club," Ned said. "Malcolm, can we borrow you and two of the footmen?"

"Yes, of course –"

"We're looking for an inlaid writing desk." Julian sketched the shape with his hands, and saw the others nod. "It has a mahogany varnish, with brass and mother-of-pearl filigree, a sort of flowering vine pattern."

"It could have a different shape," Ned said. "If there's anything strange in the room, any object or piece of furniture you don't recognize – don't go near it, but tell me at once."

"We should stay together," Julian said.

Malcolm nodded. "I'd rather you were close at hand, gentlemen. How do you want to proceed?"

Julian looked at Ned, who gave a tiny shrug. "Start at the top of the house, and work our way down."

They began in the bedrooms at the top of the house, small and spartan, with only the larger bedsteads to betray their most common use. There was nothing out of place there, no open windows, no mysterious or unfamiliar objects in any of them or in the bathroom, and Malcolm gave a sigh of relief.

"There's just my rooms, then, and I would have noticed."

"You're the only one who lives in?" Ned asked, and the steward nodded, reaching for his keys.

"A bit inconvenient, sometimes, but – just as well, tonight."

His rooms were small but pleasant, the sitting room lined with books and the bedroom almost filled by an old-fashioned tester bed. Malcolm's personal taste was austere, and it was easy to see that there was no sign of a writing desk.

"Or anything else I haven't had for ages," he said, sounding relieved.

"We're not done yet," Julian said, and the footmen exchanged unhappy glances.

"Those rooms downstairs are – highly decorated," Ned said. "Do you think you'd recognize if something had been added?"

"Actually, I think I would." Malcolm gave a wry smile. "I'm expected to replace things when they get broken, you know."

"That's a help," Ned said, but the words were more encouraging than his expression.

"Let's begin with the front rooms," Julian said. They were smaller, and somewhat less over-filled with objects, and he felt there was more chance of finding the writing desk if it were there. As long as it remained a writing desk, of course.

Malcolm led them back down the main stairs, and turned up the lights in the first floor hall. In the unusual radiance, the wallpaper looked tired and a bit old-fashioned, and everything could use a touch of fresh paint. Five doors stood ajar, and Julian glanced at Ned, who gave another tiny shrug.

"It doesn't really matter where we start, I suppose. Just be sure to close the doors firmly when we're done."

If the writing desk had to open a window to get in and out, it was unlikely to be able to pass through a closed door. Julian nodded, and pushed open the nearest door. The light from the hall spilled in, showing it empty, and he turned up the lights inside. Like all the first floor parlors, it was crowded and a bit fussy, with two large sofas and a velvet ottoman, and the rug was thick and soft underfoot. Every available surface was covered with bric-a-brac, and he heard Ned give an unhappy sigh. The footmen exchanged another look, and the stouter of the pair said, "The candlestick?"

Julian looked where he was pointing, a five-branched candelabrum in the shape of a tree twined with a snake, and Malcolm said, "No, that's ours. A gift from a member."

A regrettable one, Julian thought, but managed to swallow the words. This was something he did well, and he took a steadying breath, closing his eyes to conjure up his memory of the room. He'd been in it recently, which was a help, and he let himself imagine each of the pieces of furniture, each statue and carafe and cluttered tabletop. When he was sure he'd placed them all, he opened his eyes, looking for any deviation from the pattern. It was all there, familiar and slightly tawdry, cut glass decanters rather than crystal, their silver labels polished but obviously plate, and he looked at Ned.

"I don't see anything new."

"Nor do I," Malcolm said.

"And there's no sign of the writing desk," Ned agreed. "Malcolm, can you lock these doors as well?"

Malcolm produced a ring of keys from his pocket. "Oh, yes."

"Then you can go ahead and do it," Julian said.

Malcolm obeyed, turning down the lights again first, and they moved on to the next room. Once again, there was no sign of a writing desk or anything out of the ordinary, though Malcolm tutted over the near-empty decanters. The next room had a statue that neither Julian nor the footmen recognized, a Mercury feeding the infant Dionysus, but Malcolm identified it as another gift.

"And a nicer one, too," he added. "We could actually sell that one if it came to it. But that's neither here nor there."

"No," Julian agreed, and Malcolm locked the door behind them. The other rooms on the floor were empty of any writing desks; there was a desk on one of the ottomans in the downstairs back parlor, but they all recognized it as belonging to the club. It was japanned ware, too, black with a gold foil wreath, and when Ned sketched a sigil over it, it remained inert and unchanged. There was nothing in the main parlor, either, and Malcolm locked the door behind them with a sigh of genuine relief. The footman who had been watching the door edged closer, looking glad of their return.

"Everything all right?" Ned asked, looking at him, and the man nodded.

"Yes, sir. It's turning foggy, though."

"You can take the rest of the night off," Malcolm said, to the footmen. "You'll be paid for your work, of course."

"Thank you, sir," the tallest of the group said, and looked at his fellows. "If there's anything else we need to do…"

"Best just to leave now," Ned said, and they let themselves out gratefully. A tendril of fog curled in after them, smelling of damp and soot, and Malcolm shot the heavy bolt behind them.

"Did you mean it when you said the police were likely to come, or was that just an excuse to get people to leave?"

"A bit of both," Ned said.

"It all depends on whether Kennett tells the inspector in charge the addresses of Farrell's clubs," Julian said. He was past caring about protecting anyone's reputation. "I think he will, if he's pressed, but I don't know if Hatton's going to push him."

"I don't think you should stay here, in any case," Ned said. "I don't really think it would be safe."

"But if the police come –"

"Then the club is closed up, and they'll have to come back," Julian said. "I agree with Ned. Is there someplace else you can stay, just for the night?"

Malcolm blinked once, then nodded. "Yes. Yes, I can take a room at a hotel, though I'll have to send a telegram –"

"Why don't you do that?" Ned suggested, and Julian glanced at the office again.

"Yes, and I'll finish with the books. Just to be sure."

He slipped back into Malcolm's office, glancing quickly around as he turned up the lights again. There was nothing, neither a writing desk nor anything else that hadn't been there before, though the room was even colder than before. He shut the window, cutting off a finger of fog, and turned his attention to the club's books. The glamour was solid, responding only to the key Malcolm had given him, and he carefully resealed the stack before returning to the hall.

"They'll have to get a metaphysician to open them, and they're not going to find a willing one at this hour of the night. Or a judge willing to authorize opening the club." He handed Malcolm the key, and the steward returned it to his chain.

"Surely they have a metaphysician on staff."

Ned winced. "That would be me. And I don't intend to be found. Not until morning, anyway."

Malcolm let them out by a side door, and they traced their way down the narrow alley between the club and its nearest neighbor, emerging onto the street beside the steps that led down to the area. He stopped in dismay, staring at the fog.

"Bloody hell, I'll never find a cab on a night like this."

It was getting thicker, Julian thought, though he'd seen worse, and it was true that the cabs seemed to vanish at the first hint of close weather.

"There might be one once you reach the Edgeware Road," Ned said soothingly, "or at least an omnibus. And at worst you'll have your choice of railway hotels. But it won't come to that."

"I suppose so." Malcolm looked around nervously. "Will you be all right?"

It was not a question Julian had expected, and impulsively he reached out to squeeze the steward's shoulder. "We'll be fine. And you'll be better off without us."

"Oh." Malcolm blinked. "Well. Do be careful." He started off into the fog, and Julian looked at Ned.

"Well. I suppose that went better than I expected."

"Yes." Ned looked exhausted, and for an instant Julian wanted nothing more than embrace him. Instead he looked down the fog-shrouded street, as empty of pedestrians as it was of vehicles.

"Should we try to find a cab, or take a 'bus?"

"We won't get a cab tonight," Ned said. "But if we cut through Dorset Square we might be in time to catch an omnibus."

"Not our best route," Julian said, but started into the fog.

"I don't want to walk all the way to Oxford Street. Though if you have a better idea..."

Julian shook his head. Ned was right, it was the closest way, and the sooner they were indoors, the better. "Have you given any thought to keeping that thing out?"

"Honestly, Lynes, when would I have had time?"

Julian touched his arm in apology. "No, of course not. But there has to be a way."

"There was a remedy in one of the grimoires that purported to keep a Hand of Glory out of the house," Ned said. "But the ingredients aren't exactly things I have on hand, and I hate to try substitutions. For now, I'm inclined to try locking all the windows and sleeping in shifts," Ned said. "Or – perhaps we ought to take our own advice and sleep at a hotel."

"That's not such a bad idea," Julian said. They were coming up on Marylebone Road at last, the streetlights flaring brighter through the fog, and he could hear the sound of traffic, the steady rumble of wheels and the slow beat of hooves. Probably they were safer in company – the thing was supposed to take by stealth, and presumably would be reluctant to commit murder in front of witnesses, though if a witness could only say, "it turned into smoke and the man dropped dead," perhaps there was less reason for concealment. Still, if no one had seen it yet, they could hope crowds would be a deterrent. Especially since he wasn't at all sure what he could do if the thing did attack again.

They reached the road without incident, only to see the most recent omnibus disappearing into the fog. Julian swore, startling a well-bundled woman who had just dismounted, and apologized. Ned added his own apology and a winning smile.

"You might be better off walking, if you're in such a hurry," she said, mollified. "The 'buses are that slow tonight, with the weather."

"We might well be," Ned agreed, and they moved off, the fog damp on their faces.

They walked as far as the next stop without being overtaken, and Julian paused irresolutely on the corner, considering their next move. There were fewer and fewer pedestrians about, most sensible people kept within doors by the thickening fog, and even the traffic seemed unnaturally light.

"We could wait a bit," Ned said, doubtfully, and Julian peered around again. In the fog, everything looked strange, buildings turned unrecognizable without their familiar cornices, and he frowned. He knew where they were, knew these façades as well as any street, and suddenly the anomaly leaped out at him: there were only two posts at the edge of the tobacconist's area, not three.

He caught Ned's sleeve, dragged him toward the street. "Quick, we have to cross now."

"But –"

There was nothing visible through the fog, and no sound of wheels. Julian took a tighter hold of his elbow and urged him on, breasting the rolls of fog like water. Hooves sounded to their left, louder and closer than he'd expected, and it was Ned's turn to swear. But then they were across, and safe, and Ned grabbed him in turn.

"What was that about?"

"There were three posts where there should be two." Julian turned, peering back through the fog, and Ned stared with him.

"By that tobacco shop? I only see two."

"There were three. I'm sure of it."

"And you think –" Ned stopped abruptly, frowning.

"I think it can change its shape," Julian said. His voice was oddly taut, and he cleared his throat. "Damn it. It's gone now, but –"

"It won't stop," Ned said, grimly. "And we shouldn't stand still, either. Come on, Lynes."

They hurried away, not quite running, their own footsteps muffled by the fog. A cart passed them, a shadow in the fog, trailing the smell of the driver's damp pipe, but the sidewalks were empty. Everyone with any sense had stayed home tonight, and it was late enough that even on a fine night the traffic would have been reduced. Buildings loomed ahead of them, weirdly distorted by the fog, and it took a heart-stopping moment before Julian could be sure there was nothing alien on the steps and railings. A carriage loomed out of the fog, horses blowing unhappily, and lumbered past, momentarily throwing them into shadow. For an instant, Julian was sure there was an extra spike on the railings across the street, but the fog cleared for an instant, and he saw nothing had changed.

"There's never a cab," Ned muttered, and Julian looked quickly behind them, counting the iron knobs on the nearest railing. Surely there had always been an even dozen...

"We need to go somewhere safe," he said. "Have you warded your flat, Mathey?"

"Not against this." Ned looked around himself, his forehead creased with worry. "The Commons. If we can get to the Commons –"

Julian nodded. "This way."

He caught Ned's sleeve again, pulling him across the empty street. St. Marylebone loomed ahead of them, scaffolding wreathing one side of the building. The railing and gates seemed normal enough, and he unlatched the gate, slipping into the churchyard.

"Lynes," Ned began, then followed silently.

It was darker in the churchyard, but the fog seemed thinner. Julian led them along the side of the building, skirting the pale stone obelisk that dominated the smaller memorial stones, until they emerged at last on High Street and the safety of the gas lights. Julian looked around again, seeing nothing, and Ned caught his arm.

"Wait."

Julian heard it then, the steady clop of hooves and the dull mutter of wheels on the cobbles, and a moment later a dray lurched past them, barely more than a shadow in the fog. He glanced over his shoulder – was that an extra urn beside the low marker? – and started across the street. Ned followed this time, and they crossed safely into Beaumont Street.

"If it comes," Ned began, and shook his head. "Almost anything I can try to stop it might set the street on fire, or worse."

"What's the metaphysical word for milk?" Julian asked. It was the only thing that had worked without unanticipated extras, and Ned gave a quick smile.

"That's worth a try, I suppose. If we have to." He looked around. "Which way?"

Beaumont Street to Devonshire Street to Portland Place, Julian thought, and then on through the maze of little streets to the Commons. He knew the big streets well enough to be sure he'd spot something out of place, even with the fog; once they left the main roads, however, he was less certain. Of course, they could hold to the larger streets, double back down Cleveland Street, but that would take time, take them out of their way, and he didn't think they had the time to spare.

"There," he said, pointing, and turned left onto Devonshire Street. A fountain loomed out of the fog, black and shapeless, and for a moment he was sure he saw an eagle perched on the topmost basin. It resolved to a familiar dolphin, and he caught his breath. All they could do now was hurry.

New Cavendish Street was dimly lit enough that there seemed no chance of noticing some object out of place. There was nothing for it but to plunge blindly through the fog, expecting at any moment to feel it swirl around them like a coiling serpent. If it gave even that much warning before it sank through clothing and skin to reach their beating hearts.

They crossed Cleveland Street to see the familiar shape of the metaphysicians' wing of the Commons rising up before them. Something touched Ned's arm, and he flinched violently away before realizing it was Julian's hand.

"How many posts at the cab stand?"

"How should I know?" Ned said.

"You see it every day."

"You've seen it enough yourself," Ned said, but he sped his steps, hurrying into the dark walkway that led into the square. On the other side, the gas lamps were lit along the walk, but every window of the metaphysicians' wing was dark.

"Up to your chambers?" Julian asked, already turning toward the stairs.

Ned caught his arm to tug him back. "They're not warded," he said. "It's not needed here, they'd always be tangling with all the enchantments thrown around –"

"Where, then?" Julian glanced around like a hunted animal in search of any shelter.

"We have to get to the metaphysicists' wing," Ned said. "The fastest way is through the garden, but…" He shrank from the idea of crossing that foggy expanse of garden beds and sculptures, with the more nocturnally active of the plants rustling to themselves in the dark. "Maybe round the walk would be best."

Julian glanced again at the staircase up to Ned's chambers, and then down the walk, and then sharply back at the staircase. "Are there seven stairs up to the first floor?"

"I don't know."

"All the others on this row have six."

"Run," Ned said, and plunged forward into the garden.

Julian was at his heels, his footsteps beating staccato on the flagstones. It was hard to see more than an arm's length ahead, and Ned stumbled off the path at the first turning, into a bed of flowers that snapped angrily shut around him. He stepped back and turned to follow the path, Julian still beside him.

"It could be anything in here," Julian said.

"I know." Ned bumped into something cold and waist-high, flinched away from it, and then realized it was the familiar plaque warning visitors not to eat the fruit of the Commons's single miniature lotus tree. He tried to let his feet carry him by instinct, finding his way around the next few turnings, and only once blundering unwisely into a hedge of thorns.

He ripped his coat free of the hedge, gave the fountain in the garden's central square a wide berth, and hurried forward through the herb garden, its mingled scents hanging in the fog. Around the first turning toward the metaphysicists' wing, and he could see the gaslights at the edge of the courtyard glowing through the fog as he came out into a small paved square. The row of hedges in front of them stood at the edge of the garden, and beyond that, the path led straight up to the metaphysicists' wing. They could take that at a run.

He started for the path through the hedges. "Mathey," Julian said, putting out a hand to pull him up short. There was an urn set in the middle of the path, with a curling tangle of bramble growing out of it. Ned didn't remember it, but the Commons gardeners moved the plants around, they were always bringing in new specimens –

He turned all the same, crossing the square to the other path that led through the hedges toward the metaphysicists' wing. Another urn stood in the middle of the path, topped by a similar tangle of bramble. He let out a breath, beginning to relax.

"They're identical," Julian said flatly. "It can't invent new shapes, it can only copy them, but it copies them *exactly* –"

Ned backed away. He could only make out the outline of the other urn through the fog. They could retrace their steps, but every step would be further away from safety, and sooner or later it would get tired of playing with them and close in for the kill.

He felt something twine around his ankle, and leapt away. It rustled, and he realized it was the bed of *Urtica mordax*, woken from its usual night-time immobility, and reaching curiously toward him. He evaded it easily, and it reached out toward the nearest urn, and then began to twine investigatory tendrils around it.

The outline of the urn softened, its edges dissolving into fog.

"Run," Julian said. Ned didn't need the prompting. He ran for the other path, dodging around the solid urn and pelting up the stone walkway toward the nearest circle of gaslight. Julian was at his heels, gasping for breath but not falling behind, and Ned threw himself at the nearest door.

It was locked, of course, at this hour. He found his wand, and then thought better of it. "Get the lock open, Lynes, you're better at it –"

Julian had his wand out already, and spoke sharply as he gestured. Sparks flew from the lock. "It's warded –"

"It's in an old style," Ned said, "there are rules against people experimenting on the locks, let me try –"

"No, I think – I've got it," Julian said, with one more sharp flick of his wand, and the lock turned over with a thud.

Ned threw the door open. Behind them, the gaslight dimmed, as if something was throwing a shadow between them and the light. The fog began to swirl around them, although there was still no breath of wind.

Neither of them needed to be told to run. Ned pelted toward the staircase and then up it, taking the stairs two at a time and then waiting an agonizing moment for Julian to catch up at the top of the stairs before he took off running again.

He skidded to a stop in front of the door at the end of the hall. It opened into a lecture hall, and his chest clenched. He was abruptly sure he was in the wrong building entirely. And now it was between them and the stairs –

He turned and saw a second door across the hall. He shoved at it, and found it far heavier. He pushed through and stumbled across the threshold, turning to pull Julian through behind him. A hooded shape rose up over Julian's shoulder, gold flecks glittering like eyes, drawing back to strike.

Ned put his shoulder to the door and slammed it closed. As it shut, the elaborate silver figures that lined the walls flickered for a moment, as if limned by moonlight, and then dimmed again, leaving them in utter darkness.

Ned stood gasping for breath, wand at the ready.

"Where are we?" Julian asked, touching his sleeve in the dark.

"The experiment room," Ned said. "These are the best wards in London. If it can get to us in here – there's no ward that would stop it."

"The wards at the Dionysus at least discouraged it," Julian said.

"We may be safe here." He took out his pocket-watch and opened it, using its dim luminescence to find the nearest wall, and then the sconce set into it; thankfully, there was a candle still in it, burned only halfway down. He lifted his wand and traced the word for "fire" over it, and was rewarded by seeing its wick light, throwing a golden glow throughout the room.

He leaned against the wall, and then slid down to sit against it, feeling weak with relief. After a moment, Julian joined him, his shoulder against Ned's.

"Now what?" Julian said.

"I'm not sure," Ned said. "It may return to Farrell when it can't get at us – before, when we drove it off, it didn't come back that night."

"Do you want to open the door and see?"

"Not at present, no."

They waited, both of them unsure how long it would take the creature to lose interest in them and return to its creator. Ned would have thought it was impossible to fall asleep under the circumstances, but it had been a harrowing day following a sleepless night, and the room was warm and dim. He woke with a jerk to the sound of footsteps in the hall outside, the candle guttering low. Julian's head was on his shoulder, his weight numbing Ned's fingers.

"Lynes," he said, and nudged Julian with his elbow. Julian woke and pulled away immediately as the footsteps stopped outside the door.

The door opened, sunlight spilling in from the hallway outside. Oppenshaw stood in the doorway, frowning in at them over his spectacles. "Mr Mathey," he said. "What have I told you about touching the walls?"

"I'm sorry, Mr Oppenshaw," Ned said, climbing to his feet.

"Metaphysicians are not authorized to use this room without express permission. And the door to this building was left not only unlocked but ajar. As we are not generally in the business of inviting burglars to walk in and make themselves at home, I do hope you have an excellent explanation."

"We were being pursued by a writing desk that eats men's hearts," Julian said.

Oppenshaw considered that. "Interesting," he said.

"We have to get to Scotland Yard," Ned said. "But, quickly – the creature seems to be based on the Hand of Glory. It's – at least startled – by milk. Would it be safe to use the metaphysical word for milk to attempt to drive it off?"

"I can't say it would be safe," Oppenshaw began guardedly.

"Is there any chance it would work without disaster? I'm likely to have to try something."

"It might work," Oppenshaw granted. "It's a traditional element of pre-modern metaphysics that can typically be replaced by a descriptive sigil in modern metaphysical practice." He shook his head, his mouth tightening to a severe line. "But I wouldn't want to have to be the one to try it."

"I don't expect you will be," Ned said, and hurried out to find a cab.

NED FELT UNCOMFORTABLY CONSPICUOUS ARRIVING AT Scotland Yard in evening clothes, and Hatton gave him a black look as he came in.

"Late night?"

"We were nearly killed," Julian began hotly. Ned put out a hand to stop him, feeling that a less confrontational approach was called for.

"The creature was hunting us. We took refuge at the Commons, within a warded room, but there wasn't any way to know if it was still outside short of opening the door. Which would have let it inside to eat our hearts."

"It seems to have eaten Farrell's instead," Hatton said.

Julian stared at him. "What?"

"Farrell's dead. He was found at the Bedford Hotel, stone dead, with a wand in his hand and what looked like a half-chalked circle around him; my guess is he was trying to ward the thing off, but not making a good job of it."

Ned tried to feel regret rather than shameful relief, and couldn't quite manage it. "And the creature?"

"There wasn't any writing desk found in the room."

"It might have looked like something else," Julian said. "It can change its shape."

"Lovely," Hatton said. "The hotel servants didn't notice anything out of place in the room, but Farrell had bags with him – we've got them here."

Ned exchanged looks with Julian. "We had best take a look at them."

The bags were crammed into a cluttered corner that served as an evidence room, and appeared to be unremarkable leather cases. Ned regarded them warily, considered metaphysical approaches and their chance of wreaking havoc, and finally opened one, gingerly. It proved to contain an assortment of men's clothing, as did the other case.

"I think they're just his luggage," he said.

"That's what we thought. We've got the other gentleman's bags as well, if you want to open them up for us. I'd be obliged."

Ned turned, frowning. "What other gentleman?"

"When we cleared people out of the hotel, we found the manager dead as well. I woke the Yard's surgeon at an unfortunately early hour – he gave me an earful for it, believe me – and had him open them both up."

"Their hearts were missing?"

"So they were. And the hotel's cash box was found empty."

Ned let out a breath. "So either Farrell sent the creature back out after it attacked us, and then it turned on him even after it had killed its target –"

"Or it killed Farrell and then began hunting on its own," Julian finished. "Which of them was killed first? I know we can't do the standard metaphysical tests –"

"No need," Hatton said. "Farrell was stone cold, with rigor well set in. The manager was still warm when we found him. We cleared our men out in a hurry, and I'm not letting anyone back into the hotel until we find the creature."

"I doubt it's still in the hotel," Ned said. "It can move about, and take the shape of any object around it. It requires some form of nourishment, probably the hearts it's eating. If it's free to attack whenever it gets hungry…"

"Then I should expect some poor sod somewhere in the city to have his heart eaten tonight," Hatton said.

"Or sooner. It killed Farrell, and then killed again hours later. It could be out hunting as we speak."

Hatton scowled. "How do I stop this thing? We can't tell everyone in the city to be on the watch for any household object that seems out of place. You can't imagine the panic we'd start."

"If it's no longer under Farrell's control, we may be able to set a trap for it," Ned said, trying to think through how it could be done. "We have Kennett, and he was involved in the ritual that created it. There's a link there, and we may be able to strengthen it." He was thinking of the packet that Farrell had given Challice, but he hated to explain that to Hatton if he could avoid it.

Julian gave him a sideways look. "Then what? Not that I'm opposed to using Kennett as bait –"

"I can't officially approve of using prisoners as bait for monstrous creatures," Hatton said. "On the other hand, I'd very much like to catch this thing. If the gentleman is moved to volunteer, the Yard might be moved not to press any charges. But I would need to feel some confidence that he won't simply be eaten."

"I've been thinking," Ned said. "Strong enough wards seem to be able to hold it. And there's a traditional ointment that's supposed to keep it from crossing thresholds."

"Why didn't you say that before?"

"Because it requires the gall of a black cat, the fat of a white hen, and the blood of a screech owl, and can only be compounded during the dog days of summer," Ned said. "Which were weeks ago. But I've been talking to Oppenshaw – our best man on non-conforming metaphysics – and he thinks that modern substitutions may not interact disastrously, as long as they're merely symbolic representations of the original component."

"Speak English, Mathey."

"If I enchant the ointment using sigils representing the astrological influences during the dog days, it should work without setting things on fire. And I can probably work out substitutes for the other ingredients as well."

"You may not have to," Hatton said. "We've been taking all sorts of disturbing things off unlicensed practitioners. Garmin!" he added, raising his voice to carry. Garmin stuck his head up over one of the stall dividers.

"Governor?"

"Have a look through the evidence room and see if you can find Mr Mathey here gall of a black cat, the fat of a white hen, and the blood of a screech owl. If not, see if Carruthers has any in that museum he calls a workroom."

"I'll need a mortar and pestle as well," Ned said. "If we can trap it in a room, I may be able to bind it or destroy it using milk, or the metaphysical word for it."

"That didn't work for Leach."

"Leach wasn't a metaphysician.."

"All right," Hatton said. "Let me know what you need."

"To change out of evening dress, to begin with."

"You'll excuse me if I'd rather not let you and Lynes go wandering off again just now," Hatton said. "Suppose I send a constable to your lodgings and Mr Lynes's to pick up a change of clothes for you both."

"If he'll bring my metaphysician's bag as well."

"Done. Now let's have a talk with Mr Kennett."

Kennett had spent the night in a cell, and looked haggard and unshaven. "Mathey, will you explain to them that I had nothing to do with the deaths –"

"Farrell's dead," Ned said.

Kennett blanched. "No."

"The creature ate his heart, Kennett. And now it's on the loose in the city, and it's already killed one innocent man. You're going to help us stop it."

"I don't know how."

"We're going to set a trap for it," Julian said. "You're the bait."

"If you volunteer," Hatton said.

Kennett stared at him. "Why would I do that?"

Hatton shrugged. "Public-spiritedness?"

"I'm not that public-minded."

"Mathey here felt it might influence you to offer to release you without any charges," Hatton said. "Which goes against the grain, I'll admit, because you certainly deserve to be charged with practicing non-conforming enchantment, being an accessory to murder, and certain unnatural acts I won't mention. But if it'll keep anyone else in the city from dropping dead, I'm willing to make the sacrifice."

Kennett hesitated. "What would I have to do?"

"I'll be the one doing all the work," Ned said. "The most I'll need from you is for you to stand still where I tell you and refrain from distracting me. And I'll want a drop of your blood." Kennett hadn't been part of the original ritual with Challice, but if his vital fluids were added to the talisman, Ned thought it might confuse the issue sufficiently to attract the creature's attention.

"I'm not sure I like that."

"Think of it this way," Julian said. "You're in as much danger as anyone in the city from the bloody thing, and it knows you. Wouldn't you like us to actually catch it?"

"I had thought of leaving town."

"Practicing non-conforming enchantment," Hatton said. "Accessory to murder. And buggery. We may not have anyone left who's willing to testify to the last, but once you're hanged for abetting a murder, it won't much matter."

"All right," Kennett said. "You don't leave me much choice, do you?"

"That's the spirit," Hatton said.

Garmin managed to unearth what he claimed were the ingredients needed for the ointment, although the gall was a shriveled and unidentifiable scrap and the fat looked like ordinary enough chicken fat, gone somewhat rancid with age. "Suppose this is the remains of someone's dinner?" Ned said, turning the vial of blood back and forth in his fingers.

"Then they've got peculiar tastes, governor." Garmin took out his wand, made of some kind of bone Ned wasn't sure he wanted to identify, and sketched a series of cantrips over the dried gall, muttering over it as he did. "It's cat, all right. There's other parts of a black cat that have their uses – so I'm told, you understand – with plenty left over for the stew pot if you want."

"Ground up for sausages, more likely," Hatton said. "It's amazing what they'll put in sausages and sell them as beef. Will this do?"

"I hope so." Ned reached for the mortar and pestle and set about the business of compounding the ointment, trying to ignore the way it smelled.

Julian came to look over his shoulder, with more interest than distaste. "Where were you thinking of doing this?"

"There's the experiment room at the Commons, but in all conscience we'd have to clear the building, and it'll be hard to persuade metaphysicians to go away for their own safety when something interesting is happening. Or wait until after hours, but we'll be giving the creature a chance to kill again."

"Besides, it's already learned that room is warded," Julian said. "I'm not sure we could lure it inside."

"The Commons owns some other property in town," Ned said.

"The Half-House? I'm not sure that's a good idea."

"It wouldn't be," Ned said. "But there are some other buildings used for experimentation. If we ask Oppenshaw, he can probably find us a place."

"We put Kennett inside the room to lure it in –"

"In a protective circle drawn with the ointment," Ned said, wrestling with the pestle to work the stiff concoction into something like a smooth paste. "As tempting as the idea of just tossing him in with it and shutting the door after it may be."

"That would work for me."

"Lynes."

"Yes, all right. So you're proposing that we'll be in the central circle, and once the thing's in the room with us, Hatton will use the ointment to seal the door –"

"I'll be in the central circle," Ned said. "And you'll seal the door."

"From the outside?"

"It'll have to be from the outside. And it'll have to be you. Hatton doesn't know anything about metaphysics. He'll be lost if anything goes wrong."

"There's Garmin."

"I don't want to trust my life to Garmin."

"If I'm outside, I won't be able to help you."

"Do you have a better idea?"

"Let it eat Kennett."

"Lynes."

"I could bind it."

"I'm a better metaphysician."

"Damn it, Ned –"

"There's no point in arguing," Ned said, in what he hoped was the tone an intrepid explorer would have used before marching off to search for shelter in a raging blizzard, although a raging blizzard would have been a great deal easier to face than the idea of dying with his heart ripped from his chest. "Send for Oppenshaw, won't you?"

Julian went off to do so, looking mutinous, and Oppenshaw arrived within the hour, shortly after their clothes. Julian's were accompanied by an emphatic note telling him that Mrs Digby ran a respectable house, was not in the habit of receiving policemen, and didn't expect a repetition of the day's indignity. His clothes appeared to have been hastily snatched up off the floor, and showed it. Ned's were out of his wardrobe, neatly folded, and accompanied by a packet of biscuits from Mrs Clewett "to keep up his strength."

When Oppenshaw made his appearance, looking about him curiously as if the police station was a foreign country of which he wasn't sure he approved, Ned explained to him what he needed and what he intended to do.

Oppenshaw nodded. "Yes, I believe we can provide appropriate facilities. On one condition."

"Name it."

"There cannot be another Half-House. If you can bind the creature using the traditional formula, or modern substitutions for its elements, you are welcome to do so. But you will make no wild experiments." He regarded Ned over his glasses. "We have a duty to the city, Mr Mathey, an old and important duty that is often forgotten as we rush about enchanting our umbrellas to ward off the rain. You will take no risks with non-conforming enchantment, no matter what the personal cost."

"I understand," Ned said. It was an effort to keep his voice even. "If it kills me, at least you can seal the room up for good with the creature inside."

"With the greatest of regret," Oppenshaw said. "But we've done it before."

CHAPTER EIGHTEEN
Facing the Serpent

J ULIAN RESTED HIS ELBOWS ON THE battered tabletop, frowning at the untouched pile of paper in front of him. Across the table, Ned bent over his notes, carefully translating astrological correspondences into modern sigils, and Julian reached for his own pen. Ned clearly had the ointment well in hand; the next question was how to draw the creature, and that was…more complicated, at least if one was not going to feed it Kennett. And besides, with Farrell dead, the connections to the ritual that had created it were growing more and more tenuous. It clearly needed to eat fairly often – probably each time it exerted itself – and Julian was willing to bet that the hunger would override whatever cloudy purpose the thing might still remember. Which meant they needed something that would get its attention, only – what?

"Would you look this over, old man?" Ned slid a sheet of paper toward him, and Julian took it.

"Of course." For some reason, possibly the lack of breakfast and Scotland Yard's execrable tea, his mouth was dry. He bent his head over the neatly in-scribed page, Ned's familiar legible hand refusing for a moment to come into focus. He should be the one to perform the enchantment, he had more experi-ence with non-conforming magic – but Ned was the better metaphysician and always had been. He focused on the sigils, tracing each strand of Ned's work. It was neat and accurate, as always, and once so purely clever as to make him smile in spite of everything, and he pushed the drawings back across the table. "Exemplary."

"Let's hope so."

"Have you given any thought to luring the thing in?"

Ned made a face. "There's the talisman you gave me. I think we can use that, if we add a drop or two of Kennett's blood. The two rituals were tangled up to start with. There must be a hook in one of them that we can use to draw it."

"Do you have the talisman here?"

"It's in my case," Ned answered, and shoved it across the floor.

Julian caught it, withdrew the crumpled packet, and carefully unfolded it on the table, grimacing at the stains. "I'm worried about Challice."

"There's nothing we can do," Ned said, and Julian sighed.

"I know. I'd warn him, but – against what? His own furniture? His wife would think I'm mad."

"Very likely."

Julian drew his own wand, tracing an experimental sigil over the talisman. For an instant, the curves blazed blue, then faded to ash, dappling the locks of hair for an instant before vanishing. "Ah."

Ned reached for his pen. "Square of Venus – well, it would be – but if we begin there –"

"'Heartless' can become – no, you're calling the eater of hearts –"

Ned swung the paper around to reveal the new sigil. "Calling it and compelling it to attend. At least, that's how I'd translate the old quasi-demonic conjuration that it's hooked to."

Julian traced the sigil in his own mind, teasing out the individual words. "Mathey, that's brilliant! You should write it up for the *Journal*."

"If –" Ned bit off whatever he had been going to say. Julian suspected it was *if I live long enough.* "I doubt the Commons would let me publish."

"Pity." Julian looked at the sigil again. "That's going to take quite a bit of energy, though. Why don't you let me enchant the ointment? Save your strength."

Ned considered for a moment. "I think I want to do that myself. It's not that energetic, and I want to feel how it responds."

Julian couldn't argue, much as he might like to: Ned did need to have that visceral sense of the enchantment. He glanced over his shoulder, saw that Hatton and his men were out of earshot, and lowered his voice. "There has to be a way to do this that doesn't require you to be in there with it."

"Believe me, I've tried to think of one. But if I'm not there, Kennett has no protection, and I'm not going to send him in there to get killed."

"Serves him right," Julian muttered. "What about a simulacrum? Use that for bait instead of Kennett? Then we could stand outside and just seal it up."

"I thought of that," Ned said. "But, first, I'm not sure if a simulacrum would be, well, attractive enough, not to mention that it would take a good deal more energy to make one. Second, I'm not sure that another sealed room that no one dares enter is really the best solution."

There was no arguing with that. Julian looked away as Ned pushed back his chair.

"I'd best be getting on with it, if Hatton will give me the space."

"Yes." Julian watched him go, though it took all his self-control to keep from following him. There was nothing he could do to help, he told himself firmly. He would only be in the way. He had managed to shave when the constable brought his clothes, which at least made him feel a little less as though he belonged in the cells with Kennett. Some while back, Garmin had stuck his head in to say that there was more tea and sandwiches in the main room. Julian wasn't precisely hungry, but he knew he'd want the energy later on.

The tea was hot and black, astringent enough to taste through the sugar and milk, and the sandwiches were simple but good. After the first bite, he ate rapidly, and Garmin gave him an almost friendly nod.

"Likely to need that, we are."

"Sadly," Julian said.

"Your friend's in the workroom," Garmin said. "Which I hope he won't be setting on fire or exploding anything."

"Unlikely," Julian said, through a mouthful of ham. He was speaking as much from loyalty as conviction, and Garmin gave him an old-fashioned look.

"What's more, his boss is in with the governor. Apparently he's got a place we can try to trap this thing." He paused. "Is it really a writing desk?"

"Yes," Julian said. "The idiots enchanted an actual writing desk. So now it's a writing desk that will eat your heart. It's not really funny at all."

"Why a writing desk?" Garmin asked. "Of all the bloody things –"

He broke off as Hatton's door opened, and Hatton and Oppenshaw emerged. The inspector was scowling, though Oppenshaw looked as serene as ever.

"It look as though we've got a place to try to trap it," Hatton said, to the room at large. "Nice house in Battersea, currently untenanted. And you're sure, Mr Oppenshaw, that this thing will be able to – pick up the scent – that far out of its usual haunts?"

"If Mr Mathey's reports of the creature's behavior are accurate, and I see no reason to think that they are not, the creature can translocate as soon as it senses its desired prey." Oppenshaw paused, considering Hatton's raised eyebrows. "It can appear where and when it chooses, Inspector. So, no."

"Lovely," Hatton said. Garmin swallowed hard, his Adam's apple bobbing above his soft collar. "But it's the best we've got."

He turned away, beckoning for Garmin to follow, and Julian took a deep breath. "A word with you, Mr Oppenshaw."

"Of course, Mr – er, Lynes, is it?" Oppenshaw managed a vague smile, one that did not reach his eyes.

He'd never forgotten a name in his life, Julian realized, any more than he'd forgotten a sigil or a cantrip or a rule of opposites. It was all a façade intended to make one feel safe, when in fact the specialists in non-conforming magic were as dangerous as the subject they studied. "Yes. I gather you're going to come with us?"

Oppenshaw nodded. "I am."

"Then I'd like to ask you to seal the circle. I was planning on it, but if you're there – you're certainly qualified to deal with anything that goes wrong. If you would do it, then I could help Mathey in the circle itself."

Oppenshaw considered him for a long moment, his expression opaque. "No, Mr Lynes. I don't think that would be wise."

"Mathey shouldn't have to deal with this by himself."

"Your loyalty is commendable," Oppenshaw said, "and believe me when I say I do mean that. But it is unwise. First, the number of metaphysicians involved in an enchantment increases the likelihood that something will go drastically wrong. It is almost impossible to match energies well enough to make a seamless join."

"Non-conforming magic was often done in groups –"

Oppenshaw lifted his hand. "Yes, and that's one of the reasons it's defined as non-conforming. Hear me out, Mr Lynes." He waited until Julian nodded abruptly. "If something does go wrong, I would prefer to lose two men rather than three. That is another compelling reason. But I can't trust you, Mr Lynes. Mr Mathey is a member of the Commons, and he will, if this attempt fails, allow himself to be killed rather than cause a greater disaster. You would not."

"I would," Julian said. "I give you my word."

"You couldn't keep it. I do not think less of you for it – it is an understandable and in other circumstances entirely admirable trait – but I cannot allow it. You have seen the Half-House. There must never be another." He adjusted his glasses. "If we are to make this attempt at all, only Mr Mathey and Mr Kennett can be within the circle. Otherwise, I will withdraw the Commons's sanction."

Julian nodded. "I understand." And the trouble was, he did. Oppenshaw was, if not right, at least not entirely wrong. It wasn't in him to stand by and let Ned die – let anyone die pointlessly, not if he could do something that might prevent it. He could hear his Oxford tutor's dry voice in the back of his mind:

Mr Lynes, the laws of metaphysics are not like the rules of the college, which you persist in breaking. You cannot bend the Law of Similitudes any more than you can break the Law of Gravity. There was always a part of him that had been compelled to try. He closed his eyes for an instant, grappling for calm, and the workroom door swung open.

"The ointment is finished," Ned said, "and if Kennett is willing to cooperate, I believe I can draw the creature to us."

Oppenshaw nodded gravely.

"Right," Hatton said. "Garmin, bring Beal and Crofts. It's the next train to Clapham Junction, gentlemen, and look sharp about it."

It seemed to take forever to reach the station, though Julian was aware they made perhaps better time than average, and he took a solid grip of Kennett's elbow as they forced their way through the crowd. Kennett gave him a betrayed look, and settled to a decorous pace. So he had been thinking of making a break for it, Julian thought, with some satisfaction, and tightened his hold.

The Commons's property proved to be a handsome Georgian house surrounded by a high brick wall topped with short iron spikes and, when Julian looked more closely, broken glass as well. He saw the constables exchange glances, and was not surprised to see tiny sigils set into the bricks at regular intervals. The Commons was taking no chances with uninvited visitors.

The gate was an elaborate wrought-iron structure with gilded Tudor roses at the intersections of the bars, and more enchantment woven into the pattern of the iron itself. The main lock had no visible keyhole. Julian's eyebrows rose, and Ned cleared his throat.

"Mr Oppenshaw –"

Oppenshaw drew his wand, sketched a sigil over the lock. The keyhole obligingly appeared, and Oppenshaw produced an old-fashioned key and proceeded to open the gate. "Yes, Mr Mathey, the protective enchantments would interfere with your experiment if I were to re-engage them. That is why I am going to ask Inspector Hatton to leave a man by the door to keep watch."

"Not if that thing's going to make a meal of him," Hatton said.

"Highly unlikely." Oppenshaw's voice was even more disapproving than usual. "The creature will be entirely focused on its target. However, we cannot risk interruption. Your man is only there to stop other people from taking undue interest in the house."

Hatton looked as though he would have liked to argue further, but nodded instead. "Crofts. You stay. Beal, you're with me and Garmin."

Kennett took a half step backward in spite of himself, and Julian tightened his grip, feeling for the sensitive spot just above the elbow. "Come along, Kennett," he said, with what he hoped would pass for cheerfulness. Kennett winced and obeyed.

Inside, the house was ordinary enough. A parlor opened to either side of the hall, and a flight of stairs led up to a landing lit by a tall window. Both parlors were sparsely furnished, chairs and one long table under holland covers, and the air smelled dry and old, as though the place were rarely used. Gas had been laid on, however, and Oppenshaw meticulously turned up the lamps, then led them down the hall and under the stair to the equally bare kitchen. There was a second, servant's stair there, and Oppenshaw turned up the lights there as well, motioning for Ned to precede him up the stairs. Ned shifted his bag to a more comfortable grip, and did as he was told. Julian scrambled after him, and they found themselves in a bare back hall, with one open door that gave onto an empty, windowless room.

"Yes, that's it," Oppenshaw said, coming up behind them. "The best I could do on short notice."

"It'll have to do," Hatton said, and looked at Ned. "Won't it, Mathey?"

"It'll work, all right." Ned set his bag down in the middle of the room and looked around, looking assured and professional and calm. "Give me a hand with the circle, will you, Lynes?"

Julian gave Garmin a look, received a nod of understanding in return, and stepped past Oppenshaw into the little room. Behind him, he saw Garmin step up to block any chance of Kennett's escape. The room itself was very nearly a perfect cube, ideal for this sort of work; the floor was well-sanded board and the walls smooth plaster, all of which would take the symbols of the circles nicely. He held Ned's notes while Ned constructed the inner, protective circle, leaving the last bit incomplete as a door, then went round the walls, drawing a second circle there. Again, they left it incomplete, just one final sigil to be set in place across the threshold, and Ned handed him the pot of ointment.

"You know the pattern?"

Julian nodded. "I have it." It was simple enough, a hook and a curve to catch the dangling links of the circle, easy to draw in a single movement.

"Right." Ned squared his shoulders. "Kennett! It's time."

"I'm not at all sure this is a good idea," the poet began, and both Julian and Hatton glared at him.

"You'll be safe inside the circle," Ned said, with more patience than Julian could have managed. "But right now, I need a drop of your blood." He unfolded the charm as he spoke, and Kennett gave it a look of mild distaste.

"I'd really rather not."

"Come along, old man," Ned began, for the first time sounding a little ragged, and Hatton straightened.

"Now, now, Mr Kennett, if you'd rather we pursued some of those alternative charges…"

"No, no, that's – I'm fine." Kennett held out his hand with a martyred air. Ned pricked his thumb and squeezed out two drops of blood, which he wiped onto the stained paper. He folded it closed again and set the packet carefully in the center of the circle.

"Just stand there, Kennett, and don't distract me."

Julian held out the pot of ointment, and Ned dipped his finger in it, drawing the last of the sigils with his finger. Julian felt the circle close, a silent thud like a tumbler turning in a lock. They were committed now, and he licked his lips, unable to walk away without a final word. "Ned, I –"

He stopped, aware of the others behind him, too close not to hear, and Ned smiled. "I know," he said. "Get ready, old man, I'm going to call it."

Julian retreated quickly to the hall, to find that Oppenshaw had moved Hatton and his men further down the hall. "And I will join them there, Mr Lynes, if you and Mr Mathey are ready."

"I'm ready," Ned said, and Oppenshaw nodded.

"Very well. Good luck, Mr Mathey."

He turned away without waiting for an answer. Julian took a deep breath, wiped his hands on his trousers for fear he'd drop the ointment. Within the second circle, Ned closed his eyes for a moment, centering himself, then lifted his wand. He gestured, shaping the enchantment, and Julian could feel it hovering, power in potential, as Ned added layer upon careful layer, rebuilding the old forms with new metaphysical words. Newer, more precise, more powerful: the force building behind the gestures was suddenly alarming, but Julian closed his mouth firmly over any protest. It was too late now; they were hunting tigers, and just as in the books he'd read as a boy the goats were tethered beneath the tree to draw it in. He saw Ned brace himself before he spoke the final word, but even so the force staggered him for an instant, and in that instant, the thing was there. The writing desk lay on the bare boards, its edges already thinning to smoke. Kennett cried out, and in the same moment Ned shouted, "Now!"

Julian already had the ointment in his hand, inscribing the sigil in its spot in the circle. He felt the enchantment take hold, a fist twisting in his guts as the circle sealed itself, trapping them within, and the door slammed shut in his face. "Ned –"

He swallowed whatever else he might have said, leaned his forehead against the rough wood. It was in Ned's hands now. He had never felt more alone.

€❀

THE DOOR CLOSED LIKE A TOMB being shut. The serpent reared up, a hooded shape trailing yellow smoke, its gold eyes gleaming. It surged forwards, and Kennett stumbled backwards. "Bloody hell –"

Ned caught him by the arm and the collar and held him in an iron grip as the serpent rushed at them. It balked at the line of ointment and wound around the outside of it instead, wreathing them in smoke. "If you break the circle, we're both dead."

"What if it can get in?"

"Then we're dead anyway. Now will you stand still?"

"I'll be still," Kennett said, and Ned let him go, raising his wand. He stepped forward, and the serpent rushed round the circle to meet him, rearing up again inches from his face.

He made himself stand still, no matter how much he wanted to bolt himself. Instead he visualized the square of Mars, calling it up in memory until he could see each number clearly, and then connecting the numbers that represented the letters of the word "milk." The familiar discipline brought an icy calm with it, and he moved his wand crisply, tracing the lines of the sigil.

The smoke burst apart, dispersing into a loose cloud, and for a moment Ned dared to hope it had worked. But the smoke was already reforming, knitting itself back into a serpent that began angrily circling them again, lashing its whole body as it went as if it could batter through the protective circle by sheer fury.

He kept his wand raised, trying to think. He'd tried to disperse it, and Julian to freeze it in place, and neither had worked. There were bindings, though, to keep something like a writing desk closed, and that was a simple enough cantrip that it might not be too great a risk to try.

If only the serpent would slow down enough for him to aim. He turned, trying to match its pace, and sliced the air furiously with the sigil for "close yourself."

He felt it go wrong before he finished the last stroke of the sigil, but it would be worse to leave it unfinished. The cantrip flailed toward the serpent, tangled in its enchantment, and then rebounded back at him. For a heart-stopping moment Ned wasn't sure which would be worse, to throw himself out of the way and through the protective circle, or to stand and be bound in a warped version of his own enchantment, unable to move, or maybe to breathe –

He felt the energy of the cantrip hit the protective circle on its way back to him and shatter, and he gasped for breath in sheer relief. Kennett cringed away from the walls of the circle, trying to stand perfectly in its center as the serpent circled them again. It was better than panicking and bolting, and Ned put a hand on his arm for a moment, trying to steady him.

The creature reared up before them. Kennett flinched and took a step back. "If you run, it'll be on you in a moment," Ned said. "It's trying to make you run. It can't get into the circle –"

As he spoke, the serpent whipped its head forward, and something glittering rushed forward at him through the circle. Ned put up his arm by instinct to shield his face at a hail of something cold and hard. Kennett cried out, and Ned grabbed hold of him again to hold him.

"Sixpence," he said, plucking one from Kennett's sleeve. "It's only money, damn you, it's doing what you made it to do, bringing you the money it stole –"

He broke off as he saw the litter of cash on the floor. There were coins scattered throughout the circle, some of them lying over the line of protective ointment, and a pound note with one corner inside the circle and the rest outside.

"It's trying to break the circle," Ned said, his voice as level as he could make it. "It can't touch it, but it doesn't have to as long as it can break it."

"It's going to kill us." Kennett's voice cracked "It wasn't supposed to kill anyone, I never thought something like this could happen –"

"Be quiet." Ned said. Kennett hadn't thought, that was the problem, none of them had thought. They'd been sure that all rules were arbitrary, and gloried in breaking them. But he couldn't afford to think about that now. "And for God's sake be still."

A binding, he thought desperately, a binding. It couldn't be closed like an object, but that wasn't really what he wanted, anyway – he wanted it to revert to its proper shape, go back to being an inanimate and harmless writing desk. And that should be easy enough, the sigil forming itself in Ned's mind, *take your shape.*

He raised his wand and then hesitated. There was something wrong with that, something that twisted in his gut at the thought. He could see how the energies would flow into the sigil, see how it would catch on the serpent's own enchantment, but it didn't feel like it would rebound. There was a lock for that key to fit into in the original enchantment, some part of it that let the serpent change its shape, it ought to work –

He was already reaching out to trace the first line of the sigil when he saw the trap opening up before him. *Take your shape*, and it already knew how to *take* things, how to put them somewhere that wasn't inside a box or inside a cloud of smoke but – somewhere else. He could see with sickening certainty how it would happen, the energy not rebounding but folding itself *away*, the serpent folding itself inward smaller and smaller into nothingness, and going on folding, until the room began to fold itself in with it. And after that –

Ned lowered his wand. That was what they'd done to create the Half-House, he was suddenly certain, that or something like it, and he had come so very close to doing it again, a breath away from disaster. He had promised not to experiment, and it was time to keep his word.

"I can't stop it," he told Kennett.

There was another patter of coins and notes against the floorboards. "It's going to break the circle," Kennett whispered.

Ned's own voice sounded almost calm in his ears. "I know."

The serpent threw itself at the barrier, and this time it roiled against it for a moment before it drew back, as though it were no longer facing an invisible wall but something soft that it could press through. It reared back again and struck, and this time it came flowing halfway through.

Ned scrambled back, barely out of its reach, but the creature was changing its shape, surging forwards towards them. Where it touched the barrier, its edges dissolved into smoke, but enough of it was writhing through, and he was backed against the other edge of the circle. One more step would take him out of it entirely.

The serpent still poured off smoke where it touched the circle, and it writhed, trying to free itself entirely. In the moment while it was distracted, Ned cursed himself for not thinking to bring in more of the ointment with him. If he could have circled it with the protective ointment while it was caught in place –

Modern substitutions, he thought, and raised his wand. There was no time to think it through, only a heartbeat to decide whether to trust instinct or not.

The serpent reared, preparing to strike.

He lashed out with his wand, slicing the air with the symbols. *Fat of a white hen, blood of owl that screams* – for a moment he blanked at "gall," but his hand was already moving, muscle memory from some long-ago Oxford classroom more obedient than his conscious mind – *gall of a black cat*, and then the astrological correspondence to tie them all, its influence called into being through symbol and will as if the very planets moved in their places to answer him, *the dog days of summer* –

The serpent struck, met the enchantment, and exploded into smoke. At the least he'd bought a moment, he thought, a few more heartbeats. It writhed, trying to re-form but flinching away from the sigils he'd drawn in the air, caught between them and the barrier.

"Kennett," he said. "Mend the circle."

"I don't know how –"

"Smear the ointment across it!" For a moment, he thought Kennett wouldn't move, but then he stumbled to one knee, reaching down to close the breach in the circle.

The serpent whipped around toward him, and Ned raised his wand over Kennett's shoulder, beginning the sigils once more. The serpent turned and rushed for him, but he finished the sigil a heartbeat before it touched his chest, and it exploded again into smoke. As it re-formed, it realized it was fenced, with only one way to escape back out into the circle. It whipped about to take it, rushing round the inside of the circle toward them, and Ned tugged Kennett up to his feet and pushed him out of the protective circle.

He scrambled over the line himself and spun to face it. The creature was caged now, and hurt, swirling from one part of the circle to another wildly. If he gave it a moment to think, it would seem that it was as easy to break the circle from within as from without.

He flicked his wand and traced the sigil for *milk* and the serpent dispersed into smoke. As the wisps roiled, Ned's wand slashed through the air the more complex sigil as if he were performing before an Oxford lecture hall. Every gesture crisp and correct. *Fat of a white hen, blood of an owl that screams, gall of a black cat, and all under the dog days of summer* –

The smoke filled the circle, and then rushed together, like an explosion in reverse. An inscribed writing desk clattered to the floor, and lay in the middle of a circle of coins and banknotes, perfectly still.

For a few heartbeats, Ned stood and looked at it. Then he crossed to the wall and scraped up a handful of the ointment they'd used to anoint it. He stepped carefully over the circle and went down on one knee beside the writing desk before he could think better of it. He smeared the ointment around the seams of its lid, and then across the seam and round it. It felt perfectly ordinary in his hands, as if he might want to prop it on his lap and write a letter.

Kennett was leaning against the wall, breathing as if he'd run a race, his face ashen. Ned ignored him and stepped cautiously out of the circle. He regarded the writing desk for a while, waiting for any signs it was more than a wooden box.

Finally he crossed the room and opened the door. "You can come in now."

"Mathey," Julian began, and then seemed to run out of words entirely. Ned felt his expression was reward enough.

"Got it taken care of, then?" Hatton said, as if he'd merely dealt with a nasty infestation of rats. Julian drew himself up to protest, but Ned put up a hand to ward him off, finding Hatton's manner as steadying as Hatton probably intended it to be.

"Come and see," he said.

Oppenshaw was the only one who immediately took him up on the invitation. He circled the writing desk, examining it both through and over his spectacles. "Well done, young Mr Mathey," he said finally. "You would make a decent metaphysicist, should you choose to pursue the proper education."

"I'm afraid I prefer practice to theory," Ned said.

"So many young men do say that."

Julian came in then, with Hatton at his heels; Julian seemed to have recovered from his moment of sentiment at Ned's survival, and looked cautiously fascinated. Hatton stopped just short of the protective circle and stood looking down at the writing desk.

"Well, what are we going to do with the bloody thing?"

"I expect we can find a place for it in the Commons's museum," Oppenshaw said. "We have a collection of items requiring special care."

Hatton circled it, regarding it warily. "I suppose just chucking it in the fire is out of the question?"

"I wouldn't advise it," Oppenshaw said.

Ned took the opportunity to pick up the paper-wrapped talisman, lying discarded among the coins and notes, and handed it to Julian, who took it with a somber nod. It at least could go into the fire now, and he hoped Challice would be the better for it.

"It would be far too risky to attempt to destroy the object," Oppenshaw went on. "But we will ensure that it remains contained, and available for study. From a safe distance."

"Be my guest," Hatton said. "I'll send Garmin with you to keep an eye on it until it reaches the Commons, and then I'm happy to turn all responsibility for it over to you." He turned to Kennett. "Mr Kennett, if there were any justice in the world, I would now be charging you at the very least with using non-conforming enchantment to create a bloody mess."

"We had a bargain," Kennett said.

"So we did. Get out of my sight before I think the better of it."

"I never meant for this to happen."

"That won't bring back the dead, Mr Kennett."

Kennett looked away without a word, and Hatton walked him to the door. "Show Mr Kennett the way out," he told Garmin. "He's finished assisting us with our inquiries for the present time." He turned back to face Ned, who squared his shoulders wearily for another ordeal. "Mr Mathey, kindly take a walk with me."

Julian's eyes followed Ned as they left the room, but there was clearly nothing he could say that wouldn't make matters worse. It was uncomfortably reminiscent of their school days, and he had to shake his head to banish memory as Hatton led him down the stairs and into the dusty parlor, shutting the door behind him. The house was very quiet.

"I'll resign, of course," Ned said to break the silence.

"Will you?" Hatton's tone was unreadable.

"Unless you insist on sacking me. But that would cause more of a scandal."

"A scandal wouldn't be good for the Metaphysical Squad. Or for me." Hatton crossed to the window and pulled the curtain back enough to let a cold gray light into the room; it was raining again. "Every now and again we get reformers who want to tell us at the Yard how prostitution ought to be a crime outright. I nod, and agree that it's an ugly business, and wonder if they've ever actually set foot on the streets of our fair city."

Hatton stood still facing the window, watching the rain. "We do our best at the Yard to stamp out the worst kinds of vice. Girls under thirteen we find walking the streets when they ought to be skipping rope in the schoolyard. Little girls from the country who only wanted a decent place as a scullery maid, and wind up in a bawdy-house being slapped about by the madam and robbed of every sixpence they earn. Boys sleeping ten to a room in the worst kind of lodgings because it's better than the workhouse, and getting lessons in every indecent act you can do for a shilling. Not that they wouldn't learn that in the workhouse as well. There's rape and brutality and ill-treatment I wouldn't wish on a dog, and we do what we can to stop it. And we might as well try to empty the sea with a spoon.

"If we had twice the men and twice the hours in the day, we couldn't stop even the worst of it. Not to mention have any time left over to pursue metaphysical creatures that are eating the populace." He let the curtain fall, finally, and turned to Ned. "I'm not saying I approve of your friends' vices, but it seems to me that they're all grown men and not in need of the Yard's intervention."

"Thank you," Ned said.

"Don't thank me, damn it. I'm not doing you special favors as a friend. I'm only saying we've only got so many hours in the day, and I'll be damned if I'm going to spend them hunting down gentlemen who don't make their private arrangements my business. Mind you, if this business with Farrell had made it into the papers, I would have had to give you the sack. And I expect I'd have been sacked as well for hiring you once the newspapers got onto it. Probably with the implication that I shared your tastes, since I haven't yet managed to persuade any young woman that she wants to be a policeman's wife."

"I will resign."

Hatton shrugged. "I wish you wouldn't. You're a good metaphysician, the best we've ever had at the Yard. You're willing to work for the little we pay, and unlike Garmin, I don't worry that you're stealing the spoons. And, all right, you have your vices, but if we sacked everyone at the Yard who's ever broken marriage vows or visited women of ill repute, there'd be bloody few of us left rattling around the place. And the state of your soul isn't any of my concern." He shook his head. "Just don't get yourself caught, or there'll be hell to pay."

"I don't intend to be."

"That's what they all say," Hatton said. "It doesn't hurt that tomorrow's headlines are going to be YARD'S HEROIC METAPHYSICIAN SAVES CITY FROM DEMON FURNITURE. I'll stick with that rather than YARD SACKS MATHEY IN SODOMITE SCANDAL."

"It is better press."

"And don't we both know it."

Ned started to say he was sorry, and stopped with the words half-formed. He was sorry for the risk of scandal, and sorry for the pall this must necessarily throw over what he had hoped was becoming a friendship. But there were other things he didn't regret, and he couldn't say the words when they would be taken as an apology for Julian or for his own nature.

"That is, if you're willing to stay on after all this excitement," Hatton added. "You didn't exactly sign up to run the risk of having your heart eaten."

"I don't mind a bit of danger."

Hatton snorted. "I suppose you mustn't."

"I'll go and help them clean up upstairs," Ned said, after an awkward moment's pause.

"I'd appreciate that," Hatton said. "I'll tell you, I won't be happy until that thing is tucked into the Commons museum with a sign on it saying 'man-eating writing desk, do not touch if you value your vital parts.'"

"You and I both."

"And, Mathey?" Ned had turned toward the door already, and turned back at the words. "Well done," Hatton said.

Ned nodded. "Thank you," he said, and then went up to see the writing desk safely squared away.

€✹

JULIAN MADE HIS WAY THROUGH THE Commons's garden in the deepening twilight, refusing to look too closely at the plants that rustled in their beds in spite of the still air. It would be foggy again tonight, too, and he didn't entirely care for the reminder. At least the writing desk was locked away safely in the metaphysicists' wing, secure in a well-warded case, but it would be some time before serpents of smoke ceased to haunt his nightmares.

He made his way up the stairs to Ned's chambers, unsurprised to see the outer door still folded back, but as he reached to knock, the door opened before him.

"– and I do think it's more suitable," Miss Frost said, over her shoulder. "Oh, good evening, Mr Lynes." She was already bundled in her neat wool coat, a dashing if made-over hat perched on her severely pinned hair, and drew on her gloves as she spoke.

Julian lifted his hat. "Miss Frost."

Behind her, Ned had a bemused expression. "Good evening, Miss Frost."

"Good night, Mr Mathey." She bustled down the stairs, her heels striking a smart tattoo on the oak treads, and Julian came into the little office, closing the door behind him.

"What was that all about?"

Ned leaned his hip on his desk, shaking his head. "Her friend Miss Barton has applied to be Hatton's police matron."

"The schoolteacher?" Julian asked.

"She's the least likely schoolteacher you've ever met," Ned said.

Julian blinked, remembering the untidy red curls and the outrageous alibi, a married lover and a blackmailing gardener. "True enough. And I can't see Hatton caring if she goes on writing romances. As long as she speaks well of the police."

"I wouldn't think it would matter as long as she stayed anonymous. And Hatton isn't one to preach."

"Evidently not," Julian said, with a sidelong glance. Ned was looking much better, the lines of worry erased from between his brows, and he risked the question that he hadn't dared ask the night before. "Speaking of Hatton – now that he's not going to sack you, what conditions did he make?"

"For my continued employment?"

Julian nodded. It had taken most of the rest of the day to install the writing desk in its new home, and by the time they'd returned to Ned's lodgings they'd wanted nothing more than to fall into bed. They'd made love, silent and a little frantic, determined to prove they were both still alive and well, only to fall asleep with any number of conversations unfinished.

Ned shrugged. "None, really. As long as I'm discreet…"

Julian nodded again. That was the game, and they both knew how to play it; perhaps it was better that Hatton knew the truth, even if it meant that matters were likely to be awkward between them for some time. He was, he admitted, a little sorry for that: he'd begun to like the man in spite of his better judgment. "I had a note from Kennett today. He's going to Italy for the winter."

"I hope he stays there." Ned shook his head. "He deserved to be prosecuted."

"He didn't mean to do it," Julian said. "Not for anyone to die. Anyway, I doubt he'll gain the reputation he was seeking. If he's gone all winter, while his book is in the stores – some other clever young poet will take his place, wait and see."

"Six men are dead. Maybe more that we never found out about. And Kennett doesn't get to be a literary figure. It's not just."

The shutters were closed against the thickening fog, and Julian dared to squeeze his shoulder. "I know. But we don't want to see anyone else ruined."

"No. Of course not."

"I heard from Lennox, too," Julian said, after a moment. "Both Jacobs' and the Dionysus are reopening tonight. He thinks there won't be any permanent consequences from all of this, and he says he's grateful to both of us for handling it so sensibly."

Ned's expression lightened. "That's kind of him."

"It was brilliantly done, you know."

"I was bloody terrified."

"So was I." Julian hesitated, but there was no reason not to try to say more. "I am –" *I'm very glad you aren't dead.* No, perhaps that was not the best way to phrase it. He cleared his throat, and tried again. "You know I care very much –" That sounded as though he were trying to break things off, and he stopped again, feeling the color rising in his face.

"I love you, too," Ned said.

Julian stopped, his face flaming. Ned's smile held no mockery, however, and Julian reached out before he could think better of it, drawing Ned into an awkward embrace. He felt as clumsy as a schoolboy, but Ned returned the kiss with enthusiasm, and Julian held him tight for a long moment, all too aware of the faint sound of Ned's heartbeat. It would be a long time before he could hear that without a shiver of worry, and he disentangled himself cautiously.

Ned straightened his coat. "You know, if the Dionysus is open tonight, we could always have dinner at Blandings and then go there after."

Julian considered that for a moment. "Actually – if you've no objection, Mathey, I'd just as soon have a chop at the Mercury."

"Lynes?" Ned gave him a look that suggested he felt some concern for Julian's sobriety.

"You have to admit that the chances of being dragged into something metaphysically dangerous is rather less there than at the Dionysus."

Ned winced. "Unless it involves billiard balls. But, yes."

"I feel capable of dealing with that," Julian said austerely, and Ned grinned, reaching for his hat. Julian waited while he dimmed the lights and locked the chamber door behind them, and they went down the stairs in perfect amity.

Acknowledgement

Thanks, as always, to the First Readers on LJ. Thanks are due also to Alex Jeffers for edits and his lovely design, to Ben Baldwin for the cover, and to Steve Berman for both his edits and for taking on this project in the first place.

About the Authors

MELISSA SCOTT is from Little Rock, Arkansas, and studied history at Harvard College and Brandeis University, where she earned her PhD in the Comparative History program with a dissertation titled "Victory of the Ancients: Tactics, Technology, and the Use of Classical Precedent." She is the author of thirty science fiction and fantasy novels, most with queer themes and characters, and has won Lambda Literary Awards for *Trouble and Her Friends*, *Shadow Man*, and *Point of Dreams*, the last written with her late partner, Lisa A. Barnett. She has also won a Spectrum Award for *Shadow Man* and again in 2010 for the short story "The Rocky Side of the Sky" (*Periphery*, Lethe Press), as well as the John W. Campbell Award for Best New Writer. She can be found online at mescott.livejournal.com.

AMY GRISWOLD is the author of *Stargate SG-1: Heart's Desire* and the co-author of *Stargate Atlantis: The Lost*, *Stargate Atlantis: Allegiance*, and *Stargate Atlantis: Inheritors*, as well as "Caden's Death," in *Sword and Sorceress 25*. She lives in Chapel Hill with her partner Jo, daughter Beth, and two opinionated cats. She can be found online at amygriswold.livejournal.com.

Death by Silver, the first book in this collaborative series, received the Lambda Literary Award for LGBT SF/Fantasy/Horror.

For entertaining Victoriana and series updates: matheyandlynes.tumblr.com

CPSIA information can be obtained at www.ICGtesting.com
Printed in the USA
LVOW07s0121240816

501564LV00005B/235/P

9 781590 215302